Roric turned slowly to greet the rider. Valmar, behind him, was too frozen to move. This was a creature out of the recurring nightmare Valmar had had as a boy, a nightmare he hoped he had finally outgrown, coming to meet him in broad day.

The rider had no back. He had a face, a front, but it was only a hollow shell, but Roric didn't seem to notice. "Have you decided then that you need me!" he asked the rider evenly.

"We want you, Roric No-man's son," said the rider, in a voice so deep it seemed to come from the earth. Valmar could see blue sky through the holes of his eye sockets.

"You will come now."

"Roric!" hissed Valmar. "*He has no back!*"

Roric whirled on Valmar and seized him by the shoulders. "Don't bother me with children's tales," he hissed in reply. "Now listen carefully. Take this message to Karin for me. Tell her I have found at last a place for a man without a family—or that such a place has found me. Tell her I have gone with the Wanderers, but that I shall always love her."

"That's not a Wanderer!" protested Valmar.

But Roric had already turned away and was mounting his stallion.

Valmar looked after them in amazement as Roric and the being who could not be a Wanderer rode quickly away. Suddenly he jumped on his own horse. "Roric!" he screamed, his voice thin and high. The two figures were about to disappear into the forest. "Roric! Wait! I'm coming with you!"

His gelding ran all out, but he was too late. When he reached the forest edge, they were already gone.

ALSO BY C. DALE BRITTAIN

Tales of the Wizard of Yurt

VOIMA

C. DALE BRITTAIN

BAEN

VOIMA

A Baen Books Original

Baen Publishing Enterprises
P.O. Box 1403
Riverdale, NY 10471

ISBN: 0-671-87637-6

Cover art by Gary Ruddell

First printing, January 1995

Distributed by Simon & Schuster
1230 Avenue of the Americas
New York, NY 10020

Typeset by Windhaven Press, Auburn, NH
Printed in the United States of America

CONTENTS

PART I: Lords of Earth and Sky

CHAPTER ONE

1

Roric put his sword across his knees and his back to the guest house wall. When they came to kill him in his bed asleep, they would find him neither in bed nor asleep.

Swallows swooped through the twilight air, then disappeared back toward the barns as the sky went from yellow to darkest blue. He shifted on the hard bench, listening but hearing nothing. Even the wind was still. He reached into the pouch at his belt and with his thumb absently rubbed the charm there: the piece of bone cut in the shape of a star that had been tied into his wrappings when he was first found.

It would be good, he thought, to see Karin one more time. But it did not matter. They had said their farewells as though they knew they would not meet again short of Hel.

The moon rose slowly above the high hard hills to his left. His shadow stretched at an angle, dark and liquid, across the rough surface of the courtyard. He bent to tighten a shoelace and turned his head to be certain the soft peep off to his right was nothing more than a night bird. There was another shadow next to his. Someone was sitting beside him.

He was on his feet with his sword up in an instant. But the other, seeming for a second less substantial than his shadow, did not immediately move. When he did, it was to stretch out weaponless hands, palms up. "Would you attack me unprovoked?"

Roric did not relax his guard. "You intended to do the same to me!"

The other gave an amused chuckle. He wore a wide-brimmed hat that shadowed his face from the moon. "So *that* is why you are sitting outdoors when all others are asleep."

"If you are not come to kill me," said Roric cautiously, "and you have not come to warn me, why are you here?"

The other did not answer for a moment, and when he did it was in a soft voice. "Perhaps it is because we could use you."

"Me?" said Roric bitterly. "A man who may be dead before morning, and if he lives will be an outcast at least, and probably outlawed as well at the next Gemot? No one needs me."

"I do not think you will be dead before morning. But I must agree," with another chuckle, "that you will be of less use to us if you are. I need to ask you several things, and I am interested in your answers."

Roric leaned on his sword, listening but still hearing nothing ominous among the quiet sounds of the night. The other person, whoever he might be, was not a wight or he would not cast a shadow. But his soundless materialization on the bench suggested someone of great voima: a Weaver, perhaps, or a Mirror-seer—even a Wanderer. But if he was one of these, he should already know the answers.

"All right, then," said Roric, and a smile came and went for a second across his face. "We may as well talk while we're waiting for the attack to come." In the moonlight this man—if he *was* a man—seemed so unreal, so much a product of his own vision, that he could have been talking to himself.

"Then what have you done, Roric No-man's son, to make your fellows want to kill you and cast you out?"

"I've loved a high lord's daughter," he said shortly.

"And so your king has come to kill you?"

"How did you know a king wants me dead?" demanded Roric, raising his sword again. This person who knew his name but apparently not much else could in fact be one of the king's men, here to distract him from the coming attack, only seeming insubstantial because of night and moonlight.

But the other again gestured with upturned palms. "This is a royal manor, and the crown on your shoulder-clasp suggests royal service. Is your king planning to kill you himself?"

"No, not with his own hands. He couldn't!" with a grim laugh. Roric lowered his sword again; whoever this person was, he did not seem one of Hadros' men. "The king is my sworn lord, and he would be outlawed himself. But I wondered at the time why he sent me to this manor on such a trivial errand. Still, I did not suspect treachery until I saw the warriors arrive by stealth: three of them, my king's fiercest fighters. I would not have seen them at all if I had not forgotten my knife in the hall at dinner and gone back for it."

"Sit down by me," said the man. Roric had still not seen his face. "I do not like having to look up at an armed man when I'm trying to talk to him. Now tell me," when Roric had slowly seated himself, his sword again across his knees, "do you intend to kill these warriors?"

"I will not stand quietly while they kill me!"

"But are they not beneath your notice?"

"One of them I could certainly outfight," said Roric, "probably even two. Three I think will be harder . . . My tale is already short, because it starts with me, but the end should be very interesting."

There was another faint chuckle from beneath the broad-brimmed hat. "So your intent is to give up your life to make a glorious song? I would not have thought a life for a song a good bargain. The song will not cause your king much distress, nor comfort the lady."

Roric did not answer but stared straight ahead at the moonlit side of the barn on the far side of the courtyard.

"And tell me," added the other, "why loving your king's daughter should be such a crime."

"She's much too high-born for a man without kin, but she is not really his daughter," he started to say, then stopped. He thought again that if this person with a shadowed face— if he even had a face—was a Wanderer, he should already know this. For someone of great voima, he seemed remarkably ill-informed. "And you tell *me,* who it is who wants to use me, and for what purpose!"

"We have enemies," said the other, still in that mildly ironic tone, "whom we made deliberately, made ourselves, and are now finding a little harder to *un*make. We have watched you for some time, Roric No-man's son. If you come with us, it must be of your own free will. A mortal, a man like you, may be able to help us, as well perhaps with another issue we are considering . . ."

"Then you are not a mortal yourself?" Roric asked slowly. It was sometimes said that warriors on the field of battle saw the Wanderers striding in their midst, but his battle was not yet joined—and he himself had never expected to see one of the lords of voima out of legend come to meet *him.*

But before the other could answer there came the sound Roric had been straining for the last four hours, of stealthy feet scrunching on gravel.

He was on his feet in an instant, his back pressed against the guest house wall. The moon in rising had left a slice of darkness here, and he would see the warriors well before they saw him. No time now to wonder about the lords of earth and sky. "It's been pleasant having this little conversation," he muttered to the person beside him, "but I think we will have to postpone the rest."

Good, they had brought a torch with them; the fir rosin smoked and sizzled, and the flame burned orange. Their dazzled eyes would never pick him up. Especially now:

clouds came up abruptly in a clear sky and darkened the moon.

He breathed very quietly, thinking fast. He had intended to sell his life as dearly as possible, but now he had another plan.

The guest house door was around on the side. They knocked; the sound was of a sword hilt wrapped in a cloak. "Open the door for us, Roric," called a guttural voice. He recognized it; it was Gizor One-hand, whom he had distrusted even when still a boy. "We just want to tell you something."

I'm sure you do, he thought. The falsely friendly note in Gizor's voice would have been a warning even if he had been lying inside asleep.

They knocked again when they got no response, then tried the handle and seemed surprised to find it unlocked.

"Be ready," Roric hissed, glancing back over his shoulder. "We'll move as soon as they go inside." But the other had disappeared so thoroughly into the darkness he could no longer see him.

Then all three warriors shouted together and crashed through the door, the torchlight flashing from their naked blades. Roric moved like lightning, across the courtyard, past the barns toward the stables, with no spare attention to wonder where the other had gone.

He had, he thought, something under a minute. No time for a saddle. He found Goldmane's stall in the dark, took a few precious seconds to rub the startled stallion on the neck and say some calming words, then led him out by the halter.

The housecarls had been roused by the shouts and were running toward the guest house, and he thought he could see the provost of the manor silhouetted against the doorway to the great hall. But the bobbing torch was already starting toward him.

"Is he there? He's there! He's got his horse! Don't let him get away!"

He leaped onto the stallion's back, and Goldmane began to run even before he had his balance again. He lay sprawled across the horse's neck, levering himself into position with his legs. Goldmane whinnied and sprang upward—clearing a wall or a ditch, he could not see what—almost losing him in the process.

"Good horse, good boy," he muttered, seizing handfuls of mane to pull himself up. "Are you still mine, or have you joined Gizor's employ?"

But then he laughed, the night air whipping across his face. Clouds tore away from the moon. He could see now where they were, coming out of the lane onto the high road. He slapped the stallion joyously and settled down to ride.

Even if the king's warriors managed to get away from the manor without answering the questions the provost would doubtless pose them, they would never catch him before he reached the castle. Goldmane was a stallion of voima, who had triumphed in every race since Roric had won him from the troll.

The king might be plotting his death in new ways within the week, but he was not yet an outcast, and he would see Karin again. The moon floated in a clear sky as the stallion's long strides ate up the miles.

It was dawn when he came out of the dense woods at the top of the sandstone cliff, and Goldmane slowed to a walk for the narrow and steep descent among the ledges. Roric shifted his stiff fingers in the stallion's mane, now matted with sweat. It had been a long run even for a horse like this, but after the first mile all sounds of pursuit had been left behind. King Hadros would not be expecting him unless he had had a raven-message, and Roric did not think Gizor One-hand was one who spoke to ravens.

The rising sun glinted on the sea, several miles off. But as the road reached the cliff's base the sun was hidden again. Here oaks grew on sandy hills, with nothing but long grass between their massive trunks. Roric urged his horse into a trot for the final stretch through the trees and across the stream on the old stone bridge. Goldmane's hooves rang hollow, but this morning there was no sign of the troll.

The hall of the castle and the walls that surrounded it were built of yellow sandstone from the cliff. The whole great mass, including the weathered oak outbuildings within the walls, seemed to grow naturally out of the hill. Smoke rose from the cooking fires in the kitchen as he clattered through the open gate into the courtyard, then slid from his stallion's back at the entrance to the stables.

Goldmane's head drooped, and now that he had arrived exhaustion seized Roric as well. The man—if it was a man— who had spoken to him, four hours of tense waiting, the long ride, were all jumbled together. But he forced himself to stay on his feet long enough to rub down the stallion, put a blanket over him, and be sure there were oats and water in his stall.

His thought had been to burst in on the king in the hall, flaunting his escape from treachery, defying him openly before his sons and his other sworn men. But at the moment sleep seemed even better. He tried to remember precisely what he had planned to say.

As he started out the stable door, there was a quick step outside, and then Karin was in his arms.

She pressed her face against his chest, filthy and sweaty as he was, and for a second he felt her shoulders quivering under his hands. But then she lifted her face, cheeks smudged but eyes clear.

"I knew you would escape alive," she said in a voice that just barely did not tremble. "I went to the Weaver who lives by the cliff and burned an offering. But— But dare you be here? They'll say you killed the men unprovoked."

He pulled her back into the stables and kissed her slowly and thoroughly. "I did not kill anyone. Did the king boast to you that I would be dead?"

"Of course not," she said sharply, as if irritated for a

moment. "It was only because he has been acting so oddly this last week that I was watching, and I saw Gizor One-hand and those cutthroats of his slip away—even Hadros may not have known when they left."

"The king must have hoped at a minimum I'd be outcast for wounding or killing one of them. Maybe he intended to get rid of Gizor and me at the same time."

They were talking in low voices, their arms tight around each other. "But are you sure they meant to kill you?" she murmured. "After all—you escaped."

He pulled his lips into a thin line. "Are you doubting the strength of my voima when it's three against one?"

She shook her head hard. She had hair the color of wheat fields in July, gold tinged with russet, and it was undone and tangled as though she had been up all night.

"I ran," he added, then stopped, feeling it was less than honorable to tell her this. He shook his own head. "Come, and we will face King Hadros together."

But she stepped away from him as he went into the great hall. King Hadros sat with his warriors and housecarls around him, finishing his morning porridge and beer. Roric spotted the red hair of Valmar, the royal heir. The king was bent over his flagon, his elbows out as though to keep the others away. He gave a great start as Roric walked toward the table, and his brows rose sharply. Although he managed to put the flagon down without spilling any more beer his eyes stayed round. A strange expression went across his face—was it relief?

Roric changed all at once what he had planned to say. "I finished my business at the manor more quickly than I expected," he said loudly. His heart was beating hard though he strove to keep his tone casual. Exhausation was gone.

"So I left last evening," he continued, "and rode all night to be here today. Oh, I happened to spot three of our warriors arriving when I was leaving. One was old Gizor One-hand. I hope they'll think to bring Goldmane's saddle home with them; I must have left it at the manor. I expect they had come on some special errand or other, but I knew it could have nothing to do with me, so I didn't wait to speak with them."

He let it hang in a profound silence, wondering how many of them knew, letting them wonder how much he had guessed. As long as he did not say openly that he had been attacked where he slept, he should be able to resume a normal life here at the castle. King Hadros would not want his other sworn men to know he had plotted the death of one of them, and certainly not that his plot had failed utterly. Not only had he escaped Hadros' assassins alive, he had put the king in his debt by not accusing him here.

But as Roric played again with the star-shaped bone charm, he did not feel the triumph he had expected from facing down Hadros before his men, telling the king in covert fashion that he knew all and had outwitted him.

Maybe it was because running from danger suddenly seemed a dishonorable thing to have done, the act of a man without a family.

He pulled out the knife from his belt, felt a momentary surge of satisfaction when Hadros' eyes for a second went even wider, tossed it into the air and caught it. "But now I'm tired," he said, deliberately turning his back on the king, who had still not spoken. "If you have no more errands for me this morning, I'm going to sleep." As he reached the door, feeling somewhat better, he turned back for a moment and bowed.

He slept until noon, sprawled on the straw in the men's loft, and woke to find Karin sitting beside him. "Is this wise?" he asked with a smile. "If Hadros already wants me dead because he thinks your affections are turning toward me, what will he think when he finds you here?"

But then his smile faded as he looked at her face. She

was still pale, and her jaw was clamped tight as though to keep it from trembling.

"Gizor's back?" he asked, sitting up abruptly.

"They came back a little while ago," she said as though it was of no interest. "They looked shamefaced."

He put an arm around her. "What is it, then, my own?" he asked softly. "Were you so worried about me? Don't you see that I'm safe now, as long as I'm in the castle?"

"It's not you," she said, her eyes averted.

"Then who do you love better than me who can make you this sad?" he asked mockingly, then stopped all at once. "Hadros— He hasn't dared— If he's forced you, then I don't care if he is my sworn lord, I'll—"

She squeezed his arm. "It's my brother," she said, still not looking at him. "I found out yesterday. The messenger came to Hadros the day before, but he did not tell me until after he had sent you off to that manor. It's as though he wanted you away from here when he told me. And then last night I thought I had lost you both."

He pulled her toward him and stroked her hair. The straw crackled beneath them. "Tell me what happened. Your brother has died?"

"It was a shipwreck," she said indistinctly. "A calm sea, a clear crossing. But they were all young men on the ship, and they had all been drinking. They went right against the Cauldron Rocks. There were no survivors."

"I'm so terribly sorry," he said, continuing to stroke her hair.

She pushed him angrily away. "You don't understand, Roric! Of course I'm saddened to have lost my brother, but I hardly knew him anymore—I hadn't seen him in over ten years, not since I came here as a hostage. And I've never been able to feel the same toward either my father or my older brother since. After all, they gave me into the hands of the enemy."

When Roric said nothing, she added after a moment, "I was much sadder back when I heard my younger brother had died, only a few months after I arrived. He and I had been playmates . . . But you wouldn't remember that!" she finished brusquely.

"I didn't really know you then," he said, looking at her with his head cocked. "You were just the pretty little girl who had come to live with us. You were an outsider—I did not then realize that you and I were both outsiders here. I do remember you crying, and I wondered why."

"You still don't understand," she said through her teeth. "Now that pretty little girl has become an heiress."

He considered her in silence for a moment. "So will you still love me when you're queen?" he asked with a grin.

She gave him another push. "Don't joke, Roric! You, of all people, should realize what this means."

His attempts to take the anguish from her eyes a failure, he said soberly, "Then you'll be important to a lot of people as well as to me."

"Not just important. Valuable. I've been valuable all these years as a pledge for my father's good behavior toward King Hadros. Now I'm the heiress to my father's kingdom. That makes me doubly valuable. A marriage would unite the kingdoms, ensure that war would never again break out between them."

"And as a future queen you couldn't refuse," said Roric grimly. "You'd marry Valmar, of course, because he's the oldest son."

"I could do worse than Valmar," she said, her eyes distant.

"Now don't *you* joke!" he cried, pinning her arms.

She focused on him again and shook her head. "I only meant that I would prefer to marry Valmar than to marry his father."

"But you can't marry Hadros!" Roric cried. "He's old enough to be your father! He almost *is* your father!"

"Older men marry young heiresses every day."

He clenched his teeth in silence for a moment, then thrust a fist into the straw. "I wish he was in Hel! Why is he doing this? Hadros is my sworn lord, and I used to love him like a father myself."

"Until last week," said Karin.

"You knew we quarreled?" he asked, turning around.

"Everyone in the castle knows it. Both of you have good voices for calling the hounds in the hunt—or for hurling insults."

For a second he thought he saw a smile on her face. Encouraged, he took both her hands. "Then let's run away, Karin, you and me. Neither Hadros or I will have to break our sworn word by killing each other, and you won't have to marry anyone but me."

She pulled her hands free and stared icily over his head. "Sometimes you're as dense as Valmar. If I go, King Hadros will invade my father's kingdom, while the whole court is in mourning and no one expects it. I'm going to be a sovereign queen someday. I cannot run away."

Roric turned away abruptly and thrust his fist into the straw again. When he turned back toward her she had risen to her feet. "As a queen," she said, "I also cannot compromise my good name by being found in the men's loft." But then she looked at his expression and bent to kiss him swiftly before scrambling down the ladder.

As the sky went red and shadows stretched long across the castle courtyard, Roric slipped out the gate on foot. He stayed away from the road but cut through the oak forest, across the sandy hills, toward the base of the cliff.

The sun had set by the time he reached it. He stood for several minutes at the cave entrance, waiting. Above him, the first bats darted across the sky, squeaking on the fringes of audibility.

He lowered his eyes from the cliff to find a short personage standing before him. "Greetings, Roric No-man's son," said a voice that could have been either a high-pitched man's or a deep-pitched woman's. No one had ever been able to say for sure if Weavers were men or women, or if the distinction had any meaning for them. This one, or one just alike, was said to have lived here since before the castle was built.

Roric reached for his belt. "I've brought you my best knife," he told the Weaver.

The pommel was set with rock crystal and the blade was polished steel. The Weaver took it and examined it, turning it over as a squirrel turns over an acorn, before finally whisking it out of sight beneath dark robes. Roric followed as the Weaver stumped back into the cave where a tiny fire was burning.

"And what would you ask of voima and of fate?" asked the Weaver, arms and legs huddled together until the robes looked like a pile of empty clothes, though yellow eyes glinted in the firelight. Roric too sat down.

"I met someone last night," he said after a moment. "Weaver, Mirror-seer—or Wanderer. I want to know who he was."

"And why do you ask another's name when you have no true name of your own?"

"He said he might have use of me," said Roric, trying with an effort to keep the edge out of his voice. It was no use becoming angry with a Weaver.

"And that use might be—?" When Roric said nothing more, the Weaver's hand disappeared again into the shapeless robes and emerged this time with a piece of string. Fingers moved quickly as the string took shape, first a series of loops, then triangles and diamonds, finally a web so dense it looked as though it must contain much more string than when the Weaver had begun.

"Tangled," came the voice at last, neither man's nor woman's. The Weaver always said that. "Lives are tangled here. The change, the upheaval, may be closer than anyone thought, and some beneath the sun may be sought to withhold it, or even to hurry it."

"I gave you my best knife for a clear answer," said Roric testily. "I'm not burning an offering to influence the future—

not that I'm sure that often works. I'm asking you something that has already happened."

"What has happened," said the Weaver enigmatically, "depends on your perspective. Who has appeared, and what he seeks, depends on whether he seeks a man without a name or a man with a mighty father."

"And which one do you think you're talking to?" asked Roric fiercely.

"It might also depend on which the Wanderers could use most readily . . ." The light and shadow from the fire accentuated all the Weaver's deep facial lines.

"So it *was* a Wanderer!" The Weaver did not reply, which Roric took as assent. He stared unseeing for a moment into the fire. "Such a thing has never happened to my certain knowledge to any I know," he said at last, very quietly, "only to those of the old tales."

"And are there not Weavers as well in the old tales?"

Roric did not answer but cocked his head as though listening to the high voices of the bats outside. "He never did tell me what he wanted," he said after a minute, "but if he wants *me* it's because I was nearly an outcast when he spoke to me. Does that mean— Does that mean the Wanderers have reasons of their own for hiding from me who I am?"

"You are Roric No-man's son," said the Weaver loudly.

"Yes, and that's who they said they might need. But why would the lords of voima want a mortal to help them?"

The Weaver examined the web of string again, picking at a few threads until the knots were even more tangled. The silence stretched so long that Roric had decided he would have no answer to his question when the other suddenly spoke. "Even the Wanderers may not have full control over their own fate."

"Listen. I haven't tried this since I was twelve." Roric tugged in sudden resolution at his ring, the one Hadros had given him when he became a man and received his sword, when they had first sworn their oaths to each other.

"If I give you this, will you give me a straight answer? Will you tell me my father's true name?"

The Weaver made little rasping noises that could have been a cough, could even have been a laugh. "That is not an answer I give for a ring—or for the silver-decorated halter you tried to give me years ago. This is an answer that gives a man his identity and takes it away in the same instant. The price of your question is knowledge that will destroy you."

"I don't understand you any better than I did when I was twelve." Roric rose abruptly. "I've wasted a good knife," he said with a shrug. "The Wanderer—*if* he was a Wanderer, and *if* he appears again—can tell me himself what he wants. In the meantime, I know who I am, and I have no intention of waiting for my fate to reach me. I am King Hadros' sworn man and bitter enemy, and I am the man Karin loves."

As he left the cave, there came a metallic clatter almost at his foot. He paused and glanced down. It was his knife.

He stood motionless for a second, then picked it up and returned it slowly to his sheath, looking back toward the cliff. A fitting conclusion to the last day's events, he thought with a mirthless smile. Even in the oldest tales, no Weaver had ever refused payment. It was now full night, and there was not even a glint of firelight from the cave.

2

Karin had never told anyone, not even Roric, about the faeys.

She slipped out of the hall very early in the morning, an hour before the maids would rise to stir up the fires for morning porridge. The room was still completely dark. Hadros and his sons snored peacefully in the other cupboard beds as she went on slow silent footsteps across the hall, finding her way by feel to the great door. She kept the bolts oiled, and they slid back effortlessly. The hinges gave the faintest creak as she swung the door open, but the note of the snores did not change.

Roric, she knew, would also be asleep, up in the men's loft with the king's warriors and housecarls. She hesitated for a moment as she pushed the door soundlessly shut behind her, with a disquieting image of him quietly knifed. But even Gizor would not dare an attack among so many men.

She pulled her cloak around her against the pre-dawn cold and hurried across the courtyard to the apple tree that spread its trellised limbs against the outer wall. They would assume she was in one of the other buildings in the castle when they woke to find her gone from the hall. She had been climbing this apple tree since she was small, and it would still—just—hold her.

She scrambled upward quickly, pausing at the top of the tree to free her cloak from a twig on which it caught. The last ten feet she went by toes and fingers, but the sandstone was soft enough that she had been able to chip away holes over the years. Then she went lightly along the top of the wall toward the back of the castle, where an oak branch stretched near. Since Hadros had won the war with her father, he had neglected such things. She seized it, scrambled, and worked her way down the tree until she was low enough to jump.

The faeys would want to know she was going to become queen.

The long grass brushed dew against the skirt she had hitched up while she climbed, and roots caught at her feet. She never liked to come out while it was still fully night, for fear of meeting the troll, but if she waited for sunrise the faeys would be gone. She hurried in the opposite direction from the cliff, darting between trees whose shapes became clearer and clearer as the sky lightened above her.

But she was in time. As she came over the last rise, she could see their lights still burning with a cold green glow.

Many of the faeys had already gone into the hill, but others lingered in the dell. She paused above them, pushing back the hair she had not taken time to braid, and whistled three times.

They ran around in panic for a few seconds as they always did, as though they never could remember they had taught her that whistle themselves. But then they spotted her and poured up the hillside to meet her.

They came up to her knees. They leaped and frolicked like puppies, crying, "Karin! Karin!" in shrill voices, snatching at her skirts and all trying to get closer to her than the others.

Even miserable she had to laugh. "Yes, yes, I'm coming to visit you! I have news you'll like to hear. Yes, I'll tell you when we're all inside."

For ten years, the faeys had been the only ones with whom she could be not a princess, not a hostage, not even a woman, but only herself, Karin.

They poured back down the slope into the dell and gathered up the lights. She went on her knees to crawl into the hillside behind them. The stone swung shut, closing them in.

In all the years she had been coming here, she had never liked this disorienting moment when natural light was abruptly gone, leaving them all illuminated only by the faint green light that put weird shadows across their features. She took a deep breath and shut her eyes, then carefully opened them again.

It always became better in a few minutes. The faeys brought out wild strawberries and honeydew from the bees and ate happily, apparently not noticing that she was not eating hers.

"Yes," said Karin. "I told you I have something to tell you. I'm going to become a queen."

"A queen! A queen!" the faeys cried in delight. "And will that pleasant young man you told us about become your king?"

"I don't see how he can. But I love him, and I don't want to marry anyone else."

The faeys gave her more strawberries as though that would solve her problems and finally noticed she was not eating. She ate a few to make them happy.

· "And that's not all," she continued. "I shall have to leave here, go back to the kingdom where I lived when I was little."

This caused consternation. "But how could you go away? That would mean you'd leave us! Don't leave us, Karin! Maybe we could come with you!"

She looked at them between exasperation and affection. She had stumbled across the faeys when wandering at twilight the first summer she had come to Hadros' kingdom, within a week of when her younger brother had died. She had not then been much taller than they were, and the faeys had since told her she was the first mortal they had successfully tamed.

"If you came with me," she said, "you'd have to leave your dell. The trip is too long for a single night, and much of it is by ship."

They had not thought of this. They conferred urgently among themselves for a moment, then announced, "Then you'll have to give up being queen! That way you can stay here and still marry that nice young man."

They gave her arm and hair reassuring pats, happy to have solved her problem so easily. Karin shook her head. She had come hoping the faeys might have some ancient wisdom to offer, but years of visiting them should have made her know better.

"The king here would like me to stay, I think," she said.

"There! What did we tell you? You know you wouldn't want to move away from us!"

"But he will want me to marry his son, rather than Roric, the man I love."

For a reason she could not understand, there was immediately further consternation among the faeys. They jumped up, knocking over their bowls, and several darted off down the tunnels while others started making little piles of pebbles in the dim green light.

"What's happening?" she asked in a minute when no one seemed about to tell her.

One looked up from a pile of pebbles that kept falling over every time he tried to balance another on top. "Is your Roric— Is he sometimes known as Roric No-man's son?"

"That's right," she said with a frown. "He was found at the castle gates when he was a baby, no more than three months old. The queen had pity on him, especially since she had no children of her own yet—or so I've always heard. He was brought up as King Hadros' foster-son and became one of his warriors, but he is a man without family."

"Should we tell her? You tell her. Don't you think she'll be upset if we tell her? We don't want to upset Karin. But queens have to deal with upsetting things every day."

"What's going to upset me?" she almost shouted.

"Oh, nothing!" the faeys cried together. "Nothing at all! Just something we heard, but it must have been another Roric altogether. Nothing to do with you!"

She rose to her knees, as high as she could go in the cramped space. "If you do not tell me at once," she said resolutely, "I shall leave here and never visit you again."

There was a horrified silence, then several spoke up, although hesitantly. "Well, it's probably nothing serious. But maybe it's better if— We may have been mistaken, of course . . ."

"Tell me plainly," she said grimly, "and tell me at once."

Only one dared speak now. "We've heard— That is, someone said— We've heard the Wanderers want him."

This was so unexpected she sat down abruptly on her heels. "But why would the Wanderers want Roric?" she asked in wonder.

"Well, you know," said the faeys unhappily, "even you

mortals must realize— Even for the lords of voima, fate does not always go well. Or for faeys!"

"Yes, I know the faeys have their problems," she said absently. "But— But could it mean they need him because of who he is?" Her face lit up in the green glow of the lights. "Could he really be a son of a Wanderer all this time?"

"What?! Why would you even think that? Don't think that! It's not right for mortals to have such notions!"

It had been a nice idea for about two seconds.

"They want him because he is a mortal, but one who has no ties with other mortals!"

Then they don't know about me, she thought. This was disconcerting; it was almost as bad to think that the Wanderers could have important gaps in their knowledge as it would have been to think that they were watching all the time.

"What use would they have for a mortal?"

"Maybe he can help them," said one of the faeys slowly. "We sense the time of upheaval is coming, the time even creatures of voima fear . . . Soon we may have to seal our burrows against the outside world; sometimes we have to seal them for hundreds of years. Would you like to stay inside with us when we do, Karin?"

She deliberately ignored this, not sure what upheaval the faeys could be talking about and certainly not wanting to be sealed up anywhere for the rest of her life. "But how did you find out about Roric? Do you yourselves speak to the Wanderers?"

"Not us! No, not us! Even the Wanderers don't come into our tunnels! Only faeys and mortals we invite. And we only invite you!"

"Then who told you?"

Here their answers were so contradictory, so confused, that it was at best a guess that they might have learned this from the Weaver.

"And what do the Wanderers want with him?" she tried a third time.

But either the faeys really did not know, or the prospect of telling her was even worse than her threats not to see them again. After a few minutes, agreeing somewhat reluctantly that she would indeed come visit soon, she crawled out, back into the dell, and pushed the stone shut immediately behind her, knowing the faeys would all be huddling far back in their tunnels until the threat of direct sunlight was gone.

She adjusted her cloak around her and hurried back toward the castle. She had to speak to Roric as soon as she could get him alone, to discover if he knew anything of this. She was still reluctant to tell him about the faeys, though he was certain to ask how she came by the startling information that the Wanderers wanted him.

Had he in fact already met a Wanderer himself? His eyes had looked strange yesterday morning when she found him at the stables, but anyone who had escaped death and ridden all night would be wild-eyed, even without a conversation with the lords of voima.

There might still be some things, she thought, that he felt reluctant to tell her, as she kept the secret of the faeys. They had had, both of them, to learn control, to use caution in a castle where they were at the same time family members and outsiders. She passed the little valley where an oak's low-spreading branches made a hidden bower. It was here, three weeks before, that she and Roric had lain together for the first and only time, wrapped up in both their cloaks, laughing and kissing and pledging eternal love to each other.

Their future together had looked so hopeful then, and Roric had been so sure that Hadros, who had been a father to him his whole life, would raise no objections. That hope had lasted until last week when he had finally decided the moment was right to raise the topic.

Karin scraped the last of the porridge out of the pot and sat down to eat at the opposite end of the table from King

Hadros. "I went for a walk," she said shortly when he looked a question at her. Her firmly set jaw and lowered eyes kept anyone else from speaking to her.

The king's sons were discussing the horses. It was the season to bring the mares and the young foals in from pasture, to introduce the foals to humans and rebreed the mares, and almost time to start breaking the yearlings for riding. She listened absently to their conversation as she finished breakfast and braided her hair.

"We'll have to see how well the foals came out this year," said Valmar with a laugh. He was the king's oldest son, two years younger than Karin, and had red hair and dark blue eyes with lashes that had always seemed to her too long for a boy. She still thought of him as her little brother, even though in the last few years he had shot up from boyhood to young manhood. Though most men stayed clean-shaven until marriage, he had managed to grow a somewhat patchy beard. "And we'll have to see if the mares will be satisfied to be covered by an ordinary stallion this time. I'm afraid Roric's troll-horse may have sired some of this year's crop!"

His younger brothers, Dag and Nole, laughed too, then glanced toward her as though recalling her presence and stopped abruptly. They all knew better than to say anything that could possibly be considered crude or lewd in her presence, but King Hadros did not seem to have noticed.

Valmar rose. "Coming with us, Father? Or is your knee still bothering you?"

Karin looked up sharply at that. The king sat with one leg extended straight out from the bench. "Oh, my leg is fine," he said easily. That was the leg, she recalled, that he had broken in the fall last year—or was it the year before? "But perhaps I shall let you go ahead and catch up with you."

His three sons clattered out, taking the housecarls with them. Karin stood up with a swirl of her skirt, thinking that she would work in the weaving house; it did not require much concentration, once the pattern was established, and the tension burning inside her needed an outlet. The maids would be impressed at how fast she threw the shuttle today.

But King Hadros motioned to her. "Come here, Karin. I would speak with you."

He smiled when he spoke, and she went somewhat reluctantly to sit beside him, looking at him steadily. Hadros was no taller than she but twice as wide, all of it muscle. He had little white scars all over the backs of his hands and arms and a long one on his cheek, which just barely did not reach his eye. Ever since she was fully grown, she could usually manage to talk and smile him into being agreeable.

Today she was less sure that she could control herself. This was the man, she thought, who had ordered Roric murdered.

But the man she saw now was the one who had taught her to ride, the man who had given her the direction of his household when the queen had died and she was still only a girl herself. She had known him both in riotous good humor and in black rages, especially when he had sat drinking long with his warriors. It was Hadros who, when she had first started developing a woman's body, and one of the housecarls had made a remark to her so coarse that she had been another year older before she understood it, had seized the man by the neck and smashed him to the floor with such force that he died. But at some point, almost without her noticing, Hadros had developed lines in his tanned face and gray in his hair. And she had never before not known him to lead when they brought in the foals.

There were voices and the sound of hooves in the courtyard. She glanced through the open door to see that Roric, riding Goldmane, had joined the king's sons. His rather ferocious good looks, straight dark eyebrows over deepset eyes, a muscled body always in motion, usually made her heart turn over, but today she felt more irritation than anything else. In the one glimpse she had of him he appeared carefree, and he did not glance at all in her direction. Could he have forgotten already?

"I had not realized your leg was bothering you again," she said, turning back to the king.

He shrugged. "I have not spoken with you for nearly two days, Karin," he said, "since I had to tell you about your brother. By now I hope you have adjusted to the news."

Oh no, she thought. Here it comes. He's going to ask me to marry Valmar—or even himself.

Instead he smiled and tucked a finger under her chin. "So sober, my little princess." He had not called her that in years. "I know you realize this makes you heiress to your father's kingdom. The All-Gemot of the Fifty Kings will be held at his castle this year. Would you like to accompany me across the channel?"

This was not at all what she had expected him to say. The All-Gemot, she thought wildly. She had contemplated it during the long hours two nights ago when she had sat up, dressed, in the dark, listening to the restless tossing from the king's bed. If Gizor and his men had killed Roric, she would have found some way to accuse Hadros before the Fifty Kings.

She had not known the All-Gemot would be held in her own father's kingdom. She tightened her lips. They had sent her out a prisoner, a little girl, someone less important than Hadros' offer of peace. But she would be coming home a woman and a future queen.

"Yes," she said gravely. "I would very much like to accompany you."

"There are a few sovereign queens already among the Fifty Kings," he said. "And I'm sure you know it is not always fifty anymore. Last year I think there were sixty-three in attendance, including several from those little kingdoms up north—though it was quite an act of courtesy to call them kings!"

"How soon will we leave?" Roric might be among the warriors to accompany the king—or Hadros might use the opportunity to try again to have him killed here at the castle while his own hands stayed clean. She wondered if there was any way to ask the king to bring him along.

"Ten days. And you will want to bring your finest clothes. I am sure you remember the standards those kings south of the channel set for themselves! We will not be thought another little upcountry kingdom."

She had not considered that, and for a few seconds she ran in her mind through the fine clothes stored in the bottom of her chest—the red silk dress she had worn when she came here had not fit for nine years. She did recall that, when she first arrived, this court had seemed crude, unrefined, but she had been ready to hate everything about it. She could scarcely remember her own mother, who had died when her younger brother was born, but now that she thought about it she was quite sure the queen had not worked in the weaving house or done her own brewing.

"And the All-Gemot will be an excellent opportunity to announce your betrothal to Valmar."

Karin took a sharp breath, then bit her lip. He had brought it up when she had almost forgotten to fear he would.

The king smiled at her as though he had just offered her a treat. "I could not of course urge Valmar on you while you were a hostage here. No man could say that King Hadros made war on girls. But once you are home you shall be able to make your choice freely. You two have spent a lot of time together ever since you were children—I helped make sure of that. By now you must know he'll make you a fine husband."

It was his expectation that she would be delighted at this generous offer that made her answer hotly. "Valmar? But why should I marry *him*? The beard can't hide it. He's nothing but a stripling boy!"

She stopped, seeing his surprise and, yes, disappointment. Whatever she wanted to argue with King Hadros about, it was not the manliness of his oldest son.

But where she had expected hot words in return, he

said quietly, "He is still young, Karin. Perhaps you would prefer to wait a year or two. There has mostly been peace of late among the Fifty Kings, and even the upcountry bandits and southern booty have provided little opportunity for boys to be hardened into warriors. Most of the ships now on the channel are merchants' ships, not war ships. I had already killed three men in combat when I was Valmar's age." She thought he was finished, but then he added, almost under his breath, "Of course, there are some, like Roric, who do not need war to make them men."

She clenched her fists until the nails bit into her flesh. "And he is the man," she said in a voice that she was dismayed to hear tremble, "that I shall marry."

Again she expected a hot answer, but Hadros only went perfectly still for ten seconds, then turned to look at her gravely. "He did not say he had spoken to you already . . ."

She caught herself just in time from shouting, "And would that have made any difference in your ordering him killed?" Instead she kept her fists clenched at her sides and asked as evenly as she could, "And how can you possibly object to my marrying him?"

"You have always been a princess, even before your brother died. You were a hostage, but I intended to treat you as though you were my own daughter, and no man without a father could marry a daughter of mine."

"*You're* his father just as much as you're mine." She spoke in a low, intense voice. No one else was in the hall, but there might be highly interested maids outside the open doorway.

He pulled out his dagger and started trimming his nails, not looking at her. "Don't be childish, Karin," he said, and it was only the faintest unsteady note in his own voice that kept it from being patronizing dismissal. "You know I never formally adopted him, even though my queen loved him, even though the lords of voima had not yet granted us sons of our own. He is my sworn man, but I would as soon see you married to Gizor One-hand."

"Well, small chance of my wanting *that!*" she said, trying desperately to laugh. She started to ask why then, if he never intended to adopt the baby found at the castle gate, he had had his own wife raise him, but she closed her mouth without asking.

Hadros glanced at her from the corner of his eye. "And Roric is too young to marry anyone," he said slowly.

"He's five years older than Valmar!" she thought but did not say.

"He could still carve out a lordship for himself, maybe in the upcountry, maybe somewhere along the coast. My own grandfather won this kingdom in war, and even in these more peaceful times—and maybe *especially* in these more peaceful times—there is room for a man of courage to rise high through his own strength. I would not see him shackled to a wife and a fancy southern kingdom."

Karin slowly digested what this implied of the king's attitude toward his own oldest son. At last she said, very quietly, "But Roric could be fated to die in his first battle as easily as to win renown."

"And I," said the king, just as quietly, "would rather see him dead than wasting the strength within him." He rose abruptly to his feet. "I had better see how those lads are getting along with the foals."

3

Valmar shouted and waved his hat to turn the mare, then dug his heels into his gelding to pursue her down the line of trees. She saw the pen at the bottom too late, and before she could turn again both she and the foal running at her heels had had the gate slammed behind them.

He pulled up, panting and wiping his forehead with his sleeve. "Is that all of them?" he yelled to Roric.

Roric sat on the fence, relaxed and self-assured, counting horses. He wore a sleeveless leather jerkin that showed all his muscles—Valmar hoped he would have arms like that someday.

Even though the mares had been running free all spring and were nervous about letting anyone near their babies, they were used to King Hadros' men and were already calming down. "I think we're still short one mare," Roric called to him. "Has anyone seen the spotted one?"

Just then the spotted mare, with a jet-black foal beside her, appeared at the top of the hill. Nole, Valmar's youngest brother, was right behind her, but she wheeled and darted away again, Nole and a half dozen housecarls at her heels.

Roric swung back up on Goldmane. "Should we give him a hand?"

Valmar smiled and shook his head. "Let him catch at least one by himself."

Roric stilled his stallion with a firm hand on the reins and looked at the pen full of circling mares. But Valmar, watching, thought he did not see them. Ever since he had quarreled with the king last week, and especially this last day and a half, since he had returned from his errand to the manor, Roric had not been himself. He could still joke with the king's sons and ride a horse who would not allow anyone else on his back, but any time there was a pause his face took on an expression as though his thoughts were a hundred miles away.

And his own father was also acting strangely. Valmar was still not sure what Roric's remarks had meant when he came home the morning before, or why his father had listened to them without saying anything at all.

"Tell me," said Valmar suddenly, "why you and Father quarreled."

Roric gave a start, then smiled what appeared to be his normal smile. "I gather we were heard all over the castle. But men sometimes say things when they have sat too long drinking that they later regret."

"Is that why you slipped away last night rather than

drinking with us?" But as he spoke he remembered: that shouting match in the hall with the door closed, the voices loud though the words were indistinct, had taken place in the middle of the morning.

"I just had somewhere to go," said Roric offhandedly, though Valmar, watching his face, thought there was more here than he wanted to say.

"Even though you quarreled with Father," Valmar asked, "will you stay at the castle? Will you continue to serve him— and," he added almost shyly, "once I am king, will you serve me?"

This time Roric looked disconcerted, as though he had not thought this through. "I do not know," he said, not quite meeting the other's eyes. "There are reasons—the lords of voima know what powerful reasons—for me to stay, but something has happened that may mean I shall go away for a while. . . . How about you, Valmar?" he added suddenly and with a grin. "Are you going to travel far and boldly, to win a fortune and a place in all the songs?"

It was Valmar's turn to be disconcerted. "But I could not leave," he said slowly. He had grown up knowing he would someday inherit this kingdom and had never seriously considered going elsewhere—even if the day he would inherit always seemed impossibly far in the future. "Without someone directing the castle, nettles would invade the fields, deer roll in the meadows, geese nest in the forest clearings—"

"Here comes Nole," said Roric. "He has her this time."

As the spotted mare galloped down the hill, a band of shouting men on her tail, Valmar glanced up to see a single rider in the distance, silhouetted against the sky. Father was coming after all, he thought. He would try to talk to Roric privately some other time.

The three brothers, Roric, and the housecarls leaned on the fence to look at the foals. Valmar was glad now that his father had not accompanied them. When Hadros reached here in another minute, he would find everything as it should be. Valmar had showed he could be trusted with the horses, and the housecarls had all obeyed him today without any of the humoring he sometimes sensed, the faintest suggestion that he was still a child.

"The mares should have all been bred to Midnight this year," he said. "Father said that black colts have been doing especially well at market recently. So tell us, Roric," with a elbow for his ribs, "where did those two sorrel foals come from?"

"Don't ask me!" he protested. "I do not set my stallion at stud without charging for it!" In the middle of a laugh, his face changed abruptly.

Valmar whirled to look where he was looking. His father had ridden to within a dozen yards of the pen.

Except that it was not his father.

The housecarls and Valmar's two younger brothers fled, kicking their horses wildly. But the mares in the pen went dead still, and the birds above them fell silent. Roric turned slowly to greet the rider. Valmar, behind him, was too frozen to move. This was a creature out of the recurring nightmare he had had as a boy, the nightmare he hoped he had finally outgrown, coming to meet him in broad day.

The rider had no back. He had a face, a front, but it was only a hollow shell.

But Roric did not seem to notice. "Have you decided then that you need me?" he asked the rider evenly.

"We want you, Roric No-man's son," said the rider, in a voice so deep it seemed to come from the earth. Valmar could see blue sky through the holes of his eye sockets.

"I shall be with you in half an hour," said Roric. He suddenly tossed back his hair and grinned. "There is one other person who wants me."

"Not half an hour," replied the rider in the same deep, vibrating voice. As he spoke storm clouds moved across the sky, and the air temperature began to drop precipitously. "You will come now."

"Roric!" hissed Valmar. "You can't— Don't you see—
He has no back!"

"Don't bother me with children's tales," Roric hissed in
reply. "Two minutes!" he shouted to the rider.

Then he whirled on Valmar and seized him by the shoulders. "Listen very carefully," he said in a low voice. "Take
this message to Karin for me. Tell her I have found at last
a place for a man without a family—or that such a place
has found me. Tell her I have gone with the Wanderers,
but that I shall always love her."

"That's not a Wanderer!" protested Valmar. As Roric shook
his head, Valmar took in what else he had said. "You mean—
you mean you love my big sister?"

The corner of Roric's mouth curved up slightly. "Yes.
Tell her that. And take care of her if I do not come back—
especially if you marry her yourself."

"I couldn't marry her!" Valmar started to object, but Roric
had already turned away and was mounting his stallion.

Valmar looked after them in amazement as Roric and
the being who could not be a Wanderer rode quickly away.
Could this be not a nightmare but a dream, the dream he
had sometimes had of all-powerful beings realizing they
were not all-powerful but that they needed something,
someone, him? But that he might marry Karin! One of his
most vivid early memories was of her, only a few weeks
after she had first arrived at the castle, coming to him and
saying, "You're my little brother now. And I'm going to
teach you the games you have to play with me."

He glanced back over his shoulder. His father, really his
father this time, was galloping toward him, a crowd of warriors and dogs and housecarls with him.

Valmar suddenly jumped on his own horse. "Roric!" he
screamed, his voice thin and high. The two figures were
about to disappear into the forest. "Roric! Wait! I'm coming with you!"

His gelding ran all out, but he was too late. When he
reached the forest edge, they were already gone.

Long, long ago, in your grandmother's day or your great-grandmother's day, lived a man and woman who loved each other with all their hearts. He fished in winter in the briny sea, and grew barley in summer in his fields on the hills, while she kept the cow and brewed the beer and made the cheese and bread. Their only sorrow was that they had no children.

Their only sorrow, that is, until one stormy winter's night his ship did not return from the briny sea.

And in her despair she came home from drinking his funeral ale to a silent hall, and she called on the lords of voima to hear her. Her man was dead such a short time, she argued, he could not yet be in Hel, in the realm of the lords of death. Voima must still reach him. She demanded the lords of earth and sky to listen, demanded incessantly for three days. And on the third day, when she had almost lost hope and had returned to her duties on the farm and was once again brewing the beer, a Wanderer came to her.

"So you want your man again," he said, standing in the door of the brewing house and looking at her from under his broad-brimmed hat. "All it will take in return is that which is between you and the vat."

"Between me and the vat?" She looked down and saw the silver funeral buckle at her waist. "Of course," she said. "I shall gladly meet your terms." But even while she was loosening the buckle the Wanderer disappeared.

She looked wildly for where he had gone, then forgot him, for she heard a voice in the yard and a step she had thought never to hear again. But as she turned to rush from the brewing house she suddenly gave a great cry and collapsed in agony.

For the lord of voima had not meant her buckle. And she had not known until that moment that she had been with child.

CHAPTER TWO

1

Across the meadow, into the forest, through the tangle of the alder thickets, Roric followed the rider. The other's horse went effortlessly through the densest underbrush, and Goldmane followed.

It disturbed him that he could not see the rider clearly. Maybe it was the sun's glare, or the speed they were going, or the thin blue mist that rose from the boggy soil under their horses' hooves, but when Roric looked at him directly all he could see was a shadowy outline.

And yet he had seen his face, thin and yellow, dark eyes within enormous bony eye sockets burning like the last coals on the hearth on a winter's dawn. If it was a Wanderer who had sat and talked with him outside the manor's guest house, this could not be the same one.

They came up from the boggy lowlands at last, their horses scrambling on the thin soil that overlay a steep rocky hill. Roric looked around, thinking they could not have come so far so fast. This hill marked the western boundary of King Hadros' kingdom, and even by road and sea it should have taken a full day to reach here, yet it seemed that only an hour had passed since the rider appeared at the mares' pen.

"Where are we?" he called to his companion. "Where are we going?"

The other did not answer or even acknowledge that he had heard. Roric looked ahead, toward the top of the hill, and saw two lichen-spotted standing stones that he could never before recall seeing, leaning together as though to form a gate.

The rider went straight through. Goldmane made to follow, but Roric held him back for a moment, looking off toward the distant sandstone escarpment that rose over Hadros' castle. Whoever this person was, he seemed able to move space and time.

But then the stallion jerked his head against the bit and followed through the gateway of the standing stones.

And emerged into a world Roric had never seen.

2

The sea wind blew in Karin's face, stinging her eyes and whipping her hair. She took a deep breath of clean salty air and abruptly felt awake for the first time in ten days.

It had been like a dream during a bad fever, events rushing at her too fast, incomprehensible. She must have slept during that time, but she could only picture herself working, or else lying fully awake in bed, longing achingly for Roric. She had prepared for the trip to the All-Gemot with no conscious memory of having done so, packing her clothes, making sure that Hadros and Valmar had their own finery, choosing what herbs to include in her medicine chest, preparing food to take, instructing the maids on what would need to be done in her absence.

When Valmar had tried to talk to her about a person he said could not possibly have been a Wanderer, when the king raged so that the men went to their loft immediately after dinner without drinking with him, she went about her chores with her face placid and her eyes devoid of any expression.

Now she seemed suddenly aware of herself again, the skin on her cheeks, the way her cloak tugged at her shoulders, the feel of the smooth railing under her hands. For ten days she had been constantly busy, constantly moving, but all at once there was nothing to do except watch the sailors and the sea. She ran a finger along the broad links of her gold necklace; it had been much too heavy for a child, but her father had given it to her to wear when she went to Hadros' castle, and she would wear it coming back.

The king joined her at the railing. The ship ran with its red sail taut, rising up on the long swell that had come across hundreds of miles of empty ocean to the channel, then sliding into a trough rimmed by waves that seemed they must surely sink the ship in the next second. But the ship always rose again, the foam white under its bow, and the lines creaking overhead.

She looked at Hadros thoughtfully. He too looked almost himself again. While she emerged from a fevered dream, he was waking up from a furious nightmare.

"Be glad I did not let you marry him, little princess," he said with a visible effort at good humor. "You would not want to be coming home to your father to tell him you had married a man who ran at the first challenge."

"He did not run," she said, then wondered if she had already said this. If so, the king had apparently not heard it.

"He ran from me, to save his skin if not his honor," said Hadros, looking grimly out across the waves, "and he had best not come back with a wheedling tale in search of forgiveness."

Karin wondered if this was an admission by the king that he had indeed intended to have Roric killed—even if he had regretted his intent. If he did run, Hadros, she thought, it was so he would not have to kill *you*. "The Wanderers want him," she said, "and no one can refuse a summons from the lords of voima."

"Do you actually believe the boy's story?" he asked with a frown.

"Of course I believe him," she shot back. Valmar was up in the prow. She had a vague memory of him looking miserable, but now he eagerly strained to see the distant line of land ahead. "All the housecarls—your younger sons—support Valmar's story."

"Crazy stories," growled the king. "Glad he's gone."

Karin thought without saying that Hadros did not seem glad he had driven Roric away. Instead she said, "Do not think of Roric as someone who ran. Think of him as someone who has gone to use his strength and his courage to win renown for himself."

And who went without saying farewell.

"The lords of voima do not appear to mortals except in the old tales," said the king, "and then only to great heroes." He was no longer frowning but instead looked uneasy, as though he had been using his fury to avoid thinking about something disturbing. "A person with no back," he muttered. "There *are* plenty of creatures of voima walking this earth . . ."

"Did you ask the Weaver?"

Hadros did not answer for a moment. Waves slapped against the side of the ship, and white spray danced in the air. "I went to his cave to burn an offering before our voyage, of course," he said at last. After another long pause he added, "Weavers have never been known for answering questions they did not want to answer."

The Fifty Kings were encamped in the broad meadow before her father's castle. Tents of linen, of elkhide, or of silk stood side by side, their lines tied to the same posts. Rough men like Gizor One-hand and graceful warriors with curled hair and delicate stilettos hanging from slender hips met and talked while their masters waited in their tents for the Gemot to begin, or else went with hoods pulled up for quiet conversations with other kings.

Next to the royal tents was another encampment, this one of merchants. "There have always been peddlars," King Hadros commented, "but this is the first time I have seen an entire fair next to the All-Gemot. Perhaps it is because recently the Fifty Kings have met north of the channel, where fewer merchants trade."

Late in the afternoon, he took Karin through the tents to meet a woman who was one of the Fifty Kings.

"So this is the heiress who has been gone so long," said Queen Arane, beckoning her into the tent. Hers was one of the silk ones. Her bodyguard she told to wait outside.

King Hadros greeted her as though they were very old friends, though Karin had never heard him mention her— but then he had already given familiar slaps on the back to kings of several kingdoms she had not even realized existed.

At first Karin thought the queen young, for her unbound hair was a deep chestnut, and her figure as she rose slim and lithe. But then she saw the little lines on her forehead, the veins blue on her hands, and the eyes—not quite cynical, because they still looked ready to be amused, but as though they had already seen everything someone could expect to see and then much more.

"You can leave us, Hadros," said Queen Arane and motioned Karin to a cushioned seat. Her straight eyebrows gave her a look of determination and firmness that everything else about her seemed intended to belie. She said, "I am very sorry your brother was drowned. He would have made a good king."

"You may have known him better than I," said Karin, "for I knew him only as a boy."

Arane's eyes glittered as she turned. "I did indeed know him well. He was excellent friends with my nephew, my most probable heir—who was also on the ship when it went down."

Karin murmured, "I too am sorry then," and sat in silence for a moment. She had no sense, she realized, of how old her own father was, how soon she might have to become sovereign queen herself, but she would have to learn the affairs of the Fifty Kingdoms—or sixty-three, or however many there were.

"It is not all bad," said the queen with a wave of her

hand. Rings were thick on the fingers. "It will keep my cousins busy for at least several years again plotting against each other." She took a handful of the rich cloth of Karin's sleeve. "Fine clothing for a princess living in one of the northern kingdoms," she said approvingly. "Growing up in King Hadros' court has not made you want to be a warrior, I hope?"

"Hadros has taught me to use a knife to defend myself," said Karin uneasily. "I had not expected to be a sovereign queen, so I never thought about leading an army . . ."

"And do not begin to think of it now," said Arane, tapping her on the knee. "Women can use their wits, their smiles, their tongues to maneuver most men, most of the time—have you not already noted this yourself?"

"At least if they have not sat overlong drinking," said Karin with an answering smile.

"But the lords of voima did not give us the strength of arm they gave to men—the strength which men foolishly but predictably think gives them power over women. That belief itself, of course, can be very useful . . . But I warn you, Karin, not to challenge men on what they consider their own ground, as a warrior. There was one young queen who had won a kingdom for herself, up north of Hadros' lands, but she was not content to plan the strategy and map the battles. She had to ride out with a sword in her hand herself, and when she disagreed furiously with one of her lieutenants, he challenged her to single combat. It was regrettable—she had ten times the wit and the spirit he did, yet she answered his challenge, with the result you could predict." Arane shook her head. "I do not believe he lasted long as king either; that land has sent no representative to the All-Gemot for three years now."

Karin saw a hundred issues and problems and possibilities opening up all around her, when she had thought her only concern was to face the man who had sent her off as a hostage but was still her father. She was not sure she agreed with the wise eyes facing her, but she was unable to shape a response while she still felt as though she had been dropped into deep waters without knowing how to do more than splash.

"And you have not yet made any plans to marry, I trust?" Arane asked suddenly.

"I do not believe I shall marry soon," Karin answered quietly.

The queen nodded briskly. "Good. I knew you had wit in you when I saw you—even aside from being your brother's own sister. It is your greatest weapon, the threat that you may at any time marry. I am sure that you have already considered the possibilities, the ease with which you can rid yourself of an enemy by letting a quiet word slip to his rivals that he may soon become the man of your heart."

Karin wiped her forehead. It was suddenly very hot in the silk tent. Was that what she had done to Roric by agreeing that he, rather than she, should talk to King Hadros—treated him as an enemy she would dispose of through his rival? But Hadros was not, she hoped, a rival for her hand.

But what did that make Valmar? She still called him her little brother, and had often felt him the only person in the castle she could count on unreservedly, without having to plan or maneuver, but what would he do when he realized he and Roric were in competition?

"There is a young warrior who lives in Hadros' castle, I believe," the queen said casually, "Roric No-man's son. I used to know him. How is he?"

Karin gulped, wondering wildly if the queen could read her thoughts. She forced herself to answer calmly. "He's fine. He left recently on a trip." She smiled as well as she could. "I am very glad to have met you, Arane, and I shall ponder all the things you have told me. Now I think I should return to Hadros' tent, to make sure the evening meal is prepared properly. Since I am not yet a queen, I must use the means I have to keep the men happy."

*   *   *

Leaving Valmar and Gizor behind, Hadros and Karin went at twilight up to the castle.

It took King Kardan a minute to recognize his daughter. They were announced by a page, and for a moment he did not look directly at her but instead behind her, as though in search of the little girl he had sent away.

But then he focused on her, tall and russet-haired, looking at him from sober eyes rimmed dark with weariness.

She had imagined coming home many times in ten years. At first she had pictured her father picking her up and tossing her over his head in joy, laughing and teasing and telling her it was all a horrible mistake and he was so glad to see her safe. Later, she had imagined herself telling him scornfully what she thought of a man who would let his own daughter go to the court of the enemy, perhaps to be cherished but more likely to be made into the lowest kitchen slut. But she had not expected the hall to be more familiar to her than her father.

The very stones of the wall seemed to rush at her like the faeys, laughing with delight to see her again. When she turned to the man who was too short and too old truly to be her father, she had to force herself from beginning her greeting by saying, "You've moved the high throne to the other side of the hall."

Instead she bowed formally to him and offered him her hand. He was wearing black, mourning that contrasted with her own jewelry and brightly embroidered garments.

"I am— I am glad to see you again, Karin," he said. His voice came out half-choked. "By the Wanderers, you look like your mother." He paused for a moment, then found his voice again. "We have put your brother—your brothers—into the same burial mound as your mother. Before you leave again, we can go there together if you wish to burn an offering."

"I have brought her home, Kardan," King Hadros said behind her. "You will find her as pure a maiden as when you first sent her to me." She stiffened for a second, consciously trying to keep any expression from her face. "After more than ten years of peace between our kingdoms, our warriors have forgotten how to make war." He held up a piece of parchment, dangling with seals, then crushed it and threw it into the hearth. "I remit you the tribute from this year forth, and I send you back your hostage."

And suddenly it was as she had imagined ten years ago it would be, crushed in her father's arms while he laughed with joy and kissed her. She kissed him back enthusiastically, feeling tears at the corners of her eyes. All at once, beyond expectation, she was home and safe.

But if she was not going back to Hadros' castle, who would direct his household, whom would the faeys try to tame in her place, and what would Roric think when he came back again?

"So—you mean I am to stay here?" she asked King Hadros, turning in her father's embrace. As she turned she realized that he had not said one word of regret or apology for sending her away.

"That is what I said, little princess," Hadros said with a smile. "Acquaint yourself with your kingdom before you come to rule it. And that other matter—the matter of which we spoke—there is no haste for you to decide. Your dower chest will be safe for now in my castle. But accompany your father to the All-Gemot next year, and I shall bring Valmar with me again, and perhaps then we can reach an agreement."

King Kardan lifted one eyebrow at her, but she shook her head. Valmar, she was quite sure, had no idea of any of this. For a second she wondered wildly if the rider with no back had been summoned by Hadros himself, to take Roric away permanently, and if he hoped that here, away from his castle with all its associations, she would quickly forget him.

Well, he might hope she would forget Roric, but she did not think any mortal king could make the Wanderers do his will. She gave Hadros a long look, not wanting to insult him and certainly not wanting to agree. "I shall consider," she said gravely, "but I fear my answer will remain the same."

They had not realized here any more than she had that Hadros intended to bring her home for good. The maids ran about madly preparing a suitable place, finally putting a bed for her in her mother's old private parlor, off the royal bedchamber.

Karin lay between linen sheets, under a green brocade coverlet, her eyes open in the dark. She thought that they all acted as though treating her with the respect due the heiress to the kingdom would make up for the last ten years.

Here were no cupboard beds, and she could hear the sound of no one else's breathing. The horsehair mattress felt hard and awkward to someone who had slept for years on rye straw. Her pillow was small, not the large pillow stuffed with goosedown she had plucked herself. Though one wall of the room backed up to the fireplace in the royal chamber, she had no fire, no coals to wink at her in the dark.

She thought over what Queen Arane had said that afternoon, and as she considered it King Hadros' castle seemed simple, comfortable, even welcoming. The faeys, she remembered, had told her that queens had to deal with upsetting things every day.

And without the fogged perception through which she had gone the last ten days, she could also think about Roric clearly. She had not been able to ask him—and now perhaps never would—if he knew why the Wanderers wanted him. Hadros had spoken truly that the Wanderers did not appear to mortals except in the oldest tales. Even if the faeys were right, the housecarls' story—which had taken on additional wild embellishments each time it was told— was not the story of a Wanderer.

What could a mortal do against beings like that, armed only with his own strength and a little bone charm? And where could he possibly be now? But Roric was indubitably gone, and since he had been gone for days already without a word, he might well be gone forever.

Suppose she was carrying his child? She had not really considered the matter before—first they had assumed they would soon be wed, and then she had been too worried for his safety, even before her life had passed into a fevered dream. But she had thought of it when Hadros told her father she was coming home a pure maiden. Would her father reopen the war himself if her waist began to thicken?

She put her hands on her stomach. It felt the same as it always did, except perhaps a little uneasy. But even worse might be to lose Roric and not even have his child.

And in the meantime, what could she possibly do with herself tomorrow morning? She could not relieve her tension with weaving, would not have the milking and churning and brewing and sewing to keep her stepping. She put an arm across her eyes and gritted her teeth, homesick as she had not been since she left this very castle.

3

Valmar slipped away from the All-Gemot.

He had often attended the royal Gemot back home, held four times a year, but he had expected the conclave of the Fifty Kings to be different. To his disappointment, the proceedings within the cords that marked the Gemot-field were very similar, whether accusations were made, sworn testimony given, or evidence—a bloodstained cloak or a sealed agreement—handed around.

The only markedly different aspect had come at the very beginning, when the two kings new since the last All-Gemot stood forward and announced their rule, and those kings who had brought their heirs with them for the first time introduced them to the rest. King Hadros introduced Valmar, and

Karin's father showed her to all the other kings. Several of the younger ones, and several of the older ones whose heirs were reaching marriageable age, made low and appreciative comments that made Valmar frown as though they had been insults. She wore a heavy gold brocade gown slightly too big for her, and she seemed not to see him or anyone else. Once introduced, she returned to the castle with the maids and warriors who accompanied her.

But after that the All-Gemot was very much like the quarterly Gemots Valmar knew. Karin's father, King Kardan, presided, as Valmar's father presided at home. Even though the Gemot began at dawn, when everyone was sober and most men still sluggish, there was the normal arguing and shouting. Men leaped at each other, reaching where their swords should be except that no one was allowed weapons within the cords, and were pulled back by their friends. The most exciting part was when the conclave voted to outlaw a king who had not even attended, for killing a man secretly in a fit of jealousy, according to the testimony, and then hiding the body.

Any man could kill an outlaw with no blood-guilt falling on him. Valmar drummed his fingers on his belt and wondered if it would be hard to kill him, if the outlawed king would fight with desperate, inhuman strength. But he would not even know him if he met him.

When Valmar finally slipped away, he noticed that many of the attendants who had accompanied the kings had also left the proceedings, and even two men he was fairly sure were kings themselves stood some distance off, talking to each other. No one paid him any attention as he went up to the castle.

It was a castle like none he had ever seen, its smooth walls reaching high above his head, towers on every corner. Pennants snapped from the towers, and all the stones were whitewashed. There was a moat where swans glided, seeming to ignore him pointedly. A guard in livery as elegant as his own best clothing stopped him at the bridge.

"I would like to see the Princess Karin. Tell her— Tell her it's her little brother."

When he was escorted a few minutes later across the bridge and into the courtyard, he was amazed to see that everything here seemed built of stone, and built connecting with everything else. There was nothing like the cluster of weathered oak buildings that surrounded the stone hall at home. He was led up a long stair, through a narrow room, back outside, and up another set of stairs before reaching the great hall.

Karin was sitting in a window seat, reading a book he recognized, a book she had made herself by sewing together sheets of parchment. In it were written, in a firm though childish hand, the favorite tales she had heard as a little girl. She had told him once that she had made it before coming to Hadros' kingdom, not realizing that many of the same old tales would be told there as well—and also not yet realizing, she said, how much different tales, or even different versions of the same tale, might contradict each other. She read it now with a frown and her full concentration, as though hoping in it to find certainty.

Valmar had not been sure of his welcome, but at the sound of his step Karin sprang up to meet him and took his hands as though she had last spoken with him much longer ago than yesterday. She sat him beside her in the window, from which they could look out at the tents spread across the fields between the castle and the river. He looked at her carefully, expecting to see her somehow different inside the elaborate gold dress. But she was still his big sister.

"I've wanted to talk to you for days," he said. "Everyone heard about the—the man Roric went with, and you know Roric told me it was a Wanderer. But he said something else too."

Karin bent closer, her gray eyes so intense he had to look away.

Now that it came to it he found it unexpectedly hard to

say. "I should have told you this before, but, I don't know, I didn't like to say it before Father and my brothers. Roric said to tell you he would always love you."

Karin sat back slowly, her hands folded and her eyes closed. "Thank you, Valmar," she said after a moment.

He had expected more reaction from her. "Did you already know he loved you?"

She opened her eyes and smiled with just the corners of her mouth. "Yes. I already knew."

"Well, I did not," said Valmar, then stopped himself when he realized he was sounding petulant. After a brief pause he went on, "I know he is not really our brother, but I was still very surprised—we'll probably all marry someone someday, but I think I had assumed it was someone we had not yet even met. I don't want to say it's not right, but . . ."

Karin was still smiling, this time at him rather than at her thoughts, as though pleased with him. Valmar remembered what else Roric had said, that he should take care of Karin if he himself married her, but decided this could not have been part of the message.

"Did he say anything else?" she asked.

"That was all his message—no, he also said to tell you that he had at last found a place for a man without a family."

"Did he seem—happy to go?"

Valmar hesitated. "Not happy. But also not entirely grim. It was almost like—this may not make sense—like a fierce joy." He fell silent a moment, remembering his own wild yearning, the ache akin to homesickness for something he had never seen, which had sent him galloping fruitlessly after them. "But, Karin! I can't believe it really was a Wanderer. And why would he want to leave home anyway?"

"He has chosen honor over love," said Karin, staring fixedly out the window. Every now and then, distant voices from the Gemot reached them.

Valmar sat thinking that any warrior should make that choice, but neither of them spoke for a moment.

"Are the Fifty Kings well occupied?" she asked suddenly, her hand closing on his arm.

"Yes, I think so. Your father read a list of all the cases they had to hear today, and they hadn't gotten very far down it when I left—and then several people raised additional issues."

"Good. Then no one will miss us. There used to be a Mirror-seer living at the lake just a short way up the valley."

They took horses from the royal stables to ride south, up along the river. Karin had hurried straight from the hall to the stables and been polite only with a visible effort when the chief ostler had welcomed her and then carefully selected the finest and most suitable horses for the princess and her companion. She settled herself on a side-saddle, which Valmar had never seen anyone use before, as they rode away from the castle.

Hills rose on either side of the valley, steep-sided and almost bare of vegetation. But the valley itself was lush and green. The road followed the river's winding for three miles, then zigzagged up the side of an escarpment that formed a natural dam. Beyond a lake was tucked, brilliant blue and smelling faintly of mud.

"I know you're supposed to be able to influence the lords of voima by burning them offerings," said Valmar. "But what will you have to offer them to make them tell you why they took Roric?"

"In the old tales," said Karin distantly, "the more desperate the request, the more precious the sacrifice. You may have heard the story of the woman who called on the Wanderers to restore her dead husband. One finally came to her while she was brewing and offered to restore her man, but demanded in return 'that which was between her and the vat' . . ."

Valmar looked at his big sister in horrified surmise a moment but said nothing and forced himself to dismiss the thought.

The Mirror-seer was where Karin remembered, living in a tree-sheltered cabin on the shore. He was as round as a ball and completely bald, and he was fishing from the dock in front of his cabin when they rode up. Waterstriders made constant little ripples in the water by the dock, and the fish were coming up to feed.

"And you expect me to tell you the doings of the Wanderers?" he demanded, apparently highly displeased to be taken from his fishing. "Shall I also explain the workings of fate?"

"It would be most agreeable if you would," said Valmar. He felt he ought to speak on Karin's behalf, even though he had never met a Mirror-seer before.

But she interrupted. "I am the heiress of this kingdom," she said, looking levelly at the round little man, "and would like to establish a close relationship with you." She reached up slowly to unfasten her necklace. "A man named Roric No-man's son has been taken away, perhaps by the Wanderers, and I would like to know if he still lives beneath the sun."

The feel of the heavy gold links in his hand did much to restore the Mirror-seer's good humor. Valmar, watching him, was surprised and a little relieved at how ordinary he seemed, not like the Weaver, who could have been any age or any gender and who always appeared just when one thought oneself completely alone.

"Then you are the little princess who went away as a hostage," said the Mirror-seer. "Wait here."

He ducked into his cabin while Karin and Valmar waited outside on a dock dappled by sunlight falling through the branches overhead. Back down the valley, they could just glimpse the white spires of the castle.

Valmar jumped when the man reappeared. He was draped completely in black, only his eyes showing through slits in the cloth, and he carried two mirrors.

Karin motioned Valmar back. She stepped forward herself onto the dock with the Mirror-seer, but he waved her away as well. Valmar shivered involuntarily. The Mirror-seer's eyes through the slits were an intense sky blue.

The man first mumbled words so low they could not understand them, but as he spoke the breezes dropped, the insects and fish were still, and the lake itself became as flat and smooth as a mirror. Then he bent over the end of his dock so that he could see his reflection and positioned the two mirrors not quite facing each other. He moved them slightly, until Valmar caught a glimpse of tiny repeating figures. For a second, he thought one of the repeating figures in the reflection was different from the rest.

After several long, completely quiet minutes, the Seer moved the mirrors again, put his own head between them, turned them both on his reflection in the lake, and suddenly stood up.

"What do you see?" asked Karin urgently.

"I see a disturbance among the Wanderers," the little man answered slowly. He reached up to pull the black cloth off his bald head. Valmar saw with a sudden shock that he was much thinner than he had been only a quarter hour before, as though his flesh had been consumed like a candle. "I might guess what this means, but I would prefer not to say . . ."

"I gave you a necklace worth twenty Mirror-seers' hides," said Karin fiercely. "I think you will say."

He sat down on the dock, the mirrors faceup in slack hands. Valmar, looking at them, thought that now they reflected nothing, not even sky. "It is said," the man answered after a moment, "that the Wanderers have not always ruled earth and heaven, that there were rulers of voima before them and will be others after them . . ."

"Even for the lords of voima," said Karin as though she was quoting someone, "fate does not always go well."

"An end is fated for everyone, not just for mortals," said the Mirror-seer, giving her a quick glance.

"But where is Roric?" she demanded.

"I did not see him with the Wanderers." He held up a hand against her protests. "I cannot say what that means. I can only tell you what I saw. And you have heard more from me than you will hear from any other Seer."

None of this made any sense to Valmar. "Then if you cannot tell us where Roric is," he put in, "we'll have to find him ourselves. Even if you won't tell us the fate of the Wanderers, you can certainly tell us where to find them." When the man turned to stare at him, he fumbled at his cloak. "Would this clasp make the telling easier?"

But the Mirror-seer unexpectedly smiled, a wide crack in his pale face. "Save your jewels. I can tell you where a mortal is most likely to meet a Wanderer without consulting my mirrors."

Karin interrupted. "And where is that?" she cried.

He went on speaking to Valmar as though he had not heard her. "But I warn you, that which you must offer the Wanderers themselves may be far more than a Seer or Weaver will ask you." He then turned to Karin. "I am surprised, as princess of this kingdom, that you did not know. A Wanderer may often be glimpsed at twilight on the top of that bald hill at the head of the valley. How you reach him and what you say to him," turning his back abruptly, "is your problem."

"You don't have to come with me," said Karin as she and Valmar rode on up the valley.

"Yes, I do. Roric told me to take care of you if he didn't come back."

She smiled suddenly as though very pleased. But she said, "King Hadros will wonder if you are not there at the end of the day's meeting."

"Will they not wonder in *your* castle?"

She stopped smiling. "Let them wonder. Let them imagine anything they like about you and me. I could not stay in my castle, not knowing what has happened to Roric, surrounded by those people and doing nothing."

Valmar was momentarily disconcerted by the implications of what she thought people might imagine. But he said, "If fate does not go well for the Wanderers, I wonder if that means they are being attacked by people with no backs."

The valley was narrowing, with little room for more than the track and a few firs beside the river under steep rocky walls. The water beside them dashed white over tumbled boulders. At first the tracks had led on either hand up out of the valley, toward villages perched on the hills above it. But now their path seemed little frequented, shaded and strewn with brown fir needles. Valmar, looking ahead, saw no pass, only the river cascading as a thin white line out of a cliff face.

Karin reined in where the path died out completely. "The Seer must have meant that hill," she said, pointing. "It's called Graytop. I came up here on a picnic once, not long before the war, with my older brother and our nurse. We decided we were going to climb it. I doubt if we made it more than a quarter of the way up."

Valmar looked at it critically. The hill stood out, separated from the valley walls and higher. It rose sharply from the far side of the river, its lower slopes green, the upper slopes bare granite. "If you made it a quarter of the way up, you were doing well."

"I have always been good at climbing," said Karin with a small smile. She dismounted. "If the Wanderer comes at twilight, that should give me about two hours. I think I can make it up there in that amount of time."

"How shall we cross the river?" asked Valmar.

"As I recall, a little way along the bank there's a place where we scrambled down to the water. The river's course is very narrow there—I could jump it even when I was eight." She turned her eyes full on him. "But I am going alone."

Valmar swung off his own horse and seized her by the hand. "I told you I have to take care of you! I couldn't wait

here quietly while you tried to climb—perhaps slipping—
and then maybe met—"

She put her free hand over his mouth. "I cannot climb
in my mother's brocade dress, so I am taking these clothes
off. I am quite sure," and for a second her lips twitched in
amusement, "that your father would not want you beside
me as I went up the hill naked."

The shock silenced Valmar for a second. He dropped
her hand and stared at her, wondering if she could be serious. Then he said resolutely, "In that case, you can wait
here and I shall go alone."

"You have never been as good at climbing," she said,
unfastening her cloak and turning around while she started
on the lacings of her bodice. "You can help me and Roric
most by staying right here. If I fall, drag me out of the river
and get me back to my father's castle if I am still alive. If I
do not return, try if the Weaver back home will give you a
clearer message."

"But why do you want to risk your life like this?" he
protested.

"I love Roric. Now turn your back, or you really will
have King Hadros furious with you."

He turned his back obediently, hearing the rustle of clothing coming off. He considered trying to wrestle his big
sister back onto her horse, tying her to the saddle and leading
the animal back down to the castle. He would seize her
with his own cloak, he decided, making it hard for her to
fight back while also covering up a nakedness that he startled
himself by beginning to picture.

And then he realized there was silence behind him. He
spun around to see a slim figure, wearing only riding gloves
and a shift caught up above the knees, springing across a
narrow place in the river course and scrambling up the far
side.

He slowly gathered up the clothes she had dropped and
folded them neatly. There were two long, blond hairs caught
in the hood of her cloak. He picked them up carefully,

then pulled two of his own red hairs out with a sharp tug. He leaned several tiny fir twigs together and laid the hairs across them, then struck a spark with the flint and steel at his belt. The dry twigs caught at once. The hairs twisted as though alive as they burned.

He ground out the embers with his heel and looked up the hill. Karin was now a small pale shape, higher than he had expected and apparently climbing easily. He hoped his offering was acceptable to the lords of voima.

4

At first when the cool afternoon air touched Karin's skin she shivered, but the exercise of climbing quickly warmed her again. She wished for the sturdy boots she normally wore at home, as her toes cracked against still another stone. She had left her elegant slippers with Valmar as worse than useless, but at least her hands were protected by her riding gloves.

The hill was as she remembered, its lower slopes made up of stones that had long since wedged themselves firmly into position, now grown with weeds and moss. It made for surprisingly easy climbing, with plenty of chinks for toes and fingers. She and her brother had stopped eleven years ago because it was growing late, because their nurse, from whom they had slipped away, had finally spotted them and was shouting terrible threats, and because they were getting tired.

She felt the strain especially in the muscles between her shoulder blades. Every now and then there was a small tree, well-rooted among the rocks, and she allowed herself to rest for a moment within its crook, trying to stretch out the stiffness. But the sharp twigs caught at her skin and the light fabric of her shift when she moved again.

As the afternoon advanced the sun disappeared behind the high hills and a wind began to blow, moaning softly, not quite shaping intelligible words. Karin glanced back down into the valley, heavily shadowed now so that it was impossible to pick out detail although she could see a dark mass that must be the horses.

Then she looked up the slope before her, becoming ever steeper. Soon she would be out of the area where the stones were well lodged, into a region where no plant life grew because the stones were still constantly shifting. The sky was a thin and pale blue; she did not dare rest longer if she wanted to be at the top before twilight.

As she continued upward she startled birds nesting in crevices on the steep slope. She thought about the Mirror-seer, wondering if his willingness to give information so openly, so freely, was all a deception, that he knew it was no easier to meet a Wanderer on Graytop than anywhere else in mortal realms. If so, he must be having a hearty laugh at her expense, watching in his mirrors as a woman wearing nothing but a ripped shift risked death on a steep slope for no reason at all.

Karin kept on climbing. She had reached the gray rocks that gave the hill its bald appearance. She was high enough that she now looked down on the little clusters of distant houses that perched on the hills above the valley, and the setting sun touched the granite with a deceptively warm light.

Here she had to go very carefully, testing each step before she shifted her weight. Several times as she started to pull herself up a piece of rock broke loose and plummeted back toward the valley, sending the birds whirling dismayed out of their nests. If she fell, she thought grimly, Valmar would have trouble finding enough of her body to make it worth carrying the pieces back down to her father.

Her heart was beating so hard it shook her whole body as she reached up again and again in search of a solid grip, forcing her battered feet to follow. But then suddenly she realized that the slope against which she pressed was less steep, that she was crawling more than climbing. She raised her head. The air was darkening, though the sky above was still light, and she had reached the top.

If there was a Wanderer here, she certainly did not see him. She scrabbled away from the edge and stretched out in the minimal wind protection a large stone provided, sucking at a deep scratch on one wrist. The cool air quickly dried her sweat.

"Are you an outcast?" came a quiet voice behind her.

She spun around, wrapping her arms around herself and keeping her knees together, suddenly deeply ashamed to be found undressed.

But the Wanderer—if it was a Wanderer—gave no sign that he had noticed. He sat on a stone a short distance away, his face hidden by a wide-brimmed hat, seeming to look northward toward the sea.

Karin stared at him as though paralyzed. She had been so glad to reach the top of the hill alive that she had forgotten that she would have anything else to fear. But if the Mirror-seer was right, this was one of the immortal lords of voima who controlled mortal destinies, whose power over earth and sky, life and death, was limitless.

Somehow she had expected him to look more impressive.

Then she found her voice, forcing herself to speak without trembling. "I seek information. I regret that I have climbed up here nearly naked, with nothing to offer you, but I have come because I am trying to find Roric No-man's son."

As she spoke she wondered wildly if he might be right, that she really was an outcast. She had been taken out of the only home she had known for ten years, to be returned to the home that had sent her away.

The man chuckled. "Then you and I seek the same thing."

She took a moment to analyze this. "You do not know where Roric is? But he left to go with the Wanderers!"

"When you say he left," said the man a little sharply, "what exactly do you mean?"

Karin frowned. Wherever Roric was, this person ought to know it. "I mean that a being came and summoned him away from home, and no one has seen him since." The twilight was rapidly hastening toward dark. Either a late-flying bird or a bat darted past her head. "Those who saw it, said the being had no back."

The man in the wide hat, sitting half turned away from her, certainly had a back. But as she finished recovering her breath, trying unsuccessfully to see his face—if he even had one—the chill that gripped her went far deeper than the touch on her skin of the evening air.

He did not answer for a moment. "Then I fear we will not be able to use him," he said at last, with what sounded like a sigh. "We do not force mortals against their will, and he has made his choice." Something about his voice sounded, not aged or creaky, but still extremely old.

"But where is he?" Karin cried.

"You, on the other hand," he said, not answering her question but turning fully toward her for the first time, "might be useful to us. It is a rare person who has the strength and the will to climb this high, seeking someone who might be nothing more than a shadow."

She thought she felt his eyes on her, but she was now too angry and too disappointed to feel shame. "I do not intend to become 'valuable' for anyone else," she said bitterly. "I climbed here because I hoped you could tell me where Roric is. I know I have nothing to offer you, but I could bring you a bracelet or rings tomorrow—" She paused, not liking to think of climbing up here *again*. "Or we could meet somewhere else . . ."

"Do you think me a Weaver or a Seer," the other asked, sounding amused, "that you must offer me a bracelet as a gift? Think what you put in the flames when you burn an offering: some hairs, a scrap of wool or parchment, a bite of flesh or some grains of wheat— Are these not gifts that symbolize the yearning spirit more than iron and gold?"

Then he really is a Wanderer, she thought, even if he does not shoot flame from his fingers.

"You are a princess, Karin Kardan's daughter. Why is Roric No-man's son important to you?"

"I love him," she said defiantly. "He and I are sworn together."

She trembled now as she spoke, weak with exhaustion and fear for Roric. But at least with this strange figure, on this bald hill in the dusk, she did not feel any need to hide and control her feelings and her words.

"You have, I recall, long been a hostage in a foreign court," said the shadowed figure thoughtfully. "It is not surprising that you would swear yourself to someone else out of desperation—it cannot be easy being an outcast."

"I did not choose Roric out of desperation," she said heatedly. "I chose him because I love him. Now, are you going to tell me where he is?"

"Not unless I know myself," he said with a low chuckle. "But you yourself have possibilities . . . Tell me, what did you think to do next?"

"Get off this hilltop, because the only thing I've found here is someone who claims to be a Wanderer but doesn't know anything!"

"I make no 'claim' to be anyone," said the other, quietly and good-naturedly. He rose, stepped behind a large rock, and disappeared.

Karin jumped up and ran around the rock, knocking her toes again in the shadows. There was no one there; she had not really expected that there would be.

She walked over to the edge and looked down. Though there was still a little light off to the west, the rocks below her disappeared into blackness. The bottom of the hill was completely hidden. There was no way she could descend that rock face in the dark and still live till morning. She listened, hearing nothing but the distant sound of the rushing river.

Valmar would be worried. She put her hands on either side of her mouth and shouted, "I shall pass the night up here! I'll see you tomorrow!"

Again she listened but heard no reply. Maybe he had already gone. But she could not climb down in the dark. This looked, she thought uneasily, like a good place for a troll, and not even the semi-domesticated one who lived under Hadros' bridge, whom Roric at least had dared face.

She settled herself stiffly against a rock so that her back was protected, then realized how cold it was growing. On the hilltop the wind blew steadily, with a bite as though it reached her fresh from distant icefields. If she fell asleep up here she might not wake. She pushed herself to her feet and groped until she found a fairly broad expanse of smooth granite on which to spend the night pacing.

Long, long ago, before your grandfather's time or great-grandfather's time or even *his* great-grandfather's time, there was no glory or honor on the earth. The earth was ruled by women, and their only thought was for their children and for their children's safety, even when those children were grown, even when those children had become men and yearned for adventure and far places. The men were at most allowed to travel to market, to hunt bears who had threatened the flocks, to fish on the deep and dangerous sea, but never to go to war.

And in those days there was one young man named Laaiman, brave and glorious, whose mother kept him from everything but taking care of the cows. But one day, coming home from pasture, he saw something shiny lying in his path, something made of steel, long and sharp with a handle that just fit his hand. It was a sword, but he had never before seen one.

He left the cows and went to the Weaver who lived in a cave nearby to ask the Weaver what it was. And when he had burned an offering, and the Weaver had woven its web, he was told, "It is the sign. The end of women's rule has come."

Laaiman did not know what this meant, but the Weaver would say no more, and as he left sealed up the entrance to the cave. And that night there was blood on the moon, and wolves howled all around the cow barn, and in the morning came blizzard snow though it was midsummer. Snakes writhed in the sea and fish on dry land, and all the women went into labor and brought forth monsters. And beings appeared who had never been seen before, like tall and shining men whose faces were concealed—Wanderers, they called themselves, lords of voima.

only one with a sword, defended his manor and his mother and sisters against the other men. The Wanderers applauded him and gave him greater strength yet, so that he could conquer all others even when other men too began to make swords.

And when Laaiman had conquered a kingdom and won himself eternal fame and honor, he saw a woman crossing his fields, walking lightly on the very tops of the barley stalks. She was slim and dark-haired, with eyes like the deepest night. A woman of voima, she named herself, made for the pleasure of the Wanderers. But he took her into his own bed, and on her he fathered a race of great men, of heroes, and of kings.

CHAPTER THREE

1

The ale horn came down the table again, and Roric drank deeply before passing it on. The ale here tasted even better than Karin's brewing, and as far as he could tell he could drink any amount without it going to his head.

His companions, however, had already reached the stage of laughing for no reason, shouting good-naturedly but incomprehensibly, and struggling for possession of an ale horn that always had enough left for one more drink. They were all slightly bigger than he was, and all had the disconcerting trick of becoming blurred and shadowy if he looked at them directly. They now seemed to be competing in boasts, who would do the most now that they had a mortal with them—but exactly what they intended to do with him remained unclear. Two took their boasting to the stage of jumping up and seizing each other by the neck. But they stopped their squabbling to cheer when a well-endowed young woman with a strangely vacant expression rose and began to dance.

Roric shrugged off his unease, forcing himself to relax and enjoy this feast. He had stayed constantly alert, constantly watching, in the three days—if indeed it was three days—while the person who might be a Wanderer had led him across a startlingly lush and beautiful countryside, but led him furtively. They had kept behind the tall hedgerows,

64

plunged deep through woods that seemed to glow green, galloped the other direction if surprised slipping past the barns.

When he had left Valmar, fervent to take his fate into his hands, he had not anticipated spending long hours and days crossing a rich realm, trying not to be seen. But when he demanded to know where they were going the other had only said, "Do heroes ask questions when they go to meet their fate? You will know soon enough."

In this land Goldmane seemed tireless, able to gallop for hours, and he could ride almost indefinitely. At first it was like being in the heart of a tale, galloping wild and free far, far, beyond the narrow fields of Hadros' kingdom, the wind whipping and singing around them. But in the tales the heroes were always galloping *toward* a glorious goal. When this being had first appeared riding up to the mares' pen, he had seemed terrible, a force before which trees and clouds must bow abashed. But someone who could have stepped out of a nightmare in mortal realms was in contrast here timid and easily frightened by even the most trivial threat.

They must, Roric thought, be covering scores, even hundreds, of miles a day, and yet the countryside did not change. The entire time he watched for landmarks so he would know his way back again, yet as the miles disappeared behind them he became less and less sure he could find the way. There were plenty of distinctive features, steep hills overlooking bright lakes, the clustered outbuildings of manors, rocky outcroppings that looked to his eye as though they should have castles on them although they never did, wide rivers with meadows on either side of the ford; and yet these features seemed to repeat themselves endlessly with very little variation.

It was like the countryside he had always known and yet different: larger, much greener, with no weeds among the grain, no stones pushing up in the hay fields, no marshy thickets in the bands of trees between manors, no tumbledown buildings on those manors, no biting insects—and no sunset. Every hill they climbed, every valley they entered glistened as though seen through freshly rain-washed air, yet no rain fell. When they paused in their riding to sleep, it was warm enough that he was comfortable curled up under a tree without even a cloak to spread over him.

It was late spring—or had been—yet here the wheat was nearly ripe, the lambs well grown, and the rowans in the manor courtyards hung with swollen red berries. He had the disconcerting sense that perhaps here it was *always* summer, for none of the manors by which they slipped had the woodpiles that should by this season be readying the dwellers for the sharp bite of winter.

In late August, when all nature seemed to have forgotten colder weather except for the sea-ducks whose mournful calls marked the end of summer, Roric had often thought that it would be good if winter were not fated, had wished idly that each day could continue as warm as the day before. But here he began to think the lash of snow and the killing frost might in themselves be purifying, that without them lushness would blossom into overripeness, and then into rot.

They saw a number of housecarls and maids, usually in the distance, but no one who could be the great folk who must live in those well-tended manors. And on the second day of riding, he realized what else was missing: there were no fairs and no market towns. It was as though all these fine manors were self-sufficient, that the folk who owned them spent their days inside tooling the leather or hammering the iron or spinning the wool, so that none need go to market and buy.

Not until they reached this hall had his companion relaxed his vigilance. The manor was built on top of a steep rise, hidden beyond a pine forest. After a short ride among the trees they passed under a wooden gateway, and the trees immediately began to thin out. And once past the pines and up a sharp slope they had found verdant meadows and spacious stone buildings.

Others then had come running to meet them both. The buildings, at least, remained solid when he looked at them. The manor's fields were bursting with grain; its cows, larger than Goldmane, were heavy with milk; and the ale horn never needed to be refilled.

Everyone had seemed delighted to meet Roric.

At first, he had thought the being who summoned him must be a chieftain, even a king, until he had refused to answer questions. Then he decided this was a warrior like Gizor One-hand, sent to bring him here, and asked nothing further. But when he arrived the band of men who greeted him still included no one who seemed to be the leader.

Roric cut his meat with the knife he had tried to give the Weaver and glanced toward the open doorway. It was late afternoon, motes of dust dancing in horizontal ruddy rays, but it had seemed late afternoon the entire time he was here. The beef was so tender the juices ran down his chin. He wiped them with his sleeve and wondered if this was Hel. If so, it was unlike anything he had ever imagined; for this kind of Hel he and Karin should have been dead together months ago.

But he had never heard, even in the oldest tales, of a man looking on Hel with living eyes. He would have thought it was the Wanderers' realm into which he had stumbled, except that they had traveled so furtively. They might instead be somewhere in the far southern lands, even beyond the realms where landless men sought booty. If so, if he got home again, he would take Karin, take a ship and a few good men, and return here to make a kingdom for himself. Karin and he between them would make sure their men did not overripen into softness.

In the meantime, these people had not yet told him why they wanted him.

❋   ❋   ❋

It was not the next morning, because there was no morning here. But he had slept and wakened when one of the slightly indistinct men—he might as well think of them as men—came to find him. As they went outside he hoped, feeling itchy for action, that at last he would be told why he was here. But the other did not speak at once.

Birds chirped blithely as buxom maids finished milking the oversize cows and set them loose in the pasture. Neither maids nor housecarls had yet spoken in his hearing. Roric leaned on the fence and considered the disconcertingly misty person beside him. He thought he was the same one who had brought him here, but it was difficult to be sure. Last night in the hall, he and all the others had seemed so jolly almost as to be foolish. If these were the lords of voima, Roric thought with a half smile, it might explain why mortal life was often so disordered and hard to understand. But his smile faded as he added to himself that here *he* at least was going to do all with his strength that fate allowed him.

"You said you wanted me," he said. "I have followed you without demur, but now that we are here I must know why."

"First you must swear yourself to us, Roric No-man's son." The other's voice took on again the deep, vibrating tone it had had when he first rode up to Roric and Valmar. "Swear on iron and the bloodred sap of the rowan tree that you shall obey us and never go against us."

Roric gave him a quick sideways glance, but he was scarcely more solid viewed from the corner of the eye than directly. "That in honor I cannot do. I am King Hadros' sworn man and Karin's sworn lover. To another I cannot swear myself unless I am very sure my new oaths do not counter my old ones."

"Here your previous oaths have no meaning."

"Not to you, perhaps, but they do to me."

The cows had ambled off. Housecarls went out from the loft house toward the fields, scythes over their shoulders.

"You came into immortal lands of your own free will," the other said in a voice that could have come out of the ground. So this *was* the Wanderers' home country, then. No use trying to find it again by ship. "Perhaps we can test if your unsworn loyalty will be enough. For I tell you that there are beings here that would destroy us."

Roric drummed his fingers on the fence. "So far—" he started to say. But suddenly, unbelievably, an enormous bear appeared around the corner. It stood eight feet high, and its fur was black and its eyes yellow. Bitter claws twice as long as a man's fingers reached toward Roric's companion.

It opened its mouth in a roar, showing razor-sharp teeth and a hungry gullet. In one motion, Roric seized the man by the shoulder, whirled him away, and snatched up an axe that leaned against the barn.

He had about two seconds while the bear looked at the empty air between its claws. In those two seconds he threw the axe with all his strength, hurtling it end over end, lodging it in the skull between yellow eyes that turned just too late to spot it coming.

Roric grabbed the man and vaulted the fence into the pasture, then looked back. The bear crumpled with a soft moan and lay still.

"They're especially dangerous when they're wounded," said Roric, drawing his sword. The man beside him rose rather shakily to his feet. He was still a little misty around the edges, but at least he had *felt* solid.

Roric stepped cautiously up on the fence's lower bar for a closer look. But the bear did not look wounded. It looked dead.

A few hundred yards away, the cows, clanging their bells, looked toward them as though puzzled. Roric found a pole and poked without response, then finally, emboldened, rolled the bear over. It was indeed dead, its skull split open.

"Now do you believe me, Roric No-man's son, that there are beings here that would destroy us?"

Roric leaned on his sword, looking thoughtfully at the dead beast. "Are any of the men here on the manor good tanners?" he asked casually. "This is a fine bearskin. I would like it as a winter cloak." But he was thinking, "That was too easy."

Roric and the shadowy figure went inside, and the latter said offhandedly that a tanner would start preparing the fur at once, but Roric never saw it again.

The men were finishing the breakfast porridge and beer, yet they seemed curiously at loose ends. The housecarls had gone without anyone supervising them, and these warriors—he had to think of them as warriors even with no chieftain or king to command them—were not sharpening their knives, or trying, laughing, to train new puppies, or repairing their harness, or even telling old tales to boys or doing any of the hundred small tasks Hadros' warriors always did in odd moments at home.

But as he hesitated in the doorway all these slightly oversize, indistinct men suddenly sprang up to begin preparations for war. They took down battle-axes and heavy swords from the walls, found leather helmets strengthened with steel, and swung their shields on the saddles of the horses assembled in the courtyard. At home, they would have gotten out the polishing stone and the sharpening wheel, but all their weapons were already keen and brilliant, as though fresh from the blacksmith's. Roric looked critically at his own sword; fortunately he had sharpened it the first day he was back at Hadros' castle from the manor. No one offered him any weapons or armor.

Their voices rang out in the hall, all of them talking at once, some still boasting about what they would do with their mortal, some complaining irritably when another got in front of them, others speaking excitedly of honor and glory. Roric, standing in a corner out of the way, started to play with his star-shaped bone charm. With it in his hand the people here seemed slightly less misty, slightly more concrete. For the first time he began to see the variety among them: skinny legs, enormous and bulbous bodies, extremely long torsos, misshapen humped backs, and powerfully muscled arms. But their faces, for the most part, remained hidden.

He clenched his fist around the charm, then put it away. Whoever these people really were, he had thrown his fate in with them.

Their horses were perfectly solid. These stood quietly, unspooked by their masters, as an array of heavily armored shapes clambered into the saddles. Roric used his teeth to tighten the leather lacings on his gloves and set his foot in Goldmane's stirrup.

The warband shouted and clashed their swords against their shields, and all the dogs began barking and trumpets blowing. It only missed the women seeing them off. The only women he had seen at the manor had been the maids with their vacant expressions.

After riding boldly down the hill into the pine woods and through the gate, the band became furtive again. They shushed each other and rode at single-file, glancing from side to side. Roric came to a decision. He kicked his stallion to the front of the band, then pulled Goldmane sideways across the road to block it.

The others reined in before him, looking at him with eyes of cinder in shadowed faces. "I am not one of you," said Roric in a voice intended to carry, "nor sworn to you. I came to your land because one of you told me you wanted me, even as a man without a father. I have waited patiently to find out what you wanted, intending to win here renown and a place for me and the woman I love. But if I am to accompany you to war I have to know why."

One of them—he thought the one he had talked to before—came forward and slapped him on the shoulder with a hand that felt reassuringly solid. "You're our mortal, of course!" he said heartily.

"But I do not know," said Roric loudly, "why the Wanderers would want a mortal."

This caused some consternation among the warriors. Some motioned as though to shush him. But the man answered after a very short pause. "Mortals have unusual powers here in the realms of voima—or so we hear! Of course, it is hard to test, because mortals can only come here if a rift has been opened, which we cannot do ourselves, and they must come of their own free will."

Goldmane suddenly made as though to bite the other's horse. Roric had to pull him up hard. "You still have not told me why I am here," he said levelly, a suspicion growing darkly in his mind. "Do you love to fight battles with each other, but since you yourselves are immortal, you all need to take mortals with you to war so that *someone* can die?"

The man put his hand on Roric's shoulder again. "We do not intend for you to die, Roric No-man's son. Now are you satisfied?"

He was not satisfied, but having ridden out with these people he now had very little choice.

"Let us continue," said the man heartily, "and perhaps we can discuss issues of mortality as we ride, if that is your interest."

At the first manor they reached, several of the men broke down the pasture fence and sent in the dogs. These chased the cows, setting the bells clanging wildly, until a shout came from the manor house. Then the dogs were quickly whistled back, and the whole war party galloped off with laughs and jeers.

"We're making war on cows?" Roric asked with an eyebrow raised, once they had come to a stop in a patch of woods.

"No, we just like to disrupt things a bit."

Roric thought this over as they continued onward. For beings of voima, immortality itself might make them petty.

Since they would live on forever, they had no need for brave and glorious deeds to make their memory live in song. They need have no goals or even hard work in a land of unending fruitful summer. All that mattered was the moment, the enjoyment of a joke at someone else's expense, the glow of drunkenness. Even quarrels need not be settled because ultimately the outcome was always the same.

But he, who was not immortal, did not like the particular quarrel building behind him, which the quarrelers made no effort to keep from his ears: whether they should be delighted to have a mortal, or whether he was too independent-minded and too dangerous.

"If you are not Wanderers," he asked slowly, voicing his suspicion at last, "who are you?"

"We are the third force," said his companion as though it explained it all, and with no attempt to apologize for having misled him. "The Wanderers thought they could persuade you to help them against us, but we reached you first!" The face that Roric could not always see came into focus, grim-mouthed and not at all foolish.

A force distinct from the Wanderers, he thought, immortal and imbued with voima, could be dangerous to the Wanderers as well as to mortals. This would explain their furtive progress through this land. If it *had* been a Wanderer he spoke to originally, had these beings come to claim him in the hope he would come without question?

He slid his fingers into his belt pouch to feel his bone charm, tapped the hilt of his sword, and stroked Goldmane on the neck. He had come here with these and his wit, the same weapons he had used against King Hadros. There he had won. Here he was not sure what winning entailed.

2

"The Wanderers know less about us than we had assumed," said Karin. She could barely stay on her horse, but she seemed determined to talk. Valmar had wakened, after a long night in which he had dozed fitfully sitting against a tree, to find dawn breaking and Karin trying to pull her clothes back on. She had trembled so hard and her fingers were so numb that he had finally had to tie the lacings for her.

"But you said he knew your name," said Valmar.

"And not much more. Either he was asking me questions because he was interested in how I would frame my answers, or he really did not know I love Roric."

Valmar considered for a moment in silence. His horse picked its way carefully down the track, and in the distance ahead he could see the spires of King Kardan's castle. His father would be furious; he hoped his big sister would volunteer to talk to him before he had to.

"But if they don't know very much," he said slowly, "then why do we burn offerings to them?"

Karin stared at him with eyes that had become enormous. "I shall burn no more offerings."

"Maybe it's better like this," declared Valmar suddenly. "We shall ask nothing else of voima, but make our lives into the best tale that fate allows us, with our own strength and honor and our own manhood—or, in your case, womanhood." He sat up tall and stiff in the saddle as he spoke.

"But if we decide to ignore the lords of voima," said Karin quietly, "we cannot forget that *someone* has taken Roric."

King Hadros met them as they reached the meadow that circled the castle. He stood with his massive fists on his hips, scowling, but he did not speak at once, instead taking in his flushed son and Karin, her clothes all disordered, clinging desperately to the reins as though afraid any moment she would slide from the saddle.

Valmar observed what looked like several very different comments rise to his father's lips and fade away again. Finally he said in a low growl, "I had taught you more honor than this, son."

Karin tried to pull herself straighter, then gave up and
slid from the horse. She winced as her bare feet touched
the ground; they had been too swollen for her slippers.
Valmar immediately dismounted in case she needed support, but she remained standing. "Your son behaved himself in perfect honor," she said slowly, staring straight at
the king. "He helped me and assisted me. Everything I
asked he performed."

And then, completely unexpectedly, Hadros smiled. "Well,
you have changed your opinions quickly enough, little princess," he said gruffly, but he sounded almost pleased. He
gave Valmar a slap on the back that staggered him. "It is
not what I would have recommended, but it may be for
the best . . ."

Valmar, shocked, tried to deny what his father seemed
to have assumed and found himself only sputtering. He
stole a glance at Karin. There was the slightest amused
twitch at the corner of her mouth.

"I told your father that after a tiring day of riding and
exploring with Valmar you were spending the night in my
tents," said Hadros to Karin. "He seemed disturbed that
you were not in the castle at the end of the day's Gemot—
nearly as disturbed as I was to find my son missing! But it
seemed best not to reopen the war at the All-Gemot." He
smiled a little. "Shall I speak to him today of your por-
tion?"

"No," said Karin, weakly but determinedly, her eyes cast
down. "Not today. Not until I tell you. Valmar is, after all,
not yet of age."

"He has my permission, of course," said Hadros slowly.
"Did you hope to hide from your father this shame until
you are well wed?"

"I hope to hide this from *everybody*," she said on the
brink of tears. But then she pulled herself together with a
visible effort, took the reins of both horses, and walked up
toward the castle, leaving Hadros and his son looking after
her.

Then the king turned, striding toward the corded circle where the Fifty Kings were gathering for the day's decisions, taking Valmar with him.

He was still trying to work out why his father, whom he had expected to be livid at the shame of his having ridden off with Karin and not come back all night, instead seemed delighted at the thought of what might have taken place. Karin had misled Hadros deliberately, as though she had suddenly decided she wanted to marry Valmar. If he could see his big sister again before the All-Gemot finished, maybe she would let him know what she really intended.

In the meantime he remained silent as they walked, wishing himself invisible, but it still seemed, inexplicably, as though his father was pleased with him.

3

King Kardan was sitting on the side of Karin's bed when she awoke. She sat up, pulling the sheet around her shoulders, and glanced toward the window. She still felt exhausted, almost as though she had been beaten, but from the angle of the sun she had slept the entire day.

"Is the All-Gemot finished?" she asked.

"There are still two more days of deliberations, but we have finished the most important business." He smiled and patted her hand. "I can understand why you would be loath to part from the people with whom you have spent the last ten years—especially since, I can see now, you have even become friends with them. I can even see why you would want to reacquaint yourself with your kingdom by taking a long ride with Hadros' heir. Perhaps I was too quick to assume you would be as happy to be home as I am to have you. There has not been a day since you left, Karin, that I have not thought of you. But I do wish you had told me you intended to stay with Hadros last night, so I had not worried."

"Suppose—suppose I told you I had met a Wanderer

last night." She spoke quietly, looking down, wondering how likely he was to believe her. She no longer felt she knew this man, and yet they had to learn to trust each other again.

"I would say I had not heard a story like that from you since—well, since you went away!" He tapped her lightly on the cheek. "Do not tell me they still believe in those little upcountry northern kingdoms that the Wanderers appear to ordinary mortals. And in the meantime," with a smile, "could you warn me if you decide again to take a long ride with your friends?"

"It shall not happen again." She looked him over, her head cocked at an angle. Gray hair, certainly, and somewhat of a paunch, but he appeared no more ready to die or to step down from the throne than did King Hadros. She might not become sovereign queen until many more years had passed. "It has been a strain," she added apologetically, "learning about my brother, the journey here—but I shall come down to dinner. Do you think you could invite Queen Arane to the castle this evening?"

She sat with the queen on a window seat—the same place, in fact, where she had talked to Valmar the day before. Karin saw her childish book of old tales still lying there and quickly tucked it under a cushion. As Arane settled herself gracefully, Karin thought that she did not quite trust those wise eyes. The queen was ready to give advice, probably extremely good advice, but she would not help anyone else for a second if it stood in the way of her own plans.

But here Karin did not think her affairs would collide with the queen's. "I need your counsel," she said in low voice. "I may be forced into a marriage for which I am not ready."

The queen lifted her eyebrows. "Two days ago you told me you did not think to marry soon."

"And I still hope I shall not. But yesterday Valmar, King

Hadros' heir, and I went up the valley for a picnic, and we did not come home last night."

"Who knows this?" asked Arane sharply.

Karin glanced quickly across the room, but there was no one within earshot. "No one knows. Or no one here. King Hadros does."

"This is not the story you want told around the Gemot of the Fifty Kings, Karin!" said the queen with a mocking smile. "Could you not have been more discreet? If your father and Hadros cannot come to an agreement, your lover will at the worst be declared an outlaw for raping a high-born woman, and you at the best will start your rule with a reputation for wantoness. Not that you must always sleep alone!" raising a hand to forestall what she seemed to think was Karin's objection. "But leave it all a guess for slanderous tongues, never sure knowledge."

"You don't understand," said Karin, able to find a space for her own words at last. "Valmar and I could not have had purer relations if we had slept with a sword between us. We are to each other as brother and sister, and for all I know he is a virgin still."

"And you are not," said Arane, as though pleased with this discovery.

Karin had not meant to let that slip, but it was not important now. "But I fear that no one will believe us. My father and Hadros have only just concluded their hostilities toward each other. I did, I think, persuade Hadros that his son had not taken me by force, but he still thinks he took me willingly. And my father will not be concerned with such niceties."

"So what would you have me advise you?"

"How to avoid marrying Valmar while keeping my honor intact."

Queen Arane shook her head as though hard put to believe Karin's naïveté, then smiled and settled herself, preparing to map a battle strategy. "Do you have any men you could trust? Someone who could arrange for the boy to have a small accident? You need not harm him permanently or even badly, but a certain kind of wound, you understand, would mean the wedding would at least be postponed . . ."

"No!" Karin started to jump up, then remembered herself and sank again to the cushions. "I have no men of my own, none I could trust with a mission this delicate. And also," she added defiantly, "I would certainly not wish such a wound on Valmar."

"You need to acquire some trusty warriors as soon as you may," said Arane thoughtfully. "Or perhaps, if you are squeamish, you could arrange for Valmar merely to be threatened. Does he have a rival for your affections, someone who would at a word from you make threats against the boy to frighten him away? Then Hadros' wrath would turn against his son rather than against you. His temper is swift, as I know well, but he can also think clearly once his fury is past. If Valmar himself shrank from the marriage, it would be in Hadros' own self-interest to keep this matter quiet."

Karin shook her head. "The only rival Valmar has for my affections is gone, and I do not know where he is." She was certainly not going to tell the queen that Roric had left with someone awe-inspiring and terrifying, who still was not, it seemed, one of the Wanderers. But she did wonder if King Hadros would be content to hush this whole affair up if Valmar himself did not want to marry her, or if his rage against his heir would become murderous as it apparently had against Roric.

Queen Arane was silent for a moment, looking out the window at the twilight, a small smile on her lips. "What does young Valmar think of this?"

"He has had no idea, I think, that we might marry. As I said, we are to each other brother and sister."

"So Hadros is your principal opponent here. He will take it as an insult to *his* honor, I judge, if you flatly refuse to take his son, especially in these circumstances." She turned a jeweled ring thoughtfully on her finger. "Before you reject this marriage utterly, be certain there are not reasons why it would be beneficial. A young and malleable husband offers certain advantages, even if the advantages do not compare with those of being single." The queen reached out to turn Karin's face toward her. "For example—are you quite sure that you are not with child?"

Karin kept her eyes cast down. "Quite sure. There was a time, a few days ago, when I wondered—but no." She did not look up, regretting bitterly now that she had asked the queen to come.

"You could try to win Hadros around with clever words," said Arane. "I must believe that in the years you have lived in his court, a woman of your wit has found ways to do that. Tell him, for example, that you are already pledged to someone else, someone far away—perhaps even this rival you mentioned—and that you need the king's help to cover your shame."

"I think I already tried that," said Karin gloomily. "It was of no use." She did not dare add what she now thought fiercely, that with Roric she had hoped to be an equal, part of a couple who trusted each other and spoke openly to each other, and that even without Roric she did not want to be a woman who directed the men around her with wiles and manipulation and never affection.

"You are making it very difficult, Karin, for me to help you!" said Arane with an exasperated laugh. "You are sure you could not make the best of the situation at this point by marrying young Valmar?"

"I am sure."

"How did you come to do something so heedless as spend the night with him?"

Karin wished again that she had not asked the queen for counsel. She had no more good ideas than she had had before, and another of the Fifty Kings now knew she had not spent last night peacefully sleeping in Hadros' tent. "We had not so intended," she said quietly, thinking now only how she could ease Arane away. "But dark overcame us before we could get down." That, she commented to herself, was an understatement.

"You perhaps could tell King Hadros that you and Valmar spent the night with me," suggested the queen, as though having been asked for advice she could not leave without finding *some* way to save the situation.

"No, although I thank you," said Karin, shaking her head and keeping her eyes down. As she had asked herself all last night while pacing the rocky hilltop, and as she awoke today, she wondered where Roric could be if not with the Wanderers—and what they could now possibly want with *her.* "I think the only way this could easily be resolved would be if Hadros were to die."

Queen Arane started back. "Karin, my dear! I know I counseled you not to be squeamish, and that you are feeling somewhat desperate, but—do you not think this might be somewhat too drastic a step?"

Karin stared at the queen in horror. "I did not mean I planned to kill him! I was merely saying that while he is alive—I was just explaining that . . . He is almost my second father!"

"Then your first father had best beware," said Arane briskly. She rose and gave Karin her hand. "I doubt we shall meet again before the end of the Gemot."

A page appeared as she started across the hall to escort her out to where her bodyguard was waiting. Karin, looking after her, felt a laugh rising in her chest that was almost a sob. She had after all discovered a way to get rid of the queen.

4

"The Wanderers in your world bring death and life."

They sat in an apple orchard, the fruit so thick overhead that the leaves were almost hidden. Roric had been surprised when they reached the orchard to see no green and no rotten fruit among the long grass under the trees. But several in their band had taken sticks and began beating the branches, and after the downed apples lay on the ground for several minutes the flesh softened and the skin split. Roric wiped a hand on the grass after accidentally leaning on an apple and getting his hand covered with sticky fermented pulp.

"Are you trying to tell me," he asked slowly, "that in this world *mortals* bring death and life?"

The man did not answer. He only turned on Roric a face shadowed and without detail, then looked away.

They had paused in their riding, stopped for the night except that there was no night. But most of the band had eaten, traded a few songs and stories, and curled up under the trees to sleep. Now only Roric and this man, this being, were left sitting up, while the sun hovered low in a sky without a sunset.

Roric was not sure whether to believe anything he might say; but he still felt he had a better chance of getting a reliable answer out of him than any of the others. He wondered if this sense was only a result of having been in his company longer than any of the others'.

"If you will not tell me that," Roric said after a few minutes of silence, "then perhaps you can tell me who constitutes the first two forces, since you say you are the third."

This the man apparently thought he could answer. "The first are those you call the Wanderers. The second are those who oppose them."

"But do you not oppose them yourselves? Who are you riding to war against if not the Wanderers?"

"We fight *both* sides." The man suddenly drew his dagger and threw it, as though playfully, past Roric's ear. It lodged in the trunk behind him.

He jumped involuntarily, then reached back as calmly as he could and pulled it out. He weighed it in his hand, then looked up with a forced smile. "Is this then your guest-gift to me?"

The man snatched it back. Too bad—it had what looked like gold inlay on the blade.

"The lords of voima, they call themselves," said the man suddenly and in what Roric thought were bitter tones. "They are proud and self-righteous, roaming earth and sky, watching over mortals, shaping their own land in imitation of mortal lands— Men, they call themselves, yet I in the form of a stallion have begotten colts on all of them!"

"How do they treat you when they are not mares?" asked Roric carefully. This was an insult they used at home, and he could—he hoped—discount its validity, but he had never heard such an insult hurled at the Wanderers.

"They ignore us, scorn us, laugh at us, treat us as beneath their notice. They *say* they created us, but if we are their creation you would think they would show us more respect."

No question about it. The man was feeling bitter.

"Did they not create all those who live here?" Roric asked carefully.

"Well, they *shaped* it all, as they put it. But we are all they have ever created completely: the third force, the only beings besides the two major forces to have individual thought and will."

"And those who oppose the Wanderers?"

"They only wish to replace the old lords of voima with new ones—themselves."

"And where does that leave you?" asked Roric, trying to sound sympathetic.

The whole situation had a quality of a dream, or of a story told about someone else. Somewhere in this beautiful and frustrating land there had to be glory for a fatherless man to seize, but it was rapidly growing harder to believe in it.

"We still have our own voima," said the being, sounding crafty now. "And even your Wanderers are not fated to rule forever. We disrupt them whenever we can."

"Including capturing a mortal," provided Roric, "and sending him to attack the Wanderers. Will my steel overcome them when yours will not?"

"You were not captured, Roric No-man's son. You came willingly."

But I did not know where you were taking me, he thought—and still do not. If he now accompanied these beings willingly, it was because he had not seen an alternative since they arrived here.

He got no more useful answers out of the man. A short time later Roric lay down himself to sleep, under a different tree from everybody else.

Sleep did not come easily. He lay on his back, an arm across his eyes to shield them from the sun. He thought of Karin, picturing her going about her daily activities directing Hadros' household, hoping she was not worried for him. Then he tried to picture a "third force" where he had always expected there to be only one.

There had always been creatures of voima abroad in the world, trolls, dragons, hollow beings without backs, faeys—although he had never seen any of these but trolls, unless the strange green light in the dell he had seen only once, when out walking in the evening, had indeed been faeys. There might well be more creatures of voima here in the Wanderers' realm, beings who did not share in their full power although they were immortal themselves, creatures of spite or tricks or dangerous sullenness.

He rolled over sharply and looked toward the sleeping warband, half hidden in the grass. It had always been disquieting that he could not see them properly, even with his charm in his hand. They had been too timid, too foolish for him to fear them here, but at least one of them had terrified all of Hadros' housecarls. What were they really like? Valmar had gasped out something about someone with no back, and although he had paid no attention at the time, he now wondered what the boy might have seen that he, expecting a Wanderer, had not.

He rose to his knees, considering saddling Goldmane again and slipping away while they all slept. But if they wanted him, he had little doubt they would be able to catch him, and if he ran he did not know where he would go. "And even a man without a father should know he cannot run from fate," he growled to himself.

But then he smiled a little as he lay back down. If he lived to see mortal realms again, he would have a tale that would take several nights' singing to tell.

They came quietly up out of a valley, not talking, not blowing their trumpets, and saw a large manor house in the distance. Again there was no sign of the masters. But the warband spread out, forming a large half circle. They communicated by hand signals, keeping silence. Helmets were secured and spears readied.

Roric unfastened the peace straps on his sheath and glanced back down the valley. "Look," he said suddenly. The man next to him turned on him with the beginning of an irritable exclamation, then stopped when he saw what Roric had seen.

Coming up the valley behind them was another warband.

These riders were sharp and vivid, no shadows here. They were clad all in steel from which the sunlight flashed. They seemed small and slender in comparison with his own band, but there was nothing small about their spears. A white banner without device floated above them. Horned helmets completely covered their faces.

They had spotted him. They reined in their horses, then the rider in the lead raised a horn and blew.

The note was piercing, sending the blood pounding in Roric's ears. At last, he thought. After days of inaction, it had finally begun. Every horse in both parties reared and charged toward the other.

And he was among them, standing in the stirrups, his hair tossed back, his sword in his fist and bellowing. But as he and the horned warriors rushed together he wondered for a second if he was on the right side.

The two bands met like waves crashing together. Screams

of horses and the clang of steel on steel surrounded him. Goldmane raced in the lead, and he struck out again and again, using his sword to deflect blows aimed at him. His own strokes bounced off shield and armor.

All around him was an unfocused blur. He had no attention to spare for his companions. It felt as though the entire horned band were attacking him personally. All he could see were swords and spears aimed at him, as he ducked a javelin, parried a sword stroke, seized a spear and jerked it out of one warrior's hand one second and thrust it against another the next.

He was still untouched, but as he whirled to face another blade the back of his mind asked, as though mildly curious, how long he thought this could continue.

In the distance came another horn call.

This one was different, poignant, almost melancholic. The people at the manor, he thought, had joined the fray at last.

And at that note the fighting fizzled out. Warriors fell back on every side, and no one met his strokes. In a few seconds the clang of steel on steel had ceased. He looked around wildly, his own sword still upraised. He saw no fallen men, only both sides turning to run.

And Goldmane ran too. He had never felt his stallion go this fast. First in the middle of the group of galloping steeds—from both warbands, he thought, though it was hard to see with the wind in his eyes—then in the forefront, then out before all the rest. Shouts blew back down his throat, and hard tugs on the rein were of no avail. The stallion had the bit between his teeth, and he ran effortlessly, leaping streams and hedgerows until it seemed he was flying, only putting down a hoof occasionally to guide them on their mad course.

Roric clung like a bur to the saddle, his eyes almost blinded and a fierce smile on his lips.

"Well, I'd like to know where you learned a trick like that," said Roric to his horse.

He sat with his elbows on his knees while the stallion, unsaddled and unconcerned, grazed peacefully beside him. "Could you always run that fast, but you just never bothered before?"

Goldmane had finally begun to slow, and Roric had gotten the bit away from him at last. He tethered his horse firmly to a tree in a little meadow on top of a ridge, but the stallion showed no more interest in speed.

"The troll should have known better than to let you go," Roric added appreciatively. They were completely alone. He had not seen anyone of either warband for hours.

"Tell me," as the stallion continued to tear off mouthfuls of grass, "were those trolls we were with? I hope you knew what you were doing this time. Did you recognize whoever we were fighting against? Were they Wanderers, or whoever the 'second force' might be? And were we really in danger of our lives, either from the horned band or from the manor, or did it just feel that way?"

Goldmane lifted his head, looked at Roric quizzically, then returned to grazing. "And I really would have questions for you," said Roric, "if you started to answer me."

He rose to his feet and laughed, slapping his horse on the shoulder. "You're almost as informative to talk to as the man who brought me here. Wait for me. I'm going to get some water."

A narrow, muddy trickle came from a spring and cut through the meadow, and while Goldmane had lapped it up, Roric hoped that if he followed it a short distance he would come to a pool or at least a place where it ran a little deeper.

He followed the trickle with the conviction that he would not return to the people from whom Goldmane had carried him away. Soon limestone rocks sprouted up through the grass. The trickle took on force and size until it shot over the edge of a little cliff, its spray making tiny rainbows in the horizontal sunlight.

Roric went to his knees to look over the edge. The cliff

was less than twenty feet high. Below the water shot into a hole like the mouth of a cave, but he could hear its splash so the hole could not be very deep. He went around and found a way to scramble to the bottom of the cliff, then lowered himself carefully into the dark, damp crevice down which the water disappeared.

In a very short distance, he found the pool he had hoped for. The stream splashed and whirled, then flowed away, broad and quiet, over dimly lit stone. Here the water appeared perfectly clear, so he drank, dipped his head to wash the grime from his face, then lifted water in his palms to drink again.

That was when he saw the light.

At first, kneeling with water dripping from his chin, he thought it his imagination, a green spark in the distance. But it remained even when he moved his head. He stood up slowly, listened without hearing anything but the waterfall, and walked forward cautiously, his hand resting on his sword.

As he walked, the green light became brighter. He ran a hand along the damp stone roof over his head, then stopped when it sloped rapidly lower. But now he thought he could hear voices ahead of him.

"What's that sound? I don't hear a sound. Listen, that sounds like footsteps! It's just somebody outside. No, I tell you, someone is in the tunnels and coming this way!"

The voices were high, almost squeaky. He continued forward with a wondering smile, on his knees now.

"I don't hear anything! That's because it stopped. Do you want to go look? All right then, I'll look. But you have to come too. But you're the one who heard the sound!"

Now he himself heard footsteps, light and quick. He waited in the near darkness while the green light rapidly approached.

But he was not prepared for the shriek.

"A Wanderer! A Wanderer! They've come for us! Flee while you can! We can't get out! What can we do!?!"

He sat back on his heels to appear less threatening to the very short people who now ran in circles before him. They had dropped their light, but it still burned, giving their faces, already distorted by panic, an unreal quality.

"I am not a Wanderer," he said, not shouting for fear of frightening them worse but speaking very clearly. "Who are you?"

"It's not a Wanderer! He says he's not a Wanderer. Is it a mortal? But how did a mortal get in our tunnels? Who are *you*?"

They were all around him now, jumping to get a better look over each other's shoulders, pushing forward and then scrambling back if he shifted.

"I am indeed a mortal," he said slowly, "but I have been in the Wanderers' realm. I followed a stream into the back of your cave."

"There is no stream! What does he mean, a stream? Do you see a stream?"

And indeed the tunnel floor was dry. He could not even hear the splash of the waterfall. Goldmane! He looked over his shoulder into blackness. I've gone somewhere, he thought, I don't know where, like stepping through that stone gate, and I've left Goldmane behind.

"Can I return to the Wanderers' realm by going back?"

"No! You can't go anywhere! There's nowhere for mortals to go! And if you really are a mortal, you should be here, in mortal lands!"

These were certainly not the mortal lands he remembered. He looked at the excited group before him. "Are you perhaps faeys?"

"Yes, yes, of course we're faeys! And we don't like mortals here in our tunnels! They're too dangerous! We've only ever tamed one successfully."

"Then I shall bother you no more." He groped back the way he had come, on his knees, his head bent beneath the low ceiling. But in twenty feet he reached a solid wall.

He turned around slowly. They were clustered, watching him. "We *told* you mortals can't reach the Wanderers' realm that way."

"Then how can I?"

"You can't! We already told you that you can't! You have to stay here, or at least not *here*, but in mortal lands. As soon as it's dark outside we'll put you out the door."

And the lords of voima only knew where he would be when they put him there, without even his horse. He might be a thousand miles from Hadros' court and from Karin. At least he seemed to be back in a land with sunsets. He settled himself cross-legged to wait until evening.

But the faeys did not go away although they retreated a little down the passage. "Maybe we could try taming this one," someone suggested, but the rest shushed him. Roric ran his thumb along his jaw, realizing that his beard had not grown in the week—or however long it had been— that he had been in the Wanderers' realm. "You haven't told us your name," another faey said boldly after several more minutes had passed.

There seemed no reason to hide his identity. "I am Roric No-man's son."

"There! I knew we should try to tame him! But are you sure? Suppose it's a different Roric?"

He leaned forward. "What do you mean?" he asked sharply.

"Do you know someone named Karin? She's going to be queen!"

Long, long, ago, when the earth was new and men and women first came, blinking wide-eyed, out from the forests, there was life but no death on earth, and the lords of death waited without taking anyone. The lords of voima brought birth and growth, but very soon the earth became crowded, for children did not replace their parents but were added to them, and even the insects and the birds and the trees constantly multiplied.

And at first humans were happy, thinking themselves eternal, knowing that fate could not touch them. But then the wisest among them realized that all was not well. Where there was no end for men to fear, there was no goad to complete any task. Deeds were left ever undone, songs were left ever unsung, and there was neither growth nor change among men or women, only more and more persons, each like all the others. The wise, and at last even the foolish, understood something was wrong, but none knew what to do.

Finally Sielrigg the hero said, "I shall seek out Fate and see if something different can be arranged, before we crowd ourselves into the very sea and fall into a torpor that would make even life itself no longer worth having."

So he went to the Weaver's cave and burned an offering, then he took his sword and swung astride his great warhorse. He rode for miles, for days, for months, for years. He rode from the north to the south, from the east to the west. And at long last he came to a hut in the deep, deep woods, where a wizened old woman waited all by herself, and he knew that she was Fate.

"We need to grow, we need to change," Sielrigg told her. "Humans are not made to sit idle. But our immortality makes it hard for us to treat anything seriously, and there are too many of us for anyone to hope he may do any new thing."

"What you are missing," said the wizened old woman, "is a needful balance, a balance between life and death, ceasing and becoming."

"But I did not come to ask for death," said Sielrigg, hefting his great sword although he knew well that the old woman could not be wounded any more than he could. "I ask for a way for us to find again the sense of purpose the lords of voima meant us to have."

"And I give it to you in my own way," answered Fate. "Henceforth the lords of death shall have powers to balance those of the lords of voima even in the present world. All were fated already to come to Death at the last, when even Time shall end; now I shall allow Death to take men and all other creatures even from the very midst of life. When all humans know that their end must someday come, that if they do not grow the food they shall starve, that if they do not sing their songs they will go forever unheard, then you shall see renewal."

Then Sielrigg the hero said, "Very well. But I ask a boon of Fate. If this will help my people, then I ask that I be the first to die."

And his wish came true on the spot, for his sword turned in his hand and stabbed him, and as his body sank to the forest floor his spirit went forth, a shadowless wight. It went down to Hel, which until then had stood vast and dusty and empty, and he became the first mortal spirit ever to reach that realm. But then many more humans began to die, and insects and animals and trees as well. Hel then became the place of despair and unfulfilled plans for all who went there untimely, but the earth was a land of ceaseless striving, where glorious battle was worth fighting, where the food had to be grown and the young children cherished, and the songs that were sung kept the spirit and memory of the dead alive.

CHAPTER FOUR

1

"I think you misunderstood something important," said Karin. "Please listen to me."

The All-Gemot of the Fifty Kings had ended, and after it several days of games and feasting, and at last King Hadros was preparing to start back to his kingdom. The whole area where the kings had camped was full of tents being struck, attendants packing up the gear, and kings saying good-bye to each other for the year, either with assurances of good fellowship or with threats. Ships were spreading their sails and rowing out of the harbor, the skiffs swift as birds, the great longships slower until their sails filled.

Hadros had changed out of his finery and was again dressed as roughly as his warriors. He looked down quizzically at Karin but as though his mind was already on the voyage.

"Absolutely nothing passed between Valmar and me," she said as firmly and clearly as she could. "I know you think it did, and that we did not contradict you as we should have, but I had just spent a very long and very cold night climbing around in the dark—"

Hadros frowned. "What story is this? Where were you?"

Karin stopped herself from saying that she had climbed up a rock scree to talk to a Wanderer. Hadros would never believe she had spoken to one of the lords of voima, though she was now trying to be as truthful as she could. Instead she said, "We went to visit a Mirror-seer. I remembered him from when I was a girl. I asked him for information on where Roric had gone."

"And did he give it to you?" said Hadros in almost eager tones.

She shook her head. "He said he could not see him beneath the sun." But then she added quickly, "And since therefore nothing untoward happened between Valmar and me, give up this idea that we should soon be wed."

He put a hand on her shoulder. "I have not yet made an offer to your father for him, little princess. I thought to let a few weeks pass, so that if the two of you were spotted coming back together there would be no gossiping tongues saying your marriage had to be made up overnight! But I shall certainly cross the channel again soon with suitable gifts. We can drink your betrothal ale here and have the wedding at home when the harvest is in."

"But don't you believe me?" she said desperately. "I love Valmar as a brother, but I could never marry him, or he me."

Hadros massaged her shoulder with his massive hand. "That is why it is counseled that young women leave the experimenting until after their parents have concluded the marriage bargain," he said, looking off somewhere over her head. "Many do not enjoy it when they first begin, but if they are already wed it does not matter, whereas if they could come and go and try different partners from the ones their parents chose, it would lead to upset and confusion."

Karin took a deep breath. She should have known better than to try to persuade Hadros with a simple plea for understanding. "Then grant me a boon. Let Valmar stay here with me."

For a second Hadros looked as though he would laugh. "I realize his training at the hands of the maids may have been of the roughest sort, Karin. Are you planning to teach him a better technique before your wedding?"

She realized with a cold shock that Hadros had never spoken to her like this before, as though she was an experienced woman from whom he no longer had to keep even the slightest tinge of an off-color remark. It was this more than anything else that told her it was hopeless trying to persuade him that her night with Valmar had been completely innocent.

But when Hadros, with Gizor and his attendants, left a short time later, Valmar stayed behind.

King Kardan was bemused that his daughter would want him there. "Did you perhaps become even better friends with Hadros' family than I thought, Karin? I know captives sometimes grow to love their captors, but in this case! Hadros has not spoken to me; is not the boy a little young to make an offer for you himself?"

"I am not planning to marry Valmar or any other king's son," she said, meeting her father's gaze levelly. "And that is why I want him to stay. His very presence will keep away other offers for at least the summer—I saw the way the Fifty Kings eyed me when they realized I was now your heiress. But I have become fond of Valmar as a brother. At Hadros' court we were children together."

Everything she said was true, but she still thought bitterly that this was a strategem worthy of Queen Arane.

King Kardan smiled understandingly. "You and your own little brother used to be inseparable. I remember the two of you racing around underfoot, telling us you were trolls one moment and heroes the next. At the time, I thought it just as well that you were no longer here when he took ill and died . . ."

The evenings were long, and after dinner Karin and Valmar walked in the meadow before the castle. Beyond the meadows, beyond a narrow oak wood, they could catch glimpses of the channel, dark blue in the fading light, and the wind that rustled their hair was tinged with salt. Only the trampled grass of the meadow and the blackened scars of fire-rings showed that the All-Gemot had been held here. Even the merchants had sold the last departing kings final gifts to take home to their families, packed up their booths and left.

"I don't understand why you've spoken to my father as you have," said Valmar at last. Karin could hear in his voice an effort to be mature and detached fighting with boyish irritation. "He now assumes that you and I shall soon marry."

"It already seemed like a good idea to him," she said. She turned away from him to look up the valley, past the lake, invisible from this angle, where the Mirror-seer lived, toward the peak of Graytop. "Our children, his grandchildren, would rule two kingdoms."

"But you encouraged him!"

"Would you rather let him think you'd raped me?" she said in exasperation. "Or have him announce to my father that I had been carried off by the strong hand to become your concubine? Youthful love can be rectified by marriage; youthful violence cannot. I'm sorry, Valmar, I'm no more pleased about this than you are, but I was very tired and it was all I could think to say."

"But have you told him you love Roric?"

"I told him. Especially since Roric is gone, he did not think it mattered."

Valmar took her hands and turned her toward him, looking down at her as though he had never seen her before. For a second, watching his expression, she feared that she had insulted him deeply by rejecting so readily the idea of marriage with him. But after a moment he laughed loudly and tossed her hands away. "It's useless. You're my big sister! I would be just as content to marry Dag or Nole as you!"

"Yes, but your father doesn't want you to marry your brothers." For a second Karin started to smile, but only for a second.

In the morning they all crossed the fields and splashed through a brackish stream to the royal burial mound.

Karin's earliest clear memories were of when her mother had died and been put into it. The grass had long since grown over the spot where they had sliced into the mound for her, and also the spot where her youngest son, whom she had died bearing, was buried six years later. But the earth was still fresh where Karin's drowned older brother had been buried.

Valmar stood back with the royal attendants, but Karin and her father climbed up to the top, twenty feet above the ground. Standing there, swaying slightly, she had to squeeze her eyes shut for a moment to regain her composure. She had not been back on the mound since the old queen's funeral. For a moment the soft mud that lay over her brother's body was the fresh earth where her mother was buried, and Karin was not a proud young woman, a future sovereign queen, but a very frightened little girl.

King Kardan lit a small fire with tinder he had brought with him. Once it was burning, the small orange blaze licking and popping in the ocean wind, he laid in it a strip of silk, a twig from the rowan in the castle courtyard, and three gray hairs from his own head. Karin hesitated a second, remembering that she had told Valmar she would burn no more offerings to the Wanderers, then glanced at her father's profile and reached up to pull at her own hair.

As she laid the strands across the fire, she was not sure if she was offering them to the Wanderers, to the dead older brother who had seemed oddly unsaddened when she left as a hostage, as though just as happy not to be going himself, or to her living father, whose pain and loss were so visible on his face that she had to look away.

After a minute, Kardan reached out to squeeze his daughter's hand. She forced herself to meet his eyes. He was no longer looking inward, at his loss, but directly at her, and it struck her that she was now all he had left. Standing on the mound where her ancestors had been buried since time out of memory, standing above their very bones, she felt the full weight of their tradition fall on her. When the dead were gone, it was up to the living to remember them, to honor them, to carry on all that they had begun.

Her mother and both her brothers were now in Hel where all mortals went, the brave and the honorable, the depraved and the cowardly, venerable grandfathers and babies who had lived no longer than to take one breath.

People did not return from Hel except in the oldest tales, but then beings without backs also did not appear to mortals except in those stories. Even so, those who had died peacefully or in accidents should not walk again if suitably buried. She had heard somewhere when very young, probably something the serving-maids had said that she was not supposed to overhear, that one could reach Hel by digging into a burial mound. But if so there must be more involved, for all castles and manors had large mounds into which new graves were dug every generation.

The stories had never given a clear picture of Hel, though she had the impression that it was a murky and confused land, where one's memories and even identity slowly disappeared. But on one point all the stories were explicit.

There were no Wanderers in Hel.

2

Roric picked his way through the oak woods. It was an overcast night and hard to see, but the cold damp air was exhilarating. He sucked it into his lungs as he proceeded slowly in the direction of the castle. He did not know if the Wanderers would try for him again, since the "third force" had reached him first this time, or how King Hadros would react to his return, but very soon he would see Karin again.

He smiled in the darkness. He could understand why Karin had never told him about the faeys. He and she had come to trust each other so recently, and had had so little time for conversation in the short weeks since they had first declared their love for each other, that she might not have felt easy in telling him about these foolish friends from her childhood. But he had a message for her from them. They were becoming worried because they had not seen her in a long time.

He stopped, a hand against the rough bark of a tree, listening. Something was moving across the ground ahead of him, something heavy. It rustled the grass and twigs and made a curious spongy sound as it came. He drew his sword, slowly so as to make no noise, and put his back to the tree.

And then the clouds above him lifted for a moment, and the moon shone down on the oak woods, several days short of the full.

Crouched on the hill before him was the troll.

Mostly head and mouth and long powerful arms, with a small soft body that it had to drag along when out of the stream, it lay on the hill looking at him with eyes bigger around than ale horns. "What have you done with my horse, Roric No-man's son?"

Its voice was deep and indistinct, soft like its body but packed with menace like its teeth.

Roric turned his blade so that the moonlight flashed on it. "Get out of my way, troll, unless you wish to test my steel. I have no time for riddles and games of chance tonight."

The clouds obscured the moon again, and Roric could hear the troll laughing. Its laugh was much worse than its voice, wild, irrational and threatening. But something else was wrong. The moon had been just past the full when he galloped away from Gizor and the manor, and he could have sworn that was only a week ago, not nearly four weeks. How long had he *really* been gone?

"You should know mortal steel will not be much use against a troll *here*," came the soft dark voice again.

"It will slow you down if you intend to eat me."

"No, not tonight, Roric No-man's son. I caught a deer last week, and I am still feeding nicely. Did you never wonder why I didn't eat that horse?"

Roric had been about to rush past. Now that he knew where the troll was, he should be able to get by it and on to the castle well ahead of it. The troll was certainly dangerous, and no children had ever been allowed out of the castle alone after dark, but it moved slowly enough that Hadros had never felt it a threat worth rousting out from under his bridge. Rather, he left it there as an additional guard to his castle.

But instead of hurrying away Roric went still, judging the troll's position by its snorting breath and the squishing sounds it made when it moved. It might know something he should have known himself long ago. "Goldmane is in the realm of the Wanderers," he said slowly. "Is that where he came from originally?"

At the time, two years ago, he had not questioned where the troll had acquired the horse. All he had seen as he stood by the troll's bridge at twilight was the magnificence of the stallion. It had seemed unsurprising that a creature of voima like the troll should have it. All that was surprising was that the troll had been willing to engage in riddles and a game of dice for Goldmane—the dice had come back to his hand wet and sticky from the troll's—without insisting that if Roric lost he should be eaten on the spot.

And now that he thought about it, he had beaten the troll rather easily. It must surely have known the old riddles about the egg and about the creature that goes on four legs, then two, then three.

The troll chuckled. "I am not sure if the one who sent you your horse originally will have time to send you another now that you've lost him, especially with the change coming."

Roric moved along the sandy hill a short way to keep his distance, thinking hard. The trolls of the Wanderers' realm, the "third force," must already have had their eyes on him two years ago and deliberately given him his horse. It was Goldmane, he thought with dismay, who had taken the bit in his teeth and gone through the stone gateway out of Hadros' kingdom while he was still hesitating. If he could not trust the stallion, he was back to his own voima and the little bone charm.

But it was also Goldmane who had carried him away from the horned warriors and had brought him home.

And he had something else he needed to know. "When you say my steel will harm you but little here, do you mean it would do greater damage in the Wanderers' realm?"

The troll did not answer his question and did not even laugh. "Be proud of your association with the Wanderers if you like, Roric No-man's son," it said indistinctly. "But be careful wandering these hills at night if I am not well fed." It gave a booming belch, and then it did chuckle again.

Roric made a wide circle around it, his sword still in his hand. Ahead of him through the trees he could see faint lights from Hadros' castle. Soon he would learn if he *had* really been gone for close to four weeks—or, he thought grimly, even for several months.

An oak tree around the back of the castle reached a branch toward the top of the wall. Roric scrambled up it, as he had many times since he was a boy, coming home after the gates were already shut and not wanting to have to knock and explain himself. With luck, he would find Karin before he had to talk to anyone else.

Hadros had neglected things like the oak branch since the end of the war, he thought with a hard smile as he dropped inside the wall. If he had been a scout for an invading army he would have had the gates open for his companions in no time.

Even in the dark, he knew the castle like he knew his own skin. He slipped across the courtyard, hearing the voices of maids and of housecarls from the hall. Flickering firelight came through the open doorway. He was slightly surprised, because normally the maids did not sit with the warriors and housecarls in the evening, instead retreating to the weaving house or the bakehouse. He glanced in both in search of Karin and found them dark and empty. In the bath house, even the stones were cold.

And certain voices seemed to be missing. He stood close by the doorway into the hall, listening. He could not hear the king's deep voice, which usually rose over all the other men's. And now that he thought about it, he also did not hear Valmar or Gizor One-hand, though both of them might long sit silent on the bench in the evening. But he thought he heard Nole, the king's youngest son, his voice high and excited.

As he hesitated outside the hall, he heard in the distance the sound of hooves. He slipped across the courtyard again to look out through the crack along the edge of the gate. A band of men, carrying torches that lit up the night, were riding up the hill toward the castle. Their harnesses jingled, and all of them had shields slung from their saddles.

And the man in the lead was King Hadros. Roric stepped back into the shadows with a smile as the king pounded his fist on the gate. He would let the king enter his hall before surprising him with his own return.

"I am home!" roared the king. "Open the gate!"

The housecarls poured out of the hall. "They're home! They're home from the All-Gemot!"

The All-Gemot. Roric had completely forgotten about it. It was still ten days or so in the future when he rode away, which meant he really had been gone under a month, not the entire summer. That at least was a relief. He wondered if he would have accompanied Hadros if he had been here; he had been among the king's warriors at the All-Gemot the last few years.

The big gate swung open, and the king and his warriors came through. Gizor One-hand was among them. Roric mingled with the back of the crowd as Dag and Nole hurried forward to greet their father, and as housecarls took the horses and baggage. Roric thought it a little surprising that no one seemed to notice him.

"But where is Valmar?" he heard Dag ask. "And where is Karin?"

"They are in Kardan's kingdom," said Hadros. From his tone it was impossible to tell if he was pleased or not. "Karin will stay, because someday she will be sovereign queen there."

"And Valmar?"

"I shall tell you when I've had something to eat. You!" to one of the maids. "Is there no one here who will offer a man food in his own home? Karin would have had something hot ready for us," he grumbled, heading into the hall.

King Kardan. That was Karin's father. Roric went into the hall with the rest, forgetting to keep himself hidden although still no one seemed to pay him any attention. She had told him, of course, that she was her father's heiress now, something the faeys seemed to find very exciting, but it was like having half the castle suddenly disappear to have her gone.

Tonight he would not bother the king, hungry and tired as he was. But in the morning he would ask to be released from his oath of loyalty to him. Since Hadros had tried to have him killed anyway, he should be happy to have him go. Then he would go to Karin and offer himself to her as her warrior as well as her lover.

He tried uneasily to remember where Kardan's kingdom was. He knew it was somewhere across the channel, but he had never crossed the channel in his life.

The king's younger sons asked about Valmar again once Hadros and the warriors who had accompanied him had wolfed down bread and cheese and stewed mushrooms and had started the ale horn around for the second time.

"Well," said the king slowly, leaning back on the bench with his elbows behind him on the table. "Valmar will stay in Kardan's kingdom this summer with Karin. In a few weeks I shall return there with suitable betrothal gifts, and they shall be married after the harvest."

There was a shocked silence. I've gotten back just in time, thought Roric.

The king's younger sons were nearly as surprised as he was. "Did— Did you decide for them, Father?" Dag asked at last, hesitantly as though fearing his father was about to choose a wife for him as well.

"No, although I am well pleased with their decision." The king showed his teeth in a smile for a second. "It seems they had fallen in love themselves, something Karin, that sly lass, tried to keep from me. Valmar," with a shrug, "was happy enough to fall in with her plans."

"But she does not love Valmar!" cried Roric. "She is in love with me!"

No one appeared to hear him.

The maids and housecarls began talking at once about the upcoming marriage, until Hadros looked up with a frown. "Enough of this chatter. I shall not have those who serve the royal family engage in idle talk about us. Karin and Valmar will be married here and live here at least half the year, until her father dies. Or I," mostly under his breath. "That is all you need to know."

The men started drifting off toward the loft house, some of them still speculating—and once they were out of Hadros' hearing, in language he would never have tolerated—about how far Karin's and Valmar's love had progressed. The consensus seemed to be that Valmar was quite a lad to have won the cool princess.

Roric went up to the king, who was yawning now and pulling off his boots. "I meant to wait until tomorrow to speak to you," he said, "but I can wait no longer."

Hadros looked straight through him and unbuckled his sword belt.

Roric leaned against the wall for support. No wonder no one had said anything to him. No one could see or hear him. He had returned from the Wanderers' realm but returned in such a form that he might as well not be here.

He wandered out of the hall, picking up a piece of cheese and eating it distractedly as he went—at least food was still real to him. But the troll could see me, he thought.

How far did this extend? Would others still be able to feel him? Would a sword still cut him?

He followed the warriors and housecarls up the ladder to the men's loft. Someone bumped against him in the dark and said, "Excuse me." So he could still be felt then, even if not seen.

Exhausted and shaken, he stretched out in the straw. Invisible, he would have to stow aboard a ship across the channel in the hope that once there he could find Karin and her kingdom even though no one would hear when he asked directions. But what good would it do him to be there, the silent and unseen observer, if Karin and Valmar really were in love?

He awoke to the sound of his name. "Roric! What are you doing here?"

He sat up abruptly. Early morning sun came through the small window. One of the warriors who had accompanied King Hadros leaned on his elbow next to him. "I didn't see you last night! Did you come back while we were gone? Did you really meet the Wanderers?"

"Can you see me?" Roric demanded.

"Of course I can see you," with a laugh.

So he was back. The lords of voima only knew what had happened to him, but at least it was over. He jumped up. "I have to talk to the king, find out more about this marriage between Valmar and the Princess Karin."

"I can probably tell you more than Hadros is likely to." Roric sat down again slowly. "You know he always treated the princess very delicately, as though even her ears were made out of glass. Not that he minded her doing all the work to direct his household! But she seems to have decided to take matters into her own hands as soon as she was out of the kingdom. I'd heard, of course, of sovereign queens with a whole string of lovers, who still profess their purity and keep serious suitors dangling, but I'd never believed it before."

"But what happened?" asked Roric through cold lips. This could not be Karin they were discussing.

"The second night we were there, she took young Valmar with her on a ride up into the hills and did not come back until the next morning. I saw them when they returned, and I don't think there can be much doubt what happened," with a chuckle.

Roric kept his hand from his knife by sheer will.

"I think King Hadros moved fast to make sure his son *wasn't* just one more in a string of lovers, by getting her to agree to their marriage. But I don't think he's made a formal offer to her father yet; that's why we have to go back in a few weeks. If you come along, you'll see for yourself.

"But what about *you*?" the man added. "Was that really someone with no back? And where did you go?"

But Roric was no longer there. He went down the ladder in one long jump and strode across the courtyard. Since Valmar was not yet of age, he had not yet sworn himself to him, and no oath would keep him from killing him.

Roric had almost forgotten his own voyage to the Wanderers' realm in the news about Karin, and he was not prepared for the stunned face Hadros turned on him when he interrupted the king in the middle of his porridge and beer.

"No, of course I did not run away," he said quickly. "I've been in the land of the Wanderers, though it turned out it was not a Wanderer who summoned me. But I intend to leave this kingdom now to cross the channel, and I ask to be freed of my loyalty to you."

The king stared at him as though he had not understood a word, then very slowly began to smile. "Both Valmar and Karin tried to persuade me you had gone with the Wanderers, that the lords of voima might really take a personal interest in people like you and me. Perhaps I should have believed them." He reached out abruptly to clap Roric on the shoulder. "How does it feel to be a warrior of voima out of the oldest tales?"

"No, you do not understand," said Roric. "One thing I

did learn in the land of the immortals is that they are *not* creatures of honor and glory—or at least not the ones I was with. I never spoke with the Wanderers themselves. There is much more purpose in life here as a mortal than there could ever be in that realm."

"Are you sure you were not hiding in the woods this whole time?" asked the king with a gleam in his eye, as though not quite daring to believe him.

"No, of course not! I shall tell you all about that realm someday—the fields are rich with grain, and the sun never sets. But right now I am going to Kardan's kingdom."

"Of course you can accompany me when I go in a few weeks. I need to start assembling suitable betrothal gifts."

This was becoming as frustrating as trying to talk to the beings of the "third force." "I am going *now*," said Roric as distinctly as he could. "I would prefer you to release me from my oath before I go so that I can swear myself to Karin's service, but if you do not I shall go anyway."

"And why are you so eager to go there now?" Hadros asked suspiciously.

Roric was not about to tell the king he intended to kill his oldest son, but at this point he scarcely cared if he guessed. "Because I love Karin."

"Out!" roared the king to the others in the hall, who had been following the conversation with intrigued expressions. "All of you, out!" They fled in panic, and Hadros jumped up to slam the door after them.

The hall was dim now, lit only by the smoke-hole and the small windows up in the eaves. Hadros sat down again, favoring one leg and breathing hard.

"You came to me with this nonsense last month. I told you then to forget the whole idea, that Karin would not wed a fatherless man."

"And you were furious enough," said Roric, still standing, his hand on his hilt, "that you told Gizor you would not mind if I was dead."

Hadros started to jump up again, then changed his mind.

"Threatening you has not, it appears, taught you sense," he said with steely calm, but then for a second Roric thought he smiled. "Sit down so we can face each other at eye level."

When Roric sat down cautiously at the far end of the bench, the king continued, "You are my sworn man, and I am your sworn lord. Gizor overreacted to something I said in anger. Let us not allow that princess to make either of us kill the other."

"I love 'that princess.' You tell me a man without a father should not aspire so high, but she loves me herself. A princess can marry any man she chooses."

King Hadros was still breathing hard. "Maybe you did not hear," he said quietly, as though not wanting his words to carry outside the hall. "She has taken Valmar for her lover." Roric shut his eyes for a second to try to stay calm but did not interrupt. "I could not allow Valmar, any more than you, to speak to her while she was still a hostage here, because it was my responsibility to send her home to her father as pure and unfettered as she came to me. He paid the tribute faithfully each year, and I do not war on girls.

"But now—now that she is a royal heiress and home again, she can make her own decisions. She has many better men to choose from than a warrior without kin. And she has chosen my son."

Roric clenched his fists. "If you told him—if you told him to take her by the strong hand, then even if I am your sworn man, I—"

King Hadros snorted, and Roric caught again that very fleeting, very strange expression, almost as though the king was pleased. "Not at all. I think it was her idea. Forget her, lad! Do not waste your strength thinking of women. Think instead of this.

"Valmar can afford to marry young. He shall be king here someday, unless that new bride of his leads him such a merry chase that I outlive him! But you, Roric, you cannot tie yourself down. You have grown into the most formidable of my warriors, but you need to use that power to win a realm for yourself. You know you have the strength and the voima within you to be as good a lord as most of the Fifty Kings."

Roric glanced at him from under his eyebrows; Hadros looked concerned now, even fatherly. "Wisdom, they say, is for old men," Roric said slowly, "but action is for the young. But I can't just act as a housecarl or even dependent warrior after you brought me up as your foster-son, and I also can't act like a man with a family behind him. So what do you wisely recommend?"

"There are always thrones to be won by the valorous," said Hadros. "Several of the Fifty Kingdoms sent no one to the Gemot this year, and I am sure even now there are second sons preparing their warships to see if the region might be ready for a new lord."

"I had thought," said Roric bitterly, "that the lords of voima might have a place for me."

"That too," said Hadros quickly. "Now, if you want a ship of your own the best I can do is lend you one of mine, and I'll let you have a few warriors. How would you like Gizor One-hand?"

Roric stared for a moment, then started to laugh. "Are you still trying to get me killed, or is this one more challenge by which I prove my manhood? No, Hadros," rising to his feet, "if the Wanderers still want me they will be able to find me, and if they do not, I see no reason to attack an unsuspecting kingdom. I simply do not believe that Karin loves Valmar rather than me. Tomorrow—no, today—I shall leave for Kardan's kingdom to see her myself. I would prefer you to release me from my loyalty to you first."

The king rose stiffly, glaring. "Valmar is my son and heir. You are pledged to him through your pledge to me. And I do not release you from anything!"

"Then I forswear my loyalty to you!" He tugged at the ring Hadros had given him when they first swore their oaths to each other, the ring the Weaver would not take. This time he got it off. He held it in his hand for a second, breathing hard, then hurled it at the king's feet. "And I defy you as an untrue lord!"

Roric slammed out of the hall and rushed toward the stables, half expecting Hadros to shout for his warriors. But there was no sound behind him.

Also no Goldmane in the stables. He saddled one of the geldings as rapidly as he could. No time to go back to the loft for his small store of possessions. The knife the Weaver had returned to him should buy him passage if he could find a ship going to Kardan's kingdom.

He galloped through the courtyard, hooves echoing, out the gate, down the hill and across the troll's bridge. This was a fast horse, one of the fastest in the kingdom after his stallion. But there was no sign of pursuit.

Twenty miles along the coast was the little market port where Hadros sold his horses every year. There should be a ship in the harbor there, Roric thought, willing to take him. A mile from the castle he saw a raven perched in a tree, watching his approach with its head cocked to one side. Roric pulled up hard. He would send Karin a raven-message if the bird would carry it. It would take him at least two days' traveling to reach her, and if she had turned to Valmar in despair, thinking him gone forever, he wanted to let her know he was coming.

He whistled to the bird, trying to remember just what one said when speaking to ravens.

3

Valmar and Karin walked by the seashore. She was restless all the time now, and Valmar walked or rode with her wherever she went, but if she knew herself what was wrong she was not able to tell him.

King Kardan, Valmar thought, did not yet seem to realize that his own father was busy planning their wedding. Karin had not spoken of it again, and it seemed too impossible to be real. But last night he had surprised himself into wakefulness from a dream of lying in her arms.

It was only the sudden change from his father's court to this castle, he told himself, only the unusualness of seeing Karin dressed like a queen, that made him think of her as other than his sister. And it was the same change that had made him begin to think there might be more to life than the future his father had laid out for him, that his attempt to run after Roric had been more than the folly of a boy. At this rate he would soon want to be like King Thaar in the old tales, he thought, riding out to protect Karin from a dragon—except that no one had ever seen a dragon in this part of the world.

Karin looked out to sea; the north coast of the channel was too far away to be seen. Valmar looked instead at her, her great gray eyes, the angle of her cheekbones, the fine blond hairs around her forehead which were too short to be worked into her braids and blew back in the breeze. If she too had dreams, they were certainly not of him.

"Look at the ravens," said Karin. "I wonder what they've found."

A pair of ravens hopped along the strand, giving harsh cries and disturbing the gulls. Their jet-black plumage stood out among the light-colored sand and pebbles. They stayed just ahead of the waves that broke rhythmically against the shore. But there was nothing obvious washed up on the sand to attract them.

And then one of the ravens spoke. "Karin," it said.

The word came out all sharp-edged and harsh, but it was certainly her name.

"It's a message!" Valmar cried. "It must be a message from—" But here he stopped. His father, he knew, was one who spoke to ravens, but this was a strange way to send word to his foster-daughter.

But she had already rushed forward and dropped to her knees on the wet sand, heedless of her dress. "Yes, I am Karin," she said, looking from one raven to another.

One spoke: "Karin. Roric is coming."

And then the other: "Karin. Valmar. Beware of Roric."

Then with deep caws the birds rose, almost in her face, and flapped away, back over the dark, foam-dotted waves of the channel. A single black feather drifted down to the wet sand.

Valmar hurried to Karin and helped her up. "Was that one message," he asked, "or two?"

But her face was joyous, transformed. "Roric is coming! That means he's safe!"

"But the other raven said to beware of him!"

"It must only have meant to watch for him. Valmar, he's coming!" She startled him by hugging him hard, then took his arm to walk back to the castle.

"So he's returned from the land of the Wanderers—or wherever he has been," said Valmar. "Do you think he's won treasure there?"

"I don't care," said Karin, still smiling so widely everything she said came out as a laugh. "I just want him with me again."

"It will be good to see him," Valmar agreed. With Roric here—although he did not say this to Karin—this plan to have him marry his big sister would all be forgotten. He told himself he would be glad for that.

Karin turned suddenly. "I cannot return to the castle. I must go down to the harbor. He may be crossing the channel even now!"

Valmar held her by the arms until she looked up at him. "Karin," he said quietly, "it's time for dinner. I don't know if you've noticed these last few days, but your father is worried about you. That's part of the reason I've always been with you—to keep him from sending his warriors along to watch you. Do you want him asking Queen Arane to come analyze what is wrong?"

"No, no, of course not," she said with a laugh, but she looked yearningly toward the harbor as he steered her back home.

❊ ❊ ❊

But at first light she went down to the harbor alone, not waiting for Valmar, not saying anything other than that she would not be back all day.

King Kardan took Valmar aside. "This may sound curious coming from her father, lad," he said, striding back and forth in the middle of his hall, hands behind his back and his eyes down. "But I no longer feel I know my daughter. She grew into a woman in the years she was away, and I cannot hug her or tease her back into good humor the way I might have ten years ago. I had expected her to be joyful to be home again."

"Oh, I'm sure she's happy to be here," Valmar stammered.

"She may have been at first," said the king, shooting Valmar a quick glance. He had the same direct gray eyes as Karin. "But since we went to the burial mound—or even since that second day she was here, during the All-Gemot, when she went on that long ride with you and suddenly decided to spend the night in King Hadros' tents again—she has been distracted, uneasy . . . I would have to call her miserable."

Valmar actually agreed but did not want to say so.

Kardan put a hand on his shoulder so that Valmar had to join him in his restless pacing. "She told me she thinks of you as her little brother."

I am *not* her little brother, Valmar startled himself by thinking. I am going to be her husband.

"She seems more content to be with you than with anyone else," said the king, who fortunately could not read his thoughts. "Do you understand why she is miserable? Can you stay with her, cheer her as you may?"

An unexpected vision of how he might cheer her flashed through Valmar's mind. He pushed it firmly away. Karin had been too distracted to sense his changing feelings for her, and he hoped to hide them from her forever.

"I think she misses our foster-brother," he said. "His name

is Roric; he was brought up in Hadros' court along with the rest of us. But he should be coming here shortly to see her, and then I expect she will be more content to settle down. You see, he was away from the castle when we left for the All-Gemot, and she never had a chance to tell him good-bye."

"Curious," said Kardan. "She has never spoken of him."

"You see," added Valmar in what he hoped were friendly and confidential tones, "she doesn't like to speak to you too much of life in Hadros' court. She's afraid you'll think she considers it more her home than this, her real home. But I'm sure in a few more days— And especially once she's seen Roric—"

The king nodded slowly. "Then if she is waiting for this Roric at the harbor, I hope he comes soon." He slapped Valmar on the back. "You are a good little brother, lad. And when you are twice as old as you are now, I am sure you shall be a worthy successor to your father. At least I will not need to worry on my deathbed of a renewal of war between our kingdoms!"

Valmar kept thinking of the strangeness of the raven-messages. Who had sent them? Roric himself, King Hadros, or someone else entirely? Raven-messages were by their very nature brief, so if one had more than a few words to convey one needed more than one bird, but one of these messages and not the other had been addressed to both of them.

He did not like to say anything to Karin, who looked forward to seeing Roric with a joy that bordered on pain. Her face was openly eager, and her eyes looked right past him to the ocean beyond. But the message to beware of Roric suggested that something important had changed. Had he come back from the Wanderers' realm with no back?

Three ships came into the harbor that day, but none of them bore Roric. As the sun grew lower, Karin's eagerness became mixed with misgiving. She stared at the waves, rough under a strong wind, and kept murmuring about the Cauldron Rocks until Valmar realized that that was where her older brother's ship had foundered.

She did not return to the castle that day even for meals, but ate the bread and cheese Valmar arranged to have brought to them while standing on the headland above the cove, straining to see into the distance. She was dressed like a queen in gold brocade, but under the imperious façade lay the terror of a girl whom Valmar longed to take in his arms and comfort.

But he did not dare. He knew that her expression had nothing to do with him. The moon was rising, when at last he took her by the elbow.

"Karin, listen to me. No more ships will arrive tonight."

She turned toward him sharply, as though she had forgotten his presence, then clutched at him for support. "Do you think— Do you think—" He could sense all the questions she could not ask: did he think Roric's ship had gone down, did he think Roric might have fallen overboard during the crossing, did he think Roric had been knifed in the night?

"I think he will be here tomorrow, or perhaps the next day." He had both his arms around her, his beard in her hair, and rocked her gently as though she was a child. "You know there are not nearly as many merchant ships that cross the channel as there are that stay on this side," he murmured reassuringly. "None of the ships we saw today came from the north. And with the sea this rough the ships will postpone their crossing anyway. It may take Roric a few days to find a ship coming here—I doubt my father will lend him his! Or he may have to take passage to another of the southern kingdoms, then ride over here."

"Then he may already be back at the castle!" cried Karin.

"No, no, of course not." Her face was clear and pale in the moonlight before him. "You know they would have sent word. But you have already frightened your father enough. Come back home now, and be yourself again."

"I could do it in Hadros' court," she murmured, mostly under her breath. "Why cannot I do it here?"

They walked slowly back toward the castle. She shivered without a cloak, so he wrapped his around both of them. His arm went around her shoulders, and hers around his waist. The west darkened, but the eastern sky was light where the nearly full moon floated. He could feel her breath warm against his neck, her softness against his side. This, he thought, was how lovers walked.

What was he going to do? If Roric was suddenly here, he would have trouble explaining that he was merely supporting her as a solicitous little brother, yet he would not care to have his foster-brother furious with him. He might be able to conceal his feelings from Karin, but could not imagine *him* fooled. If Roric appeared tomorrow, their brotherhood could be broken forever. Would Valmar have to fight him, either kill him or be killed himself?

Anyway, Karin loved Roric, not him. This was terrible, he thought, tightening his grip around her. One point however was clear. In the last few days he had changed his mind. He would much rather marry her than Dag or Nole.

They had walked over half the way back to the castle and could see its lights beckoning them when Valmar abruptly stopped. Karin stumbled and caught herself with both arms around his waist.

There was a third person on the path beside them.

He wore a broad-brimmed hat that hid his face from the moonlight. "I have spoken with the others, Karin Kardan's daughter," he said conversationally, as though his presence there was unsurprising. "We can indeed use you."

Karin clutched at Valmar. "It's the Wanderer," she hissed. "The one I met on Graytop."

He stood frozen, unable to move, while the Wanderer tilted his head as though looking toward him. "You are a long way from home, Valmar Hadros' son. Have you perhaps been outcast?"

But Karin did not give him a chance to answer. She broke away from Valmar to whirl on the Wanderer, her fists on her hips.

"Do not come here," she said in a low, furious voice, "picking out mortals you think you can use like someone picking out apples at a market stall. You may think you want me, but I have no use for you!"

There was a momentary silence. "This outlook will certainly make things more difficult," the man then said dryly. "Would you like to tell me why?"

"*That* is why! Because you do not know anything! You make us pay a terrible price, but then do not even give us the little information we ask for that price!" Her voice was shaking, but she still had it under control.

Valmar remembered his wild surmise of what that price might have been. If she was already Roric's even more truly than he had thought, that meant— He did not know what it meant, except that he could never ever tell her now what he felt.

"I had thought I did you a favor," commented the man, "rather than exacting a price. And I think you tell the story wrongly—the woman was not visited by a lord of voima, but by a lord of death."

Karin gave a half-choked cry, almost a scream. Valmar tried to take her arm, but she shook him off.

"I must say," added the man in the broad-brimmed hat, "that your absolute commitment to what you believe helps make you appealing to us. Since we do not take mortals against their wishes, it certainly is irritating to have that stubbornness turned against us . . ."

Karin managed to answer, coherently if furiously. "Lords of voima, the great, terrible beings to whom we burn offerings! And all you do is try to make us carry out your will, without any ultimate power or knowledge of your own."

"It bothers you that we are not all-powerful, that even

we are governed by fate? I would have thought a mortal would be flattered to be asked to help at all."

"I doubt if you have any powers at all!" Karin shot back. "I am going to live here on earth, then go to Hel when I die, and never associate with anyone but other mortals!"

"Oh, we have powers all right," said the other, sounding amused. "I had assumed you would prefer not to see them."

And abruptly the ground beneath their feet was gone, and they were suspended over a pit of orange flames and molten rock. They swung ever so slightly back and forth, as though suspended by a thread no stronger than cobweb. A belch of hot gas broke through the lava, then suddenly the road was again solid beneath them.

Valmar and Karin clung to each other. But she had not changed her mind. "Try to frighten me all you like," she got out between chattering teeth. "Ever since I saw you on Graytop I have not been mistress of myself. I do not belong to you, and I will not belong to you. I am Roric's alone!"

"By the way," said the other, "I meant to tell you. You were asking about Roric No-man's son. He was spotted in our realm."

"And again you do not know the real truth!" she said triumphantly, though the tears were pouring down her cheeks. "He is back under the sun, and he is coming to me even now!"

They still had not seen the man's face. He turned his back toward them and addressed his remarks to the sky. "You certainly have courage and will, but as I say we force no one to our bidding."

He began then to walk away, and as he walked it seemed that his feet did not touch the road, but rather that he walked on moonlight. He grew smaller and smaller as he strode on the moon's rays up over the headland.

Valmar stared immobile after him. Karin had shoved him away, sobbing hard, when he tried to put his arms around her again.

And suddenly Valmar began to run, pounding back down the road toward the harbor. Moonlight washed all around him.

The man stopped and turned toward him.

"Wait for me!" Valmar cried. "I'm coming with you!"

CHAPTER FIVE

1

"No, of course I am all right," said Karin to her father. She tried to stay out of the direct light to hide the tear streaks on her cheeks, but he had already seen them. "I am only upset because Valmar has left."

"Left! But where has he gone? Has he returned home already?"

At this rate, she thought, swallowing the sobs before they could break out, she could give lessons to Queen Arane. "He has always wanted adventure, I gather, and when we were coming home from the harbor just now we ran into someone—someone I had known before—who gave him an unexpected opportunity. He had to take it immediately."

"But to leave so suddenly— And I was growing fond of the boy—" He tipped up her face toward his with one finger under her chin, as Hadros sometimes did. "Karin! Are you sure he did not have some kind of accident that you are trying to conceal from me?"

"No! I told you, he simply left!"

"Well," said King Kardan in wonderment, "I do hope he will be all right. What shall I tell his father?"

"I shall write to Hadros myself, next time there is a messenger or a merchant going from here to the northern kingdoms."

She turned to retreat to her room, glad now that she

had her mother's private parlor. But her father took her arm. "Karin, I can see you are terribly upset. Are you quite sure you had not set your heart on this boy?"

"Quite sure," she said, meeting his eyes with an effort of will.

He kept hold of her arm, studying her face. At last he said in a low voice, "Would you like to tell me what really happened? I know there was something more."

For a second she had the terrifying sense that he suspected her of having murdered Valmar, of having pushed him over the cliff. It was that fear that made her say, even though she knew he would not believe her, "Valmar went to join the Wanderers."

He shook his head and turned his face away. "I hope that you can learn to trust me again someday," he said, so quietly she barely heard him.

And then she remembered something the Mirror-seer had told her. "Listen, Father!" she said, wanting to take at least some of that heart-wringing bitterness from him. "You know there is a Wanderer often seen at Graytop at twilight! Well, it's the same one, I believe, and he—"

But Kardan looked both puzzled and alarmed. "Karin, where have you heard these stories? In all the years I have been king here, within sight of Graytop, I have never heard of a Wanderer walking there, or at least never one visible to mortal eyes."

2

The broad-beamed merchant ship came into harbor at dusk. It had been a difficult crossing, and indeed the wind had come up so briskly that most of the other ships setting out from the north shore of the channel had soon set back into harbor. Then they had been blown far off course and had reached the southern shore of the channel nowhere near where either Roric or the merchants wanted to be. They had had to beat against the wind almost an entire extra day to reach here, and only the size of this ship had allowed it to weather the waves. Roric's arms and hair were caked with salt.

In the final light he could see someone standing alone on the headland looking down into the harbor, someone shining like gold in the dimness.

But she could not see him.

"Well," said the captain, once they had secured the lines, "that castle you were asking about—" And he looked straight through Roric. He shrugged. "Gone already," he said to himself. "Good thing I had him pay in advance," and slapped the new knife in his belt.

And then Roric did go, vaulting over the gunwale, running up the road from the sheltered little inlet where ships made harbor.

Being invisible at night had been very difficult on the ship, where he had had to crawl in between boxes of cargo each sunset to conceal his fading away. He could emerge again once it was fully dark, but always with the danger of being stepped on by the sailors. But here, he thought, invisibility would be an advantage. He would stalk Valmar, learn what Karin really thought of this marriage Hadros had planned.

But seeing her standing on the cliff alone drove jealousy, at least temporarily, from his mind. She had gotten his raven-message, then, and must have been waiting for him through the long days of contrary winds on the channel. If she was waiting for him, did this mean she did not love Valmar after all?

She had now started back toward the castle and did not hear his feet coming up behind her. "Karin," he said urgently, getting in front of her, "surely *you* can see me, even between sunset and sunrise."

She kept on walking without any response, and he got out of her way. If she touched him without being able to see or hear him, she would be terrified. He could not see her face well in the twilight but it already looked anguished.

He went at her shoulder up to the castle, longing to take her into his arms and not daring. On either side he could just see armed men walking parallel to the road, watching her. She did not appear to notice.

He looked around in amazement at the size of the castle and the intricacy of the masonry as she walked through the great doors. The warriors came in behind them.

Karin went to speak to a gray-haired, richly dressed man who must be her father. Roric prowled the candlelit hall, stepping quietly out of instinct even though no one would hear him, looking for Valmar, catching fragments of conversation from the others there but nothing about the prince. He kept expecting to be seen when someone looked toward him, and kept feeling when they did not that his very existence was only a creation of his own mind.

There was no sign of his foster-brother. Where could he be? This was like no castle Roric had ever seen, but it seemed Valmar ought to be here in the hall if he was in the kingdom at all.

Karin then took a candle and went up a broad stone staircase, Roric hurrying to climb beside her. They passed through a wide chamber with an enormous bed in the center, then into a much smaller room. He just managed to dodge in before she shut the door in his face.

Inside, she turned the lock, set down the candle, and stood for several minutes with her face in her hands. Then she slowly undressed, dropping her luxurious clothes carelessly on the floor, unbraided her hair, and got into bed. When she snuffed the candle he could no longer see her in spite of the faint moonlight through the window, but he could hear her softly crying.

Roric clenched his fists. The woman he loved was within a few feet of him, but she might as well be a thousand miles away. She was crying because of him but he could do nothing to comfort her. All that the strange Wanderers' realm had earned him was the inability to touch the woman he longed for.

That is, he *hoped* she was crying for him and not for Valmar. He shook his head hard. Since he had defied King Hadros, and since the Wanderers apparently no longer wanted him, Karin was all he had left. Besides, he thought with a grim smile, if she was crying for Valmar it might be because that prince had already had a fatal accident.

After a minute he started rubbing at the caked salt on his arms. He had not seen a bath house in the castle, and although there must be one he did not want to leave this room to try to find it. But in the corner the moonlight showed him a pitcher and basin. He pulled off his own clothing and began to wash. It felt good to clean away the sweat and salt. Karin did not hear the splashing. He used her comb on his wet hair and crossed back to the bed.

She was asleep now, the deep sleep of exhaustion. The pale light had shifted and touched her smudged cheeks and the dark hollows under her eyes. But her breathing came evenly.

After looking at her a few minutes, Roric lifted the covers and slipped in. She gave a little snort but did not waken. He settled down carefully on the far side of the bed from her.

The linen sheets were startlingly luxurious against his skin. He had not slept between sheets since before he could remember, since— But then he did remember. He had been very small then; it was even before Valmar was born. He had slept with King Hadros and his wife in their cupboard bed, and he could just remember the reassuring bulk of the queen when he had wakened from a nightmare.

He lay back with his hands behind his head. He was exhausted from the journey, and in a few minutes he too was fast asleep.

Sometime in the night he awoke, wondering at first where he was. Karin's warm back was snuggled against him. He rolled over, put his face in her hair and an arm around her, and went back to sleep.

✳   ✳   ✳

He awoke again at dawn. Karin slept on, her eyelashes long on her cheeks, her russet hair spread across the pillow. At sunrise, ever since he had returned from the Wanderers' realm, people could see him again. He gently pulled her to him and began to kiss her cheek.

Her arms went around his neck even before she opened her eyes. Then she abruptly gasped and pulled back, realizing this was no dream, and her eyes flew open.

He watched her expression from two feet away: dismayed shock that there really was a man in her bed, then recognition and disbelief, and abruptly a joy that made her glow as brightly as the early sun. She threw herself on him and kissed him passionately.

In a moment she turned her lips from his, and he loosened his grip enough that she could lean back and look at him. "Roric! I've been waiting for you for so long . . ." Her smile covered her entire face, and her eyes were so intense he could barely meet them. "How did you come here?"

"I came in on the last ship into the harbor last night. You did not see me, but I followed you back to the castle." He would explain later his invisibility at sunset. "I slipped in here with you during the night."

She laughed and kissed him again. "My father will not be pleased with his guards! He knows I have been awaiting you and will be happy to meet you, but for you to come in unseen! It is good we are not at war if the watchmen are so careless."

He did not want to do anything to take the joy from her face, but he could not help himself. "When you put your arms around me—even before you saw it was me—did you think it was Valmar?"

She frowned in what looked like genuine surprise. "Valmar! Why should I embrace him?" She smiled and took hold of him by the ears. "I have dreamed of you every night, Roric."

"Everyone in Hadros' court is preparing for your wedding. And the king told me— He told me you and Valmar had become lovers."

She drew back and frowned again. "And you believed him? But I forget. You have been gone so long, you do not know what has been happening. I climbed at twilight to the top of a high peak near here to try to find a Wanderer."

Now he frowned. "And did you find one?"

"Yes." She shivered a little. "I was trying to find where *you* had gone."

He reached out and put his arm around her waist. The strange land where he had apparently passed more than three weeks was much less interesting than mortal lands. "Did he tell you where I was?"

"He did not know. But you are here now!" she added with a new smile. "What did you find in the Wanderers' realm?"

But he had not forgotten his question. It came out harsher than he intended. "Tell me, and tell me now, if you have taken Valmar for your lover."

She closed her eyes. "You are the only person I can trust, Roric. Please do not doubt me. In Hadros' court I could keep myself in control, allow my emotions out only when it was safe to do so. Here, I do not know why, maybe it is all the memories of my childhood, maybe it was meeting the Wanderer, maybe it is because I have been so worried for you.

"But I am in much greater danger, I realize," she went on, "than I ever was at home. I did not know then how much King Hadros shielded me. And yet, when firmness and courage are called for, I have constantly been on the verge of breaking down. I wanted Valmar with me because he was my only link with the world I have known for the last ten years, and because I could trust my little brother."

"You have not answered my question," he said very quietly.

She tightened her lips for a second, but the joy was still in her eyes. "I was starting to tell you. I spent the entire night on the peak where I met the Wanderer. When I returned, Hadros assumed I had spent the night with Valmar. But of course Valmar no more intends to marry me than I do him, and although he remained here in the castle when Hadros went home, so far we have kept any word of this foolish marriage bargain from my father. I can swear to you on steel and rowan, Roric, if you are still unwilling to believe me, that no one has lain in my arms but you."

She looked at him seriously, but a smile tugged at her mouth. "If the situation had been as you feared, who would you have killed first, him or me?"

He laughed then and crushed her to him. But he could not resist asking, "You are sure he did not intend to father a child on you while he was here, to make you surely his?"

"Of course not!" For a second a very strange expression flitted across her face, but she turned it into a smile. "In fact Valmar has left— But I can tell you all that later," kissing him hard.

"In that case," said Roric, "are your maids likely to come disturb you? Perhaps I should try fathering a child on you myself!"

Karin put her head out of the room just long enough to tell the maids that she felt ill and would not see *anyone* all day. Late in the afternoon she and Roric lay on the tumbled sheets, letting the warm air from the open window wash over their skin, talking.

"So Valmar has gone now to the Wanderers' realm," said Roric in wonder. "If they could not get me, and you too refused them, maybe they were happy to take whatever mortal was willing to come with them. It is a strange realm, Karin. Here mortals try to create a life, a story, that will live on beyond them, but the immortals, at least the ones I met, have no honor . . . Maybe it will be different for him."

"My father is concerned about him. He would not believe me when I told him where Valmar had gone. For a moment I even feared he thought I had done away with him myself, but he has said nothing more about it."

"Are you sure he is not planning your marriage to Valmar himself?" said Roric with a laugh. "May he not think you have found a way to rid yourself of an unwanted suitor, especially with me appearing so soon afterward?"

She did not laugh in return. "Even if my father does not think I shoved Valmar off the headland, I fear King Hadros may think so."

Roric's face went sober. "I defied Hadros before coming here. The sea was too rough for a ship the size of his, but he may soon be after me. It will indeed be hard to explain Valmar's absence, especially since I think Hadros guessed I intended to kill him."

She took his face in both her hands, and her eyes were teasing. "Hadros did send a raven to tell us to beware of you. But you would not really have done that, would you? Killed your foster-brother, violated all your honor, because of jealousy?"

"Hadros himself," he replied somewhat distantly, "tried to tell me that love conflicts with honor."

3

As sunset came, they dressed and combed themselves, preparing to go out. "You may not grow invisible this evening," Karin said hopefully.

But Roric shook his head. "I have thought that each evening since I emerged from the faeys' tunnels."

"I hate to have you spend all night outdoors," said Karin, "but this time of day, right after sunset, is the only time that I will be able to smuggle you out of the castle. I can think of no way to explain your presence here to my father unless he first meets you walking up at sunrise from the harbor."

"It will be a warm night," said Roric with a smile, "and besides, you may want your sleep."

When the sun touched the horizon, Roric began to fade. Karin clenched her fists, then threw herself into his arms for a final kiss.

"You do realize," Roric said just before his voice became inaudible, "you will still be able to feel me."

They went down the great stairway to the hall side by side, but King Kardan, looking up surprised, saw only her.

"Yes, I feel better," said Karin. Her voice in her own ears sounded calmer, less wild than it had for several days, and her father nodded almost with relief. "I shall take a short stroll in the evening air to clear my head."

They unlocked the doors for her, and Roric stayed at her shoulder. As she went out the great gates of the castle, she saw two members of the guard following her. She stopped, then walked up to them.

"It's your father's orders, Princess," she was told. "It is not safe for a young woman to walk alone."

She had the vague sense they had followed her the day before as well, but yesterday was a blur. "Of course," she said, "but keep your distance so I can enjoy a little solitude." She returned to where she thought she had left Roric and had to stifle a startled outcry when he unexpectedly took her hand.

But she squeezed his invisible hand as they walked, trying her best not to remember any more of the details of the story about the daemon lover. It was another of the old stories about a woman who had lost her man. In this story the woman had longed for her husband so passionately that he had returned from Hel to her, but had returned as a wight, without his now rotting body.

Her feet found their way down the harbor road to the headland as they had ever since she heard the ravens' messages. The western sky was still shot with scarlet, but the light was going fast. "Perhaps I should go back to the castle soon," she started to say, but then she caught motion on the water's dark surface from the corner of her eye.

She hurried to the edge for a closer look. The wind had dropped at last, and the ship, with lanterns hung on bow and stern, was coming into harbor on its oars as well as its nearly slack sail. Color had faded with the onset of night, so she could not see if the sail was red.

But she still recognized the ship well—she had come here on it. It was Hadros' ship, and the heavily muscled man who was first onto the shore, his shield on his arm and his sword in his hand, was King Hadros himself.

She started to run, not back toward the castle but directly inland. She still clenched Roric's hand in hers. "I can't face Hadros—I *can't*!" She did not know where she was going, but there was no way she could explain to the king so that he would understand, at least not tonight, that neither she nor Roric had killed his son.

There was just enough light to show the startled guards closing in on her.

Karin tried to go faster but could not. "I can't outrun them in these clothes," she gasped.

Suddenly Roric's hand was gone. She struggled onward, then heard a surprised cry behind her. She turned to make out a shape that seemed to be struggling with the air—one of the guards. He doubled over suddenly and dropped to the ground. The second guard ran up beside the first, his sword out, but there was a sharp clang, his sword was struck from his grip, and his head jerked backward as he was knocked down by an invisible fist.

Holding up her skirts, Karin kept running, but she smiled as she ran. In a moment she felt a hand under her arm, supporting her, helping her to greater speed.

When they had passed beyond a hedgerow she paused to catch her breath. Moonlight and shrubs made crazy shadows around her. She firmly pushed away the thought that this might be someone else from the realm of the Wanderers beside her. "I hope you didn't have to kill them," she said, then realized he could not answer. "Squeeze my hand twice if you did."

He did not squeeze at all. "Good," she said. "When my father dies they will be *my* guards."

She listened but heard only the ordinary sounds of the night: a chirping of insects in the meadow, small creatures rustling in the hedgerow, and in the distance the slow sound of waves. King Hadros had apparently not yet come up from the harbor.

Karin suddenly felt fully herself again, unafraid, able to assess dangers, able to plan. In fact, since Roric did not know where they were and could not speak, she had to plan for both of them. Would Queen Arane approve of this new method of manipulating men?

She smiled at this thought and started walking rapidly. In the darkness it was a little better; the solidity at her shoulder felt like Roric as long as she did not look toward him. "We have a head start," she said. "By the time they realize in the castle that I have been gone too long, by the time those guards recover consciousness, by the time Hadros comes up from the harbor and demands to see his son, we will be well on the way to the Mirror-seer's lake. They will not think to look for us there tonight."

Her feet found the track that led up the valley. "As long as we are *both* gone, Valmar and I," she said to the silent presence next to her, "it will be hard for King Hadros to start the war again on the presumption that Valmar was murdered here. Hadros and my father may even agree that they both were cruelly deceived by *you*, who first killed Valmar and then kidnapped me. But I am afraid the two of them will agree together that Valmar and I will have to marry if we can be recovered."

She felt the tension in the arm that touched hers and laughed. "No, Roric, I really do not want to marry my foster-brother. He *is* better looking than you," she added teasingly, "but I thought today would have answered all your questions about my intentions. By the time he returns from the Wanderers' realm, I will have thought of something to change Hadros' mind—women can always outmaneuver men if they want."

But a thought nagged at her, driving away her laughter. The Wanderer had asked all three of them if they were outcasts. He might have been deliberately looking for someone with no ties because whoever went to assist the Wanderers against fate would not be coming back.

"You probably don't know about the Mirror-seer," she said to Roric because she did not want to think about Valmar. The track was beginning to rise, and they had to go slowly in the dark. "It was he who told me I would find a Wanderer on Graytop—but could not tell me where you had gone. Now that the Wanderers have their mortal he's *got* to tell us more."

The way seemed much longer in the dark and on foot than it had in daylight and on horseback. The moon was well into the western sky by the time they topped the escarpment to see the lake's surface calm before them, reflecting stars.

As she picked her way along the damp shore the calls of the frogs grew silent, and there were splashes as they leapt from shore to water, but behind her their song began again. The Mirror-seer's house was a black, indistinct shape.

She stood hesitating on the dock before it, realizing he must be asleep, wondering if he could see anything with his mirrors in the dark. But this was no time, she told herself, for timidity. She lifted her fist and rapped boldly on the door.

There was a confused banging inside, while the frogs went silent again and a little wind sprang up among the reeds. Then through the small window she could see a candle come to life, and the door opened before her.

"Princess!" said the little round man in surprise, pulling disordered clothes more firmly around himself. His eyes were hidden by shadow. "What can have brought you here in the darkest night? And this?"

He turned toward the emptiness where Roric stood, holding up his candle. She turned too, eagerly, but saw nothing but the candle's flickering flame.

"Then you are back in mortal lands, Roric No-man's son," said the Seer gravely.

"You can see him?" she asked urgently.

"Of course. And you cannot?"

He turned then, seeming to listen to something. "I understand," he said soberly. "You were not with the lords of voima themselves but with a simulacrum of them. That is why your beard did not grow while you were there, and why in the realms under the sun you are only fully real when the sun is shining." To Karin the Seer added, "My own voima allows me to see him. But there may be something I can do . . ."

"We need to find someone," said Karin, "Valmar Hadros' son. He walked out over the sea on moonlight to join the Wanderers." She realized the Mirror-seer was tapping the fingers of one hand against his thigh and added hastily, "You can have this ring. It used to be my mother's; I think it is very valuable."

The Seer took the ring she handed him but did not look at it. "You will soon exhaust your father's treasury with all these people you want to see, Princess," he commented. "And you should know I cannot see someone no longer under the sun."

"We do not need to *see* him," said Karin, and from the way the Seer turned his head Roric apparently said something too. "But we need to bring him back from the Wanderers' realm. King Hadros will kill somebody—maybe my father—unless we produce his son very soon."

Again Roric seemed to add something, for the Seer said dryly, "Those who seek the Wanderers usually have deeper concerns than recovery of a horse."

"If we cross the channel again," said Karin, "and go to the stone gateway where Roric followed the—followed whatever the being was, will we be in the Wanderers' realm?"

"There is no gateway there that mortals can pass unaided."

For a second she could feel despair starting to mount. Coming here had been useless, at best a temporary delay until she had to face the two kings, whose men were even now doubtless searching the woods for her.

But she was not going to give up now. She set her jaw

and asked, "I am not asking you to *see* anything by darkness. I only want information. Before you told me where to find a Wanderer. Now I want to find the rest of them—and the knowledge you tried to keep from me before."

"I kept no knowledge from you," said the Mirror-seer, but he seemed uneasy, and his turned his face away toward the lake.

"You told me that an end is fated for everyone, even the Wanderers. Now tell us what role they want all of us—Roric, Valmar, and me—to play as they fight against that end."

For a moment the Seer played with the heavy ring, tossing it up and catching it one-handed. The gold glinted in the candlelight. Then suddenly he closed his fingers around it. "I am not doing this for a piece of jewelry," he said. "But you are the heiress of the kingdom in which, after all, I have to live. The mirrors will sometimes show something different by night . . ."

He turned then abruptly and disappeared back into his house. Karin stood waiting on the dock, listening to the little waves against the shore. Although she strained to hear, there was no sound of pursuit from the castle. It grew colder, and Roric put an invisible arm around her shoulders.

In twenty minutes the Seer was back, completely draped with black cloth, so that at first the candle he held up seemed held by a disembodied hand. She pressed against Roric, either to reassure him or for reassurance herself.

"This is for you, Roric No-man's son," said the Seer, holding out another black cloth. Roric let go of her, and in a second the cloth had disappeared, although with the moon low virtually everything outside the range of the candle flame was invisible.

The Mirror-seer went to the edge of the dock and held up the candle so that its light was reflected in a dozen shining shards on the waves below. He held a mirror over the candle, then went perfectly still. He kept his eyes turned to the mirror, bringing his face closer and closer as the candle smoke gradually spread a dark stain over the glass. To Karin, waiting with indrawn breath and heart pounding, the Seer seemed to stand motionless for an hour.

Abruptly there came a loud splash, followed almost instantaneously by another. The candlelight was gone, but something was thrashing in the water by the dock.

Karin froze in terror and uncertainty. "Help me out, Princess!" came a voice from the water, the Mirror-seer's voice.

She knelt down and extended an arm over the black water. The Seer seized it so powerfully that she was almost pulled in, and had to brace herself to tug him out.

He came up all dark and wet. She could only make out a lighter gray spot that must be his face as she helped him onto the dock and he pushed back his drapings. A short distance down the shore there was further splashing, as though something very large was coming up on land.

"You are halfway back," said the Seer, his face turned away from her. "When you reappear at sunrise, you shall be fully returned to the land of the mortals."

"Roric?" said Karin tentatively, but if he answered she could not hear his voice.

"Listen to me, Kardan's daughter," said the Mirror-seer then. "I have seen more than even a Seer can safely see. If I tell you this now, I shall be unable to tell you anything more for a long, long time, if ever. It is your choice—difficult information now, or many small seeings in the years to come."

"We may not have years to come," she answered. "Tell me what you know, and tell me plainly."

But the Seer did not speak at once. He sat on the dock, Karin beside him, and water dripped from him onto the planks. He seemed to be trembling, either from the effort of his seeing or from chill. She could feel exhaustion stinging the backs of her own eyes. This night already seemed to have lasted years, and it was not over.

"No one can choose their fate," he said at last, so low

that she had to bend close to him. "Not even the Wanderers. Their realm of endless day must sometime move toward night, only to be reborn if new powers take control."

"I knew it," said Karin between her teeth. "I knew they had no ultimate strength."

"But they do," said the Seer, even more quietly. "Mortals cannot choose not to die. Although the Wanderers cannot avoid their fate, they have a way to alter it . . ."

Karin thought about this for a moment. "What would happen to mortal realms if the Wanderers died?"

"If *no* one replaced them—then chaos like the chaos out of which the earth was originally formed."

"But there are other beings of voima! Won't *you* still be here?"

"Voima persists even without the lords of voima. The change has come before. I believe—I hope—that *some-one* will take over—the same Wanderers reborn, those who now challenge them, or even, perhaps, those others that took Roric No-man's son. The Wanderers' realm should not be an empty night for long. But then— Mortals may still burn offerings, but the answers they will receive will be very different . . ."

There was another long silence. "But what do the Wanderers want with *us*?" she asked at last. "And why do they want outcasts?"

The Seer shifted as though unwilling to answer, but when he spoke it was louder than anything he had said so far. "There is only one solution for the present Wanderers if they want to reverse their fate. And that solution is in Hel."

"But there are no Wanderers in Hel!"

"Exactly. It is reserved for mortals. That is why they need a mortal: to go there, to find what they need, to bring it back."

"And that is?"

The Seer shifted again, and she thought he was shaking his head, though it was hard to be sure. "I am not an ordinary mortal. I do not know."

"Well," said Karin abruptly, determinedly, pushing herself to her feet. "I for one am *not* going into Hel on behalf of the Wanderers. And I will not let them send either Valmar or Roric. None of us will sacrifice the rest of our lives for them. You say the Wanderers want a mortal to bring something to them, but that person would come back as a wight, without a body."

"That is possible," said the Seer colorlessly.

"There is one thing you still have not told us," she said, standing over him now. "How can we find the Wanderers, get into their realm to rescue Valmar? Will I still find that Wanderer on Graytop, the one who told you to send me there?"

"He will not meet you there again," said the Mirror-seer, still in that distant, expressionless voice, confirming her guess that he had been instructed to send her there.

"Can we reach their realm through the faeys' burrows?"

"There is only one path you can take, Karin Kardan's daughter, only one route mortals may now pass unaided. And that is far to the north of here, far beyond the channel, in the mountains of the hot rivers."

"The Hot-River Mountains?" said Karin thoughtfully. "They are indeed far to the north. In fact— I think there is a king there who was outlawed at the All-Gemot. How will we find the right place in the mountains to enter immortal realms?"

"When you find it, you will know it."

"That is not an answer."

The Seer rocked back and forth in the damp pool his wet drapes had made around him on the dock. "Then ask for the Witch of the Western Cliffs when you reach the mountains. She will direct you to the doorway. And that," he added in a louder voice, "is the only way you will reach the Wanderers, and the only answer you will have from me."

She stamped her foot abruptly on the planking. "It is *not* the only path to the Wanderers' realm. But I see it is the only path they intend to let us take. Are they still testing our ability and resolve? We shall certainly go there, go there at once, but only to recover Valmar from being persuaded to offer his own life for beings whose fated end has already come."

She turned, took two steps, and turned back. "Thank you," she said gravely to the Seer. "If I ever become sovereign queen here, unless the world is changed beyond recognition, I shall ensure that you have the respect and the comfort any Seer would want. Roric?"

She held out her hand to emptiness, and someone or something took it. If this was not Roric, she thought grimly, if something else had climbed out of the lake and taken his place, then she would find out at dawn.

Karin kept stumbling on the dark, uneven track as they went back down the valley. She had not eaten all day and was almost unbearably weary. When they had ascended, her own footsteps had been the only sound; now there was the sound of another set of feet beside hers.

"I think we shall be at the harbor shortly before sunrise," she said. "We cannot stop for conversations with my father or with Hadros. As long as they are uncertain what has happened to any of us, that uncertainty will bind them together—I hope."

She pictured Hadros flying into a rage and running her father through in the middle of his own hall. A gasp of horror almost escaped her, but she closed her mind against the image. If it was going to happen, it had already happened, and she could not find out without exposing Roric and herself to new danger.

"We could flee to Queen Arane's court," she said thoughtfully. "I think the queen would take us in—she even asked about you when we first met. But that would do nothing to save Valmar." She realized she kept waiting for Roric to make some response, but she alone would have to make this decision.

"No, we will have to find some way to cross the channel. There may be a skiff down at the harbor that you and I could sail alone. We have to get up north, have to rescue Valmar before he reaches Hel—if the Wanderers have not sent him there already. Bringing him alive to his father is also the only way to rescue *you*. We could try to explain that there was not enough time between when you left Hadros' court and Valmar's disappearance for you to kill him, but he will not be interested in dates and times. The only thing that will interest him will be his son . . ."

She was so tired it was hard to think clearly, but suddenly she laughed. She heard the sound of her laugh disconcertingly loud, almost wild again, but still she smiled.

"I know how we can cross the channel," she said to the presence beside her that she hoped was Roric. "We'll steal Hadros' ship!"

He pulled her to a stop, and she felt hands on her shoulders. "No," she said firmly, "it is no use arguing with me. I cannot hear what you say. And this will work! Come on." But she did not start walking at once. Instead she asked, against her will, "Are you sure you *are* Roric?"

For answer he took her in his arms and kissed her. She laughed again as he released her, this time in relief. "If you are not Roric, I think I like you even better! Now, we must make haste to be there before Hadros sails again."

She gave his hand a tug and began to walk. "Men worry too much about rule and honor. I *like* my kingdom, like its luxuries—the food is better than Hadros serves, and no one expects a princess to toil! But I will cheerfully give it all up to save you."

Karin hurried down the track with new energy, her slippered feet finding a sure footing. No longer was she bound by the generations who lay in the burial mound, or by the necessity to hold herself in check in a court where she was an outsider. She and Roric together were fleeing for their lives, and she smiled as she squeezed his hand.

The darkest part of the night had passed and the eastern

sky was lightening toward yellow when they came down the harbor road. Roric was still invisible. "Wait here behind these bushes," Karin told him, thinking that men really were much easier to deal with if they could not raise objections. "As soon as the sun rises come join me. No one should observe you regaining visibility. We want the sailors to obey us, not fear us as dead wights from Hel."

She straightened out her clothes as well as she could by the half light and took the narrow road down to the edge of the sea. She would know in a moment whether Hadros had told his men why he had suddenly decided to come here, or whether, as she hoped, he had given the orders but no explanations.

One longship, its dragon prow unmounted, lay upside down and covered with a tarpaulin on the shore. Another ship, its awnings spread, floated on the tide. The sleepy men guarding it heard her approach and jumped up. They recognized her after only a second in spite of her rich clothing.

She scanned the men on board surreptitiously as they woke and came to greet her. "Are you coming home then, Karin?" one asked eagerly. "The maid you left in charge knows nothing of your herb chest, and spends all day screeching at the other women. And we have had but poor fare since you went away!"

There were only a few warriors here with the seamen. Hadros must have taken the rest with him to the castle and spent the night there—which suggested, she thought with hope, that the king and his men had not gotten into a fight with her father and his much more numerous guards, or the survivors would have fled.

"Is the king ready to sail?" asked another seaman.

She did not answer but instead made a show of looking around. "Is Roric not here?" she asked carefully, watching their reactions.

But they only seemed puzzled. "Don't you mean Valmar? Is Roric here too? He was home for less than a day before he left again."

The edge of the sun was just peeking over the horizon. "Hadros sent me to sail home with you now," she said clearly. "Take down the awnings and prepare to set out at once. The king will be detained at my father's castle for some weeks, busy with affairs of the All-Gemot."

"Or arranging your marriage!" said one man slyly, but the others shushed him.

"Roric said he would accompany me," she continued, deliberately ignoring this remark. "He was going to meet me here."

Even if they rescued Valmar from the Wanderers, even if they all lived past the change of the world the Seer could not describe, she did not know how she would escape this marriage, which kept seeming more and more imminent until even Roric half believed in it. If Valmar had already descended into Hel for the Wanderers, this would no longer be a problem. But allowing him to die was no solution, even if Queen Arane might have thought it one.

Direct sunlight now came rippling across the sea. The sailors were loosening the awnings from the pegs. Karin cupped her hands and turned toward the headland. "Roric!" she shouted. "Are you up there? We are ready to sail!"

And he appeared, himself, solid, coming down the steep road in long leaps. "We must leave at once," she said, even before he reached the shore. "Sails up! Oars out!" By the time Roric reached the narrow quay and vaulted into the ship, the sailors were releasing the mooring lines.

"Just in time," he said in her ear as they came out past the shelter of the headland, and the wind bellied out the red sail. "I saw a group of people heading this way from the castle. Another five minutes and they would have had us."

4

Valmar ran into moonlight, the empty air churning beneath his boots. He kept closing his eyes against that brilliant whiteness, then opening them to take in its glory. He had run, it seemed, for many minutes, for hours, while the moon grew and grew, big enough to swallow him, the headland, Kardan's kingdom, the sea, the entire earth. And the man who ran at his side, whom he did not dare look at, was also growing.

His eyes flew open again as he felt solidity beneath his feet and almost stumbled. The moon had caught fire.

But it was not the moon, he realized, as his feet slowed first to a walk and then to a halt. It was the sun, and he was running into a sunset that had set all the clouds around it ablaze.

They seemed to be in a meadow of grass and clover. Cows grazed on the far side, but they kept raising their heads and lowing uneasily. Everything, even the rank grass, was tinted pink by the sky.

Then Valmar turned to look at the being beside him.

He was white, brilliant white, so white the sunset did not touch him. He was more than twice the size of a man and arrayed in robes that glowed. The face he turned on Valmar was enormously solemn, enormously wise and noble, and yet there too was an almost friendly air if such were possible, a touch of good humor.

Valmar dropped to his knees. "My lord," he stammered. He fumbled his sword free of the peace straps and out of the sheath, and held it up, hilt first, while keeping his head down.

"As I recall," commented an amused voice above him, "you were going to ask no more of the lords of voima."

"Lord, I did not know," said Valmar, his face averted. He kept expecting to feel his sword taken from his hands, but it was untouched.

"You were going to make your life into the best tale your own strength and honor and manhood could create," the other continued, "and all without asking anything of us."

Valmar put a hand across his eyes. "Do not mock me now, Lord. I did not know—I did not know that you were the source of strength and honor and manhood."

"In fact," said the Wanderer, still sounding amused, "we pattern our honor on that of you mortals. Voima flows from life, not the other way around. But as you can see, our land is hastening toward night. And while you may have decided you would ask nothing more of voima, we would ask something of *you*."

Valmar sat back on his heels, daring to look up for the first time. "I am yours to command." Strange conflicting feelings whirled through him: the way he always felt listening to the old stories of glory and death; his thoughts of Karin; his admiration for Roric, who too had been here; and his desire to make his father think well of him, all the feelings burning and swirling into a sensation that could have been a mighty song of trumpets.

"But we do not command," said the Wanderer. "Come, and you shall meet the others."

The sun did not set but remained frozen just above the horizon, though as the clouds blew across the sky an ever-changing display of gold and scarlet lit up the west. They went on foot, the Wanderer—as Valmar could not help but think of him, though he must have a different name here—slowing his pace to Valmar's. When he asked how far they had to go, he always had the same answer, "Not far. Not very far."

They traveled through shaded dells and open meadows, along the edges of woodlots and by pastures where the flocks regarded them querulously. At first Valmar thought this a perfect land, one of endless abundance and fertility, but then he started to see the gaps: shocked hay mildewing where it stood, birch trees broken so that unshed leaves were dying, pear trees whose fruit was rotting even before it ripened.

These were the sorts of setbacks every farm of every kingdom had to deal with in mortal realms, Valmar told himself, and should therefore not seem worrisome. But somehow they did. For the lords of voima *any* weakness or rot was a sign that their powers were beginning to wane.

He squirmed as he realized that the Wanderers must have been listening to the very conversation in which he and Karin had spoken of them as being without knowledge or power. How could he have been so foolish? Maybe they only had gaps in their knowledge, if indeed they had any, because of this imminent onset of night.

He would stand with them, then, he thought resolutely, stand with them against those who wanted to replace them, even if it was a doomed cause. People who glittered and who filled him with an awe beyond fear, though at the same time trying to reassure him, *must* be in the right.

He startled himself by wondering if Karin—or even Roric—would agree. Roric had been here, but had come back. Had he let down the Wanderers, even rejected them? Or had they somehow rejected *him*?

But he had not seen Roric, Valmar reminded himself; he was not even sure he *was* back except that the ravens had said so. There might be many purposes and plans here, of which Roric was involved in one set and he in another.

He thought about the being without a back, whom he had seen so briefly, who looked neither as this Wanderer had when he appeared on the headland, nor as he appeared now. And Valmar tightened his jaw as he wondered if Roric might be on one side and he on the other.

The hall where he was taken was enormous, glorious, its ceiling so high it seemed there must be clouds beneath it, its benches all cushioned and its tables laid with silver. Hammered silver bosses decorated the beams, and the upright timbers were all painted blue. The other beings there were nearly indistinguishable from the one he had first met, tall, glowing white, with faces so noble and wise he could barely look at them.

They set him on a high bench where he felt like a child and brought him food, roast beef, fried onions, soft cheese, a white loaf with honey, and an ale horn that never became

low no matter how much he drank. He was so excited it
was hard to eat, but he was, he realized, very hungry. Horizontal sunlight poured through the hall's open doorway.
The tall white beings stayed at the far end of the hall as
though not wanting to distract him from his dinner.

When at last he had eaten his fill and pushed the silver
plate away—he noted with some surprise that no maid
came to take it, that everyone here, both lords and servants, appeared to be men—the Wanderers gathered around
him. There seemed to be about a dozen of them, though
they were hard to count since he could not look at them
directly for more than a few seconds.

"You may wonder, Valmar Hadros' son," began one of
them, "why the immortals would want a mortal's assistance."

"I did wonder," he said after a brief silence, in which he
realized they really were waiting for his answer. His heart
beat almost ashamedly loudly, as it had the first time he
had prepared to face Gizor with a real sword in his fist
rather than a wooden sword, or the first time one of the
castle maids had kissed him.

"You have to understand," the being continued, "that
our realm is not exactly like mortal realms, although of
course it is patterned after them. And one difference is
that mortals are not meant to come here, and thus individual men and women, if they do come, are much more
powerful than they are at home."

"If I have to understand," said Valmar hesitantly, "I'm
afraid I don't."

"Well," said one of the Wanderers, whose slightly amused
tone made him think it was the one he had met originally,
"you might be surprised to learn that here you have
destructive powers of awesome proportions. A land modeled on that of mortals might be destroyed by mortals—
and with the land the beings in it."

"So is the onset of night caused by mortals?" he asked.
If he could just slow his heart, he thought, he might
understand all this better. They were counting on him, the

immortal lords of voima were counting on him, and he could not fail them.

"No," very quietly. "It is our fated end approaching. But a mortal can help us defeat those who are even now preparing to replace us when we are gone."

"But even if you defeat some other immortals," he replied with a frown, "will not fate still find you?"

They did not answer for a moment, as though uneasy themselves. When one did speak at last, it was with no hint of amusement.

"A seed dies and is reborn as a stalk of wheat. A mortal dies and is reborn as a voiceless, nameless spirit. Some deaths are glorious, some are sad, some merely an empty end. But because we are immortal we do not have access to Death, to its opportunity for a new beginning in a new form, which might with voima be molded into an even better form than before."

"So what do you want me to do?" Valmar asked timidly, fighting his fear but fearing he already knew the answer.

"After you have helped us defeat the others whose presence has become so much more irritating with the approach of night, we would like you to do us a favor. It is just," with a brief pause, "the smallest favor. We would like you to descend into Hel for us and find the lords of death."

PART II: Flight and Pursuit

CHAPTER SIX

1

"Tell the captain to put us ashore before we reach harbor," said Roric quietly.

Karin, standing beside him at the rail, turned toward him in surprise. The wind tugged at her braids, and the sailors were all bustling about now that they were within a few miles of King Hadros' harbor. The choppy salt water of the channel behind them was empty except for one small sail on the horizon.

"Surely *you*, Karin, in planning this theft, realized that Hadros would send a raven-message home," he continued in an undertone, staring at that sail. "Gizor One-hand may not be one to talk to ravens, but I expect they can talk to *him*."

"But Gizor may have been with the king!" she protested.

"Then he sent his message to whichever warrior he left in charge, or even to Dag. It doesn't matter which. Does your father have a blue and white striped sail on his warship, by the way? As soon as Hadros realized we were gone, he sent a raven to tell those here to capture us when we landed—probably to hold *you* until your father arrived, but to kill me outright."

Her eyes were wide. "Would he try—again—to have you killed?"

"I defied him. If that's Hadros right behind us, he may

have added the refinement to wait to kill me until he could watch." He smiled grimly. "You and I may not have been outlawed yet, but we are already outcasts for stealing this ship, my sweet. Your friend the Wanderer would be pleased. Little blood-guilt will fall on our killers. But the seamen for the moment seem ready to obey you. Make up some excuse why we need to go ashore—Birch Point should be a good place."

She gave him a last quick look and started toward the stern where the captain stood at the rudder.

But Roric reached out suddenly to catch her arm. "Wait a minute," he whispered. "Can you see them?"

She stared toward Birch Point, now less than a half mile away, then abruptly dropped below the level of the rail.

"Good thinking on Gizor's part," said Roric in admiration. "He guessed what I was planning to do and has his welcoming party all ready."

Karin tried to tug him down beside her. "But I only saw one man! And I would not have seen him except for the sunlight reflecting from his helmet."

Roric remained standing. "They know we are on this ship, whether they spot us or not. At this point, it is better if they do not know we spotted them! You can be sure that the man whose helmet we saw was not Gizor himself."

Karin pressed herself against him and he put an arm around her, to the evident interest of the seamen not too busy with the lines and oars to pay attention. "Then what shall we do?" she asked in a low voice, no longer the determined woman who had first taken him to the Mirror-seer and then stolen this ship. He held her tighter.

"Go ashore at the harbor as though in all innocence," he answered, thinking rapidly. "Gizor must feel I insulted his honor by escaping before, so he will be well prepared this time. Because Hadros took many of his warriors with him, Gizor will not have enough for an ambush at every possible place. He will—I hope—have left the rest at the castle, knowing there is little place to hide them at the harbor. If we do not suspect an attack, he thinks, we will go straight to the castle and be captured easily there. If we do suspect, he'll expect us to make for Birch Point rather than the harbor. We should have a twenty minute head start on them, maybe more. The alder thickets and the bog will slow them down, and they will not have tried to take horses in there. As soon as we hit land, we run. It is not as though we had any baggage to slow us down!"

The entry into the harbor seemed to take an eternity, as the sail drooped, losing wind, and the sailors pulled at the oars. The first approach to the dock was not quite on line; the captain, quietly cursing his own steering, had to have the seamen back water, away from the hidden rocks that guarded the harbor against those who did not know the line on which to sight, and tried again. Roric kept his eyes on the shore until they ached, but he could see no motion through the trees.

When at last the oak planking touched the dock, he was over the side in a second and helping Karin over. There was still no sign of Gizor. Roric was suddenly in high good humor. "We shall join you at the castle shortly," he called to the seamen. "Before it grows any darker, I want to go to the Weaver's cave and burn an offering for our safe passage!"

They walked the first fifty yards, straining for the jangling of armor and weapons, passed a line of trees that shielded them from the harbor, and began to run.

The afternoon was nearly gone, and the oak trees cast long, dark shadows. They ran hand in hand, their feet on the sandy track sounding unnaturally loud. "If they come around by the shore, we're ahead of them," panted Roric. "But if they cut inland from Birch Point, if they guess we are not heading for the castle but—"

Their way was suddenly barred by three helmeted men. One of them was missing his right hand and held his sword in his left.

Roric jumped back, his arms wide for a second as though

to hide Karin behind him, then whipped out his sword. "Decided to try for me a second time, Gizor?" he shouted.

The old warrior looked past him for a second, said, "Karin?" in what sounded like surprise even from inside his helmet, then turned again as if in sharp decision toward Roric. "If you give yourself up," he said in the tone Roric had never trusted, "we will not hurt the girl."

The two warriors with him spread out slowly, one to each side. Roric recognized them—Rolf and Warulf, Gizor's most trusted warriors, the two who had been with him when they attacked the manor guest house.

"You did not plan to hurt her anyway!" Roric shot back at Gizor. "Even *you* know it would be your neck if she was harmed."

"Surrender while you still have the chance," said Gizor warningly. "I'm not going to let you trick me a second time. King Hadros wants you, alive or dead."

"If you give yourself up now, I shall not kill *you!*"

"Such a braggart, when it's three against one?"

Roric laughed defiantly. "Such a coward, to make it three against one?" He moved lightly, testing out the sandy surface, almost dancing as he laughed at Gizor, remembering quickly how these men fought. Rolf was fast, so fierce on the attack that he almost forgot to defend himself, and Warulf was virtually unbeatable if you came at him on his right side, but a little slower against attacks from his left.

Gizor took a breath that made his chest rise and fall hard, but he answered quietly. "We just want to make sure you surrender peacefully." He turned his head slightly, as though watching the other two advance. "Throw down your sword now, Roric, and I give you my oath I shall not harm you."

"The others will instead?" Roric laughed again and tossed back his hair, then wheeled suddenly. Gizor had stopped a dozen yards away to threaten him, giving him a few seconds *now* before they could all be on him at once. The warrior to his left—Rolf—was fractionally closer.

It was three against one, him with no armor and no shield, but it was no worse than it would have been at the manor guest house, where he had taken the Wanderer's advice and run to save his skin.

Roric sprang in attack just as Gizor had always taught him. But then he had been fighting to prove his ability— now he was fighting for his life. The warrior's shield stopped his first sword stroke. Roric parried a return stroke, then went in low for a thrust that almost got past the shield.

Then he dropped, rolled to the side, and leaped up, dodging the sword of the other warrior coming up behind him. It whizzed along his left arm and took a nick from his hand.

But now he had them both before him, and Warulf's left side was toward him. From the corner of his eye he could see Gizor, advancing but strangely slowly. They were all men he knew, and these warriors too seemed momentarily reluctant to push their advantage.

But he could not stop now. He swung his sword two-handed, with a yell and all his strength. It ricocheted off the very top of Warulf's shield, then found the narrow crevice between the warrior's mail shirt and his helmet.

The man collapsed with a rush of blood from his neck, brilliant red in the twilight. Roric leaped back, yelled again, and parried two strokes from Rolf. Gizor had taught him well. His own first strokes bounced, first off the shield, then off the helmet. He feinted to the side, ducked a blow aimed at his face, and found the opening to thrust his sword in low and upward, into the belly.

Gizor came at him while he was wrenching his sword loose.

He tried to turn, his balance off, the track beneath his feet slippery with blood.

But the old warrior's rush was very slow, his battle cry almost a shriek. And then he saw the dagger protruding from the back of Gizor's shoulder, thrust through a slit in the mail.

It was Karin's dagger. She held a downed oak branch, and as Gizor raised his sword against Roric, she hit him with it across the head with full force.

She snatched up the dagger as Gizor collapsed at her feet and stared wildly at Roric, the oak branch dangling from one hand and her eyes half-crazed. He grabbed her other hand and began to run. She threw the branch from her with a cry. Their footprints were bloody the first half mile.

"I knew I had chosen a good woman in you," Roric gasped when they stopped to catch their breath. "But I had not realized before how good!"

Karin's gray eyes in the dusk looked almost normal again. "We should have killed him while we had the chance," she said between her teeth.

"You had the chance," he said, started to wipe his forehead with his arm, then realized it was covered with blood.

"I couldn't do it," she said in a suddenly small voice. "I could not drive my dagger into his neck. I would never have made a good shield-maiden. But *you* should have killed him, Roric."

He took her hand to pull her onward. "By the Wanderers, Karin, as we were fighting it suddenly came to me, he might be my father."

They were walking now, away from the road, across the sandy hills between the trees. "I do not think he can be," said Karin slowly. "I know you were found at the castle gate, suggesting you must be from this kingdom, but he would certainly know you were his son. Even King Hadros could not order him to kill his own child."

"He might not have known I was his," replied Roric, "if he had fathered me on some girl from one of the manors."

"You look nothing like him," said Karin firmly. "You indeed look like no one in the kingdom. Well," she added after a moment, "when I first met you, you did look a little like Nole does now."

Roric made himself smile. "All fast-growing skinny boys probably look alike. I hope you do not intend to tell me I was fathered by a boy ten years younger than I am! But they would not have taken such care of a foundling had not *someone* known who I was."

"If you want Gizor as your father . . ." she began darkly.

"No, Karin. I do *not* want to be the son of Gizor One-hand, even if his training did teach me to defend myself, with or without a shield, against both right-handed and left-handed men. Perhaps that is what the Weaver meant when he said that knowledge of my origins would destroy me."

"By the way," said Karin. "Did you really intend to go to the Weaver's cave?"

He abruptly smiled and squeezed her hand. "The Weaver has never given me a clear answer yet. I think I prefer your Mirror-seer."

He was silent for a moment then added with a frown, "But perhaps his cave at the bottom of the cliff would be our safest place. No one could kill us at such a spot without being outlawed. If Gizor is still alive in the morning, however, it will be the first place he will look for us. And I do not like the idea of sitting as prisoners in the cave until Hadros returns."

"Then where should we go?"

"Certainly not back to the castle. There will be another ambush waiting for us there, even if the ship behind us was just a merchant vessel and not my foster-father and your father."

Karin bit her lip. "I must have distressed my father terribly. He so recently lost his oldest son to shipwreck, and now he will think he has lost me as well."

"The two kings will doubtless be confused when they hear the seamen's story and learn that it was you, not me, who commandeered the ship. That was a good ploy, I thought, to prove you had not been kidnapped, even though I would have tried to talk you out of it if you could hear me! But Gizor's story—if he survives your attack—will leave Hadros uninterested in anything but revenge."

They walked in silence for a moment, then Roric squeezed her hand again and asked, "How did you know just where to put your blade to penetrate his mail shirt?"

"You forget," she said with a toss of her head. "I am mistress of Hadros' castle. I have seen that mail shirt hanging in the hall, with the slit at the shoulder unrepaired, every day for years."

And then she added suddenly, "I know where we can go, for some food and a safe place to sleep. We will go to the faeys!"

The faeys' tunnels were behind them now, closer to the castle. Karin took the lead, hurrying through the deepening night. Roric, coming after her, listened for the troll or for armed men.

The faeys had brought their green lanterns out into the dell. When she gave the triple whistle they ran around distractedly as always, calling to each other in their high voices, before they spotted Karin and Roric.

"There is voima about you, Karin," Roric commented. "I had never seen the faeys before I stumbled into the back of their burrows. You, of all the king's court, are the only mortal who can find beings who seem so incapable of defending or hiding themselves."

And then the faeys were all around them, jumping up and down and laughing. "Karin! Karin! Are you a queen yet! She's dressed like a queen! And she has Roric with her! Is he a king now? But he has blood on him! And I didn't like the way he came into our tunnels!"

But in their delight to see Karin the faeys quickly forgot their objections to Roric. Soon the two were sitting eating berries in the green light of the dell. The faeys, in some distaste, brought Roric a basin of water, and he washed off his hands and arms.

"Even if they use the dogs to hunt us," said Karin, "I do not think they will find us here." Close to the castle but sheltered from it by night and by voima, they felt temporary peace settle around them.

Roric slowly and carefully cleaned his sword, then leaned his forehead on his fists.

"I keep seeing their faces, Karin," he said quietly. "I knew Rolf and Warulf well, slept next to them, ate and drank next to them, and now they are in Hel because of me. Not a very glorious end to their stories."

"It also would not have been a very glorious end to *yours.*"

"And a very short and pointless story mine has been so far. I am not a hero out of legend, Karin. I would never have overcome three men had they fought as desperately as I was fighting, and if I had not had you."

"You stopped them in their mail and helmets, when you did not even have a shield," she said warmly, putting her shoulder against his. "You are enough of a hero for *me,* Roric. But do you think," looking toward him sharply in the green light, "you might have come back from the Wanderers' realm as a man whom steel will not bite?"

"It will bite me all right." He showed her the cut on his hand. "I was saved by fate, not any voima of my own."

They were both silent for a moment. "How many men is it," Roric asked then, "that Hadros boasts he had killed before reaching Valmar's age?"

"Three, I think."

"And they were enemies he killed in battle, not men he knew. I wonder if even *he* could be proud of killing his friends." Again there was silence for a moment.

"The warriors—including Gizor—were Hadros' sworn men," Roric went on. "I will have to pay him compensation or be his blood enemy, even more than I am already, and yet I have nothing with which to pay him that he himself did not give me."

"Then we will win something in the Hot-River Mountains."

Roric lifted his head. "A kingdom, perhaps? I thought of it too. In fact—it was Hadros' idea. I wonder if he will appreciate that I am following his suggestion while I flee for my life from him." He tried to keep the bitterness out of his voice. "Yes, that is exactly what I will do, a single warrior, capture myself a kingdom." He put an arm around her. "You will be the rest of my army, Karin."

After a few minutes, he added, "As you plan this trip for us, have you thought how we will get to these mountains? Even if Hadros is not immediately on our trail, Gizor will be—if he lives."

"I know that," she said distantly.

"The ships will all be guarded against us, so we will have to go on foot unless we can steal horses somewhere. And it is a long journey. Did you have any other jewelry on you besides the ring you gave the Mirror-seer?"

"This necklace," she said, pulling out a thin chain from inside her dress. "It might buy us food, but not horses."

"If the Witch of the Western Cliffs is anything like a Weaver or Seer, we should save it for her. These creatures of voima seem strangely fond of mortal jewelry."

Roric stretched, then lay down and put his head in her lap. "You and your friends the faeys can plan something. There may be two dozen men surrounding this dell in the morning, and I need to sleep before I fight them."

2

The faeys woke them shortly before dawn. "Come with us, Karin. Wake up, make her wake up. She has to come with us! It's not safe to stay here. There are dogs in the woods. Sunlight is dangerous!"

She and Roric allowed themselves to be squeezed into the tunnels before the faeys pulled the stone into position. With both of them inside, the space seemed even more closed-in than usual. She took deep breaths of the stale air and tried to remind herself of the alternative to being here.

"Maybe we should just stay here all day," suggested Roric. "By nightfall, we should be fully rested—we will have to be if we're going all that way on foot. And they should have called off the hunt in these woods by then."

"You can stay here with us as long as you want, Karin," said one of the faeys, giving Roric a sideways look as though not entirely sure whether to include him in the offer.

"And where are you going on foot?" another asked. "Are you not happy here?"

"There are mountains far to the north of here," Karin said, "mountains that conceal an entrance to the Wanderers' realm. We have to go there to rescue someone."

"Where does she get these ideas? It must be from Roric! She said she wants to marry him. But he just escaped from the Wanderers! Why would he want to go back? Maybe he should go back by himself and she can stay here!"

"Wherever Roric goes, I go," she said loudly, over their high voices.

Roric grabbed her arm abruptly, surprise and joy on his face. "I hear a horse."

Karin, startled, listened. "I hear it too."

Echoing down the tunnels came the faint sound of a whinney, a thud as of hooves. The faeys were seized with consternation. "A horse? A horse! There can't be a horse in our tunnels! Why is a horse here? It's all Roric's fault!"

"Could it be the way is open again to the Wanderers' realm?" he asked in delight. He started to jump to his feet, banged his head, and crawled instead, Karin right behind him. "This would certainly be easier than trying to find some way hidden in the Hot-River Mountains," he called back over his shoulder.

The way quickly became dark, and the stone floor and walls were cold to her hand. "It is!" cried Roric. "It's Goldmane!"

Karin wondered briefly to herself if he had been this pleased and excited when he reached her father's kingdom and saw her there.

The passage became a little wider here, and they crawled to either side of the stallion's head. The faeys had followed them, though keeping their distance, and there was just enough faint green light from their lanterns to see Goldmane.

He was sprawled out, legs extended. He had his head up, and his eyes were wild. The ceiling here was too low for him to stand, and the wall beyond him was completely solid.

Roric stroked the stallion's nose and rumpled his mane. "Did you come through on your own to help us, boy," he asked affectionately, "or did they push you through that one-way door of theirs back into mortal realms?"

The horse's eyes rolled, but he became somewhat calmer. "I used to think," said Roric, "that if we had access to the Wanderers' knowledge then many aspects of mortal life which seem to make no sense would become clear, but I now think they are even more confused than we are."

Karin clenched her fists. Her heart beat inside her chest as though its space was too tight. The closed-in, trapped feeling was growing stronger. "Roric," she said. "We cannot stay here all day. We must leave *now.*"

Goldmane evidently agreed. He whinnied again and tried ineffectively to kick his way free of the imprisoning tunnel.

"We can't have a horse in here!" the faeys announced from a safe distance.

"Good," said Roric. "Help me get him out."

It seemed that there could not possibly be enough space to shift the stallion, yet somehow there was. The faeys came forward first hesitantly, then more bravely, then with happy boldness once they realized the horse would not hurt them. With Goldmane scrambling himself along, and the faeys behind him pushing, they worked him slowly toward the entrance to the tunnels.

"What do you think, Karin?" Roric asked. His stallion's nose was now against the stone that closed the tunnels, and he seemed to smell the open air beyond. "Do we wait until nightfall, with both Goldmane and the faeys more and more unhappy, or do we rush out into what may be the middle of the hunt for us? The dogs will have had no trouble tracking us to the dell."

She closed her eyes and opened them again. For the last ten minutes she had had to concentrate on her breathing to keep it from becoming wild gasps for air. "We go," she said unsteadily. "I know you'll be able to fight free of whatever is out there."

Roric grinned and kissed her quickly. "At least we'll have the advantage of surprise," he said. "Gizor will never expect us and a horse to come out of a hillside!"

The faeys retreated back out of range of the feared sunlight. Karin put her shoulder to the stone, then stopped and looked toward them, feeling suddenly guilty. "Thank you," she called, "thank you for sheltering us, and," she paused for a second, "if I do not see you again, for always being my friends."

"Good-bye," they called tentatively, then, "What does she mean, if she doesn't see us again? Is she going to her kingdom now? But she said her kingdom was beyond the sea! Roric is making her do it!"

Then she pushed, and the entrance stone rolled easily away. Goldmane kicked his way through the opening, and they went with him, out of the hillside into almost blinding daylight.

The stallion scrambled to his feet. Karin, blinking hard against the sun, pushed the faeys' stone back into position. "Good-bye, Karin!" she heard faint calls from within. A piercing whistle split the air.

"They're here! I found them! Gizor! I found them!"

Roric vaulted up onto his stallion's back. There was shouting in the near distance and a single warrior standing at the edge of the dell. She reached out and Roric grabbed her arm to pull her up behind him.

They were still trying to find their balance on Goldmane's bare back when a pack of dogs came boiling into the dell, and the spaces between the trees that ringed it were suddenly full of armed men.

Roric yelled to his horse, and Goldmane sprang forward. Just one warrior barred their way on this side, and he leaped back as Roric swung his sword. Then the stallion was scrambling out of the dell and up onto the hillside beyond. As he shot under low-leaning oaks, Karin ducked down, clinging desperately to Roric.

Behind them was frenzied barking and a shouting that might have had words, though none of them made sense. But in the midst of the men galloping after them was was a wagon, and in it a bandaged warrior whose naked sword was held left-handed.

Roric shouted again as Goldmane reached the road and began to run even faster. He turned his head slightly to look back at their pursuers, quickly being left behind. She could see fierce triumph on his face.

The wind brought tears to her eyes and tore her hair loose from its braids. She pressed herself against Roric's back as the stallion's long, smooth gait seemed prepared to eat up the miles. Only a short distance before them was the sandstone cliff, and the steep road leading up away from the fields and woods directly dependent on the king.

But gathered where the road began to climb were a group of mounted men and men on foot, mostly armed housecarls, the sunlight bright on their spear points.

Roric leaned forward, brandishing his sword. "Hang on!" he yelled to Karin. For a horrified moment she thought they were going to try to run right through the men before them, and in the blur of faces she saw the king's two younger sons.

At the last second Roric jerked his stallion's head around. Goldmane half reared, then started to run along the base of the cliff, all the mounted men on their heels. She looked over her shoulder to see Gizor's group a quarter mile back, some of the riders already leaving the road, cutting across to try to intercept them.

Again Roric wheeled his stallion. Clinging desperately to the mane while Karin clung to his belt, he turned again toward the road, shot within two feet of the startled pursu-ers' horses, and raced for the way up the sandstone cliff.

Now that way was barred only by a handful of men on foot, but among them were Dag and Nole.

"Oh, no," thought Karin, squeezing shut her wind-blurred eyes. "Not them too."

All but one of the warriors jumped back involuntarily as the stallion bore down on them. But Dag came forward, lifting his spear. Goldmane reared, almost losing his rid-ers, and came down with iron hooves flailing. As the king's son leaped away, Roric leaned over and knocked the spear from his hand with a well-aimed sword blow.

And then the stallion found his feet again, sprang through the scattered foot soldiers, and attacked the slope before him. A few spears came up behind them but fell short. Twice Karin thought she was about to slide off the horse, but Roric reached his right arm back to her, the sword still in his fist, and clinging to it she was able to stay on.

At the top of the cliff, just before they entered the woods, Roric pulled up the stallion to look down. No one had pur-sued them up the narrow road, not even the dogs. But Gizor, lying bandaged in the wagon, a tiny figure far below, waved his sword at them and shouted. His words were carried away by the wind.

"He knows no horse can catch Goldmane, even with two of us on his back," said Roric. Sweat was pouring off him, and his chest was rising and falling, but the stallion seemed only slightly winded. "But the next time we meet, it will be a fight to the death."

"How did you do it?" Karin asked in a small voice. "Unarm Dag without having to kill him?"

He laughed a short hard laugh. "He was trained by Gizor too. When you're on foot with a spear against a horseman, always go for the horse's eyes. But I knew he didn't want to hurt Goldmane, and in that second of hesitation the horse reared and attacked *him*. And while watching the hooves he had no attention to spare for me."

He slid his sword back into its sheath. "We'd better put a few more miles between us and the castle, in case they follow us anyway—and I wouldn't be sure Gizor won't have another ambush waiting up ahead. So far the only reason you and I are still alive, my sweet, is that none of these warriors besides Gizor, much less Dag and Nole, want to see you dead, and some of them are even hesitant about killing me. We all know each other too well. When everyone is hesitating and trying to find a way toward peace, the most ruthless person wins—and Gizor, whether he's my father or not, is the most ruthless person I know."

3

King Kardan stood on top of the burial mound, a fresh-cut rowan twig and his dagger in his hands. The last time he had stood like this, ready to swear an oath to the massive, black-bearded king who waited at the foot of the mound, his wife had been under his feet but all his children had been alive. Now both his sons were buried here, and he did not know if his daughter still lived beneath the sun.

He slowly slit the twig lengthwise, letting its red sap run out on his palm, then touched the dagger point to his finger. He squeezed out a drop of blood and closed his fist, mixing it with the rowan sap. From here he could see the headland above the harbor, but he was too far away to hear the sounds of his ship being readied for sea.

"I swear on rowan and steel," he said loudly and clearly, "that I have not harmed in any way Valmar Hadros' son, that I have not ordered any harm done to him or had word of any. If I lie, may the lords of death take me living into the depths of Hel." The wind whirled his words and carried them far away.

When he descended from the mound, making his way carefully down the steep incline, King Hadros slapped him unexpectedly on the back. "I believe you, Kardan. You swore to me truly ten years ago, when you swore you would pay the tribute faithfully and raise no open or hidden revolt against me."

Kardan nodded, resenting the deliberate reminder that for ten years he had been a tributary king. "If we do not find Valmar," he said stiffly, "even though I did not harm him, I shall of course pay you compensation. He was here in my castle under my protection."

Hadros rested a hand on his shoulder, and his eyes flashed from beneath heavy eyebrows. "I shall take no compensation for my oldest son. If he is safe, well and good. If he is dead, his killer shall pay the blood-guilt with his own blood."

He still had his hand on Kardan's shoulder, either in fellowship or as a veiled threat, as they started slowly back toward the castle. "Now," he said, "tell me more of what your daughter said of Valmar's disappearance."

"*You* do not believe such stories?" asked Kardan in surprise. "All she said was that he had left with a Wanderer, one who had often been seen on Graytop over the years— where in fact no Wanderer has ever been seen. I know some of your beliefs and practices are different north of the channel, but even you cannot believe that the lords of voima ever appear in the flesh to mortals."

"I would not have believed it a short time ago," the other king said very quietly, "but Roric went to their land and returned again."

Sensing a gap in Hadros' confidence, Kardan asked quickly, "Who *is* this Roric, anyway? Where did he come from? And what assurance can *you* give me that he has not kidnapped my daughter at your orders?"

Kardan expected the other king to reply heatedly, but when he answered it was still in that ominously quiet tone. "Roric is my foster-son, raised in my court; he was found at the castle gates as a baby. If he has kidnapped Karin it was certainly not at my orders! You should know I do not war on women."

He took his hand from Kardan's shoulder to pull a ring from the pouch at his belt. "I gave him this when he reached manhood and we swore our oaths to each other. I ordered him, just the other day, to forget Karin, not to come here. He threw his ring at my feet, defied me, and came anyway." Hadros chuckled grimly. "Maybe the only reason I did not run him through on the spot is because I would have done the same at his age."

"You must know him well," said Kardan, hearing the desperation in his own voice and scarcely caring. The two kings had stopped walking to face each other. "What will Roric do to her? You have, what is it, another two or three sons besides Valmar? Karin was all I had left."

Hadros smiled, suddenly and surprisingly. "You fear the lad will hurt her? Not very likely." He turned to walk again; there was a slight limp in his gait. "Roric first asked, it must be two months ago now, for my permission to woo her. I refused it, of course. But she told me she intends to marry him—he must have spoken to her anyway." He watched Kardan's face as he spoke, and smiled again, although with tight lips. "She never said anything to you about that, eh?"

"No." Kardan looked straight ahead as they walked. They were almost back to the castle now. Karin intending to marry Roric! If he had appeared suddenly last night, he must be the unexpected assailant whom his guards had almost said was a wight, and she must have decided at once to go with him. But why had she said nothing to him?

"You don't like it that she didn't tell you?" asked Hadros, in a tone of commiserating fellowship that seemed intended to drive home that he knew Karin far better than her own father did.

Kardan did not answer. The other king seemed willing to forget that they had once been sworn enemies, but he himself was not yet ready to become friends with the man who had defeated him ten years ago and who must now, somehow, be behind the disappearance of his daughter.

"Well, Kardan, I think there are things neither Valmar nor Roric has told me either." Hadros shook his head. "By this time, I had expected—as had you—to be watching

my sons and my young warriors reach manhood, with all
the energy and courage I had twenty-five years ago, and
all the wisdom I could give them now. It has not worked
out quite as I hoped, but we may have to make the best of
what we have. I fear you and I are too old, my friend, to
start over."

Inside, Kardan left Hadros seated in the hall with an ale
horn while he went to change out of his ceremonial clothing. He was furious both with the king and with Karin, as
well as with Roric, this foundling who had grown up to be
one of Hadros' warriors. How could she have deceived
him like this, living here with her father in her own home,
back in the kingdom she would someday rule as sovereign
queen, saying nothing about the man she apparently hoped
to marry?

"Why had you not fitted out your ship this spring?" Hadros
demanded as he rejoined him. "If it had been in the water
we could have followed them. Such a good ship is a shame
to leave under the tarpaulins when the ice is off the channel! When I saw all you had ready were those little skiffs, I
knew we could never catch my ship."

"I was too busy preparing for the All-Gemot," said Kardan
testily, seating himself on the bench beside Hadros. He
did not add what Hadros must surely remember, even if
he feigned to forget, that he *had* had a longship in the
water this spring, the ship which his eldest son and Queen
Arane's heir had broken against the Cauldron Rocks. "Unlike
some kings I could mention," he added, "I do not need a
ship to go to war or raiding in the southlands every summer."

"Most kings do not anymore," agreed Hadros, looking
at his ale.

"And I knew that if my ship *was* ready for sea, some
young hothead among the retinues of the Fifty Kings might
decide to steal it. At least it is still here, unlike yours!"

He also did not mention that ever since the end of the
war sailing had made him queasy, so that several springs in

the last ten years he had not fitted out a ship at all. Since that last desperate dash into the harbor and flight to within his walls, when Hadros had fired his ships and rounded up all the tenants who had not been able to retreat into the castle and threatened them with the sword, when his warriors had stood ready to put the torch to Kardan's fields, and a quick inventory of the food inside the castle told them they could not feed everyone now there for more than a few weeks, he had not liked being out on the channel.

"But tell me," Kardan said with a new thought, "who could have commanded your ship from my harbor? Would your seamen obey Roric in the assumption that he acted at your orders? Or would he have had to hold a knife to the captain's throat?"

Hadros looked up sharply. "They might obey him and they might not. I had not told anyone I was furious with the lad, but since we did not keep our voices down some may have guessed." He gave a grim smile. "You had not guessed yourself, before I told you, that I came here furious with him?"

"No." This was something to consider later. "Would they sail wherever he said?"

"If he tried to take the ship by violence," said Hadros darkly, "my seamen will have killed him by now. If they sailed with him willingly, it would only have been back to my kingdom. And the raven I sent this morning will mean there's a welcome waiting for him." His lips came back from his teeth in what looked very little like a smile.

"And Valmar?"

"Valmar my seamen would obey, taking him wherever he wanted to go. And," Hadros added after a short pause, "probably your daughter as well."

"Karin?" asked Kardan in amazement. "She would never steal your ship."

"She is an active and determined lass," said Hadros. "She may be your daughter, but for the last ten years she has been living with *me*." He looked at Kardan from under his eyebrows, seeming amused. "Where do *you* think they have gone? And are all three together, or only two, and which two?"

Kardan rose briskly, wanting to reestablish some authority in his own castle. "It will take all day for them to finish the caulking. Come with me, and we will consult the Mirror-seer."

King Hadros, as he hoped, had not consulted a Seer in a great many years, if ever—he tried to appear knowledgeable, but Kardan thought he could sense both unease and a curiosity even beyond wondering what they might hear. As they rode up to the Mirror-seer's lake, Kardan explained the use of mirrors of voima to see the reflection of a reality far beyond the little valley. He let the slightest patronizing note slip occasionally into his voice.

But he had no chance to show off the wisdom and abilities of his Seer. The little round man was not in his cottage. He did not answer their knock, either the first quiet rap or repeated hammering.

The two kings stood hesitating on the dock before the closed door. Small waves broke against the shore, making the lake's reflection of the surrounding forest and mountains break and shiver. "No more use than a Weaver," said Hadros thoughtfully. "I presume he would still refuse to come to the door if you threatened to burn his house with him in it?"

Kardan glanced at him quickly, hoping he was not serious, then looked away, fearing he was.

"Or maybe he's just gone out for a stroll," suggested Hadros. He put his shoulder to the door and pushed. The wood around the lock was dry and weather-worn and cracked under his weight.

The door swung back with a creak. "What should he have in here?" asked Hadros, peering into the darkness.

Kardan looked too, but there was nothing to see. The little cottage was empty: not even a fishing rod. The only sign the Seer had ever lived here were his two mirrors on a shelf on the far wall.

Hadros tapped his foot on the dock. "Anything else worth seeing, Kardan, as long as you've brought me up here?"

Kardan took a deep breath, not wanting to admit how startled he was by the Seer's disappearance. "You can see Graytop from here," he said, pointing, "where Karin tried to tell me she saw a Wanderer."

"She did not tell *me* about any Wanderer," said Hadros. "Probably knew too well what I would answer to that! Even though," with less certainty, "I cannot doubt her as easily as I once would have. But," with certainty again and a sideways glance at Kardan, "I do know she and Valmar visited this Seer during the All-Gemot. Perhaps something they asked of him has made him retreat now. That was the night," with a slight emphasis, "those two young people passed the entire night together."

Kardan could feel the heat rising up his neck to his cheeks and ears. "For that insult I ought to kill you," he said between his teeth, fumbling his sword loose and thinking that he should still have agility on his side even if not mass.

But Hadros darted out a hand and took him by the wrist, pinning him with his sword half-drawn. "No insult, my friend," he said, smiling as though he enjoyed this. "Just a simple statement of fact. All my men saw Valmar and Karin return together in the early morning."

He gestured placatingly with his other hand. "But just because young people are sometimes foolish need not mean wisdom cannot still prevail. No one will say that Valmar made her his by the strong hand! I was planning to come see you shortly anyway, to make an offer for her. Karin deserves a fine bride-price."

Kardan, who had been struggling unsuccessfully against Hadros' grip, went still. He did not want to believe it, except that it explained too well her strange moods since the end of the All-Gemot. This too she had kept from him. And she must have spent the night willingly with Valmar, or she would not have asked to keep the boy with her.

He closed his eyes briefly as Hadros released his wrist. "A marriage between your heir and my heiress would unite our kingdoms in friendship," he heard himself saying. "But no! If she told you she would marry Roric—"

"Then she has changed her mind. You and I have both known maids to change their thinking, have we not, my friend?" with a nudge and a broad wink. "Either she now has changed her mind *again* and gone off with Roric in my ship, or she has fled with Valmar to get away from him. And," and now he suddenly became absolutely serious, "Roric had better not have touched my son."

"I know where she has gone if not to your kingdom," said Kardan suddenly into the following silence. "We do not need the Mirror-seer to tell us. And we can follow her in one of my skiffs while they finish caulking and soaking the ship, because she should still be on this side of the channel, not too many miles away. Whoever Karin is with, she may have fled to the court of Queen Arane."

Queen Arane, delicate in white silk, looked up in surprise as the two kings, their boots loud, crossed the black and white chequered stone floor of her hall. They had come straight up from the harbor, still wearing their salt-stained cloaks, and in this gracious court Kardan suddenly felt as large and coarse and out of place as the man next to him.

But the queen smiled pleasantly and summoned a page with a wave of one hand to set out a bench for them. They settled themselves slowly, Kardan wondering how best to demand his daughter, whom he had expected to see here beside her.

"King Hadros, King Kardan," Arane said, looking from one to the other with a pretty smile. "You must want some ale after a thirsty day. Or would you like wine, Kardan? I know that you, Hadros, prefer the ale of my maids' brewing. My days here are so dull that I am happy for any company, but your particular company would be welcome to anyone! And would you care to join me for dinner?"

Hadros cut her off, leaning forward on the bench with his eyebrows bristling. "We have known each other too long for such formalities, Arane. We seek the Princess Karin."

The queen's shoulders gave a slight jerk; Kardan, watching her closely, thought it surprise rather than guilt. "But I have not seen her since the All-Gemot!" she protested, lifting delicate hands. "I thought she was back home in your kingdom now, Kardan. Why should she come here?"

"I think she trusts you," he answered slowly, still watching her reaction. "She has either been kidnapped or eloped, either with Valmar, Hadros' heir, or with Hadros' foster-son Roric."

Arane started to frown at the mention of Roric but covered it up with a tinkling laugh. "And you think that she and the man she is with, either willingly or unwillingly, would have fled here? Come, both of you must know there is no room at my court for women who cannot make up their own minds!"

Kardan and Hadros glanced at each other. Now that they had set it out baldly, Kardan thought, it did rather sound as though either Karin herself or the two kings were very confused.

"I can assure your two majesties that she has never set foot in my kingdom," said the queen confidently. "If she has been kidnapped you will of course need to rescue her, as she is a strong-minded woman who will be a good queen someday. We must plan together how to find her. Let me insist you first join me in dinner, as it will soon be the hour. My page will show you to the bath house."

The stones in the bath house were already hot. The obliging page brought them towels and clean clothes, a little too big for Kardan, a little too small for Hadros, with deep creases as though they had come from the bottom of a chest.

They stripped, steamed, and scrubbed off the grime,

taking turns with the bundle of birch twigs. Kardan thought that the queen seemed much more interested in pleasantries and intrigue than in giving them answers, and, in spite of his earlier certainty, she really did not appear to have Karin with her. Somehow, he did not know how, Arane had taken the initiative away from them.

She kept the initiative all through dinner, serving them from the platter with her own hands, bringing out a honey-colored wine for Kardan, telling them amusing stories of little incidents at her court. Kardan noticed that she never once mentioned her nephew, the prince who had drowned at the same time as his own son.

"So you can assure us," said King Hadros at last, in much better humor than he had been in two hours before, "that you have no idea where the princess or my son have gone?"

"No idea at all," she said, her blue eyes wide and innocent. "You can ask anyone at my court, and they will all give you the same answer."

"What is our next alternative then, Hadros?" asked Kardan. "Back to your kingdom?"

"Faster and more likely than spending any more time sailing up and down this side of the channel."

"This is fascinating," said the queen, leaning her elbows on the table to look at them, "a princess running away with her true love, but you are not sure who that true love might be." For a second, Kardan thought she knew more than she had said, but it was too late to try to learn it from her. "And even a sense in it of the lords of voima! This is the sort of tale I love to hear."

"It's not a tale," said Hadros brusquely. "This is real."

"*Everything* becomes a tale once it has happened," said Queen Arane, still smiling. She looked from one to the other with a calculating expression. "You are both widowers, and have been for some time. My request therefore may sound the slightest bit scandalous, but with the two of you there to watch each other, scandal should not be a concern."

"What do you mean?" asked Kardan dubiously, fearing he knew.

She smiled even more widely. "When you cross the channel again to search for the Princess Karin, I shall accompany you."

CHAPTER SEVEN

1

"Lie," said Roric roughly. "Tell them some plausible story. Are not women better at manipulation than men?"

"But if this manor had a message from Hadros to intercept us—"

"They will never have heard of Hadros or Gizor, much less of us. I don't even know whose kingdom we are in now. Hadros cannot realize where we are going, and he will not have sent ravens to every manor and farm in every direction!"

"But the Mirror-seer may have told my father we were headed north to the Hot-River Mountains."

"Just do it," said Roric irritably. "I don't know about you, but after three days of hard riding, with nothing to eat but berries and that one rabbit, I intend to take food by force if they do not give it to us. I had thought you wanted fewer people dead."

Karin gave one final glance at his face and slipped off Goldmane's back. The stallion was breathing hard, his nostrils pink, but overall he seemed to be bearing up well under the burden of two riders. Roric however had said in disgust that the horse had run far faster in the Wanderers' realm.

For one moment, Karin found herself wondering what it would be like to be fleeing with Valmar instead of with Roric. But she dismissed the thought. If she were with Valmar, if he had not left with the Wanderer, if Roric had not crossed the channel to find her, she would still be in her father's castle.

She straightened her shoulders and walked firmly up the rise toward the manor. They had come into a country where high fells loomed over slopes striped by meandering stone walls, a country of unexpected valleys and of very few people. In the blue distance were a line of mountains that might be the Hot-River Mountains, though Karin tried not to calculate the discouragingly large number of days before even Goldmane's speed could take them there. The buildings here were on a bare hilltop, open to the wind, though in the dip below the trees grew thick and green.

As in Hadros' castle the hall was stone and the outbuildings were of weathered oak, but the outbuildings were roofed with green turves, and the manor was surrounded not by a stone wall but by a palisade. The gate to the courtyard was open, and dogs swarmed around her, barking, as she crossed it toward the main hall. Two towheaded children peeked at her from the hall's doorway then darted away again.

A housecarl, slouched against a building, leered at her. She glanced down at herself, at her once elegant dress now ripped and filthy. At least she must look slightly better than Roric, with his unshaven beard and a look in his eye that had become progressively fiercer the last three days.

A woman with a milk pail hurried out to meet her and drive off the dogs. "Could you please help me?" began Karin, in a note of weariness and pleading that was not feigned. She was hungry and thirsty enough to snatch the milk from the woman's hand, but she restrained herself. "I have been driven from my home and am fleeing for my life."

The woman looked at her steadily a moment. Her eyes were a pale blue, sky-colored, disconcerting in the unblinking intensity of their gaze. But she nodded then and spoke calmly. "Help me carry the rest of the pails into the dairy and tell me what has happened."

Karin shook off the strange sense that this woman might already know who she was, and followed her. Roric was right; they could not possibly have received a message from Hadros or Gizor One-hand at this isolated manor.

The two women took the pails of warm milk into one of the outbuildings, where they poured them into the pans for the cream to rise. Karin had done the same thing so many times, so many mornings and evenings in summer, that she had to catch back an unexpected gasp of homesickness. It was far too late, she told herself, to yearn for the days when she had been mistress of Hadros' household.

"I live—or used to live—on a royal manor down on the channel," she improvised, "in King Hadros' kingdom."

If the name meant anything to the woman, she gave no sign.

"Three—no, I mean five—days ago, raiders came and attacked us, firing our house and driving off our flocks." No use drawing attention to how fast Goldmane could run. "All the men were killed, and both my parents." She let her homesickness come out as a small sob. "I barely escaped with my life, accompanied by one warrior. This is the first time we have dared stop."

The sky-colored eyes watched her as she spoke, and Karin feared she was about to be denounced as a liar, but the woman only shook her head sadly. "They say there have been fewer warriors raiding the last ten or twenty years, more peace among the Fifty Kingdoms, but I fear that time has come to an end with the change so imminent now. I knew that war and raiding had started up again in the north this spring, but I did not realize it had yet reached so far south."

She covered the milk pans, and the two came out of the dairy together. "Is that your warrior?" the woman asked thoughtfully, turning her intense blue gaze down the hill toward Roric. He still sat on Goldmane, the muscles standing out on his arms and his sword swung rather obviously at his side.

"Yes," said Karin, quickly and with assurance. If she had not known him she would have been frightened by him. From this angle his profile looked like a hawk's, and he appeared to be looking into a rather ferocious distance. "I trust him completely."

Surprisingly, the woman was willing to be reassured. "I shall talk to my husband when he comes back with the sheep," she said, leading the way into the hall. The same housecarl was still leering at Karin, but the woman sent him away with a sharp word. "But I think we will let you stay here tonight."

They were given the loft room over a storehouse adjoining the hall, a bed for Karin and a pile of straw at the door for her warrior. "I cannot even remember the last time before tonight I had a good meal," said Karin sleepily as Roric slid under the blanket beside her.

"And it has been even longer for me."

"Shall we take up their offer to stay here tomorrow?"

"Goldmane could use the rest," said Roric. "And we must have lost Gizor's pursuit by now."

She thought that he was more concerned about his stallion than about her, but she was too tired, too glad to be back in a bed after sleeping rough with one ear always cocked for pursuit, to become irritated.

Roric put an arm around her and nuzzled her hair. "Remind me where we are going," he said, sounding much more awake than she felt. "We have been running *from* Gizor and Hadros for three days. After a certain point, I either have to be going *toward* something, or I shall stop running and fight."

She shifted around to face him, though the loft room was too dark to see anything; the window at the far end was no more than a rectangle of gray. "We are going to rescue Valmar, of course. We cannot let the Wanderers kill him, send him to Hel for their own purposes. With him safe, we at least have a chance to reestablish peace between you and Hadros. And you were the one who wanted to win a kingdom up there."

He kissed her on the throat and shoulders. He really is still awake, she thought with a small sigh, sliding her arms around his neck.

"Maybe this time," he said, lifting his lips from hers, "I shall meet the real Wanderers in their realm, and then I *shall* make my story something glorious."

Karin ran a finger along his jaw, now freshly shaved, starting to wake up again herself. "Do you want to kiss me or talk about the Wanderers?" she asked with a hint of laughter in her voice. "Because I can tell you, Roric, I do not believe in them anymore."

"I do," he said slowly, rolling back and pulling her head onto his shoulder. "But then I was in their realm."

"Well, I do not intend to deny their existence. After all I spoke with one twice, even if I have not been where you have gone. But I cannot believe they have any power ultimately, or that we mortals should do anything to serve them."

"Valmar has gone to serve them from what you tell me. Why should we be so determined to save him, if he is doing exactly what he wants? Especially," kissing her forehead, "since his being gone means no one can possibly try to persuade you to marry him."

She shook her head, the hair sliding across his face. "No, Roric. If I return to my father's kingdom, handfast to you and with Valmar gone forever, the war between my father and Hadros will break out again."

"And we will win it this time," he said agreeably. "Hadros is an old man now. For that matter so is Gizor—chasing us should finish breaking his strength. And Dag and Nole will be but little help to Hadros. I saw your father's castle; I would be able to defend it nearly single-handed."

"You were not there when Hadros took our castle," Karin said quietly. "I was. Even as a little girl I understood why my father had to surrender. It was either that or starve in a few weeks anyway—after seeing our fields burned and our tenants killed."

"This time I will bring the tenants inside the walls," he said, still in a voice that was almost light—but not quite.

"So that is your plan?" she asked in alarm, "double back, find a way to cross the channel, fight Hadros in open battle?"

"It is you, not me, who is so concerned about seeing your father again, about behaving as a future queen should behave. Or else you can stay up in the north country with me as *my* queen after I win a kingdom single-handed, as Hadros seems to think I can." She could not tell if he was merely joking or again fighting deep bitterness. "If the Wanderers prefer a king's son to a man without a father—leaving *him* instead for the trolls—then I shall have to win my fortune in mortal realms."

"You realize, Roric," she said, pushing herself up on an elbow, "that in trying to learn who your father is, you have never asked who your mother might have been."

She felt him shrug. "Some girl from one of the manors—probably not even a royal manor. Hadros lets his serving-maids keep their babes, but on some of the poorer manors they dread an extra mouth to feed—or even a bastard child growing up to challenge the rightful heir to the inheritance."

"But you weren't just any baby. The queen herself raised you as an infant. Do you think you might have been hers?"

Roric sat up abruptly at that. "The get of Hadros' queen and—whom? Another of the Fifty Kings? One of the warriors? Gizor? He may have been a more handsome man in his youth. But no, Karin. Hadros would never have raised another man's son as his own."

"But you weren't raised as his own," she said reasonably. "Valmar is the heir. And if he is your half-brother as well as your foster-brother, then there is even more reason to rescue him."

He flopped back down again. "If Hadros learned his

wife had been gotten with child by another man, he would have killed first the baby, then her."

"Maybe so," she said uncertainly. "But I, the last few years, have usually been able to talk Hadros around. Perhaps his queen could do the same."

"You have not been able to talk him around on marrying me instead of Valmar."

Karin did not answer, thinking glumly that he was right. Roric's father, whom he so wanted to find, was doubtless a housecarl somewhere—except that the child of a serving-maid and a housecarl would not be expected to be found with a little bone charm.

"And do not be so sure," added Roric, "that Valmar himself would have no intention of marrying you if he came back alive. He is not like you and me, Karin. We grew up as outsiders in the only castle we considered home. For years I had nothing and no one I could trust. For the last two years I have had my stallion, and the last few months you— even if you *do* insist on stealing ships without consulting me," giving her a squeeze, a smile in his voice. "But Valmar has always known that he is heir to a kingdom, and had, whenever he was hurt or frightened, the support of his big sister—you. He grew up with the knowledge that he had a high destiny waiting. Little surprise then that he should go to find adventure with the lords of voima, to seek to do something glorious to win your love, so that when he is king he will still have you beside him."

"I never felt I could count on Valmar the way you seem to feel you can count on Goldmane," Karin replied some-what stiffly, "because he *is* just a boy. But if he needs me I have to help him. I do intend to go to the Wanderers' realm to rescue him, and I would feel much better if you were beside *me*."

"I was going to suggest you and I go solve the Wander-ers' problems for them," Roric said quietly, "then live on together in their realm of endless summer, but you do not seem interested."

"In the meantime," she said, "let us stay here through tomorrow to rest Goldmane, before we decide if we are going on or doubling back." She stroked his forehead and began to kiss him again, wishing that they did not have to run, wishing there were other options than the ones they had, that it could be only she and Roric together.

She spent the next day helping with the chores on the manor while Roric spent much of the day asleep.

It felt surprisingly comforting to be doing again the tasks that she had always done at Hadros' castle, cooking, milking, drawing water from the well, sweeping, weaving, churning the butter. And her work drew a compliment. "Your manor must have been well regulated, since your mother taught you so well." The woman smiled as she spoke; she had been smiling all day.

Karin remembered that she was supposed to have had a mother until a few days before. "Yes. We were a smaller manor than this one. It's nothing but ash and scorched timber now." There were only a few maids and a handful of housecarls here, yet the woman and her husband seemed to farm an enormous number of acres, with flocks scattered across the distant fells.

"I do not think you will be troubled by those raiders again," said the woman quietly, looking out across her lands. "If anyone pursues you, they will find much to impede them."

"Do *you* ever have trouble here with raiders?" asked Karin.

"Not since I came to live here. But then almost no one travels these roads, because we are far from the sea and not on the way to anywhere that could not be reached more easily by ship."

Karin thought that she and Roric would doubtless have to cross several more kingdoms before reaching the Hot-River Mountains. "Isn't it lonely here?"

"Only occasionally. I have my children, my husband, and

those who serve us. It is enough." The woman paused for a moment, then added quickly, "But I have been very happy to have you here today. I would like to make you a guest-gift before you leave—would you accept a mare to ride, so that your warrior's stallion need not carry you both?"

"Why yes!" said Karin, flustered. "I mean, that is too generous! I could not promise ever to return your horse to you."

The women gave a faint smile, as if in reaction to something Karin had not said. "I would be honored to have you take a mare from me. And do not worry—her pace will not slow your journey."

Karin lifted the lid from the churn and reached in carefully to take the new butter from the buttermilk. "Your warrior," asked the woman casually, meeting Karin's eyes for one second, "is he also your lover?"

She found herself blushing. "Yes, he is," she said, turning away to wrap the butter in cheesecloth. It was pointless to lie.

"I thought he might be," said the woman without any particular expression in her voice, neither satisfaction at having her guess confirmed nor condemnation. "Otherwise you would not have dared flee alone with him, raiders or no raiders."

Karin held her breath, wondering what else this woman with the sky-blue eyes had guessed.

"If even a highborn woman needs to take a warrior to her bed to earn herself a little safety in this world," the woman continued, staring off across the hills where her own husband and the sheep had gone, "do you not think it time women found a source of strength of their own?"

Then she did not doubt the story of the raiders on the coast after all, Karin thought. "Women have strengths, certainly," she answered, thinking of Queen Arane. "We can manipulate men, use their own strength against them, because they sometimes concentrate so hard on action that women can outthink them."

The woman turned her disconcerting eyes suddenly toward her. "That is not enough," she said, almost fiercely. "We need to outfight them on their own terms, not just ours." She slowly began to smile again. "And our time may come, may come sooner than any man has looked for it."

2

The Wanderers taught Valmar how to fight all over again.

He, along with all the young men in Hadros' castle, had learned from Gizor One-hand and grown to expect that in a real fight he would do more than hold his own. The one time last year, when Hadros had come himself into the ring with him—it was shortly before the king had broken his leg—and had flattened him with a practice sword in thirty seconds, he attributed to his own unwillingness to attack his father all out.

"But I thought from what you said that I already had awesome powers here," he objected when one of the enormous white beings explained to him the program for his training.

"You do," said the Wanderer, turning the face on him that Valmar could not bear to look at for more than a second. "But that does not mean you are indestructible. The body must be made to serve the mind and spirit. Your powers are much greater than in mortal realms, but the forces against which we fight could still overcome you if you were unprepared."

They gave him a long series of exercises to do and often seemed to be hovering just beyond his vision while he worked, and frequently they asked him how his training was proceeding or gave him additional exercises. He labored, sweating: lifting logs, pulling himself up onto branches by his arms, running for miles to improve his wind, striking again and again with a stick against a tree. The leaves of the tree were streaked with yellow, but they did not fall.

The cows watched him, pulling uneasily at the grass as though they did not like the flavor, and lowing querulously.

When he had done these exercises for what might have been weeks, they gave him an opponent, someone who had the appearance of a man but seemed to have no knowledge of anything but fighting. He spoke very little if at all, and when he was not fighting he stood stiff and awkward, staring at nothing, but when he stepped into the practice ring with Valmar he came alive, fighting as though berserk, needing multiple blows to the head to slow him down.

The red sunset sky burned constantly above him, and Valmar quickly lost track of how many cycles of eating and sleeping had passed since he came here. But his arms were finally gaining the prominent muscles he had always admired in Roric, and his beard was coming in full at last.

His father's castle had begun to seem very far away even though this manor did not yet seem like home. He wondered, running panting through the fields, how he could have assumed for so many years that he would simply grow to manhood and gradually take over the kingdom from his father without ever having gone for adventure.

And he wanted *real* adventure, not just southern booty, even though he had trouble defining in his own mind what was the difference. He sang the old songs over to himself as he threw a ball against a wall, faster and faster, and tried to knock it with his sword as it flew back toward him. He did hope his real challenges would begin soon. Except for the sunset sky, this manor sometimes threatened to become no more awe-inspiring, no more thrilling of voima, than being back home.

And when he came in tired, and the housecarls took him to the bath house where the stones were already steaming and afterward served him juicy meat and white bread, he sometimes found himself wishing that he was serving Karin here, rather than the Wanderers. There were no women at the manor at all, and he wondered somewhat uneasily if this was another part of his training.

But when one of the great shining beings came to talk to him his heart always pounded and he looked away, trying unsuccessfully not to blush, both wondering how someone as lowly and unskilled as himself could possibly serve the lords of voima and wildly grateful to fate that he had been given the opportunity.

He tried to express this one evening—except that it was always evening—to one of the Wanderers, the one who had brought him here. As he associated with them more he was beginning to be able to distinguish them, at least a little.

"I am afraid I still do not understand, Lord," he said, trying not to mumble although it was impossible to meet the other's eyes. "Why would all-powerful, completely good lords, the creators of sky and earth and sea beneath, need a mortal's aid?"

"Have we misled you so seriously?" said the Wanderer in the amused tone he took so often. "Did you really imagine that we were all-powerful and completely good? There may be beings like that somewhere, but we are not they, and whoever they may be they do not talk either to mortals or to us."

"But you created the earth," Valmar persisted.

"No, Valmar Hadros' son," said the other, sounding mildly regretful. "The earth and sky and sea existed before any of us and will persist after any of us. All we shaped was our own realm, for even there we do not create—and we shaped it to match mortal realms. You of the northern kingdoms tell the old tales of us more than do any others, even if you do have a lot of details wrong, so we have taken your realms as our model. And as you can see, the immortals' immortal realm itself can finally change."

"But what can I do to stop the change?"

"Help us correct a mistake we made," said the Wanderer somewhat distantly. "We thought, as you did, that we *could* create, that even without women men could make their own successors if those men commanded the powers of voima. But it was not fated to be—and now that creation may be hastening the change."

Valmar thought about this the next day—or what he could not keep from thinking of as the next day: the next period after he had eaten and slept. He practiced alone today, riding a horse from the Wanderers' stables, turning it in tighter and tighter circles around the courtyard.

In part he gloried in the honor, the selection of him out of all mortals. It would make an excellent song, he thought, whether he lived to return to his father's kingdom or died heroically—except that if he never went back no one would know to sing it. But also in part he found himself, against his will, wondering if this sunset land could ever be rectified by one mortal man—or even if it was worth that man's effort.

Valmar suddenly heard a sharp hissing sound from the edge of the courtyard. It sounded like a sibilant whisper.

He pulled up his horse. Now he heard nothing. But he had an itchy feeling between his shoulder blades as though he was being watched. He sat quite still in the saddle for a moment, then turned his head suddenly.

Sure enough, there was an eye peeking around the gatepost. It drew back abruptly, but then the whispered hiss came again. He dismounted, loosened the peace straps on his sword, and stepped slowly forward.

There were words in the whisper now. "Outside. Come outside. And do not fear me."

Valmar stopped a few paces short of the gate, just long enough to throw the other off if he was planning to attack him as soon as he stepped through, then went through the gateway with a bound. Jumping back, startled, was a much smaller opponent than he had expected, armed and wearing a horned helmet but showing no immediate inclination to fight. In fact, he realized after a surprised second, in spite of the breastplate and shield it was a woman.

"Come with me, Valmar Hadros' son," she whispered

with a fleeting smile. "No, don't look back. Come quickly, and come now."

He came a few more paces toward her, hand still ready on his sword. But with another smile over her shoulder she began to walk quickly away from him, and he found himself following.

She must be, he thought, a few years older than he—Karin's age. But she did not look at all like Karin, having tight black curls that escaped from under her helmet and, in the moment that he had seen them, glinting black eyes on either side of her helmet's noseguard. He glanced back toward the courtyard in spite of what she had said. No one seemed to have seen him go.

In a few minutes he had left the Wanderers' manor well behind. She darted in and out of shadow, running on the grass between the towering trees that stretched their branches over the hillside below the manor. He followed twenty yards behind, picking up speed as she went faster, but never quite catching up. Once she looked back, black eyes flashing like mirrors in the horizontal sunlight, and grinned at him.

Valmar laughed in return, beginning to enjoy this, and ran even faster. His blood grew hot from the pursuit and the sight of her sweetly rounded form running before him. "Sprite or faey," he called, "you cannot escape me forever!"

"Do you think you are man enough to catch me?" she called back. "And man enough to make me yours when you do?"

He still did not gain on her, as her own strides came faster and faster. But when she had run over two miles she suddenly stopped and whirled around, her sword drawn and shield up. She laughed at him, her back to a tree, and when he hesitated sprang at him.

She held no practice sword but the real thing, a boy's sword such as he had had when he was twelve, sharpened to a razor point. He dodged quickly behind a tree, still rational enough in spite of his excitement to want to avoid being skewered. He drew his sword quietly, counted to three, and leaped out the other side of the tree. She was waiting for him coolly, but she did not stand a chance against a young man who had done little but exercise his muscles and practice his swordplay for many weeks.

In two strokes he had his sword wedged solidly against hers and pushed it up and back. She tried to kick him, but he stayed just out of range. His left hand snaked in and grabbed her wrist. She dropped the sword with a cry, and he kicked it away at the same time as he threw his own sword from him.

With one arm he crushed her mailed body to his chest while he pried the shield from her grip, then loosed her helmet. She was laughing again, showing a row of sharp little white teeth. Her hair, dense and curling, cascaded out from under her helmet and down her back, and he buried his fingers in it.

Her black eyes danced at him, tiny points of light at the center, and her mouth smiled widely just before her hot lips closed on his.

They lay afterward in the long grass, their heads pillowed on Valmar's rolled-up tunic, the sunset sky tinting her skin pink. Her armor and shield glistened a short distance away.

He felt comfortable, relaxed, and joyous, but he also felt vaguely ashamed now of the overpowering force of his passion, even though he told himself it had all been her idea. That she had surreptitiously called him away from the Wanderers' courtyard suggested that this would not be something of which they approved. But he put these thoughts aside as she kissed him on the ear.

"Are you then a sprite or faey," he inquired with a smile, "come to test if a mortal man can match the immortals?" He traced the smooth line of her cheek with his forefinger and kissed her red lips.

"No sprite or faey," she answered, "as you would know

perfectly well if you had ever met the faeys." She chuckled. "But I am indeed interested in mortal men, Valmar
Hadros' son—or at least one mortal man. And so far I like
very much what I have found!"

"You know who I am," he said, caressing her perfectly
formed shoulders and breasts. This was nothing like the
furtive interludes with the maids of his father's castle—
some almost twice his age, and with breath tasting of onions. He had been thinking he would give up the maids
soon anyway. This was more as he had imagined it would
be to lie in Karin's arms. He pushed thoughts of Karin
resolutely from him. "Tell me at least your name."

But she laughed instead of answering and turned around,
propped up on her elbows, to look at his face.

"You came here to find heroic deeds and glorious battles,"
she said briskly, in a tone which for a moment reminded him,
quite incongruously, of a merchant in a booth trying to persuade him of the rational advantages of buying his products
rather than anyone else's. "I am offering them to you."

"Are you a Wanderer?" Valmar asked in amazement and
almost horror. He had never imagined that he might lie
with a lord of voima—or, apparently, a lady.

Her eyes glinted at him. "What do you think?" she asked
teasingly, then shook her head. "No, I am certainly not
one of those beings you mortals call Wanderers. As you
may have noticed, they are all men! That is why I had to
get you away from them."

She referred, he noticed, to "you" mortals, suggesting
that whoever she was, she was not an ordinary person who
had somehow, like him, reached this realm. He ran a hand
down her back to reassure himself that she did, indeed,
have one.

"I shall have to get home soon," he said, beginning again
to feel guilty. Whoever she was, it was difficult to see her
as connected with the high deeds and heroism to which he
had promised his life and manhood. But it would be hard
to explain that to those dark eyes. "The housecarls will be

heating the bath house and preparing dinner for me," he added lamely.

"And that is reason enough to return?" she asked with another laugh.

"Well, I serve them, the lords of voima, you see. And if you are not a Wanderer yourself, I need to return to them. Would you perhaps like to come back to the manor with me?" he added hopefully. "I am sure they would be pleased to meet a friend of mine." The thought shot through his mind that it would be difficult to introduce her as his friend when he did not even know her name.

For answer she rolled on top of him, her elbows by his ears, and began to kiss him. After only a moment's hesitation he wrapped his arms around her warm body and held her tight to him again.

It was hard to tell time by a motionless sun. Again they lay stretched out in the long grass, the woman's head on Valmar's shoulder, her black curls spread across his chest. How long, he asked himself, had it been since he left the courtyard? An hour, two hours, six hours? And did the Wanderers even keep time themselves, or were their cycles of meals and activity only for his benefit?

"They will wonder where I am, back at the manor," he said.

She turned her head to nibble delicately on his shoulder. It tickled and made him laugh; he tickled her waist until she laughed too. "If they wanted you back," she said then, "they would have come for you long since. Clearly they do not care if you stay or go."

"But I haven't gone!" he protested. "That is, I haven't actually left their service." There were implications to what she said that he did not like.

"What lord would allow the man under his command to desert without even following him?"

Had he deserted the lords of voima? he asked himself in panic. "I am not under their command, as such," he desperately tried to explain. "They asked for my help, but

they do not compel it. I am being trained to help them
against their enemies here in this realm, before I descend
into Hel for them, to find the lords of death so that they
and their sun may be reborn."

It sounded foolish in his own ears as soon as he said it.
She laughed, predictably. "And are you so eager for death
yourself," she said in a teasing tone, "that you yearn for
steel to bite your flesh in preference to my embraces?
Because if so I could get my sword and help you out!"

"No, no, of course not," he said, pulling her to him and
stroking her hair. The Wanderers had warned him that he
was not indestructible here in spite of the powers he was
supposed to have, powers he had yet to see. And her sword
had been very sharp. "But, but— Are you one of the Wanderers' enemies?"

Her eyes glittered at him from two inches away. "Of
course I have no use for those beings—those *men*—who
claim to be lords of earth and sky. And you will have little
use for them either when I explain to you the honor and
glory that will come in overthrowing them."

He tried to draw back, but she was lying across his chest
and her arms were much stronger than they seemed.

"Do you not think there is voima in me?" she asked, giving his lip a playful bite. "Have you not considered them and
their quiet hall a little more, well, *boring* than you expected?"

It was as though she had read his mind. "But who then
are you?" he said with dry lips.

"Their fated end is coming," she said, stroking his beard.
"In asking you to help them against us—*we* whom fate has
chosen to succeed them!—they are doing nothing but making
a last, pathetic effort to change their end. Is it not better to
accept one's fate with dignity?"

"It's better to fight to the last man in a courageous, desperate battle for what you believe," said Valmar.

"When you find courage among them," she said with a
laugh, "let me know. The best they can manage is to ask
for a mortal's assistance. If you want adventure, high cour-

age, and glorious battles with the trumpets ringing, you will have to fight against them. And besides," moving her chest against his and smiling with the corners of her mouth, "if you go back to them you will have to leave me. And you do not wish to do that, do you?"

He most certainly did not. He embraced her and kissed her almost desperately. For him to have found love like this, so unexpectedly, almost better than anything he could have imagined, and then to risk losing her again just as suddenly!

But the hot excitement had burned out of him. The old tales were full of the conflict between honor and love. Roric had left Karin, the woman to whom he was pledged, to seek the Wanderers, and he, Valmar, could do no less.

Very carefully, he drew his arms from around her and disentangled her legs from his. "Think of the glory to be won in fighting heroically against the most powerful beings you have ever imagined," she tried, but he was not listening now.

"I am sorry," he said, standing up to find his clothes. "I cannot define heroism by whether it gives me daily adventure." He took a deep breath and added as firmly as he could, "Honor and courage must be reflected in keeping one's pledged word."

She sat on her heels to watch him dress, her hair tousled and eyes bright.

"Do you, uh, want me to see you back to your manor, wherever that is?" he asked, buckling on his sword.

She shook her head without answering, the smile still lurking at the corner of her mouth. He had expected her to be displeased with him. But she appeared instead very satisfied, as though some plan had all gone well.

3

The black and white piebald mare was certainly fleet of foot, Roric had to admit. At first he had frowned when

Karin climbed up to the loft room to tell him that she now had a horse of her own to ride. He feared that Goldmane would have been faster, even carrying two. But the mare matched the stallion's stride easily, even lazily, as they followed the faint track down the long hillside from the gray oak buildings of the manor.

"All right," he shouted, smiling at Karin. "We don't need to race any further—and I haven't pushed Goldmane yet!" They both pulled their horses to a trot. "And it's good to have food in our packs as well as a horse for you. I was right to trust you to speak for us both at the manor."

He was faintly aware that he had been very brusque with her several times since escaping from Hadros' kingdom, and he did not want to be—this was, after all, Karin, the woman whose love meant more to him than all the lords of voima. Her ruined finery was gone, and she wore a brown wool dress they had given her at the manor, against which her russet braids lay bright. Even though he kept being surprised that a woman could make plans for the two of them, he told himself that so far she was doing very well.

A river ran along the bottom of the hill, in a narrow defile dense with willows. A wooden bridge crossed it.

Karin's mare's hooves rang on the bridge as she started across before him. Mingled with the sound of those hooves was another sound, moist and squishy. Roric knew what it was and kicked Goldmane wildly forward. A troll eased itself out from under the bridge and directly into her path.

The piebald mare reared, front hooves flashing, teeth bared. Karin clung desperately to the mane as the horse went higher and higher, threatening to go over backward. Goldmane stopped short of the bridge, front legs stiff, almost catapulting Roric over his head.

Roric kicked his feet from the stirrups and leaped off, his sword out. "Stand back, troll, or taste cold steel!" he shouted.

This was not the nearly domesticated troll of the stream below King Hadros' castle. This was a troll of enormous yellow teeth and great muscular arms, now reaching up toward Karin: a troll that did not fear sunlight.

Roric's sword darted forward. It rang from the troll's body as though it was made of iron rather than soft flesh. But the troll turned its red eyes from Karin toward Roric, and its mouth opened, showing rows and rows of teeth and a greedy tongue. The mare came back down abruptly, Karin still in the saddle.

Roric danced out of the way of a reaching troll hand and struck again. This time his sword bit, for green blood welled from the wound. He grinned fiercely, though his next strokes bounced again. He had to keep dodging the powerful, flexible arms reaching for him. Fighting this great, wet mass of troll was not like fighting Gizor—the troll at Hadros' castle had never attacked an armed man.

He yelled and sprang closer again, raining down blows, and was just too slow to avoid an enormous hand that closed around his boot.

The hand jerked, and his feet went out from under him. Wildly he tried to scramble back up, flailing with his sword. But he was drawn closer and closer to the enormous mouth, from which a bubbling laugh came. Karin, her knife in her hand, approached warily, but the troll's other long arm snaked across the bridge surface toward her. In a second it would have them both.

"Troll!" came a completely unexpected clear voice. "Let them go!"

Roric's foot was suddenly released. He scrambled backward, his sword before him, not daring to take his eyes for a second from the troll even to see who had spoken.

The troll pulled its arms back toward its body, its mouth wide open in frustrated rage. "Troll, you should not be out in daylight!" came the voice again.

Roric dared at last one look over his shoulder. It was the lady of the manor, wearing a flour-dusted apron, her hands white with dough. "Shall I threaten you again with the powers of voima?" she demanded.

The troll snapped its mouth open and shut. It hesitated a moment, meeting her stare, then slowly, with a soft squishing noise, lowered itself back over the edge of the bridge. It disappeared into the stream beneath with a splash.

"Well," said the woman, turning toward them with hands on her hips. "I regret the troll bothered you. When you have just escaped death at the hands of raiders, you do not need to meet a troll!"

Roric remembered just in time that Karin had told this woman they were fleeing raiders.

"How did you do that?" asked Karin in wonder.

"And how did you know we needed help?" asked Roric, eyeing her carefully. She looked like a completely normal woman, with none of the indistinctness of the creatures in the Wanderers' realm, and not like someone a troll should obey.

"I was watching you go," she said easily. Roric glanced up the hill. They were at least a mile from the palisade that surrounded her manor, and she had stood at the gateway waving as they rode away. "The troll has lived here many years. We long since had to reach an agreement with it, or we would have had few of our flocks left."

"Thank you," said Karin somewhat belatedly. "Thank you very much. We owe you our lives now."

"And I may require those lives of you at some point," said the woman, still lightly.

When Roric turned to glare at her, Karin nudged him hard, and the woman laughed. "I do not seek to harm either of you," she said. "It is much better that you be alive than that you be dead, but at some point—who can say?—I may ask for your living strength. Now, I need to get back to my breadmaking. No more trolls should trouble you, Roric No-man's son."

She started back up the hill at a walk. Roric caught

their horses and untangled the reins. He went across the bridge first this time, his sword out, but Goldmane crossed now without hesitation and there was no sign of the troll.

On the far side he reined in hard and turned around in the saddle to stare after the woman, a distant figure now, trudging back to her home. "Karin," he said between tight lips, "I thought you said you had not told her our names."

Long, long, ago, even before your great-grandfather was a little boy, and many, many miles away to the north, a raider buried his treasure trove deep inside the mountain. He intended to return one day for it, but he was killed on his next raid and his treasure long lay unguarded and forgotten.

That is, until it was discovered by a dragon. He was a young dragon, coming down from the frozen Land of Ice to the Fifty Kingdoms, when he caught a whiff of treasure scent. And he flew down with a flurry of leather wings, and clawed into the mountainside with his long claws, and he established his lair there. And every month he flew out in search of more treasure and carried it home, until his trove was wealthier than three kingdoms.

But it gave him no pleasure, and as he grew older the golden rings began to pinch his belly as he lay on them, and the silver swords pricked him as he moved. He became stiffer as he grew older so that flying was more difficult, but he never stopped growing until he stretched five hundred feet long. So he went no more in search of greater treasure, but every week flew a short distance to a nearby village and ate one of the villagers.

Then the king of that kingdom, a man named Thaar, heard of the dragon. "I shall no more allow this serpent to eat my people," he said, for he was a young and strong king, the descendant of a line of glorious kings, and he desired honor more than wealth or even life. So he strapped on his helmet and shield, put his good sword Irontooth at his belt, and gave his crown to his queen for their infant son.

He sailed his ship alone along the coast to below the dragon's lair. "Come out, bloody-mouthed serpent!" he called.

He held up his sword with its long, triangular blade and rubies set into the hilt. "Come out and see what dragon teeth can do against Irontooth!"

And deep within his lair the old dragon heard him and stirred. He shook off the coins and jewels that clung to his scales and burst out of the mountainside. Like a whirlwind he descended on King Thaar's ship, breaking the mast and smashing the timbers.

But when he poked around with his long snout in the sea, he could not find the king. Puzzled, he was pulling himself back up on land when he felt something sharp against his belly, something that bit deeper than he had ever been bitten. The dragon lifted himself into the air with a roar but it was too late. For King Thaar, swimming deep, had come up below the dragon, and the triangular blade of the good sword Irontooth had thrust into his belly. And as the dragon tried to fly all his guts writhed free.

Thaar stood on the shore, dripping wet and holding his sword high in triumph, but only for a second. For the dragon, dying and in fury, descended on him, racking him with his claws and crushing him beneath his bloody body; and, just before his serpent eyes closed for the last time, his teeth bit through the mail and into the king's heart.

They buried King Thaar with his sword in a great mound that still stands by the sea, but the dragon they burned in a pyre whose flame could be seen for a hundred miles. Some of the treasure, the armbands and jeweled collars, they buried with the king; some, the golden chalices and unset gems, they offered at the Weaver's cave to the lords of voima; but to keep away the curse of dragon's gold, the rest they buried deep within the mountain. And there the treasure has remained ever since, untouched by dragon or man, for never since those days has there been a dragon so huge and fearsome, or a king so brave and full of honor.

CHAPTER EIGHT

1

"Roric has never taken my advice on anything yet," said King Hadros. He paused for a long pull of ale, ruffled the ears of the hound that lay at his feet, then glowered at Kardan from under his eyebrows. "But it is the only lead we have. We know at any rate that he went north."

"The Hot-River Mountains," said Kardan slowly. "That is where the king we outlawed at the All-Gemot has his kingdom." Hadros was back sitting drinking at the head of his own hall, with Kardan seated in the place of honor on the bench facing him. Both kings' warriors crowded together on the rest of the benches. Firelight flickered across their faces.

Queen Arane sat beside Hadros, looking completely out of place yet also completely at ease, wearing a blue silk dress and sipping delicately from her ale horn. Hadros' warriors and housecarls kept shooting the pair of them surreptitious glances and whispering whenever the king's eye did not fall on them.

"The Princess Karin's welfare must come before any concern for outlawed kings and their kingdoms," she said in a friendly tone, patting Hadros on the arm. Her own warriors were drinking too, but they stayed constantly on the alert. "Even kings need to think about the relations of men and women sometimes as well as about battle and glory."

Before eating, Hadros had ridden away from the castle, saying he would ask the Weaver where Roric had gone. "And I hope for once to get a straight answer!" He returned in half an hour glowering but in a fierce good humor, and with nothing to say about the Weaver. Kardan, who had learned already that the other king used humor to face situations he could not control, wondered what answer he had really gotten.

Kardan had drawn his sword casually as they sat down on the benches and had had it across his knees all evening. When the warriors were not speculating about Hadros and the queen, they appeared to be watching him. The only person there who seemed oblivious was Gizor One-hand, who had been using his bandaged arm to raise his ale horn unsteadily but continuously. No one sat within ten feet on either side of the old warrior.

Hadros looked across at King Kardan as though noticing his sword for the first time. "After what we've learned this evening," he said conversationally, "I hope you realize that Roric did not carry your daughter away by force."

Kardan drummed his fingers lightly on the steel. "And I hope *you* realize that he must have a powerful hold over her, for her to flee both her own father and the court here where she was raised."

Hadros looked at him thoughtfully for a moment, then worked the golden arm band off his arm, drew his own sword to slip its tip through the band, and reached it across the firepit.

But King Kardan carefully pushed the proferred arm band away. It was made of solid gold and was heavily worked and decorated, with tiny bearded faces peeking out through intertwined vines and bunches of grapes—not a product of the northern kingdoms, this, but surely something won by looting in the south. It was probably worth as much as a small manor. "Like you, Hadros," Kardan said quietly, "I do not take compensation for the life of my child. If she is dead, her killers will pay for their blood-guilt in their own blood."

Hadros pulled down his eyebrows. "Do you suggest that I would consider this sufficient compensation for a royal life, even a woman's?" His tone was brusque, but to Kardan he seemed to be mocking him. He retrieved the arm band and slid it back on. "I was merely making you a guest-gift. When *I* pay compensation, I pay it royally."

His eyes narrowed further, and his next words came out measured and cold. "But while we are speaking of compensation, think of this: The only reason Roric and Karin would flee together, slaying good men in the process, is if they shared a guilty secret, such as having killed Valmar."

The hall went completely silent except for the hissing of the fire. Kardan's hand tightened on his hilt. The queen's warriors stood up, as though casually, and moved toward the head of the hall. King Hadros' two younger sons looked up sharply, their hands on their own swords, but their faces were anguished rather than angry. Good boys, Kardan had thought when introduced, reminding him of his own dead son when a few years younger.

Queen Arane laughed into the silence, a light, almost musical laugh. "Are the two of you then more interested in blaming each other than in finding Roric and Karin?" There was a brief pause when no one answered her, and the two kings kept their eyes locked on each other. Her warriors, both kings knew, would tip the balance if it came to a fight. "Would you rather see each other dead," she added as though the question was an amusing one, "or have your heirs back again?" The kings turned slowly to look at her.

"I realize Valmar is not here," Arane said, "but from what you have told me there must be *something* to this story of his having left with the Wanderers. And you, Hadros, should know well there is a much better explanation for why Karin and Roric have fled. You yourself sent the message to capture them when they reached here—they are fleeing for their lives, probably thinking you have gone berserk, killed

Valmar yourself, and are planning on finishing them off next."

The suggestion was so outrageous that Kardan's reply died on his lips, and he saw Hadros too struggling to find something to say.

The queen laughed again, squeezed Hadros' hand affectionately, then sprang up to come around the firepit with a swish of her skirts and do the same to Kardan. Gizor roused himself as though about to speak but did not.

How did she do that? Kardan wondered. He found himself sliding his sword back into its sheath. The two kings' warriors, who had been reaching for their weapons a moment earlier, now had their ale horns in their hands again.

"So let us follow them north," said the queen, returning to her seat with a smile and a quick hand-motion to her own men. "Then we can question them as to what really happened. My ship will take us more swiftly up the coast than they can ride overland. We should be in those mountains before they are."

"That troll-horse of Roric's is *fast*," Dag piped up in objection.

But Hadros paid no attention to his son. "We'll take *my* ship, now that I have it back again," he said thoughtfully. "Yours got us across the channel, Arane, but mine has more oars." He had stopped making accusations, real or mocking, and seemed now interested only in planning for tomorrow. "We may catch them even before the mountains—there is that one spot where the peninsula narrows to almost nothing . . ."

"You have to take me with you, Father," interrupted Dag again in a high, clear voice. The king cocked his head toward him. "If Valmar— If I am now your heir, then I— That is, I think that Roric might talk to me even if he wouldn't answer questions from you."

Gizor One-hand spoke at last, lurching to his feet and spilling his ale. "Do not let this woman muddy your thinking," he said to King Hadros, his voice thick but not at all confused. "Roric killed your warriors, attacked me, and through us attacked you. We may 'question' the princess, but for him there can be only one fate. There is but one way a forsworn man may pay the blood-guilt against his lord, and that is with his own life."

King Hadros' warship came around the headland and straight into the teeth of a north wind. The two kings and Queen Arane stood out of the way while the sailors lowered the sail, its red canvas snapping furiously as though alive and fighting back. The helmsman shouted as oars splashed into the water, and the sailors bent their backs to pull.

Kardan wondered again about the "troll-horse" of Roric's. He realized he knew very little about this man, other than that Hadros had raised him from a foundling as his foster-son and had made him one of his warriors. He did not like to think of him with Karin, but the image kept coming unbidden: a rough, unmannered man, the get of some slut on one of the smaller manors, whose hard hands might even at this moment be peeling Karin's clothes from her body to satisfy his base lusts.

He should never have let Hadros take her as a hostage, he told himself, even if it meant all their immediate deaths. He had tried to deny it, but all the evidence suggested that she loved this man who might be half-troll himself. If she had never come to Hadros' court, she would never have been brought up to think a man like Roric was better than the alternatives, would not now be galloping on a horse of voima far faster than this ship could possibly take them, far away into the northern mountains.

"Worried how far they're ahead of us?" asked King Hadros good-humoredly. "My seamen are strong rowers, and the wind can't stay against us for long. Riding double, they'll be much slower than we are. And they'll have to hunt— not many people live in the center of the peninsula, and they will have trouble finding food. We'll catch them, all right."

They were starting north along the west shore of the peninsula on which all the northern kingdoms were located. The coast on their right was dark and rocky, and to the left stretched unmeasured miles of open ocean, flashing green and silver in the sun.

"I can barely remember the last ten years, now that we're under way at last," said Hadros, grinning into the wind. "How could I have spent so long at peace? This is the real life for a man—feeling the waves, hearing the creak of the mast, chasing down an enemy in a fast ship with good warriors on board and good seamen at the oars."

Kardan looked away, pretending he had not heard. He had no intention of becoming nostalgic for a war he had lost, and he would not let the other king goad him into a reply.

At the same time ten years ago that Kardan had sworn on steel and rowan to pay the tribute, Hadros had sworn to treat Karin as his own daughter—as long as the tribute was paid. He had been happy then to accept the black-bearded king's word.

But should he have done so? Had Hadros already enjoyed the princess's embraces many times, perhaps beginning when she was still a little girl? Had she then been passed to Valmar to teach him the ways of manhood, and had young Dag recently begun to take his turn as well?

Kardan closed his eyes and gritted his teeth. He reminded himself that when Karin returned home she had not seemed coarsened or abased. Hadros' offer for her to marry his heir suggested that he still considered her a woman worthy of a king's son, a maid who could command a fine bride-price rather than a discarded concubine. But she had never seemed completely happy to be home again, and especially in the few days before she disappeared her moods had been wild. She had denied any feeling for Valmar, although Hadros had said she had spent the night with him at least once, and she had kept it from her father when Roric arrived. He had to conclude bitterly that he just did not know his daughter—and if they did not find her he never would.

"I was thinking about Dag," said Hadros beside him.

Kardan opened his eyes, startled as though the other king had read some of his thoughts.

"If Roric doubles back, I hope Dag will be able to direct the castle's defenses himself. I even have doubts he'll be able to manage the breaking of the yearling colts. It should have been Valmar left in charge. Well, I *have* thought a few times that my sons might use the toughening of war! And the boy may be right; it is possible that Roric would talk to him when he wouldn't to anyone else."

Hadros glanced toward the bow of the ship where Gizor One-hand reclined in front of the mast. "When *he* insisted on accompanying us," he added in a lower tone, "I had no one else but Dag to put in authority. Roric knows all too well exactly how many warriors I have, and just what to do to spread them to maximum thinness."

Queen Arane stood a few feet away, easily balancing herself against the ship's motion with a hand on the rail, following their conversation with a faintly ironic smile on her lips.

Hadros turned to look again at Kardan. "You look terrible," he said with another grin. "Not a good sailor, is that it? Is that why your own ship had not been made ready?"

Kardan shook his head hard. He did feel queasy, but this ship's rising and falling through the waves had only a little to do with it. Besides thinking about Karin, he kept being reminded of his oldest son, dead so short a time, whose ship had risen and fallen through waves like these until it had smashed against the rocks and all had drowned.

He had thought then that he had nothing left to live for, having neither wife nor child, and a kingdom his only at Hadros' whim. Karin, restored to him, had abruptly given his life purpose again, but she had also given him a whole new array of events to fear.

"Worried about the lass?" Hadros added, this time without

the grin. "I am too. Did she tell you she took over the direction of my household when my queen died? As soon as I returned from the All-Gemot without her, I knew the castle would never be the same. I just wish she had the sense to stay with Valmar! Women," he added in a mutter.

Kardan turned from him and tried watching the waves, rising higher than the ship before they fell, their tips edged in white, then decided it would be even better not to watch them.

But Hadros was not done. "Roric won't hurt her, but neither of them can have any idea what they will find in the northern mountains. There are creatures of voima there that are worse than even those in the tales told late at night when the youngsters are asleep. I've been in those mountains—I know."

Kardan seized him by the arm. He immediately tried to make it seem that he was just trying to keep his balance, but there was more to it. Without knowing Karin's mind now that she was a grown woman, without being able to see her fate, he desperately needed an ally. As much as he considered Hadros his enemy the other king kept appearing the only ally he had.

"When I encouraged Roric to go north," added Hadros almost apologetically, "I had no idea he would take her with him. He'll find plenty there—men and creatures of voima both!—for his restless spirit. I do hope he survives the adventure, however. For one thing, I personally want to wring his neck."

They put in that evening at a cove King Hadros said he knew of old. He took the helm himself to guide them in between rocky islets, thick with brush, to a sheltered harbor as smooth as a pond. "We should be safe here," he told Kardan. "We're still too far south for any of the dangerous creatures of voima, and there never used to be any human settlements nearby."

He sent several warriors ashore anyway to check for danger

and to refill the water barrels. Gizor insisted on leading the party even though he had to be helped into the skiff. Queen Arane went with them, saying she wanted to stretch her legs after the day's journey. The two kings stayed on board as the sailors rigged the awnings, then ate some of the smoked meat they had brought along while waiting for the shore party to return.

"Why do you think the queen insisted on coming along with two widowers looking for their heirs?" Kardan asked. "It seemed like more than a woman's whim." The sun had dipped low in the sky, its light glowing on the dark pines on the shore. For a brief half hour the two kings were alone, the only sounds the quiet conversation of sailors and warriors at the other end of the ship and the steady ripple of tiny waves against the hull.

Hadros, sitting with his stiff leg stretched out in front of him, shot Kardan a sharp glance but answered casually. "You were the one who seemed to think she had become friendly with Karin."

"But why, since Karin had not fled to her court after all, should the queen have any further interest in our affairs?"

"Arane and I have been friends for years," the black-bearded king said with a shrug. "I expect she just wanted a change from that court of hers—I certainly couldn't stand it there for more than a week."

But he gave a sudden fierce smile then. "Maybe she wants to keep the peace between us. You notice she's already made it clear, my friend, that her warriors will spell the difference if you and I start fighting, so she may hope that as long as we aren't sure which side she'd support we won't start fighting at all. Or maybe she thinks she can keep me from killing Roric once we find him! Not that I really would, or at least not in cold blood," he added thoughtfully. "It takes a while to raise up young men, even if we do run out of time before we run out of fury and wounded pride. But do not let Arane's sweet demeanor fool you. Underneath she is as tough as any old warrior."

"Is there any reason you know why she should be concerned about Roric?" asked Kardan. Here at last might be some clue to this mysterious man whom his daughter apparently loved. "I would have thought she had never even met him. Could her concern for Karin and thus for the man Karin loves be enough to bring her on a dangerous journey with two old widowers?"

"Well," said Hadros slowly, "and well. She keeps her own counsel, Arane does. Your daughter will not be a bad queen if she takes her for a model." He sat for a moment with his hands on his knees and frowning, as though trying to decide whether or not to say something, then leaned back again. "Arane had a sweet maid once, years ago," he added irrelevantly and with a smile.

The rippling against the hull had become louder. Kardan stared at the dark water. Something dark was swimming just below the surface, something like a very large fish.

It was behind Hadros as he sat leaning against the rail, and he did not seem to hear it. "I did the queen a favor once, over twenty years ago," he continued.

But Kardan was no longer listening. As he watched, the fish broke the surface right next to the ship. But it was not a fish. It was a woman.

As Kardan watched in astonishment, a head of curly black hair emerged from the waves. Eyes bright as mirrors, she reached for the railing and pulled herself up. The water streamed from her naked body.

Hadros heard her then and turned his head abruptly. Kardan could see now that it was not a woman after all. From her waist down she was not human but fish, scales glittering as bright in the evening light as her eyes.

Hadros started to speak, but the siren did not give him a chance. She flashed Kardan a grin that showed a line of sharp little white teeth, then threw her arms around Hadros' neck from behind. He gave a startled cry, half-choking, as he tried to jump to his feet.

She bent his head slowly backward while his hand grasped

for the sword he had unbuckled and laid at his feet. But it was too late. As his fingers found his knife instead, the siren gave a hard jerk. Hadros' back slammed against the rail, and his kicking legs rose into the air. The knife flew from his hand, but it reached the waves only a second before he did. With a splash, the siren and the king were gone.

Kardan leaped up, kicking off his boots and tossing away his cloak. The sailors had realized at last that something was happening, but he was closest. His sword in his hand, he took a deep breath and sprang over the railing, going fast before he could change his mind.

The water was even colder than he expected. He almost gasped with the shock but managed to keep his mouth closed. He clung desperately to his sword, kicking his way downward after a thin stream of bubbles. Tiny startled fish swam before him.

The salt stung his eyes as he swam, his clothes dragging at him. But he could see the siren now on the rocky bottom, her long sinuous tail wrapped around Hadros' motionless form. She grinned again and held up a hand as though to warn him off.

Kardan thrust at her with his sword, the motion seeming unbearably slow and reaching nowhere near her. But the siren frowned and loosened her tail from around Hadros. His body slumped, the head tilted sideways.

Kardan thrust again, the sword still not reaching its goal. Bubbles escaped from his lips, rising past his eyes, and his chest felt tighter and tighter as the impulse to take a breath grew almost unbearable. The siren darted backward with a wiggle of her tail.

He kicked forward, but she stayed just out of reach of his sword. The air in his lungs was nearly gone. But he was now within a few feet of Hadros. Air still dribbled from the king's mouth, but his eyes were closed.

Kardan waved his sword at the siren a final time, grabbed the other king by the collar, and planted his feet on the stony bottom. The sharp stones bit with a pain that broke even through the cold-induced numbness.

But he kicked off with all his strength, tugging Hadros upward. The surface before his straining eyes was a wavering green ceiling, seeming impossibly far. With his sword still in one hand and the other wrapped around Hadros' collar, he could not use his arms to swim. Inert and waterlogged, the king could have weighed a thousand pounds.

He gave a great gasp as his head broke through the surface at last, the air on salty lips tasting sweeter than he had ever known it. The sailors reached over the railing, grabbing both kings. They were heaved back into the ship, the water pouring from them, as the shore party emerged from the trees.

Hadros flopped motionless on the deck. Kardan bent over him, pushing rhythmically and desperately on the shoulder blades, willing him still to be alive.

About two gallons of salt water came up all at once and ran across the deck. Kardan pushed again, and another gallon followed. Hadros gave a grunt and lifted his head.

The sailors bent to help him turn over and sit up. Kardan stepped back, shivering uncontrollably as a sailor handed him a dry cloak. Gizor and his party seemed to realize something had happened, for he shouted at the warriors as they scrambled into the skiff. Their voices seemed very distant, and Kardan's attention all focused on the black-bearded figure before him.

Hadros passed a hand unsteadily across his face, wiping away the wet. Kardan, watching him, found himself wondering why he had saved his life. This would have been the perfect opportunity to get revenge for ten years of humiliation. He would not even have had to do anything himself to harm him—all he had to do was come back to the surface alone.

But he had certainly saved him. He knelt beside Hadros again, helping the sailors strip off the king's dripping clothing. "Are you all right?" he heard himself asking concernedly.

Hadros wavered a little but managed a smile as he tried to squeeze some of the water from his beard. "While you're at it, Kardan," he said with almost a chuckle, "I expect my knife is at the bottom of the cove. Would you mind going back for it?"

Then he passed out.

King Hadros insisted on continuing north the next day, waving away Kardan's concern irritably, though he sat rather than stood by the rail and kept massaging his knee. He stationed three warriors with harpoons before the mast, close above the white water foaming around the throat of the dragon prow, watching for sirens and for other creatures from deep under the sea.

"Is it always so, well, exciting to go on a war expedition?" Queen Arane asked with an ironic expression. "My kingdom has been free of wars since my father's time, and this is my first experience of such a thing."

"This isn't a war expedition," said Hadros with a wolfish smile. "This is just a little trip."

Kardan also watched for sea creatures, but his attention was caught instead by a flock of geese, very high up, flying south fast. "That may be a portent of trouble before us," he commented. "Geese should not be flying for another two months or more."

"There have been strange rumors from the north all this year," replied Hadros. "Yet I still had not thought to see a siren so far south." But as they rowed onward against a steady wind, they saw no more creatures of voima. "The wind shouldn't be blowing from the north like this in the middle of summer," he muttered. "Does Roric have powers he's never told me about?"

"All of us have powers within us," said Queen Arane pleasantly, seating herself beside him. "The difficulty is to recognize and use them."

"Strength of mind, strength of arm—that's one thing, Arane," said the king slowly. "But there is something going on in this world that I don't like. Kardan's Mirror-seer is gone, and, though I didn't tell you this before, so is the Weaver. He'd been right there in his cave—or *her* cave, some would say—since I was a boy, and the stories say many generations longer than that, but when I went up to ask him where Roric had gone, it was as empty as though no one had ever lived there."

Kardan lifted his head sharply from watching the waves. If wild creatures of voima were growing bolder and stalking this world, and if those who interpreted the powers of voima to mortals were retreating, then they might find not just danger ahead but the lords of voima themselves. He had already this trip seen a number of things he would not before have believed.

When they pulled into a cove that evening, Hadros said grimly, "Tonight I spend on land."

"Are you not concerned for the rare *forest* sirens?" asked the queen with a small smile, but Hadros ignored her. He stepped fairly agilely into the skiff and allowed himself to be rowed to shore with a handful of warriors. Another trip brought Kardan and the queen, along with the awnings from the ship to rig as tents. The sun had set and the moon was low in the sky as they finished their bread and ale and lit a small fire.

Kardan slept only uneasily, although the other king fell asleep at once and filled the night air with loud snores. Kardan had spent just long enough on the ship that he missed its motion, and the solid earth beneath him seemed to keep slowly rising and falling, jerking him from his dreams. When he turned over, trying unsuccessfully to find a way to lie such that the pebbles did not bite into his rib cage or the cold sea breezes find the nape of his neck, the sounds of wind in the trees and waves on the shore could have been the hungry mumbling of some great creature, and even the coals of their fire looked back at him like living eyes.

The eastern sky, above the rocky ridge that followed this

part of the coast, had just started to lighten with summer's early dawn when he rolled over for the hundredth time, started to close his eyes again, and abruptly lifted himself on an elbow instead. That sounded different from the sounds he had been hearing all night.

He nudged Hadros, whose snores stopped in mid-breath, and closed his hand around his sword's hilt. He could see them now: furtive, hunched shapes just beyond the ring of their tents. As he squinted in the faint light, he saw one cautiously lift a flap of awning and reach inside.

His first thought was for Arane, but the queen's tent was on the opposite side from these creatures. He scrambled to his feet with a shout, Hadros only a second slower.

He could see now they were men, men almost naked, their hair thick and matted around their faces. "Do not attack us!" cried one as Kardan leaped toward him. His voice was low-pitched and rough, and he held up a pink palm. Yellow teeth showed in an ingratiating smile. "We just—we just want some food."

The warriors had the little group of hairy men surrounded now. Kardan's warriors especially seemed to be enjoying this. The hairy men certainly looked harmless, smaller than any members of the war-party, unarmed, eyes glinting in the dimness from out of their tangled hair. Gizor One-hand put the point of his sword under one's chin.

"Thieves," growled Hadros. "We ought to kill you on the spot as a lesson to all thieves." But he slid his sword back into its sheath as he spoke and gestured to Gizor to do the same. After a moment he grunted and complied, and the rest of the warriors did as well. Kardan, however, kept his hilt clenched in a sweaty hand. "Do we have some stale bread or rancid butter we can give them?" Hadros asked over his shoulder.

That is when they attacked. With a cry that was more bark than shout, the one closest to Hadros threw himself on him. Sharp teeth glinted in a long snout, and the claws at the end of the fingers ripped at the king's jerkin. Knocked off balance, Hadros staggered backward, and teeth snapped at his throat as he went down.

The warriors, yelling, all scrambled for their weapons. Kardan, the only one with a sword in his hand, sprang forward, all his weight behind his thrust. His blade dragged on fur, caught on a rib, then slid into the heart of the creature about to bite the king's neck.

It collapsed with a howl, falling backward as Hadros scrambled free. He had his sword out now and leaped wildly at the next hairy creature, but it melted away before him. The warriors were all shouting and swinging their swords, just avoiding decapitating each other.

Kardan planted a foot against the dying creature before him and jerked his blade free. A touch came on his shoulder. He spun around ready to thrust again and found himself looking from a foot away into Hadros' eyes.

"Back to back!" shouted the king, apparently unconcerned about nearly being run through by the man who had saved him only a few seconds earlier. But as Kardan whirled around, feeling the other's muscular back against his, Hadros commented mildly, "Unless, of course, you planned to measure swords with me this morning."

Their enemies were gone. They raced away on all fours, howling, and disappeared into the black and rocky woods before the slowly lightening sky could ever show them clearly. Gizor and the warriors, slower on two legs, pursued them.

But the one that Kardan had killed was still there. Hadros turned it over with his foot. The eyes were open, staring glassily, and a long tongue lolled from its sharp-toothed snout. It looked almost—but not quite—like a wolf.

Queen Arane, well wrapped in a cloak and with a knife in her hand, came out of her tent with her warriors on either side. She had for once nothing to say. Kardan eyed her suspiciously, wondering what powers of voima *she* might have that had, so far, protected her. The kings' warriors returned from a brief and unsuccessful chase to stare at the creature Kardan had killed. "What is it?"

one warrior asked in horror. Several turned charms over in their fingers.

"Shape-changer," Hadros said. "I should have known better than to think these were the thieves and beggars they wanted to seem. But I haven't seen a shape-changer in twenty-five years. Is it merely fate that we should meet both a siren and these shape-changers, in lands where I have never seen such creatures before, or did someone very powerful send them against us?

"If we keep on being attacked by creatures of voima," he added when no one dared answer, "we're going to have trouble catching Roric. At this rate, I'll have to take a stint at the oars myself." He kicked the creature, rolling it back on its face, exposing again the bloody hole where the sword had gone in.

King Hadros said nothing more for a moment but grunted and pulled off his jerkin, now black with the shape-changer's blood. He ran a thumb thoughtfully beneath his jaw while looking at it. "You know, Kardan," he commented, "you've now saved my life twice in two days. I should have given you better terms on that tribute, ten years ago."

Kardan had started to reach for grass or leaves to wipe the blood from his sword, but found himself sitting on the ground. He fought the impulse to collapse further. He looked up at Hadros instead and for a second found himself grinning. "You should warn a man before inviting him along on one of your little trips," he answered. "You certainly provide all the excitement a young man could ask for, but I may be getting too old for this game."

2

The Wanderers gave Valmar a sword that sang.

It sang wordlessly but gloriously whenever he pulled it from the sheath, a song that drove straight to the heart with chords of courage, heroism, and undying glory. He discovered that if he loosened the peace straps and kept it drawn even just an inch or so, it would sing to him as he rode.

Across seven rivers, across seven mountain passes, he rode the chalk-white stallion the Wanderers had given him. The wind was in his hair and the glare of the sun in his eyes. Black trees stood etched along the high ridges against an unending red sunset.

Neither the decaying algae at the fords nor the mountain fruit trees with their fruit all shriveled could detract from the mission he followed. The stallion seemed tireless, carrying him easily up and down hills. With the sunset before him and a never-repeating song of glory accompanying him he lost all track of time, stopping neither for food nor for sleep, until he saw the dark pine woods which concealed the third force.

Valmar pulled up the stallion then and found a place to settle down behind a hedge, where he hoped no one would spot him. He had not paused at any of the manors he passed, cutting around their fields with his mind already miles ahead. But he was now very suddenly weary and hungry. His heart hammered inside his armor, as he realized it had been doing for hours, even days.

He sat with his elbows on his knees, looking critically at the pine woods. It ascended a steep hill, and at the top of the hill, hidden behind the trees, should be the manor of the trolls. He had been told very little about the third force, other than that they were hollow, incomplete creatures who were distracting the lords of voima as they struggled to preserve their power; Valmar himself had decided to call them trolls. He had not forgotten the being who had summoned Roric. There was little to distinguish this from many other woods he had passed, but the Wanderers had told him his stallion would take him there, and he had kept track of the rivers and mountains he had crossed.

His mission was to destroy this third force. Not to kill them, apparently, he thought as he took out and munched the bread and cheese he had brought with him. His stallion

tore at the grass but kept shifting his location, as though
finding the grass sour wherever he was. In this land everyone, except of course Valmar himself, was immortal, and
would remain immortal unless death reached the realm.
But the Wanderers had told him he had great powers, great
enough, it seemed, to weaken those opposed to them.

He was not sure how much the lords of voima truly
wanted this force destroyed, and how much this was a
test to see if he was strong enough and able enough to
serve them. After what had seemed weeks, even months
of practicing, he felt eager to serve the lords of voima,
to be found not wanting. He put a tree between himself and the sunset and fell asleep.

When he awoke someone was bending over him, someone massive but with a face strangely blurred so that he
could not quite see it.

He sat up fast, the singing sword already in his fist, but
the being stepped back, showing him empty palms. "Greetings, Valmar Hadros' son!" he said. "Welcome to our home!
You need not lie on the ground out here when we can
entertain you within!"

Valmar rose slowly to his feet. For just one second, the
foot in the grass next to him looked as though it was clo-
ven, but then its outline too became blurred. "Why should
I trust you when I cannot see you?" he asked cautiously.
This must be one of those he had come to fight, but by
greeting him in so friendly a manner this being had kept
him from immediate attack.

"Your friend trusts us," said the other, slightly less blurred
now. Whoever he was, he looked human within the misty
outlines. "Roric No-man's son. He is our friend too and
eats in our hall."

"Roric?" asked Valmar, startled but not yet lowering his
sword. "But Roric is back under the sun. We heard raven-
messages that he was coming."

"Of course he is under the sun," said the other cheerfully, "*our* sun. Or do you mortals call that something else?"

This he seemed to find hilarious. He turned his back then on Valmar, apparently quite unafraid of him, and started walking into the woods. "Come, if you want a more comfortable bed and better food and ale."

Valmar slowly slid his sword halfway into the sheath, then picked up his pack and saddle and took his stallion by the reins, preparing to follow. Could Roric have returned here in the time he was gone?

His sword was still singing, quietly now. The other stopped and turned back sharply. "Do you *mind* making your sword stop that infernal singing?"

"I'm sorry, I like its song," Valmar started to say, then stopped. "No. I will not bother you with the voice of my sword, given to me by the Wanderers, nor will I come to your hall with you. I am your enemy, and I shall not eat your bread. I am sworn to serve the lords of voima."

"So are we, so are we," said the other hastily. "Why do you want to be our enemy? *Roric* isn't. Come to our hall, and you can meet him."

"If Roric is there," said Valmar, not moving, "then tell him to come out and greet me. Then I will consider your offer." The other started deeper into the woods, looking back over his shoulder several times, but Valmar did not follow. Whoever this was, he appeared to have a back.

Valmar sat down again, and his stallion resumed grazing. He had pictured himself coming on a warband of horrifying creatures, of sitting his horse with his singing sword upraised, defying them. He had been going to tell them to trouble the lords of voima no more or else to taste his steel. So far it was not as he had imagined.

But there was still much he could do as long as he did not make the mistake of accepting the invitation of food and a bed. He saddled his horse slowly, carefully checking all the straps and buckles, then smiled at himself. He was moving very deliberately as though waiting to see if Roric might come out to meet him after all.

He mounted then and settled his shield on his arm. Even

if these creatures of the third force were not a warband he could still defy them.

The stallion started forward, first at a walk, then, when kicked, at a trot and then a gallop. The sword sang louder and louder as he raced along a needle-littered track through the dark pine woods and up the slope beyond.

A slim mailed figure, curly black hair escaping from under her horned helmet, leaped out in front of the white stallion.

3

The mountains had been growing closer for several days, but with agonizing slowness in spite of the speed of their horses. "Gizor and Hadros may be on the king's warship, paralleling our route by sea," said Roric. Goldmane and the spotted mare trotted side by side along a grass-grown path. "A fast ship can do a hundred miles a day if the wind is right; even Goldmane can't do that day after day."

"You keep assuming they know where we're going," said Karin with a smile that was almost indulgent. "Gizor must have waited to come after us until King Hadros returned home. If the king sent out the arrow of war to the royal manors to raise an army before following, he may be over a week behind us."

"We'll find out soon enough," he answered, not wanting to quarrel with her and making himself answer carefully to avoid doing so. "I've never been this far north, but Hadros sometimes speaks of this area. The war in which he fought when he was Valmar's age involved two kingdoms up here. Before we reach the mountains we shall have to cross an arm of the ocean that nearly cuts the peninsula in two. If Gizor is ahead of us, that is where he'll be."

That took some of the complacency from Karin's face. "Then we will have fled all this way for nothing? And we won't reach the Hot-River Mountains and Valmar?"

"That is exactly what I mean," said Roric, feeling darkly glad as he spoke to be able to change her mood. But then he immediately was sorry: far better to have her singing as they rode than giving him that look of supplication and despair.

She had seemed remarkably cheerful ever since they left the isolated manor, Roric thought. She had dismissed his concerns over how the woman had known his name, saying that she herself must have let it slip, but he did not think so. There was a satisfied look around Karin's mouth that should not be there when they were running for their lives, leaving honor behind with every stride.

Though she had lain rigid next to him the first nights after they had left the faeys, the last few evenings she had fallen asleep in his arms with a faint smile on her lips, heedless of the dark clouds racing across the dark sky, the pattering amidst the leaves of tiny creatures, and the more distant creaks and calls that could have been anything from wolves to trolls. Roric often lay long awake, listening to the noises and sometimes seeing, after midnight, flashes of light rippling across the northern sky. But if Karin worried about whether they were outcasts, or whether she was behaving as a future queen should, it did not disturb her sleep.

When they rounded a hill and saw a little lake, shining like a jewel in the sunshine, and a house with a dock beside it, she said, "A Mirror-seer!" with delight. They found the door standing ajar, but she did not seem bothered. "I'm sure even Seers go places sometimes," she said.

Roric however went inside. The house was empty except for some old clothes and, in the back, the Seer's mirrors. When he held them out of curiosity to the light from the window, one mirror was empty, showing not even his own reflection, but in the other glass he saw a seated figure.

He was so startled he almost dropped the mirror, then looked unsuccessfully out the window for the source of that figure and back into the glass again. Deep in the mirror, incredibly thin, with a cat curled up on his knees, sat the Seer. He motioned Roric to silence, then seemed again to draw into himself. Roric set the mirror down carefully and, when he found Karin lying on the dock trailing her hands in the water, told her only that the house was empty.

Even the second manor they reached had not appeared to disturb her as much as it disturbed him. Like the first manor, this one was perched on a hill, but they had seen no smoke rising from the hall, and neither dogs nor housecarls came to meet them.

Roric approached cautiously, coming up behind the burial mound that stood partway down the hill. It was late afternoon, and the mound's long shadow lay across the buildings. They needed more food, having eaten everything the woman had given them three days earlier, yet the silent structures could have concealed an ambush. But the buildings all stood uninhabited, their doors open, their contents in confusion as though the people who lived here had fled something unexpected and unimaginable.

"They must have been driven out by some of the raiders that woman mentioned," Karin commented, but Roric did not think so. Raiders would have smashed everything they could not carry, and probably fired the hall as they left. The open buildings to him signaled panic but not looting. The wind whispered around the eaves, pushing the doors slowly back and forth with faint creaks. Karin, unconcerned, whistled as she found some rather stale bread and cheese, although the milk in the dairy had gone too sour.

In the hall she tidily folded up the disordered blankets on the beds. Roric had to pull her away or she might have suggested they spend the night there. The sun had slipped over the horizon by the time they were mounted again, riding out past the burial mound—and, just for a second, a form flickered on the top of the mound, seeming to raise a hand in salute or in warning. Roric shouted to Goldmane and urged him forward, knowing that Karin would take it as a challenge to race, and not daring to look back.

While daydreaming that spring, a short time ago—although it seemed like years—of the fortune he would make to be worthy of Karin's love, Roric had always assumed he would return to offer her what he had won, not have her riding beside him on the voyage to find it. Now, while trying to plan for the unknown dangers that lay ahead, he repeatedly found himself irritated by her presence—and the constant check it made on what he might dare. But if she had not been with him he would have stood and fought Gizor to the death, and he felt fairly sure whose death it would have been.

"The powers of voima are with us now," Karin now said with sudden cheerfulness, giving him a smile. "We'll find Valmar—if your stallion can keep up!" She kicked her mare and was off, galloping ahead of him down the grassy track, her braids whipping out behind her. Goldmane sprang in pursuit. For a second, just a second, Roric thought he saw a huge dark shaggy shape, the size of the bear he had killed in the Wanderers' realm, rising from behind a boulder a quarter mile ahead. He reached for his sword, but when he looked again there was nothing there at all.

At the end of a long day's riding, they reached the rift where the peninsula was nearly cut in two by a narrow arm of the ocean, cutting far inland. Roric pulled Goldmane up at the crest of the hill, looking across the valley before them. The peninsula here narrowed to ten miles wide or less. Off to the east were high, barren, virtually impassable cliffs, facing on the ocean on their far side. From those cliffs on this side cascaded a river that became salt as it ran toward the ocean away to the west. His fingers found his little bone charm, and he turned it over absently. So far, he thought, fate had been with them, but their stories might end abruptly in this valley.

The track before them dropped rapidly, then followed a zigzag path through barren grasslands and scrub, dodging boulders the size of Hadros' hall, until over a mile away it reached the salt river. Before them, according to the stories he remembered the king telling years ago, was the only easy away across the river.

The mountains they had seen for days on the horizon ahead of them rose at last on the far side of the river, their upper reaches streaked with snow. It was as though here the earth had cracked open and the ocean had rushed into the breach. The river itself was spotted with islands made of single enormous rocks, the odd tree growing from their summits.

In the distance came a high shrill whistle, a signal or else a sea bird. "A hundred men could hide among those boulders, and you'd never see them until it was too late," Roric muttered. The only sign of humanity was a wide blackened area of burnt wood and tumbled stones, open to the sun, which might once have been a castle.

"Did that castle guard the crossing?" Karin asked, pulling her mare up beside him. The wind blew the fine hair escaping from her braids across her eyes, and she pushed it back.

"It used to. Hadros said that it was fired in the last war, and if it was rebuilt it's been fired again."

Roric considered the ruin in silence a minute longer. "This must be," he said then, "the kingdom of that king you were telling me about, outlawed at the All-Gemot. If so, those deserted hills we've just come through would have been where his tenants once lived. The ford is the only way to go from the southern to the northern part of the peninsula without taking a ship. I expect too many kings— those on the sea, those to the north, and those to the south— fear control of the crossing for anyone ever to have held the castle successfully for long."

"No use us trying to make this into *our* kingdom, then," Karin said, and he could not tell if she was mocking.

There was at any rate no sign now of anyone trying to guard the crossing. "I had better go ahead," he said, "to find out if there really might be someone behind those rocks. You wait here. I don't see a ship in the river, but Gizor would know better than to leave the ship in plain sight."

He did not add that a salt river like this might well mark the end of the powers of voima that had been riding with them.

"I'm coming with you," said Karin determinedly. "It's you Gizor is trying to kill, not me."

"And I may need you and your knife to back me up again," he answered with a sudden grin. "Come on, then."

He took the lead, allowing his stallion to pick his own way down the slope while gazing around intently. There were distant, plaintive cries from shore birds—that is, he was fairly sure they were all birds—and the murmur and rustle of the wind, but no other sounds. Even the salt river was still too distant to hear.

"I don't think they will have brought horses," Roric said over his shoulder. "So if they try to jump us, we'll outrun them—give that spotted mare of yours a chance to prove she really is a horse of voima." Nothing stirred behind the boulders littering the flat area before them; when a bird rose abruptly almost under Goldmane's feet he was almost as startled as the stallion.

"Hadros always said that there were strange creatures here in the northern lands," Roric added once Goldmane had all four feet on the ground again, forcing his voice to stay calm. "But when I was little he would never tell me what they were, and when I was older I never asked. How about a sea-troll, as much bigger and fiercer than the troll we met at the manor as the sea is bigger than a stream?" He pulled his lips back from his teeth, enjoying the thought. "If there's a sea-troll here, we may not have to worry about Gizor after all."

"You know," commented Karin, "considering that you and Hadros are enemies, you are very much alike sometimes."

He looked back at her in surprise, but only for a second because he needed his attention for the narrow track. "But I am Gizor's enemy, not Hadros'," he told himself, except that he was Hadros' also. But would it be so bad to be like the king? He shook his head to dismiss such useless thoughts. He needed to act, not to worry. He turned his attention fully to watching for ambush.

The shadows from the huge boulders were dark and crooked, and half an army could have hidden in the scrubby brush. He squinted at the rocks, trying to decide if some of the darkness at their feet might be the ashes of camp fires—or even puddles of dried blood—rather than merely shadow, but it was impossible to tell. As they proceeded slowly downhill, Roric kept his back straight, trying not to feel a tickle between his shoulder blades. To look back, as though fearing an archer behind him, would only distract him from the much more likely dangers ahead.

They went slowly between the boulders until they reached the ruins of the castle, its tumbled, fire-scorched stones not yet overgrown with creepers. His fist squeezed tight on his sword hilt, and it felt as though the air itself vibrated with tension. They went quietly, cautiously, the only sounds the creak of saddles and the clink of horseshoes on stone.

"Look!" said Karin sharply. He swiveled his head, following her pointing hand. Off to the west, coming up the salt river from the direction of the sea, was a red sail.

No time for caution now. "Come on!" he shouted. "They must have reached the river before us and spotted us when we came over the crest of the hill. But we'll beat them to the crossing!" He kicked Goldmane forward, and they galloped down the stony track, past more huge boulders. The ship was coming upriver against the current, further from the ford than they were, and even with all its oars out it—

But someone else was also watching the ship, someone pressed into a chink in the outer wall of the ruined castle, his back to Roric and Karin. He heard them and spun around, yelling as he raised his sword.

More armed men boiled out from behind the boulders. Roric reined in Goldmane so hard the stallion reared straight up, but the men were also behind them. He had led Karin straight into ambush.

CHAPTER NINE

1

These were not Hadros' men. Karin had never seen any
of them before. They bore dented helmets and cracked
shields, but their glittering blades were sharp and their
war-cries ferocious.

Their only advantage was that all the attackers were on
foot. Roric bellowed and whirled his sword, and his stallion lashed out with his hooves, felling two men. Roric's
first strokes bounced off helmets, and his third struck a
shield so hard the man staggered.

The attackers drew back for a second, and Goldmane
sprang forward past them. Roric's laugh rang out over their
shouts, and he grinned as if he could have asked nothing
more of life than to die fighting for it.

Karin, on the contrary, felt wash over her all the fear she
had not felt for two weeks, as though the powers that had
protected and guided them reached no further than the
edge of this wide rift. She kicked the spotted mare, staying
so close behind Roric that she was almost on the stallion's
heels.

But armed men almost immediately blocked the horses'
path again. The men were more numerous before them
than behind them, and more and more sprang out from
behind boulders, shouting to each other. The way to the
ford seemed jammed with beards, helmets, and steel blades.

She looked back over her shoulder to what she hoped was safety, calling to Roric to retreat, but more warriors darted around behind them, and Roric could not hear her over his own yells.

A hand gripped her by the ankle, trying to tug her down, and a grinning face stared up at her. Clinging to the saddle horn, she stabbed desperately at the hand with her knife. The man shrieked and jumped away. Another man ran toward her from the other side, but the mare kicked, and her heels caught him full in the chest.

Goldmane reared again, screaming, and this time the attackers fell back further. The two horses began to run, leaping both fallen warriors and the stones pushed into their path, scattering the men still pouring out from behind the boulders. This wasn't a group of raiders, she thought grimly. This was enough warriors for an invading army.

Her vision blurred as she tried to stay on the plunging mare. Roric, immediately before her, could have been a mile away. The sun sat on the western horizon, and long, grotesque shadows took the last sense of order from this rift valley.

Somehow they were still moving forward, closer and closer to the salt river, but also closer to the red-sailed ship. Roric's sword rose and fell with great clangs, blocking a blow, knocking a man back, going for an unprotected throat. She kicked another warrior in the face and heard herself shouting threats and curses. Irrelevantly, she wondered what Queen Arane would do in these circumstances.

There was blood on her gloves, making the knife grip slippery, but she was not sure if it was hers or her enemies'. Roric bled in several places, but no wound slowed his sword—fighting for honor, his life, or for her. She tried, even while fighting herself, to keep her eyes on him, to see him in his final glorious moments before superior force finally overcame them.

But suddenly the way before them was empty of warriors. "We're through!" Roric yelled to her. "Across the ford!"

Their horses had leaped, scrambled, and kicked their way through most of the band. Even close to fifty men on foot, hampered by the boulders and broken ground, had trouble standing against a stallion of voima and a rider who attacked as though berserk.

But as their horses raced the last hundred yards, the warship with the red sail ran its keel up onto the shallow gravel of the ford, and warriors and dogs leaped over the side. The warriors already had their swords drawn as they hit the water and splashed ashore, giving their war-cries. These men Karin knew well. Many were Hadros' men, and most of the rest her father's.

The armed men she and Roric had just escaped hesitated. They halted a bow shot from the river, and several ducked behind boulders again. Looking back, she suddenly realized the ambush had not been for their own benefit. Their attackers had been hoping to catch Hadros' ship by surprise.

The first of the king's warriors ashore was grizzled and held his sword left-handed.

"Single combat!" Roric shouted to him, tossing back his hair. "This is between you and me, Gizor. Stay back, Hadros, stay back, you warriors, by all the powers of voima! You, Gizor, I challenge to single combat, immediately, on an island here in the river!"

He leaped from the stallion, throwing Karin the reins, and braced himself to meet a fully armed warrior without even a shield of his own. He was grinning again.

But the fight never began. King Hadros was only a step behind Gizor, and he grabbed him by the sword arm to spin him around. "No one touches him!" he bellowed, his face purple. "Not until I have some answers out of him! After that, I'll take his hide off with my own bare hands."

Roric hesitated, his sword still at the ready and his shoulders heaving with his breath, but there was suddenly no one before him. Karin, looking past him, saw her father clambering out of the warship, and there, standing at the rail, the last person she had expected to see, Queen Arane.

She jumped down from the mare with a shout for King Kardan. Maybe it would not be as bad as she had feared to be caught. Since Kardan and Hadros had pursued them together, they must not be trying to kill each other. With Arane's help, she should be able to persuade Hadros that Valmar was safe, that Roric had nothing to do with his disappearance. Maybe they could even help find the Witch of the Western Cliffs who was supposed to know how to reach the Wanderers from these mountains. And her own father looked so happy—

That is when the men onshore attacked.

Coming down toward the river with long leaps, shouting their war-cries, they fell on Hadros' warriors just as the sun disappeared over the edge of the world. Some attackers splashed through the ford toward the ship while the rest of Hadros' warriors sprang out to intercept them.

Roric whirled around, reaching for his stallion, but Gizor grabbed him from behind. "No flight for you again!" he bellowed. If Roric answered, she could not hear him over the yells and sounds of steel on steel.

Someone pushed her back, away from the fiercest fighting, but she tried to struggle forward. Muscled backs and shoulders were on every side of her, and she could no longer see Roric. The dogs' wild barking rose above the war cries and the ringing of sword on shield. The gravel shore on both sides of the river churned with knots of men locked in combat, but she had to find Roric among them. He needs me, she said soundlessly between dry lips, he needs my knife to save him.

Men shouted and fell on both sides of her, but she had no time to distinguish royal warriors from raiders. She had to find Roric before the end of the rapidly fading light. He's gone already, she thought wildly. But maybe he was on the river's far side. She ran through the ford, soaking her dress to the knees, scarcely noticing the cold water until she came up on the other shore and the weight of the wet wool almost made her lose her balance.

She saw him then, farther away than she had expected. He had somehow eluded Gizor but was still on foot, desperately fighting again against the warriors who had appeared from out of the boulders.

Stumbling, trying to call to him though she felt as though she had no more voice than in a nightmare, she staggered forward. With no attention to give to the men near her she focused on Roric, on her need to reach him while there was still time, to help him if she could, and if not to kiss him again before he died.

She did not reach him. She was suddenly seized from behind and her arms pinned. A hard blow knocked the knife from her hand. "Retreat!" she heard a bellow above her head. "Back to the mountains!" And all of the ambushers, hearing that bellow, hoisted up their fallen comrades and began to run.

She was tossed over someone's shoulder; she still had not seen the face of whoever grabbed her. She tried to kick him as he ran, but he only laughed loudly and mockingly.

"We've beaten them!" "They've got no stomach for a real fight!" she heard the triumphant shouts from Hadros' warriors. "Do you want to come back, boys, and get trained in *real* fighting?"

And then someone realized she was gone. Trying to raise her head, she thought she could see through her hair and her tears a group of Hadros' warriors racing after her. But they were several hundred yards behind.

"Karin!" she heard Roric's voice ringing out over all the din. "I'll save you!" But his voice broke off sharply as though he had been struck. She could not see him.

The mountains began almost immediately on this side of the salt river. The ambushers raced without hesitation up dark and narrow tracks, leaping from rock to rock like goats, turning aside where there seemed no way to go to squeeze through narrow crevices. Twice they paused to roll boulders down toward the heads of the warriors trying to follow them, giving mocking shouts.

Several times she was tossed unceremoniously from one set of arms to another. She saw then the face of the man who had grabbed her originally, a man with a fierce look in his eye but a scar at the edge of his mouth that made it seem as though he was always smiling. He laughed again as he dropped her to another warrior at the bottom of a stony ditch, then sprang down himself.

"Hope you aren't still thinking they'll save you!" he said with another laugh. And she realized she could no longer hear any pursuit.

2

Some of King Kardan's warriors half-carried, half-dragged him back to the ship. "It's no use, sire," they told him, their voices unsteady. The dogs had raced off ahead of them, but come back—those that *had* come back—without even a mouthful of enemy tunic. "We'll never catch them in the dark, and it's not safe trying to climb around those rocks any longer."

"Karin!" He meant it to be a cry she would hear wherever they had taken her, a shout such as Roric had given just before Gizor One-hand knocked him unconscious. It came out more a sob.

"We'll find the princess tomorrow, sire," said one of the warriors in completely unconvincing tones of reassurance. "They'll know better than to hurt her." It was one of the older warriors, who had known Karin well when she was a little girl, before she had first gone away.

The sailors had gotten out the rollers and worked the ship up onto the shore, away from the tides of the river. The warriors laid out the dead and injured: four dead, including one man crushed by a boulder while chasing Karin's abductors, and a number of men with greater or lesser wounds. Only one of the wounded looked likely to die.

Roric had regained consciousness and sat leaning against the barnacled side of the ship, one hand across the bruised forehead and black eye where Gizor had struck him. Both his ankles and waist were secured by heavy ropes. His boots and jerkin were badly chafed as though he had struggled against the bindings, but he now sat quietly.

Kardan sat down beside him. Roric glanced at him without interest, then looked away. But Kardan studied by the light of the fire this man with whom his daughter had run away, trying to find some clue in his unkempt appearance and bitter expression why she had left home for him. He had assumed all the way up here that he would have Roric declared an outlaw, but now he scarcely cared if he had abducted her as long as he could help rescue her from her new abductors.

"First light, we're after them," said King Hadros, "even before we sing the songs for the dead and bury them." Queen Arane was with him. She looked at Roric with interest but drew no closer. "Those warriors may know their secret mountain paths in the darkness, but they cannot hide from us by daylight. But tonight we keep the fires burning and guard the ship. Only half the unwounded men sleep at a time."

"Also tonight," growled Gizor, "we execute the traitor who turned against his sworn king and has a blood-guilt on him that can never be repaid."

He held the other end of the ropes that secured Roric, though he had also taken the precaution of running them through rings on the ship. Queen Arane said something quickly to Hadros, who walked over to Gizor. He stood there with legs apart, contemplating his oldest and his youngest warriors.

"I'll need the judgment of the royal Gemot to execute him, Gizor," he said at last. "Which means we would need to get him home first. Do you plan to lead him around like a trapped bear while we rescue the princess, then hold him like that on the ship all the way back?"

"I can kill him for you if you're too delicate!" retorted Gizor.

Hadros slowly pulled out his knife and struck him across the mouth with the hilt. He glared at Gizor while deliberately returning the knife to his belt. "Be quiet, and don't *you* decide to attack your sworn lord," he said in a low, icy voice.

Gizor put his hand up to stanch the blood and said nothing. Roric gave him a quick, grim look, but he too was silent.

"King Kardan told me," said Hadros to Roric, still in an icy voice, "that Valmar left his kingdom well before you arrived there. That had better be true." When Roric did not answer, he continued, "We'll ask the princess about this when we find her, but you'd better start preparing yourself for a judicial duel if there remains any doubt."

Hadros turned then back to Gizor. "Roric challenged you to single combat. All his blood-guilt—*if* Valmar is still alive—fell on him in a fight in which you were also involved. We may be able to settle your quarrel even without the Gemot if the two of you want to fight it out on one of these islands in the morning."

"But we have to rescue Karin first!" Kardan cried out.

Roric spoke then for the first time. "Your daughter has the power of voima in her, sire," he said in a surprisingly gentle voice. "She will still be alive when we find her."

Kardan startled himself by almost believing him, even though he was not sure Roric believed it himself.

Kardan took the first watch. He and a number of his men sat in stony silence, listening to the sounds of the night, occasionally rising to circle their encampment. But there was no sign or sound of their attackers. The loudest noises were the groans from the wounded.

He felt almost numb. He had seen Karin again but only

for the briefest moment. While sailing up the coast he had promised the lords of voima in his heart to burn a great offering if he could only know she was safe so far, but he knew now that was not enough. She *had* been safe that whole time but, as he should have known well, there could be no end of worrying about one's children as long as they were alive.

Roric had fallen asleep, or at least his eyes were closed, as he sat leaning against the ship's hull with his head at an unnatural angle. How could he have thought such bitter thoughts about this young man? Kardan was still not sure why Karin loved him, but he had to be better than whatever brigand had carried her away.

His men were right. They could not try to pursue her captors before daylight. And by then Karin would be violated at the least, he thought, perhaps killed as well—and maybe quick death would be best after all. If he had not had to keep alert watch, Kardan would have put his face in his hands and sobbed.

The watch changed in the middle of the night. "You can't find her if you're too exhausted," said Hadros brusquely. He himself had slept during the first watch. "You're not a young man to stay awake for three days and ride and fight on the fourth." Kardan wrapped up in his cloak and put his face in the crook of his arm. Across the fire, Hadros talked quietly to Queen Arane, who seemed to be finding the whole series of events an exciting adventure. Kardan himself slid into uneasy dreams, but when he awoke and rolled over the waking was even worse.

The darkness of midnight had given way to a dim sea fog in which it was possible to see faintly, but all shapes were distorted. Sunrise, he guessed, was still an hour off.

Hadros and the queen were no longer near him, but he thought he could see them twenty yards away, walking slowly as though starting off on a circuit of the campsite. He lay without moving, feeling the stiffness in all his joints, trying to decide how many men and dogs they should take in

pursuit of Karin and how many would be needed to guard
the ship and the wounded.

There was the scrape of a boot in the gravel by his head.
"Come with me," came a hoarse whisper. For a startled
second he thought someone was addressing *him*. "Fate
has brought us together this night. You want your combat,
you'll have your combat."

The voice was Gizor's. He was loosening both the ropes
that bound Roric to the rings and the ropes around his
feet, though not the bonds that kept his arms pinned to his
sides.

Kardan feigned sleep, watching from behind his lashes.

"Untie me," said Roric in a whisper of his own. "Are you
afraid I'll attack you while your back is turned?"

"I'm afraid you'll run away again!"

"I had my chance to kill you, Gizor," said Roric in a hiss.
"I let you live. You should be thanking all the lords of voima
for your deliverance, not trying to kill me!"

Gizor jerked Roric to his feet by the ropes. Kardan could
see that he had not one but two swords hanging from his
belt. "You killed my best friends and let a woman attack
me from behind."

"And *you*," hissed Roric, "kept me from protecting the
princess. The blood-guilt from her death will all fall on
you."

"You have insulted my honor for the last time, No-man's
son. I shall release the ropes when we reach the island."

They went soundlessly along the ship, past sleeping
warriors. Kardan waited until they were thirty yards ahead
and then rose to follow as quietly as he could.

Gizor and Roric stopped while two of Hadros' warriors
went by, then slipped in silence out of the campsite and
along the riverbank through coils of fog. Kardan, behind
them, kept just far enough back that he hoped they would
not notice his presence.

A half mile downstream from the camp, an island rose
from the river, a great boulder thirty feet high. The fog hid

the fires of the camp. "This will do," said Gizor. He jerked the ropes, though Roric showed no sign of trying to escape, and the two waded out into the water. The tide was out and the river low. Kardan waited until they had reached the island's edge and were scrambling up the rough stone before following them. Neither one looked back.

Off to the east above the fog, the sky was lightening rapidly. Kardan climbed slowly, finding finger- and toe-holds in the uneven surface of the stone, trying not to knock loose pebbles. The strain pulled at his stiff muscles, and his fingers felt clumsy. Karin, he remembered, had always enjoyed climbing as a young girl.

By the time he pushed his head cautiously up to the top, Gizor had freed Roric from the ropes and given him a sword. The young man stretched his arms out fully, then grinned at the man who meant to kill him. He was muscled and lean, almost the same age, Kardan thought, as his own dead son.

The top of the island was twenty feet across and fairly level, bare rock scattered with loose gravel, tufts of grass growing in a few cracks. Kardan tried to find a secure perch from which he could see without being seen. The two warriors stood facing each other in the dawn light, without armor or shield, hefting naked steel.

"Tell me one thing before I kill you, Gizor," said Roric. "Are you my father?"

3

The firepit burned bright in the mountain hall, half cave and half castle. Along both sides men sat sullenly drinking. Every now and then the voice of one or another was raised in joke or curse, but for the most part they drank in silence.

Karin sat against the wall where she had been thrown, trying not to appear as terrified as she felt. No one spoke to her, but some of the warriors looked at her over their ale horns. And then the man with the permanent mocking smile from the scar on his mouth sauntered across the hall to stand before her.

"So, what have we captured here?" he inquired, hands on his hips. The firelight, red behind him, made him dark and almost featureless, a shape and a voice that could have been a wight from Hel.

She forced her voice to be steady. "A princess," she said. "Fate has given you a princess." She had never felt less like a princess in her life, but at the moment it was her only weapon. "You may extract a rich ransom for me, but only if I am unharmed in any way. If I am, all the Fifty Kings will unite to destroy you."

"They haven't united on anything yet," said the man with a harsh laugh. "Except of course outlawing me—that, I hear, they managed just fine at the All-Gemot."

"Who are you?" she asked cautiously. If he was more than a common bandit, someone who actually cared about the All-Gemot, she might live until morning.

"Eirik, *King* Eirik to you. You don't look like a princess to me. You look like a farmer's daughter. And my warriors tell me you fight like a cornered mountain cat." He pulled out a dagger and flipped it into the air, catching it smoothly and flipping it again. She recognized the knife as hers.

"I am Princess Karin, Kardan's daughter, heiress to his kingdom," she said with dignity. Keep him talking, she thought. The longer she could keep him talking the better chance she had. This must be the king who had been outlawed by the All-Gemot for killing a man and hiding the body. In that case, the burned-out castle down in the valley had been his. "Look at my necklace." She reached inside the neck of her dress to pull out the thin chain that she and Roric had intended to give to the Witch of the Western Cliffs in return for information on how to find Valmar.

He grabbed and gave a jerk, breaking the catch, and studied it in the firelight. She furtively rubbed the spot where the chain had dug into her skin before breaking. "Fine workmanship," he said after a moment, almost reluctantly. "Either you really are from a rich family or else you're a thief."

"A thief like you?" she asked, making herself laugh. Judging from the ambush laid for Hadros' ship, into which she and Roric had ridden, he and his men now lived by raiding those who came near his old kingdom.

"Oh, I'm no thief," he answered, sitting down beside her with his legs out before him. He tossed the necklace into her lap.

Karin watched him from the corner of her eye, fearing that to face him fully would be to invite further closeness. He looked much older from close up than his youthful bravado suggested. She couldn't tell if he was really smiling or if it was just the scarred lip. Her hand closed around the necklace casually, to give the impression she hardly cared.

"I am an outlaw according to the Gemot," he went on, "but I am a lover, a poet, a berserk fighter, and a king according to *me*."

"A poet, Eirik?" she asked, her tone deliberately light. "I wouldn't mind hearing one of your poems—if you really do write them!"

He flashed her a dark look from under his brows. "I'll compose a poem about *you*," he said and yelled to one of his men. Karin noticed uneasily that the steady drinking had stopped; the warriors seemed to be following their conversation with interest.

In a moment someone shambled over with a rolled-up piece of dirty cloth that Karin thought looked distinctly unpoetic. When Eirik unrolled it, however, he took out a lyre of smooth dark wood. He slid his hands along its shape a moment as though considering. When he plucked the strings, tuning, the tone was very sweet. "They don't sing songs like this back in *your* kingdom," he said, maybe smiling for real this time.

Karin thought grimly that Queen Arane might feel herself an expert on maneuvering men, but she was quite sure the queen had never had to listen to the poems of a man who might decide at any moment to kill her.

When after a moment Eirik began to sing, his voice was still rough, but there was a deep resonance in it she had not heard before.

> "Swiftly the red-sail sought the dead castle,
> Swiftly from ambush came death-proud warriors,
> Swords and eyes flashing, giving no quarter,
> Hands firm, hearts strong, killing the seamen,
> Led by King Eirik, they slew the invaders,
> Laughed in their faces, came home to the
>   mountain hall,
> High above sea, high above river,
> Carried off a princess of mocking gray eyes,
> She'll ask not to be ransomed, for Eirik's her lover."

At least, thought Karin wildly, he seemed to accept her as a princess.

An appreciative murmur came from the men—their battle already the stuff of song. But the murmur seemed to irritate Eirik. "Is that all you can manage?" he yelled. "You should be celebrating! We killed as many of them as they did of us!" There were shouts of appreciation this time, even a few jokes, that made him square his shoulders as he turned back around.

He rested the lyre on his knees then and turned toward her the face that might—or might not—have been smiling. "So how do *you* like my poem?"

Mocking gray eyes? she thought. If he likes mocking, he can have all he likes. "Well, maybe you are a poet after all, Eirik. But how did a king and berserk warrior do something as dishonorable as conceal a body and get himself outlawed?"

He turned a shoulder sharply to her and started wrapping up the lyre in its cloth again while she wondered, scarcely breathing, if she had gone too far.

"I didn't want to upset a woman," he said after a moment, his voice low and harsh. "I told her he'd gone off raiding to the south. When he didn't come back, I knew she'd believe he thought no more of her, and she'd give up her folly. It would have worked if his brothers hadn't started poking around where they weren't wanted."

Karin thought this over. A woman, *his* woman, had loved someone else, and Eirik had killed his rival to get him out of the way. Only the discovery of the body had revealed the murder.

But where was the woman? Looking around the hall, Karin saw nothing but men, but they must have women here somewhere. In which case, even if she could distract Eirik temporarily, she would not be able to distract a woman ready to knife anyone she considered a rival to *her* king.

"Where is this woman now?" she asked. Might as well find out the worst at once.

"With the rest of them," he answered with another dark look. "Laying out the bodies *your* men killed. If you're a princess, was that your prince on the stallion?" When she did not answer, thinking that whoever Roric's parents were he was no prince of the blood, he added, "You will need to be there at the darkest part of the night when we make the offerings to the lords of death."

Karin was starting to wonder just how happy Eirik's woman could be with him, since he had apparently murdered her lover, when these last words sank in, making her bite her lip to keep from crying out. She took two breaths and then asked carefully, "You do not mean to the lords of voima?"

He held the wrapped-up lyre cradled in his arms. "Of course not. An end is fated even for the lords of voima, but death reigns forever. Even you down in the southern kingdoms know there are no Wanderers in Hel." In spite of the scar, his mouth was most definitely not smiling.

"We offer something of ourselves, of course," she stammered. Keep him talking, she thought desperately. Maybe this was not as bad as it seemed. Maybe it was. "We burn a few hairs to the spirits of those who have died in order to honor them, then make an offering to the lords of voima to thank them for letting our friends live with us beneath the sun. And of course we sing over their graves and drink the funeral ale. But the lords of death are not named among us . . ."

"We, on the other hand," he said, rising to his feet, "name them often, for we send many a proud warrior to them."

"And when you call them," she said, no longer able to conceal her terror, "do they not come?" But he did not answer, only showed his teeth in what might have been a smile and strode away.

Karin shrank back against the wall again. A king already outlawed, so that any man could kill him without blood-guilt falling on him, would have little more to fear from anyone. Her threat to have the Fifty Kings unite against him was hollow. Queen Arane's kind of manipulation was also useless if they planned to sacrifice her tonight to satisfy the appetites of the nameless lords of death.

If Roric was going to rescue her, he had better arrive soon. But his shout had been cut off—was he even alive himself?

Karin clenched her fists. At the worst, she tried to tell herself, she would see him again very soon in Hel. But there was no love in Hel, according to the old stories, and no glory, just as there were no Wanderers. The only love and glory to be found were beneath the sun or in the songs sung when you were gone.

She scanned the hall furtively, looking for a possible escape route. The great doors through which they had entered had been barred behind them; if she made a dash for it, they would be on her before she worked the heavy bars free. Smaller doors led off in several directions, but she did not know where they led and did not want to race blindly through a strange castle with pursuers right on her heels.

She could wait until they all fell asleep, she thought—

several of the warriors had already slumped over—and make her escape then. But the darkest part of the night was coming very soon, the time Eirik said they made their offerings . . .

He was not there for the moment, having passed down the length of the hall and gone through one of the smaller doors—probably to where they were laying out the bodies of the men that Roric and Hadros' men had killed. Could she try her mocking gray eyes on one of these warriors, smile and tease him into taking her off somewhere from which it would be easier to escape? But she rejected this as impractical—as well as revolting. Too many of the warriors were still awake for her to get one aside for private conversation.

She could feign illness, ask to be shown to the women's loft. That way she could leave the hall without immediately having them all in pursuit. She coughed convincingly and rested her forehead in one hand. It did feel feverish.

But as she began a weak gesture of supplication toward one of the warriors watching her, Eirik came back.

He took her wrist and jerked her to her feet, paying no attention to her cough. "The women want to see you," he said and pushed her ahead of him the length of the hall, then through a narrow passage that seemed carved from living rock. The fire in the hall behind them and a flickering red before them were the only light, and she could not see Eirik's face. She stumbled on the rough surface, but his hand on her arm kept her upright.

"Do you want to know what kind of offerings we make to the lords of death?" he asked, a harsh laugh in his voice. "Are you wondering if we slit the throats of living victims, or whether we set them out on the mountaintop for the dragon?"

She was glad he could not see her face. She swallowed twice and managed to answer calmly, even with a chuckle. "Don't tell me a berserk warrior believes in dragons, Eirik. They only appear in the old stories."

But he did not chuckle in return. "You're from the south, Princess," was all he said.

And then they emerged from the passage into a firelit room where six naked bodies were laid out. A woman with stringy black hair down to her waist turned around sharply. Several other women remained bent over the bodies, washing them, but this woman advanced to meet them with a bearing as proud as a queen.

She looked Karin up and down scornfully. Her eyes were an unexpected light green. "So this one claims she is a princess," she said. Karin kept herself from shrinking under that gaze by an effort of will. "But what *I* hear is that you were riding through the rift valley by the dead castle with no companion but one warrior—scarcely an activity for the heiress to a kingdom, Eirik!"

If they put her out on the mountaintop, Karin thought, then she might—just—have a chance to escape before a dragon or whatever creatures of voima inhabited this land came to eat her. But if this woman thought that a princess was trying to take her man away, even a man she might hate herself, Karin would never even have a chance to meet the dragon.

"I was riding with my lover, fleeing those who wished to separate us," she said, her chin high. "If you ask a ransom from my father I am sure he will pay it, and then I shall return to the man I love."

Eirik laughed derisively behind her. "Not likely. A man who eloped with a princess will be an outlaw, not someone to whom a ransomed princess will be likely to return. But here's an idea," he added thoughtfully. "Since he's an outlaw, he'll need to find new brothers. He's a good fighter, as my men can attest, and I'm now short six warriors. How about if both of you join us?"

"Eirik!" cried the woman, stepping up to him with a hand raised as though ready to strike him. She was as tall as he, and her green eyes flashed in the firelight.

But he pulled a knife—Karin's knife—from his belt and showed it to her in his right hand while making a fist with his left. "One more step forward, Wigla," he said quietly, "and I'll give you a choice between these." She stamped her foot in disgust and whirled away from him.

If he could speak of her and Roric joining him, Karin thought while the fingernails bit into her palms, then maybe she was not going to be sacrificed after all to the lords of death. Or maybe he was just mocking her again with this offer.

"Are the bodies ready for the ceremony?" Eirik asked. "It must by now be midnight." He took Karin's arm firmly again. "I'll take her along and send you some of the men to carry the bodies out to the mountainside." He laughed again at the expression that Karin was unable to conceal. There was no more humor in his laughter than there was in his scarred lip. "Not looking forward to meeting the lords of death, is that it, Princess?"

4

When Gizor did not answer him at once, Roric slapped his blade against his palm and said, "If you are my father, tell me at once, for I have no wish to be a patricide, but that is the only thing that will keep your spirit from Hel this morning."

"You are No-man's son," Gizor growled at last. "I have no sons. And if I did, I would kill them rather than know them for oath-breakers who had turned against their sworn lord."

He shifted as he spoke, and Roric, moving to continue facing him, realized the old warrior was maneuvering to put his own back to the sunrise, so that the sun would hit Roric in the eyes—one of those eyes still half swollen shut—when it rose over the eastern cliffs. A misstep here, thirty feet above the river, would be fatal.

And this battle could be fatal even if he survived it. Gizor had three times tried to kill him, and had insulted him far too thoroughly last night for Roric to let him live or his own honor would be gone. And yet that honor would also be destroyed by killing another of Hadros' oath-sworn warriors.

"When the king brought you home," Gizor said almost absently, as though in speaking he hoped to distract Roric while finding his own best position, "it was clear you were the whelp of some housecarl on one of the manors."

Roric, concentrating on the island's surface and moving himself to what he hoped would be a better position, stopped dead. "The king brought me home?" he said in a tight voice. "I always heard I had been found outside the castle gates."

Gizor froze for a second, then shrugged. "King Hadros brought you inside the hall when he found you outside."

But that was not what he had said. Roric stood absolutely still, his jaw clenched. Why had he never considered this before? If he was the son of King Hadros and some serving-girl, the king might well have brought him home to raise as a foster-son, especially since Valmar had not yet been born. How else had the king persuaded his queen to raise a serving-girl's baby herself, except by telling her that he intended to make this baby his heir if she herself could not produce a son? But then Valmar *had* been born, followed by Dag and Nole, and five years ago the queen had died.

He had never felt he knew the queen well once he grew past early childhood, had indeed talked to her but seldom once Valmar was born and he was taken to be raised among the men. Was she the kind of woman who would have taken in her husband's baseborn child? Karin, he thought and almost smiled, most certainly was not.

He did not have a chance to wonder further, for it was then that Gizor attacked.

He came at a rush out of the sunrise, with the yell he told all the young warriors would startle their enemies and even freeze them momentarily. Roric had heard that yell too many times. He braced himself to meet the charge, catching Gizor's sword on his own.

Steel rang on steel, and Roric ducked another blow as

he sprang sideways to get the light out of his eyes. He caught himself six inches from the edge. Hadros' son, he was thinking. I am Hadros' son.

"Who then is *your* father, Gizor?" he shouted mockingly. "I never hear you mention him. Was he some slave brought up with the booty from southern raids?"

Gizor did not answer, instead keeping his sword constantly moving, thrusting, slicing, cutting in great arcs at Roric's unprotected head.

Roric had fought against him in practice dozens, indeed hundreds of times. But he had never known Gizor to fight like this. His steel flashed twice as fast as it ever had then, and he used moves that he had never taught any of the young warriors how to counter, as though he had been saving them in case he ever wanted to kill the men under him. Roric retreated as well as he could on the narrow top of the island, never taking his eyes from the other's sword.

His boots slid on the loose gravel near the edge, but he found his balance and parried another blow. If I am a king's son, he thought, then no one can say I am not worthy of Karin. He grinned and tossed back his hair. "And why do you have no sons, Gizor?" he shouted from a distance of ten feet. "Did the serving-maids always put them out for the wolves rather than raise your get?"

Gizor rushed him, and again he parried the thrust and spun out of the way. So far he was fighting defensively, waiting for the other to tire himself out in fighting a younger man. But he himself was still exhausted from last evening's fight against the raiders who had sprung from among the rocks—the men who now had Karin.

He swung his sword into position to block another blow just in time, almost distracting himself by the thought that he was not just fighting for his own honor, but because he had to be free of Gizor to rescue her.

That is, he had to survive this fight, but King Hadros might still prevent him from rescuing Karin. Son or no son, Hadros could outlaw him for killing the king's sworn men and for running away with Karin, and as an outlaw he could be struck down by any man.

In the meantime, he had to win this fight against a man fighting with uncanny skill and cunning.

If he could get Gizor really angry, he thought, break down that icy efficiency of fighting, he would stand a chance. "Where did you lose your right hand, Gizor?" he yelled. "You always *said* you lost it fighting beside Hadros in the northern kingdoms, but did some serving-girl cut it off for you when you fell asleep drunk after refusing to pay her?"

He dodged and ducked the old warrior's rush, but as he spun away again he thought for a second he saw a face peeking over the edge of the island.

He barely got his sword up in time to block Gizor's next blow. Was this one of the ambushers back again?

"Gizor!" he shouted. "Someone's there!"

The old warrior answered for the first time, never moving his eyes from Roric. "Think I'd fall for a trick I taught you myself?" he asked grimly.

Their swords rang again. Both were bleeding now, and sweat ran down Roric's forehead into his eyes. "No trick!" he yelled. He dodged so that Gizor had to turn, had to look where he himself had looked a moment before.

And Gizor's eyes went past him, and for a second his attention wavered. Roric pressed the advantage, raining down blows, pushing him back. Gizor recovered almost immediately, but he was forced to take another step backward, then another, until he was almost teetering on the edge—

"Yield!" Roric shouted, his sword still ready. "Yield to me so I need not kill another of Hadros' men! Yield so we can both face—"

He never had a chance to finish. Gizor gave a wordless yell and made to plunge forward.

But as he sprang the gravel spun under his feet. He lost his balance and fell hard on his stomach, trying to hold his sword away from him. His feet went over the edge, and he scrambled with his arms for a purchase. Roric rushed forward, but it was too late.

Gizor slid, faster and faster, and with a final yell disappeared backward over the edge. There was a silence for two seconds, then a hard, shattering smack, then a splash.

Roric whirled around to see who was coming up behind him and saw King Kardan. No time to worry why he was here. "Help me get him out of the river," shouted Roric, already scrambling down the way they had climbed up. "He may still be alive, and no one will say I stood and watched him drown."

"No one will say that, of a certainty," said Kardan darkly. Full sunlight came over the eastern cliffs as they reached the base of the island. There was blood on a jumble of sharp stones just above the waterline, and the water itself was running red—no difficulty in finding the body. As Roric reached under the surface and took hold of a handful of tunic, he agreed silently with Kardan—it was quite clear that Gizor had not drowned.

And now he had the blood-guilt of three of Hadros' men on him and no way to pay it.

They carried Gizor's body back to camp between them. "One more for the burial mound," Roric commented grimly. "And the best songs will be sung of *him*."

Gizor might not have been his father, but he was the man who had taught him most of the warfare he knew. He had been bound by honor to kill him, but what honor could there be in killing a man, even a ferocious and ruthless man, who was his own king's—and maybe father's—sworn man?

Roric kept expecting King Kardan to say something, to accuse him of being responsible for his daughter's capture, of challenging him to immediate single combat himself without even giving him a chance to recover his breath. But all the king said was, "Now that it's light, those bandits can't hide from us."

When they reached the campsite, the warriors had donned their armor and Hadros, face purple, was giving orders to those who would stay behind to guard the ship. Kardan stepped up to the other king at once, even before he had a chance to react to the sight of Gizor's battered body. "Gizor gave the challenge," he said, "and they reached the outcome in single combat. I was witness, and I will swear on steel and rowan that Roric killed him honorably and indeed gave him the opportunity to yield."

So he must have been watching the whole time, thought Roric. He lowered Gizor to the ground beside the other dead warriors—the worst of the wounded had also died in the night. Everyone else stepped back to leave a broad empty space around him. No one would want to associate with a man carrying that much blood-guilt.

And then, completely unexpectedly, a young woman stepped up beside him. Roric looked at her wildly, his first thought that she must be a wight or creature of voima, for no elegantly dressed woman, wearing golden bracelets and a jeweled pendant on her forehead, should be here among the warriors.

But the others glanced at her as though they too could see her and her presence was perfectly explicable. Had she been here last night? His memories of last night, once Karin had been seized and Gizor struck him, were at best confused.

She stood for a moment considering him, head cocked, as though she found him fascinating. No one else was near. "It's hard to see for certain," she said almost under her breath, "through the grime and blood, but yes, there are certain indications there . . ." She smiled then at his expression. "You don't know who I am." He saw now that she was not nearly as young as he had first supposed, in spite of her curling chestnut hair and slim figure. "I am Queen Arane."

"Oh, yes," he said, trying to be polite. Since he could not think how to put his question diplomatically, to demand what in the name of the Wanderers she was doing here, he did not ask. "Karin has mentioned you to me."

"But I know who *you* are. You are Roric, called No-man's son. And the Princess Karin loves you."

"Not No-man's son," he said between stiff lips. If it was true, he should start claiming his real name now. "I think— I think I am King Hadros' son."

For a second she looked very distressed. "He said this to you?"

"No," shaking his head. "He does not know—not yet— that I have guessed."

The queen laughed, a small laugh that was almost sad. "I am very sorry to have to disappoint you. But do not say anything to the king of this. For I know him, and I can tell you quite decidedly that you are not his son."

Roric closed and opened his eyes. It would not have made much difference anyway. "But I am still Karin's lover." He looked up toward the mountains, the sharp stones and cliffs bathed in morning light. Hadros' warriors were ready to start, the hounds leashed now and sniffing excitedly at the ground. "If she is still alive."

CHAPTER TEN

1

Mist lay over the midnight mountainside. The moon had already set, and burning torches on either side only made the landscape darker. Karin tried to pick out landmarks or at least determine which way was south, back toward the river and her father, but it was impossible.

The door through which they had emerged was at the end of a long tunnel cut into the rock, and the transition out into the cold night air—Eirik peering around carefully before motioning to the torchbearers behind him to follow—had come like a slap after the smoky hall. They seemed now to be near the bottom of a deep dish-shaped depression. A pool lay before them, steaming and reeking with sulphur.

"Some say that Hel lies at the bottom of this pool," said Eirik, holding her arm more firmly than ever. She could picture rather than see the mocking sneer of his scarred lip. "Do you believe it, Princess?"

Behind them, the rest of the warriors emerged from the tunnel, some supported by their comrades as they reeled from ale, followed by the women, and last of all six men carrying the naked bodies of the slain.

They arranged the bodies, feet together, on a relatively level surface of stone near the steaming pool. Eirik released Karin then, but the tall green-eyed woman immediately took hold of her arm, and her grip was even stronger.

The outlaw king took first a basket of barley from one of the other women and sprinkled it liberally on the bodies. Next he took an ale horn and slopped some ale on each of their faces. There had been total silence at first among the warriors, but at this several of them chuckled, and one said, "That's right, he always did like his drink."

But when someone handed Eirik his lyre everyone again fell silent. I have as long to live as it takes to sing the warriors' praises, thought Karin. Her heart was pounding so hard that the woman must surely feel it through her arm.

He plucked the strings for a moment, a dark shape under a clouded midnight sky, then began to sing. His voice resonated over the mountains until it seemed the stones themselves vibrated.

> "In fearsome fighting six have fallen,
> Overcoming foes when dread death found them.
> Brave in battle, honored by brothers,
> Enemies in Hel will grovel before them.
> Ferocious their war cries, swift their swords,
> Yet fate ended their stories as it ends all men's.
> Welcome them, Death! Welcome our brothers,
> Make room for them in Hel's dusty hall.
> Gone from the sunlands, yet not from our songs,
> Remembered wherever the fighting is fiercest."

When he ended his song, there was a moment of stillness in which a few low voices could have been the sound of the wind. Then, at a gesture from the king, the men holding the torches took them to the steaming pool and plunged them beneath the surface. There was a great hissing, a cascade of sparks, and then the mountainside was almost completely dark.

The woman beside Karin spoke into the silence, so unexpectedly that she jumped involuntarily. "We call on the lords of death," the woman said in a deep voice. "We call on those who take whomever fate strikes down. Come, powers beyond voima! Come, nameless ones of the night!"

"We call. We call. We call on them," went voices up and down the hollow.

"We call the lords of death," cried the woman, "to take our brothers, to strike down those who struck them down, and to drink and eat what is offered!"

Karin stood immobile, not sure if she could have moved even if the woman had released her arm. Her heart was bitterly cold within her as she waited for what must surely happen next.

And then there came a soft blurping noise, something very familiar although she could not at once identify it, a sound like— It was the sound a stewpot made when on a low boil. The steaming, sulphurous pond at the bottom of the hollow was beginning to bubble.

She strained wildly to see and thought she could glimpse through the starless darkness the pond rising, a wave breaking up out of it, slithering up onto the surface of the stone as though alive— Someone yelled and jumped, brushed by boiling water, but the rest shushed him instantly.

The wave fell back into the pond, but the splash itself gave a dull boom, a sound that could have been a voice, a voice saying, "We come."

"No man escapes you," called the tall woman, her voice ringing and echoing off the encircling mountains. "No woman evades you. Dark death below, we make offering to honor you!"

This must be it at last, thought Karin, closing her eyes, the moment when they slit her throat.

But instead she heard again the blurping of the boiling pond, then a lapping of waves. Images flashed across the inside of her eyelids as though she was seeing into someone else's dream: bones, dried blood, skulls with nothing left but the hair. Against her will she opened her eyes to see a little stream of water, running uphill against nature, moving slowly toward the dead men. And then the mist became thicker, and even the stream was hidden. For several minutes there was no sound but a constant lapping of waves. A final belch, then, and the pond went still, though its rising steam continued to thicken the mists of night.

No one moved or spoke. The scent of fear was strong in the hollow, and the only sound was the wind and the faintest creaks as the warriors shifted then again went motionless. Then someone, Karin thought Eirik, broke away from the rest and opened the door back into the castle. Light from a torch within laid a path of brightness across the stony hollow to the pool. The bodies were gone, leaving only a single arm band lying at the edge.

Though everyone pushed each other in desperate haste at the narrow doorway, still no one spoke. The green-eyed woman held Karin back until all the others had passed through. When the door slammed behind them at last, several of the warriors let out their breaths loudly, and the woman released Karin's arm.

As they all stumbled back toward the firelit hall, she found the outlaw king beside her. "So, how did you like your first meeting with the lords of death?" he said mockingly, though none of the rest of his men had yet spoken. "I realize now that something I may have said could have made you think you were about to be killed yourself! I must apologize, Princess, if our rough ways caused you any distress."

She whirled in the narrow passage, furious and nearly in tears, and slapped him hard across the face. "How dare you!" she cried. "How dare you terrify me like that and then come to me with these false apologies, when it was all deliberate!"

He grabbed her by the wrist and twisted her arm until she cried out. "Mountain cat, my men called you," he said between his teeth. "Good term. But maybe I can make it up to you!" He jerked her to him and kissed her hard, though she tried to turn her head aside. "Wouldn't you rather have a king for your lover than some young warrior?"

She drove a knee toward his midsection, but he twisted out of the way. "I can see this one will take a little taming!" he said with a laugh, twisting her arm again.

She took a deep, sobbing breath and went limp. Queen Arane was right. It was no use trying to use strength against a strong man—especially when it only excited him.

Her sudden slump surprised him. "Please, I need to go to the women's loft," she said through entirely unfeigned tears. "I am with child, and I fear this has— I need the women to help me now."

He let go of her at once and squinted at her suspiciously, then took her arm again, much more gently this time. "Come on, then." The green-eyed woman was waiting at the end of the passage. She gave the king a very bitter look as he handed Karin to her, mumbling something about women's troubles. She then marched Karin off before her, down more narrow stone passages, deep into the castle.

The room into which they emerged was a little warmer than most of the castle, for a brisk fire burned in the center. High up in the wall tiny windows opened onto black night. Here were the castle's other women, though they drew back as she entered.

At least I am safe from Eirik for tonight, Karin thought, falling exhaustedly into the straw the green-eyed woman ungraciously offered her. The woman had asked her nothing about her supposed troubles—and she was too tired to wonder if she really might be with child. If she continued to try to resist Eirik, at best she would have her arm broken, but if she tried to pretend affection for him this woman with the green eyes would kill her without compunction.

A castle that had frequent contact with the lords of death, she thought as sleep claimed her, would not care very much about the death of one young woman.

She awoke before dawn, to find the fire burned down to coals and the windows high above her slightly lighter squares in a gray wall, through which a chilling wind blew. Fate had not meant then for her to die this night. As she leaned on her elbows, rubbing her forehead with her knuckles, she heard the straw rustle at the far side of the room and saw Eirik's tall woman sitting up to glare at her. Around them, the rest of the castle's women were sound asleep.

The woman rose and motioned to her. Not knowing what this meant but not daring to disobey, Karin rose too and followed her out into the passage outside the room.

Here it was even colder. She shivered, hugging herself with her arms and trying to avoid the desperate, closed-in feeling she had—usually—been able to overcome in the faeys' tunnels.

There was just enough light for Karin to see the woman combing straw out of her stringy hair with her fingers. "What do you want of us? Why did you really come here to Eirik's castle?" she demanded in a fierce whisper.

"I already told you," Karin said resignedly. She too kept her voice low. "My lover and I were fleeing the king he used to serve. We did not even know all of you were here." When the woman kept silent, as though to suggest that she did not believe her, Karin added a little more firmly, "Are you afraid then that I came here to steal Eirik from you, an outlaw and a murderer who feels he has a right to every woman he sees? Did you think a princess would be interested in *that*?"

The woman took a sharp breath. "Maybe not," she said after a brief pause, "but a princess and her lover would not choose the northern end of the Fifty Kingdoms if all they were seeking was safety. They would take a ship and go south, down to where the summers are warm and the booty is rich and unprotected, and no dragons lurk in the mountains."

"That's right, Wigla," said Karin, thinking rapidly. "It *is* Wigla, isn't it? Isn't that what he called you? Your sight is keen to know we have further reason to be here. But I too have keen sight. And I know that last year you and one of Eirik's men planned to leave here and go south, to start over again far from this death-filled realm."

Karin could hear the woman's breath hiss between her teeth, but she did not stop. "When Eirik told you *he* had abruptly left to go raiding, you persuaded yourself at first that he was seeking booty to make himself worthy of you, but you should always have known better. Your lover's brothers found his body—hidden, his spirit never celebrated in song and none of the sacrifices made for him, either to death or to voima."

She was rapidly reaching the end of what she could guess easily and was wondering desperately what she could say had happened next; maybe the castle by the salt river had been burned by enemies, requiring the move to this mountain hideout. But the woman's hands closed around her neck, ending either the need or the ability for further speech. "How did you know this? Did he tell you?" she said hoarsely, as though the words were dragged from her.

Karin put a hand up as though casually and worked a thumb between her own neck and the woman's palm. "Don't be surprised," she said when she could breathe again. "I told you I had keen sight. I tell you this only to demonstrate my abilities to you so you will understand what I shall next tell you. I also know, with my same sight, that there is near here a doorway into the Wanderers' realm."

Wigla had lowered her hands, and Karin heard her shuffling her feet, though whether in embarrassment or suppressed anger she could not tell. "The Wanderers do not come here," she said in a surly mutter. "There's nothing but death—and the dragon."

Karin did not like this repeated mention of a dragon. "Then I see more than you do," she said with an attempt at confidence. "But this I *can* tell you, and I think you will agree. If I leave here, to find my lover—whom Eirik's men left behind when they captured me—and then to find the door into the realm of voima, then I shall not be here. And *he* makes your life an agony as it is—I do not need very keen sight to see that! How much more agony would it be to see him constantly comparing you to a younger princess—especially since that princess spurns him?"

"We had already been on the edge of being outlawed for years," Wigla said, still in that mutter. "A life of raiding grows thin, as you'll see if you stay here. What are you suggesting instead?"

Karin found herself glancing over her shoulder, wondering if Eirik too might be up early and coming to see his woman—or women. "Let me out of the castle," she said. "Then I'll be gone. Tell Eirik I escaped in the night, tell him it's his own fault for not posting better guards."

The woman scowled, then abruptly made a sound that might have been a chuckle. "I think I can find things myself to tell him."

"Then you'll let me go?" asked Karin, trying not to sound as eager as she felt.

"Maybe," said Wigla, almost reluctantly. Dawn was advancing rapidly, and Karin could now see the green eyes glinting fiercely. "Tell me first how you expect to find this doorway to the Wanderers. I am not at all sure whether to believe you, Princess."

The Mirror-seer had better be right about this, Karin thought. "The doorway is hidden," she improvised, "only open or even visible at certain times. There is only one person who knows how to find it, and that is the Witch of the Western Cliffs."

For a long moment Wigla did not answer, and Karin wondered wildly if she herself might be called a witch. But when she answered it was almost agreeably. "Well, if you and your keen sight can find her, maybe you will find this doorway. But she may demand more than you care to pay!"

"Oh, I can pay," said Karin airily, keeping imminent despair from her voice. Her fingers closed over the broken necklace in her belt pouch with the sick feeling that it would not be nearly enough.

"Then come," said Wigla. For a moment she smiled, a

slow, almost sardonic smile, that Karin tried to persuade herself was an expression of sympathy and understanding. Then she turned and led the way down the corridor, stepping carefully, almost soundlessly.

Karin decided that when she emerged on the mountainside she would determine south from the sun and try to find her way back down to the river.

That is, unless the dragon was real and found her first.

2

"Yes, of course we were running from you," said Roric in an expressionless voice. They had paused in their climb and leaned against the rocks while the dogs tried to pick up the scent again. The two kings were on either side of him, not exactly holding him captive, not exactly letting him walk freely.

"Valmar left to join the Wanderers before I reached your kingdom," Roric said to Kardan. "When I appeared there— with you, Hadros, right behind me—Karin feared you would not believe us. That is why we had to go after him immediately, before you could stop us, before you could tell us we were only chasing old stories."

"This doesn't sound to me yet like an excuse for stealing a ship," growled Hadros. "You'll keep the Gemot occupied for days."

But Kardan interrupted. "What *were* you chasing?"

"We had to rescue Valmar, of course." Roric did not tell them he had let Karin persuade him he could also best preserve his own life in flight. His honor was already in tatters as it was. "The Weaver said there is a door to the Wanderers' realm somewhere here in the Hot-River Mountains."

"And you believed him?" demanded Hadros.

"I certainly believe in the Wanderers' realm," said Roric quietly. "After all, I've been there."

"And why should *you* go there safely, but not my son?"

Roric turned to face Hadros fully. He really did not resemble the solidly built king, he thought—being his son had been nothing more than a brief dream to help him overcome Gizor. "It's all changed now. I never met the real Wanderers. Valmar may have, but according to the Seer they plan to send him to Hel . . ."

"And maybe Hel is the best place for *you*," said Hadros, mostly under his breath. "I'll tell you one thing, Roric. After we rescue the princess—we know they won't have killed an attractive young woman like that—we're going straight home so you can face the Gemot. No fooling around here looking for doors into the land of voima."

They were interrupted by the abrupt baying of the dogs, who seemed to have found Karin's scent again. All of them hurried after the sound, up a steep little path almost hidden behind a boulder. Roric kept trying to look ahead, to see the fortress where they would have her, but saw nothing but bare stone.

Karin, Karin, he thought, seeing her smile in his mind's eye, her russet hair half hiding her eyes as she laughed at something he had said. If he thought of her this intensely then surely her spirit must hear him, and she must give him some indication of where they had her hidden. But he reminded himself that even when she lay in his arms it was hard to know her thoughts—so much harder therefore now, when he was not certain, in spite of the reassurances they all kept trying to give each other, that she still lived.

The morning had started clear, but thin high clouds came out of the west to filter the sunlight and chill the wind. Roric's muscles all ached from his fight with Gizor, and climbing and knocking against the rocks caused several wounds again to start bleeding. Loose stones underfoot kept turning, threatening to sprain an ankle or, worse, to crush a foot.

Sometimes they seemed to be following a path where stones had been arranged to form steps leading up narrow defiles barely as wide as a man's shoulders, but at other

times they scrambled over lichen-grown boulders that gave
no sign that anyone had ever come this way. At every turn
where there seemed more than one way to go, the kings
sent some of their men in each direction. Very quickly Roric
lost all sense of direction, seeking only to find a way upward.
Kardan and Hadros started quarreling about which direction was best, and after a few minutes started resolutely in
opposite directions. The dogs' voices echoed so that it was
harder and harder to tell where they had gone.

Roric dragged himself up onto a high dome of rock and
suddenly realized that he was alone. Without even meaning to he had eluded both kings and all their warriors, who
must be scattered now over several square miles of rock.

He sat for a moment, breathing hard and looking around.
From his perch he could look back toward the rift valley
and see Hadros' longship, looking impossibly small at this
distance, pulled up beside the salt river. In the opposite
direction, to the north, smooth-sided, nearly vertical mountains rose from the rubble through which he had been
climbing, their peaks lost in the clouds. Over to the west
the rocks were high and jumbled; they must drop abruptly
into the sea beyond.

And then he picked out motion on those rocks. For a
second he thought it must be one of the dogs, separated
from the rest, but it appeared to be human. One of the
warriors, he thought, but there was no glint from helmet
or mail. And the hair, even at this distance, looked blond
tinged with russet.

Karin! She had escaped somehow! No one seemed near
her, not Hadros' men, not the raiders. She was over close
to the western cliffs, working her way rapidly southward
back toward the rift valley, having emerged from somewhere among the rocks nearer the sea. She did not appear
to have spotted him.

He shouted but his voice was carried away by the wind,
and the tiny hurrying figure gave no sign that she had heard.
Roric strained his eyes looking for a line among the rocks

that would intersect with her path, that would take him to her.

He heard then voices yelling for him, Hadros' bellow among them, but the echoes made the voices bounce all around, and he could not have been sure which direction to go even had he wanted to obey. His stiffness forgotten, he started scrambling down, trying to keep his eye on Karin at the same time.

He paused abruptly, fingernails scraping at lichen. Very high up on the vertical mountain face, far above where it should be possible to climb, was another human figure. Roric closed and opened his eyes but the figure was still there. It appeared to be wearing a broad-brimmed hat.

Before he could react he saw something else that made him forget entirely about the figure. Closer, emerging from the rocks a few hundred yards behind Karin, came the long green head and neck of a dragon.

Unable to help her, almost unable to move, he stared as the creature worked its way out from between the boulders. It had the long, heavily muscled neck of a snake, scales glinting gold and green. The neck kept growing and growing before his horrified eyes as he realized how enormous the creature must be. The other warriors too had seen it, for the shouts from the scattered men abruptly took on a note of wild panic, clear even though he could not hear their words.

A long forked tongue dangled from the dragon's mouth, open to show the rows of needle teeth. The mouth was wide enough to snap up three warriors at once, and those teeth were longer than any spear. Fringed ears flapped above eyes that glowed like fire, eyes that looked about alertly as though in search of something to eat. Behind, far behind the head, a clawed foot emerged, pushing the serpent slowly toward Karin.

✳   ✳   ✳

3

She turned, hearing the scrape of scales on stone, and saw the dragon not a hundred feet behind her.

In a horrified second she took in the intelligent, burning eyes, the huge leathery wings folded down the back, the slow-moving neck and body, and the jaws that looked as though they could snap together very quickly around something soft and tasty.

She began to run, down the raiders' track toward the salt river, holding up her skirt and taking huge, desperate breaths. The track zigzagged, descended, doubled back on itself so that for a few seconds she was actually approaching the dragon again from lower down the slope. Muscles rippling in its neck, it lowered its head toward her.

Then the track doubled around again. She sprang up and over a boulder in the path and kept wildly running. When her legs had to slow for a series of rough steps, she looked back to see the dragon lowering itself sideways down the slope, its clawed feet tumbling the rocks Eirik and his men must have carefully levered into walls. She was running as fast as she could and it moved deliberately, not even having unfolded its wings, but its slow pace was still more rapid than hers.

Now she raced down a straight stretch, and a glance over her shoulder showed it gaining on her, sliding and scraping along the stones, its mouth open in anticipation. Faint cries came to her on the wind, so others must have spotted the dragon too, but she had no time to look for them.

She could not dodge it, and she was not going to be able to outrun it. The track turned sharply, away from the edge of a rock slide. Her only hope was to find a crevice narrow enough that the dragon could not follow. Karin sprang forward and over the edge, launching herself down a stone face so steep she immediately regretted it. She slid more and more rapidly, just managing to keep herself vertical, bouncing off stones in her path and grabbing at the stunted bushes that grew among the rocks to slow her slide.

At least, she thought, she would be dead before the dragon began to eat her.

She smacked feet-first into a dense brush and came abruptly to a halt. She looked up wildly to see the dragon's fiery eye peering over the edge of the cliff she had just come down. Before her was a narrow crevice, narrower— maybe—than the dragon's head. She plunged into it head-first. It was pitch black, but her fear of what it might conceal was nothing compared to the needle teeth behind her.

The floor of the crevice was unexpectedly smooth to her scraped hands and knees. Karin crawled rapidly, deeper in, around several sharp curves. This was more than a crevice; this was a tunnel. Behind her came a rattling noise that sounded like the gnashing of long teeth. Karin crawled even faster. Daylight was completely gone and so, she hoped, was any chance that the serpent's head could reach her.

She stopped at last, sobbing with fear and exhaustion. No wonder Wigla had given her such a strange look when agreeing to let her out of the castle. She had known that the potential rival for Eirik would be gone even more surely than she had expected. Karin could still hear a distant, echoing scraping and snuffling, but after a moment the sound seemed to move off.

She took a long breath then and leaned back against the strangely smooth stone wall, trembling and weak. In the distance she heard more shouts, muffled from where she was, then a horrible shriek abruptly cut off. Later, maybe tonight, she would try emerging from this crevice, try again to find her way back to the river, to see if the dragon had eaten Hadros and all his men.

And then, staring into blackness, she thought she could see a faint green light. For a second that light brought back visits to the faeys' burrows, of conversations with beings who accepted her as she was, neither demanding her love nor seeking her life.

She shook her head sadly and blinked to get rid of that deceptive green light, but it was still there. This was strange. For a moment she thought it must be daylight filtered through green plants, but the faint sounds that accompanied that light were not the sounds of the outside world. They sounded like high voices.

Not daring to believe, she began crawling forward again. The light grew stronger, the voices more clear. "I tell you I heard somebody! You just heard the dragon! But this was somebody breathing, and I know what the dragon's breath sounds like! Well, why don't you go look then?"

The green light was approaching her, bobbing as though being carried, though the source was still hidden by a curve in the tunnel. And suddenly she came around the corner face-to-face with someone her size.

Both of them gave startled cries and pulled back. "I did hear someone!" the being before her shouted, crawling backward rapidly. "And it's got blood on it!"

"Wait! Don't go!" she said, holding out a hand. "I won't hurt you. I just got scraped on the rocks and bushes coming down the cliff. Are you—are you a faey?"

It couldn't be a faey, she thought; he was much too big. But he stopped his retreat, picked up the lamp again, and squinted at her. "What do you know of faeys?"

"Back in the southern kingdoms," she said—of course everyone in Hadros' lands considered themselves to be in the northern kingdoms, but up here *everything* else was south—"I was a friend of the faeys." After a moment she added, "They tamed me."

"It's a tame mortal!" he called excitedly over his shoulder, then added reluctantly, "Or so she says."

"That's right," she said eagerly. She had no idea what faeys were doing here, especially such large ones, but faeys meant safety.

He called back over his shoulder again, answering excited

questions while keeping a careful eye on her. But at last he said, "As long as you're here, would you like to wash off the blood? And would you like something to eat?"

Karin groped out of the tunnels by the insufficient light of the faeys' lamps. Since it was now night, they reassured her, the dragon would have retreated to its lair and would no longer be a problem. "We never can understand why you mortals insist on being outside during daylight. Daylight is dangerous!" they told her.

And climbing around in the night was also dangerous. But there should be a moon for at least the early part of the night, she thought, and maybe, somehow, by morning she could find her way back to the salt river—that is, if the ship was even still there, if any of the men were still alive. Eirik and his men had, after all, taken her up to their fortress in no more than half an hour; all she had to do was find the path.

She felt strangely heartened by her day with the faeys. They had rubbed herbal pastes on her scrapes and bruises and fed her mountain blueberries. They might be almost as big as mortals up here in the north, but they were still the eager and easily worried beings she had first known as a girl. If beings like this could exist even here, within a short distance of a dragon, then safety might not be as illusory as she sometimes feared.

Either that, or security by its very nature was only to be found in tiny pockets in the midst of danger.

Someone was standing just outside the tunnel. He stood quietly, silhouetted against the moonlit sky, a sword in his hand.

The faeys were instantly gone and their light with them, fading away back into their tunnel without a sound. Karin remained on hands and knees, just back from the entrance, considering. Whoever it was, he did not seem to notice her. He shifted, raising his head as though listening, then again took his waiting pose.

Her choices were to retreat with the faeys, she thought, spending perhaps many more days in their tunnels, or to come out and face whoever this was. If it was one of Hadros' men, she should be safe with him. Eirik was a different consideration. But would Eirik be waiting quietly outside a faeys' tunnel?

She could not stay underground forever, in spite of dragons and renegade kings. She felt at her belt, then remembered her knife was gone. Shaking her head, she rose to her feet anyway and came out of the tunnel.

And saw as he whirled toward her that it was Roric. She almost collapsed with relief as his arms went around her.

"The lords of voima be praised," he murmured after a moment, drawing his lips back from hers. "I didn't dare hope the Wanderers would save you."

"I saved myself," she said a little testily, even while pressing herself close against him. "The Wanderers had nothing to do with it. The last one I've seen is the one who took Valmar."

"There is one here, up on the mountain. But did the raiders harm you, Karin?" kissing her scraped forehead.

"No—all my wounds came from escaping the dragon. I think their leader was planning to ransom me, but his woman helped me escape." She would tell him later about Eirik and Wigla.

"How did you get into the crevice?"

"I crawled in," she said in surprise. "There are faeys in there, large faeys. How did you find me?"

He still held her to him, rocking slowly back and forth. "I was fairly high up, watching. I saw you appear this morning, then saw the dragon coming. I was much too far away to do anything—by the Wanderers, Karin, you can't know how terrible that was! But I marked where you disappeared, and when the dragon moved off—I didn't know even creatures of voima could be that enormous!—I found the way to bring me here. When I discovered no blood and none of your clothing or hair, I even hoped you might have crawled into this crevice."

"Then why did you not follow me?"

"I've always said there is voima about you, Karin," he murmured, his lips in her hair. "I could see the crevice, its smooth walls, its flat sandy floor, but I could not enter. It was as though the air in the entrance had turned to glass. My only hope then was that you *were* there, that you were safe, and that somehow you would come out to me."

Karin looked in surprise at the shadowed crevice, then shrugged. The faeys had always had the ability to protect themselves but she did not have time to think about them further. "And the others?"

"The dragon ate somebody—I think one of Hadros' men, though I was too far away to see. I can understand someone allowing a troll to live under his bridge, Karin, but to keep a dragon as your doorkeeper!"

"They give honor to the lords of death," she said in a small voice. The person eaten could have been herself. But whoever it was, if it was one of Hadros' warriors she had known him. The days when she had managed the king's household, making sure the food was prepared and the ale brewed, seemed so distant they could have happened to somebody else.

"The dragon seemed to satisfy its hunger with just one man," said Roric. He drew back and looked at her in the moonlight. "This has been your expedition from the beginning, and if they ever make a song of it you will be at the center. Your own voima protected us as we came north, and here you escaped both raiders and a serpent. At the moment all I have is my sword and you—I don't even have my horse, not that he'd be much use now. So you tell me. Your father and Hadros must still be looking for you. Do we go home with them— Hadros intends to bring me up before the Gemot to answer for the blood-guilt on me—or do we keep on trying to find Valmar?"

"Find Valmar, of course. We haven't come all this distance to let him be sent to Hel."

"Well," said Roric with a low chuckle, "at this rate we may be seeing him there soon."

They scrambled westward across the rock scree, their way lit by the shifting and deceptive blue light of the moon. It has hard to tell distances, to distinguish between a hole and a shadow, and Roric was more awkward on a steep surface than she in spite of his much greater strength. But they gradually worked their way up and down boulders, paths, and crevices until they reached a vantage point from which they could see the stars glinting on the uneasy surface of the sea.

They sat for a moment on the rocks, catching their breaths and looking at the moon. "Wigla—the woman who helped me escape from the raiders' fortress—seemed to know about the Witch of the Western Cliffs," said Karin. "So she must live somewhere near here."

"Your Mirror-seer then directed us truly," commented Roric, which she herself did not yet entirely believe. "Where would a witch live? In a cave?"

"Look!" said Karin, pointing onward. Just a short distance beyond them, near where the stone scree dropped away in cliffs to the sea, was a spot of light. It looked like firelight, from a fire deep in the rocks, and from it thin smoke was rising.

"That wouldn't be the raiders again?" asked Roric cautiously.

"No, no," said Karin confidently. "Eirik's fortress is far behind us. It must be the witch's cave." She jumped to her feet, then added slowly, "I hope we have what she wants us to pay her."

The moon was sinking, but there was still enough light for them to scramble the last quarter mile toward the red glow. When they reached it they discovered they were looking down something of a chimney, a gap in the rocks through which they could see a fire burning far below.

"There must be an entrance somewhere near here," said Karin, smiling to herself when she realized she was thinking of the Witch of the Western Cliffs as being something like one of the faeys. "Let's try over there; it looks like another opening."

This opening did not really resemble a doorway, but at least it was not a chimney. "Should we just go right in?" said Roric, peering in. A tunnel led downward at a sharp angle. They could just see a light glowing faintly.

Karin felt gripped by a sudden strange reluctance, but she pushed it forcibly away. This was no time to let her dislike for closed passages influence her. "Yes!" she said, not giving herself time to hesitate. "We'll go right in." She crawled determinedly forward, Roric at her heels.

As they left the outer world behind, she expected to come almost immediately face-to-face with a witch, but instead the passage led them down into a broad room, burrowed out among the rocks. At the moment it seemed empty, in spite of the fire at this end. It was so tall and so wide that the far side was lost in darkness.

But there was a faint sound from the far side, not a voice, almost a rumble. Roric looked at her questioningly. This was no time for cowardice, she told herself. She took his hand for reassurance and started forward toward that sound. But they had walked only a short distance when she stumbled.

They were wading through piles of something small and hard, pebbles, she thought at first until she reached down to pick one up. It was a gold coin.

They both stopped then to look around. In the fire's faint light they could see they stood on top of an entirely unexpected and almost unimaginable heap of treasure. There were precious stones here, both in worked jewelry and unset, heaps of coins, golden helms, swords gleaming through half-decayed leather sheaths.

Could this be Eirik's treasure house? she wondered. But even a renegade, outlawed king who commanded treasure like this would not have to run for long.

And the next thing she saw was a human bone.

The sound from the far, dark side of the room became louder. Whatever was there seemed to have heard their approach and be coming to meet them with a combination of rumbling and rattling, laid over a steady scrape.

"We may be visiting the lords of death even sooner than we expected, my sweet," said Roric, low in her ear. "This isn't the cave of any witch. This is the dragon's lair."

4

"Did the Wanderers tell you they created those creatures of the third force?" the young woman asked Valmar.

He had been dozing, her head on his shoulder, and it took a few seconds for her words to reach him. But then he rolled around to look at her, propping himself up on an elbow. "Created them? No! But—they told me they wanted them overcome. I don't believe you."

She smiled at the irritated note in his voice. "If you had asked, they would have told you. I do not lie."

"You are still trying to distract me from serving them," Valmar replied, removing his arm from around her waist.

"Whose idea was it to go deep into the woods as soon as we met again and to remove our armor?" she said with a teasing light in her eyes. "But think of this, Valmar Hadros' son. When we met before, they never scolded you, did they? So you continued to serve them. But now you serve me as well."

"I cannot serve you and the Wanderers both," he said warily, sitting up now.

"The last time we met you said you would not fight against them," she said, sitting up herself. The sunset was behind her, shadowing her features. "Do you not realize that in fighting those beings at the top of the hill you will be fighting the Wanderers' own creation?"

Valmar, feeling weariness, shame, and a renewed desire

for her, said only, "The lords of voima told me that they do not create."

She laughed at this and put out a hand to touch his knee. "And they do not. Or if they do, it is only creatures like those, mockeries of men, hollow beings with no backs."

Valmar went still, his objections frozen on his lips. Her words made sense at last of something the Wanderers had told him which had made no sense at the time, that their attempts at creation were now hastening their end. He did not want to be arguing with this woman anyway—he wanted to be holding her close, kissing her, feeling her muscular body against his. Or else he should be pushing her aside, rising with his eyes fixed on the path of honor. "The man I saw, just a little while ago," he attempted. "He had a back."

"Or wanted you to think he did. In the lands of voima it is easier to mislead a mortal's eye than in mortal realms."

"And do *you* create?"

She smiled saucily at him. "I would have thought you knew that. Women create life within themselves. Men can create nothing."

He leaned his chin on his fists, considering. He still, when he could be calm, was not sure what to make of this lady of voima, who seemed both to be a human woman and to be possessed of a detachment and wisdom he felt could not have come in just a few more years' maturity than his. "Women need men to create life," he said with a frown, wondering as he spoke if even something so basic might be different here in the land of endless sunset. Then, "Have *you* ever borne children?"

She went sober, shaking her head.

"Is that because you have separated yourself from the lords of voima?"

When she did not answer at once, Valmar started reaching distractedly for his clothes, slowly coming to the horrible realization that he had lain with a woman meant for the

Wanderers. They could not have known, before, where he had gone for so many hours, but what explanation could he give them now if he did not fulfill his mission, led astray by this woman never intended for him?

"Or they have separated themselves from *us*," she said quietly when he had nearly given up on receiving an answer.

"Who *are* you?" he demanded, pausing in tying his laces.

Again she answered very quietly, sitting with her arms wrapped around a naked knee. "We are the Hearthkeepers. We stayed behind when the Wanderers left us. It is now almost the end of their fated rule, the time we should overthrow them, except—" She paused for a moment, and when she went on it was almost as though she was changing the subject. "We have voima within us, certainly, but if our full powers were going to return I would have thought to see them by now. Sometimes I even wonder if we've made a mistake . . ."

She seemed so sad suddenly, so vulnerable and unlike an immortal being, that Valmar put his arms comfortingly around her. But a thought teased at him. He did not *think* he had ever gotten any of the serving-maids with child, but might he have done so with this lady of voima?

Rather pleased with this idea, he gave her another hug, less comforting and more passionate.

She turned in his embrace to look at him. All her laughter and teasing were gone. "Originally I was sent," she said, "to lure you from your allegiance to the lords of voima, to make you serve us instead. But I have changed my mind, Valmar Hadros' son. I do not want you to fight for the Hearthkeepers against the Wanderers, any more than I want you for fight for them against us. I only want you all for myself."

"I cannot be all for you," he said, stroking her arm and trying desperately to remember why he could not. "The path of honor is higher than the path of love," he added after a moment.

Her eyes flashed at him, and the corner of her mouth

twitched. "I do have to remember that you too are, after all, a man."

Before he could answer, he heard a clanging, of swords against shields, not a quarter mile away.

"We know you're in there, Valmar Hadros' son!" came a booming voice. For a horrible second he thought it was the Wanderers, then knew it was not. "We've surrounded this woods and we're coming for you. Surrender yourself! Since you would not be our friend as Roric was, we shall take you to our manor as our enemy!"

The woman sprang up and went for her armor and sword. "We'll compromise," she said with a grin, "we'll *both* fight these beings for your lords of voima, and also be together." She had her clothes on in seconds, and was sliding on her mail and stamping her feet into her boots. "I've already seen how you do against me. Now we'll see how much a mortal can do against hollow creatures who want him dead."

PART III: Realms of Voima

CHAPTER ELEVEN

1

Karin and Roric began to run, back the way they had come, slipping and almost falling in the piles of coins. Their feet could find no purchase. It was like trying to wade through surf-swirled sand—like a nightmare in which one struggled to move until wakened by one's own kicks, but there was no waking here. The scraping and slithering behind them became louder, and the dragon's hot breath blew on their hair.

Karin clung to Roric's hand, struggling to keep her feet, staring through blurred eyes at the fire burning at the side of the cave.

Why should the dragon have a fire in its den?

She caught her foot on a jeweled sword, half-buried in the coins, and fell, nearly pulling Roric down with her. "Go!" she gasped. "Go! One of us may still escape!" Wildly she thought that it would be better to be eaten in one gulp than pursued up the narrow passage down which they had slid into the dragon's den.

Not hearing or not listening, Roric stood over her, facing the dragon with his sword out. The long snout came toward them, slowly, very slowly. For a second Karin hoped that the mind behind the burning eyes was only curious, that the dragon was at the moment more interested in their presence than hungry.

And then the enormous mouth opened, showing hundreds of needle teeth, and the forked tongue licked toward them.

Roric's armed darted out, and his sword clanged on the dragon's scales with a ring like steel against steel. The scarlet nostrils flared and the jaw opened even wider. Roric stabbed toward the closest nostril, his full weight behind the sword.

The blade hit home, and the dragon's head jerked upward, almost yanking the sword from Roric's hand.

In the seconds while the dragon bellowed in pain, Roric dragged Karin to her feet and almost carried her, not toward the passage down which they had come but toward the fire. Through tangled hair she thought she saw in the uncertain firelight a dark crevice in the rock wall next to the blaze.

The dragon's mouth behind them opened wider and the head darted forward, no longer moving slowly. Roric reached the wall a dozen feet ahead of the dragon's teeth, threw her into the crevice, and dove in behind her.

"Back! Further back!" he cried hoarsely, but she was already scrambling deeper into the crevice, for the rock here was burning hot and the dragon's teeth snicked together just behind Roric's feet.

It tried to work its head into the crevice, hissing horribly. Roric kept pushing her onward. She crawled blindly as the dragon's head blocked all the light from the firelit room.

Suddenly she cried out, for the stone was gone beneath her hands. She reached back desperately, grabbing Roric's arm, but could not regain her balance. For a second she teetered, the edge of the dropoff biting into her flesh. Then, pulling him with her, she tumbled down into a pit where no light penetrated.

They landed hard on a sandy floor, and Roric's sword clattered against the stone wall. They lay still for a moment, gasping for breath, waiting for whatever creature lived in this pit to attack them next. When nothing happened at once, they slowly sat up.

"Are you all right?"

"Are you all right?"

They collapsed into each other's arms, clinging to each other until the worst of the trembling passed.

"I couldn't have left you, certainly not to save myself," Roric said quietly.

She couldn't answer, her face pressed against his chest.

Above them they could still hear deep, angry rumblings from the dragon, but it did not seem able to follow. "If nothing's broken," said Roric after a moment, "let's follow this passage a little further and see if we can find a way out. Maybe if we go slower we won't have any more surprises like that one!"

"Roric, please! I can't crawl through any more dark tunnels. I just can't!"

"Then I'll go ahead, and you can wait for me."

"No, please don't leave me!" She was sobbing now. This was entirely her fault, from the decision to try to find Valmar to the decision to descend into the firelit room under the rocks in search of the Witch of the Western Cliffs, and if they starved to death here it would only be an appropriate end to their story.

He held her again, rocking her like a child. "I won't leave you behind if you don't want," he murmured into her hair. "But feel how smooth the floor is here. And *someone* built that fire in the dragon's den, and I doubt it was the dragon. Don't you think some of your faeys might have found a way to live close to it?"

At the thought of the faeys she sat up straight, peering about in the blackness in search of the faint green light cast by their lamps. She still saw nothing, and she realized that no faeys she had ever known, either the ones in Hadros' kingdom or the ones here, had used open fires. But imagining this was a faeys' burrow gave her courage. She took a deep breath. "Let's go then," she said.

Roric went first, crawling with his sword in one hand, feeling his way in the dark. The surface under their knees and hands remained level. "*Someone* certainly must live here," he said over his shoulder.

"Of course someone does," said a deep voice in front of them.

Karin reached forward to grasp Roric by the shoulder. The voice was good-natured and deeper than the voice of any faey, but with a detached, almost weary note that reminded her oddly of Queen Arane. "Are you—" she began tentatively, addressing the darkness and already knowing the answer, "are you a faey?"

There was a chuckle then before the voice continued. With the echoes, it was impossible to judge distance, but it sounded very close. "I have been called many things, but never that."

Karin squeezed Roric's shoulder tighter. It was very strange speaking to someone she could not see, someone who, she told herself, *had* to be human. "Then who are you?"

"Some call me," said the voice, "the Witch of the Western Cliffs."

2

"We'd like to see you if we could," said Roric when Karin fell silent.

"Then keep coming," the voice replied. "You will be able to see me—and I you—by the light of my fire. Though I must say I had thought mortals had more sense than to blunder into a dragon's den after I set the fire beacon there to warn everyone away!"

Roric crawled on, Karin right behind him. The tunnel curved around a corner, and the dark lightened to the level of dimness. The tunnel opened into a room with a high ceiling. Here again a fire was burning, and something enormous and squat reclined before it.

He came out of the tunnel and rose slowly to his feet, his sword still in his hand. "Do not fear me, Roric No-man's son," said the voice.

All creatures of voima, it seemed, knew his name. Considering how little use his sword had been against the dragon, he doubted it would be much more use here. Their best hope was that this witch really was as friendly as it wanted to sound, and he would not learn that by threatening. He gritted his teeth for a moment, then shrugged, sheathed his sword, and put an arm around Karin as she came up beside him.

He could feel her trembling, but she spoke clearly. "We have come a long way to find you. The Mirror-seer in my father's kingdom said that you would know the way into the Wanderers' realm."

The massive shape by the fire shifted but did not answer at once. It did not look human in spite of its voice. Yet the firelight glinted from a pair of eyes, human eyes. As the flame licked high for a second it bounced images from an enormous mirror on the far wall.

"Are you perhaps a Mirror-seer yourself?" said Roric politely. But he asked himself with a tightening of his lips whether all of this, their entire trip to the Hot-River Mountains, might be some sort of Seer joke.

"No, nor a Weaver," said the shape. It was impossible to place the being's voice as either man or woman, any more than it was possible for the Weavers. "Although, as you see, I too weave." Roric saw then that there was a net across the far side of the room, tightly tied, full of knots and tangles.

"But can we reach the Wanderers' realm from here?" asked Karin again, a desperate edge in her voice.

"*Everything* beneath the sun is ruled by those you call the Wanderers," the Witch of the Western Cliffs replied. Roric had yet to see a mouth but thought it must be enormous to match the creature's bulk. "At least for now, all lands are the realms of the lords of voima. But the upheaval is coming soon . . ."

"The Weaver back home," said Roric, "also spoke of an upheaval."

"And the faeys as well," said Karin quietly.

When the witch again fell silent, Roric tried to focus on the mirror. It seemed to show people moving, maybe even fighting, but too dimly to identify any of them even if he knew them.

"Come and sit beside me, Roric No-man's son and Karin Kardan's daughter," said the witch then.

Karin had not reacted when the witch first called Roric by his name, but she lifted her head sharply at hearing her own. "How do you know us?" she demanded.

"I expected you," said the witch, again with a low chuckle. Roric thought that this witch, whoever he or she might be, sounded like someone who had been alive much too long ever to hurry again, or even to worry, but was prepared to observe with interest whatever came its way. "After all, your Seer sent you to look for me; did you think I would not have *seen* that?"

"Then you know what we want," said Karin.

"And I also know that you are both exhausted, bone weary, and famished. I have watched mortals long enough to know one has to be careful with them sometimes—there was a time I watched them *very* closely. Sit with me by my fire before you try to find other realms than this one."

There was no way to judge the passing of time in the darkness of the cave of the Witch of the Western Cliffs. They ate bread and cheese and drank ale; Roric wondered briefly where the witch had gotten it but knew better than to ask. After a while, even sitting in the dark with a witch who must be twenty times the size of either of them stopped being disturbing. Karin commented that this large room was much comfortable than the cramped burrows of the faeys.

The dragon seemed far away, and then even farther away as the ale went to their heads. They had not heard any of its rumbles since they entered this room. Karin said something about tiny islands of security, but Roric was too tired for it to make much sense. Then they slept, lying on the sandy floor by the fire, their heads pillowed on what appeared to be a leathery roll of the witch's belly. They woke again to find the flames still flickering low.

The witch was working on its weaving, pulling and tugging at strings, seeming to make them even more tangled, humming quietly as it worked. It was difficult to see clearly for the shadows moved with it, but the witch almost appeared to have more than one pair of arms, like a huge spider.

Not wanting to disturb its work, Roric and Karin whispered together. She told him about the renegade king and his embittered woman, and how she had gotten out of their castle. But he did not tell her, not yet, that he had killed Gizor. For the last day he had been too involved in keeping first himself and then the two of them alive to think much on it, but he was carrying a massive blood-guilt.

"So, you two mortals have not yet had enough of the Wanderers?" asked the witch above them. "From what I heard, I thought you had turned against them."

"What have you heard?" asked Roric cautiously. This being was the first, including the humans, who seemed to realize that mortals needed food and rest, the first since they had left the isolated manor and its strange blue-eyed lady, and it inspired him—almost—with a feeling of trust. But he had never trusted anyone absolutely, except maybe Karin, and he had no reason to trust a creature of voima.

"One of those you call Wanderers often visits me," said the witch pleasantly. That is, Roric *thought* the tone was meant to be pleasant; it was so hard to tell without seeing a face. "I knew him long ago, when he was young—knew him very well, you might say. So he asks favors of me and tells things to me, and sometimes I guess even what he has no intention of telling."

"I didn't know the Wanderers were ever young," said Karin.

"Oh, yes, both small and young. Tell me, Karin Kardan's daughter," in an apparent change of topic, "have you borne children?"

"Not yet," said Karin slowly, and Roric thought that she, like he, must be wondering aghast if this strange creature was a Wanderer's mother.

"Sometimes I wonder," said the witch thoughtfully, "if their plan has any chance of success—and I think he wonders as well, though so far he still supports it, as much as he ever supports anything."

"Does their plan involve us?" asked Karin in a small voice.

They had been maneuvered, Roric thought grimly, into coming all the way here in order to rescue Valmar from the lords of voima, and all the time the lords of voima had known exactly what they were doing, were delighted to have them do it, and had no intention of letting Valmar be rescued. His eyes ached from trying to see, his muscles ached from the fights of the last few days, yet more than anything his spirit ached for a clear goal ahead of him.

"Certainly they need mortals, and you seemed like a good first choice, Roric No-man's son," said the witch. "But I am not sure, now, if they still want you, or if the mortal they have will do . . . I must say, I do not like these *changes* any better than they do, but I would have thought there was a better solution than introducing death into immortal realms."

The witch fell silent for a moment, and Roric squeezed Karin's hand. They had stumbled into a crisis of the lords of voima, a great shifting and change that might affect all mortals as well as the Wanderers themselves, and he wanted no part in it. He had gone into immortal realms originally because he wanted to do something to make himself worthy of Karin, but now he would be satisfied with having the blood-guilt removed and her beside him.

Karin seemed determined to keep the witch talking, though little they had heard seemed of use to Roric. But women, he thought, always liked talking. "You keep referring to changes, to upheavals— We mortals, I am afraid, know little of these. What is it that the Wanderers fear?"

"It was probably a mistake separating them into two," said the witch quietly, its voice very old. "But you mortals had always been separate, and so we modeled our new world on yours.

"Once you humans stopped living wild in the woods and began to group together in permanent dwellings," the witch continued, "we thought it would be better for you to be guided by beings more in your own image, beings who lived in their own realm which we made for them so that you would not be terrified by having lords and ladies of voima constantly among you. But now *they* do not create their successors, as we always did. The Hearthkeepers neither gave birth to their successors nor slid away gracefully when fate ordained the end of their time of dominance. And now they wish to rule again. If our children only replace each other the cycle will lead not to progress but to stagnation, for it will never be resolved . . ."

"Excuse me," said Karin slowly, "but I don't understand you. Who is it who have separated?"

"The Wanderers and the second force," said Roric when the witch did not answer.

Karin looked at him, her eyes dark shadows. When she spoke he could not tell if she were addressing him or the witch. "Tell me, then. Are the members of the second force women?"

"Of course not," said Roric.

And, "Of course they are," said the witch at the same time.

"I fought them," said Roric, "in the Wanderers' realm. They weren't women. They wore horned helmets."

"They, too, have decided to try something different," said the witch, again almost wearily. "They have decided to use men's own weapons against them. They did not ask me, although I could have told them. It will make no difference."

Roric tried to picture again the warriors who had attacked both him and the band of trolls with him. It had never occurred to him at the time that they might not be men, and he did not like the idea that women had matched swords with him.

"So neither the Wanderers nor the Hearthkeepers will listen to you?" asked Karin sympathetically. "In spite of all your wisdom and experience, even when they're wrong, they insist on doing things their own way?"

Roric thought with a start that he had heard Karin speak just that way to King Hadros, when the king's sons—or even he himself—had done something that angered the king.

It appeared to be nearly as effective on the witch as it was on Hadros. "Maybe we should have tried raising up mortals instead," it said, sounding slightly less weary. "You come and go so quickly it never seemed worthwhile, but maybe *you* would listen to wisdom."

Roric said to himself that he had no intention of listening to anyone, king or Wanderer, who wanted to tell him what to do, but he stayed silent, waiting to see what Karin would discover.

"We have heard the stories, of course," she said, "that before the Wanderers ruled earth and sky there was a reign of women who ruled with all the powers of voima. But do you mean that before them beings like *you* ruled? How long has this been happening?"

"Long enough for us not only to give way but to change," said the witch in a low tone. "I may be the only one left who still remembers how it was before the creation of the realms of voima and the separation of those who rule earth and sky into men and women. And I myself am not remembered, living here away from mortals and immortals alike, except of course for the dragon."

"I want to understand this," said Karin slowly. Roric did too, and it still made no sense. "Before the Wanderers and the second force appeared, there used to be cycles of creatures of voima more like yourself. But what happened to all of you when fate ended your rule? You didn't die? You changed instead?"

"We changed as you say, Karin Kardan's daughter. Even the other creatures of voima in the earth may not remember us anymore, though they remember the upheavals and the change. Many of us are built into the very foundations of the realms of voima, so that that land is made from the sleeping forms of its creators."

Karin said after a moment's pause, "So the women of the second force are trying to use armed might to defeat the Wanderers, so they may replace them, they hope, forever this time. And the Wanderers hope to use death, which has never before entered immortal realms, to overcome the women, so that they themselves will not be replaced now or ever."

"And the Wanderers want mortals because we have access to Hel," said Roric. "Maybe in that case we should try to help the second force instead."

The witch chuckled. "Oh, they would be happy to have you, Roric No-man's son. Both sides are working out their plans in ways that involve mortals. This decision to use death will be the Wanderers' second effort to ensure that they create their own succession, after their first effort resulted only in hollow men of which they are now trying to rid themselves."

Roric set his jaw, more determined than ever not to allow the one life he had to be diverted into some game played among the immortals.

"But *you* see more clearly than any of them do," said Karin. "What can they do, if neither side wants the other to rule at all, and yet neither side can triumph?"

"If they asked me," said the witch, "I would tell them. They could try once again uniting into one, as they were meant to do."

✳   ✳   ✳

The witch went back then to tugging at the weaving, and although Karin tried a few more questions it either did not hear or did not want to answer. She and Roric retreated to the far side of the room and whispered. He did not know whether the witch could overhear them or not; the lords of voima had seemed to know less than he expected, and even this much older creature did not appear omniscient. But if the witch could see all in its weaving and mirrors, then it did not matter if they whispered or shouted.

"I do *not*," said Karin, low and intense in his ear, "want to get involved in this quarrel among the immortals."

Roric was relieved to hear this; she had sounded so sympathetic that he had been afraid for a moment that she was going to propose trying to bring the sides back together. Even while they had headed north he had vaguely hoped there might be a way to solve the Wanderers' problems and win a reward of boundless glory, but this all sounded beyond the capacities of mortals.

"They have goals so much vaster than anything we can understand," she continued, "that it would be best for us to stay with what we *can* influence and know."

Perversely, this echoing of his thoughts immediately made him think that there might be something even in mortal courage and strength that the lords of voima lacked, and that it would be the path of highest honor to fight beside them. But he dismissed this thought. He had no honor left anyway.

"Would you like to stay here until he comes to visit me again?" asked the Witch.

"He" meaning the Wanderer, Roric thought—her son? "How long will that be?" he asked. Whatever he and Karin did, it might be easier if the two kings had enough time to decide that both of them were dead and go home again. He had not come all this way to be meekly taken back in bonds with nothing accomplished.

"It is hard to say in your mortal terms when he will come," said the witch thoughtfully.

"Then it may be a long while," said Karin. "I think I have seen him once too often anyway. Is there a way to leave here without going by the dragon again?"

"Oh, yes," said the witch as though surprised. "I told you I only keep a fire at that end of my cave as a warning beacon. There is a tunnel that comes out at the bottom of the cliffs, quite near the sea. Men used sometimes to come there in boats and climb up to see me, to burn an offering or ask a question of fate. I am not sure they liked my answers as well as they expected!" with a chuckle.

"Do they come frequently?" asked Karin quickly.

"I have seen none in a while, what you would call a long while," said the witch, weary again. "Since the dragon came, and since the people of the castle turned from voima to ally themselves with the lords of death, they no longer ask me for seeings or weavings."

Then they need not fear that King Eirik would meet them at the entrance of the tunnel, thought Roric. This still left the question of where they would go when they left this cave.

Karin, even more stubborn than he, asked the question she had been pursuing since her father's castle. "We need to enter immortal realms, to find our foster-brother Valmar. We heard you know the way."

"Oh, a way can be found. Even though I have not been among those who rule earth and sky for longer than even I can remember," again with a faint chuckle, "I still know the way. Leave the tunnel, dive into the sea, and you shall find yourself there."

That was it? Could it be as easy as this? Roric wondered if they had dived into the sea anywhere they would have emerged into the Wanderers' land of endless afternoon. But he shook his head. There could be no ways not guarded, no path a mortal could take unaided by an immortal.

"Thank you," said Karin gravely. "I hope they will listen to you." She started to rise, brushing sand from her tattered skirt.

"Before you go," said the witch, "there is just one more thing." There was a brief pause, and when it continued it sounded almost triumphant. "Have you forgotten to give me your payment?"

"Payment," said Karin dully. She reached into her belt pouch and pulled out a broken necklace, one Roric remembered her wearing earlier on their trip. "I am afraid this is all we have to give you."

The firelight glinted on the gold chain. "That will not do to pay me," said the witch, no longer chuckling and no longer weary. "Did you think me just another Weaver or Mirror-seer to be satisfied with jewelry? There is enough in the dragon's lair to satisfy a thousand Seers if that was all I wanted."

"Then what *do* you want?" asked Karin, her voice high.

"Even Seers and Weavers do not want the gold itself," the witch continued, "only the sacrifice of something valuable to the person who asks. It all ends up with the dragons anyway, sooner or later. A broken necklace has no more value to me than it does to you."

Roric and Karin put their arms around each other, waiting for what the witch would demand of them. They had never been able to pick up any details of its massive bulk beyond the eyes, and now it seemed to be shifting, growing, big enough to swallow them whole. The fire crackled louder, and its light flickered on soft, warty skin the color of stone.

"What *do* you hold dear?" the deep voice asked.

"Life," said Roric, quickly and cautiously. Life was less important than honor, less important than Karin.

But the witch knew better. "You have risked your life a dozen times or more, and not for the thrill but because other things meant more."

All the creatures of voima were allied against them, Roric thought.

"What then do you hold dearest?" the witch insisted.

"Our foster-brother Valmar," said Karin determinedly.

"But you are not offering to sacrifice him, I gather, since you keep asking me how to save him? And it would not be *payment* to offer another's life."

"Honor," said Roric. His honor was gone anyway. But the witch might not know that. Maybe it would let them—or at least Karin—leave alive if he offered it honor he no longer had.

"Your father," said the witch slowly and thoughtfully. "Knowledge of your father."

Roric squeezed Karin tighter. Without knowledge of his father, without even being Hadros' foster-son anymore, he would never be a complete man and would not be worthy to marry Karin. But, he thought with a grim smile, she was already his: far too late for Hadros or for King Kardan to object to their marriage. A fatherless man, an outlaw, he was still her lover.

Then he remembered something. The witch must know this anyway, so no use in prevaricating. "The Weaver in Hadros' kingdom. He said knowledge of my father would destroy me. So I cannot offer you something I do not have, something I could never have."

"The Weaver spoke truly, but not for the reason you think, Roric No-man's son. You have never been greedy for gold and always been careless of your life, and you threw down your honor in killing Gizor One-hand."

Karin turned her head sharply toward him, eyes wide in the firelight. He had no time to tell her about that now.

"That means," the witch continued, "that knowledge of the man who fathered you is the only thing that still matters to you."

And Karin. He was not going to remind the witch of his love for Karin.

The witch's voice dropped low. "A man without a goal, without something worth seeking, is a man who might as well be dead. You think your manhood depends on your identity, in knowing to whom you were born. If you had not come here you would have spent the rest of your life truly alive, with gaining that knowledge—or acting like the man you imagined your father to be—the goal of all your actions. Now I ask you something that may destroy you as surely as the knowledge you wanted the Weaver to give you. I am asking you to agree *never* to know your father, to accept a life with no further goals."

Except Karin. He kept his left arm tight around her but slid his right hand to the hilt of his sword. Even the dragon had been taken aback for a moment by the touch of mortal steel.

"Is this your bargain?" he asked, his voice clear. "You let us leave here alive, to enter the Wanderers' realm if that is our intent, and all the payment you demand for your food, our safety, and your guidance is that I give up finding my father?"

"A simple bargain, you think?"

"Unless you are playing with me, unless you plan to demand much more of me, I think it a good and simple bargain. I accept, Witch of the Western Cliffs!"

"And Karin Kardan's daughter." His arm tightened around her so suddenly and so hard that she gasped, then Roric realized the witch was not naming her but addressing her. "Do you also agree? Even if you learn what man fathered Roric, do you understand you will never tell him?"

"We have steel here," she said, recovering her breath, "but no rowan on which to swear. But I shall swear on anything you like."

"No oath is necessary," said the witch, giving its deep chuckle for the first time in a long time. "In agreeing you have bound yourself far more tightly than any oath could do. Go, then, Roric No-man's son and Karin Kardan's daughter! Evade the dragon, enter the sea, and find this foster-brother of yours. But do not expect the way to be easy, for both sides in the realms of voima will want you for their purposes."

He had dealt with the trolls and with a witch who might have brought forth a Wanderer, thought Roric. Wanderers and Hearthkeepers he could deal with as well.

The fire flared up, showing them a low, dark tunnel opening on the far side of the room, beyond the witch's weaving. Roric felt Karin take a deep breath as they crossed the room toward it.

"One more thing," said the witch, so quietly that for a second Roric thought he was hearing his fears, not an actual voice. He stopped but did not turn around. They were almost to the far wall; in two seconds they could be in the tunnel, much too narrow for the witch to fit in behind them. "We may not be able to hear the thoughts of mortals, but I do not want you to think, Roric No-man's son, that I overlook the obvious. I know what is dearer to you than life, than gold, than honor, even than knowledge of your father. If I do not ask it of you, well, my hope is still to reunite the immortals, but how can I do that if I put even mortals asunder?"

Roric stood silent for a moment, thinking this over. Karin was rigid in his embrace. Then, "Thank you," he said formally, took two quick steps, and thrust Karin into the low tunnel.

Again it was pitch dark. They crawled rapidly, his nose inches behind her feet. There was dead silence behind them. He could hear Karin taking deep, ragged breaths, but she kept going. This tunnel was smooth, slightly twisting, but with no side passages. It sloped gently downward before them.

"I found that an easy bargain," said Roric as though casually, not wanting to admit how terrified he had been of losing her. "I would probably never have known my father anyway."

"So I gather we need not fear Gizor will be waiting for us at the bottom?" said Karin over her shoulder, just as casually.

"Not unless this leads to Hel," said Roric. He kept his head down to keep from bumping it on the roof. "I did not intend to kill him, Karin, even though he has long sought my death. But he challenged me and he would not yield."

She did not answer. The tunnel led steadily downward until at last they could hear the faint sound of breaking surf before them. "If I could only see the daylight," Karin gasped.

"We're almost there," he said encouragingly, not knowing if it would be day or night when they emerged. "You're doing very well. I'm right behind you."

And then he *did* see daylight, a lightening beyond Karin's crawling form, and tasted the tang of salt air.

"Right into the sea!" he called. "If the witch is right, we'll dive into the Wanderers' realm—and if not, we could use a bath!"

The tunnel took a last turn, and the roof rose. Karin pushed herself somewhat shakily to her feet, blinking against the light. They were in a deep crevice, its rocky floor washed by the waves, and its jagged opening looking out on the foaming sea.

And standing in that opening were two people: a man with a scarred lip that gave his face a permanent sneer, and a tall, black-haired woman who looked at them with bitter green eyes.

"So you survived the dragon," said King Eirik. His expression might have been meant as a smile. "What a pleasant surprise to see you again, Princess. When we found the entrance to the Witch's cave turned solid, we thought there must be someone up there—someone it might be worth waiting to see. Now that you're here you can show us the way to the wealth and booty of the Wanderers' realm."

3

Valmar put his back against the woman's as figures emerged from the woods on every side. His sword sang of high challenge and defiance. These creatures no longer had misty outlines but showed themselves as they were: hollow, cloven-hooved, naked beneath their helmets and shields, dangling oversize genitals before them.

"This is your last chance to yield, Valmar!" one called.

"Don't let him yield," said another. "He's got a renegade Hearthkeeper! She'll be weakened from contact with a mortal—let's kill him and take her for ourselves!"

"Trust men," Valmar heard an amused voice at his ear, "to try to make something just like themselves—and have it come out even worse."

The swords and axes these creatures wielded had no mistiness at all about them. For another moment they still hesitated, leering and whispering among themselves. Valmar, watching and trying to keep his breathing regular, thought that this would be his first real fight. He shifted his grip slightly on the singing sword, thinking of his weeks of training at the Wanderers' manor, remembering everything Gizor had taught him but also remembering how easily his father had beaten him that time.

Suddenly with a cry the creatures charged. There were at least twenty of them, coming at them from all directions. The woman laughed, throwing up her shield before her. Valmar, bracing himself, thought that it was all very well to laugh at danger when one was immortal.

Then the creatures were on them. Valmar felt almost detached, watching himself fighting coolly and calmly, landing blow after blow as his sword sang gloriously, turning, parrying, deflecting a stroke on his shield, anticipating the next stroke, driving in for a sharp thrust when an opponent was off balance for even a second.

And then he realized he was actually killing them.

Where a few seconds before a mob of leering empty men had rushed at him, the ground at his feet was now littered with broken bits and pieces, looking not even vaguely human. He felt panic and nausea rising in him, but more creatures were coming, and a second's glance behind him showed that the woman at any rate was not killing those attacking *her*.

Now he lashed out wildly almost forgetting to protect himself with his shield; he did not want them to touch

him, he did not even want them near him, he wanted all
their twisted, hollow, inhuman forms far, far away. He was
not fighting for the Wanderers or for the woman at his
shoulder, but to protect himself from nightmare.

"Valmar!" He felt a grip on his arm. "Don't *chase* them!
They're leading you into ambush!"

He had not realized until that second that he *was* chasing them, that he had been about to run across the clearing with his sword high and a death-cry on his lips.

Because they had fallen back, those few who were left,
retreated hastily toward the trees. She stared at the dry
broken pieces of bone and skin—but could they actually
be bone and skin?—that littered the ground at his feet. "I
did not know," she said in a very small voice, "that anything could be killed here."

Valmar ripped off his helmet, feeling sicker than ever.
He had just killed over a dozen immortals. The Wanderers had told him he had awesome powers here, but they
had certainly led him to believe that he was the only being
in this land who could suffer death. They had told him
they wanted the "third force" driven back, made to give
up their attacks on the lords of voima, but they had said
nothing about killing them. And if these creatures really
were the Wanderers' own creation—

He grabbed the woman's hand. "Let's get out of here."
He ran through the woods, dragging her behind him, until
they emerged at the track where his white stallion waited
where he had left it. He tossed the woman onto the horse's
back and leaped on behind her. Running from nightmare,
running from the destruction of the service he had tried to
offer the lords of earth and sky, he kicked the stallion forward. They galloped down the hill away from the trolls'
manor, across rivers he did not even try to count, the terrible unending sunset blinding their vision and the wind
whipping in their faces, until after an hour the stallion ceased
galloping, then even trotting.

He slid from the horse's back, pulling her down beside

him. "I know you're not meant for me," he gasped, unfastening the clasps on her mail and pulling it off with shaking fingers. "I know you were meant to serve the Wanderers, until somehow you became separated from them. But I don't care. I must have you. They set me a test and I've failed utterly. I cannot fail any worse by taking you."

"I am *not*," she told Valmar a little testily, " 'meant' for the Wanderers. We Hearthkeepers are separate, independent, made to govern in our own right. We once ruled earth and sky, and though our powers have long been lessened, we are sure they are fated to return once the time of the Wanderers passes. And this time we intend to make sure that they do not ever end our rule again."

They lay with their heads shaded by a tree, its leaves green but withered, and their feet in the sun. The white stallion grazed nearby.

She kept wanting to talk. Valmar, feeling feverish, his heart fluttering, did not want to talk, especially now that desire was beginning to burn in him again. If he allowed himself to think about how he had failed the Wanderers he would break down completely and sob like a boy, but when he possessed her all those thoughts were very far away.

"But since you're showing no sign of trying to return now to your Wanderers," she continued with the hint of a laugh, "does that mean that you agree to leave them and serve me instead?"

He rolled on top of her and silenced her with his mouth on hers. He did not want her to remind him again of the quarrels among the immortals, of the dire need of the lords of voima that had led them to turn in their desperation even to a mortal, even to him. He only wanted to feel her body against his and her arms tight around him.

He fell asleep at last, utterly exhausted, clasping her in a final effort to find forgetfulness. He slept so deeply that no nightmares troubled him, until he rolled in slumber so that his face was toward the sun and the low red light found its way through the shriveled leaves and made images on the insides of his eyelids.

He sat up, digging at his eyes with the heels of his hands. She lay a short distance away, comfortably relaxed but with her eyes open. "If more Hearthkeepers knew of the capacities of mortals," she said with a languorous smile, "more human men would find themselves with immortal wives."

He rose without answering and walked a short distance to where a stream cut across the meadow. He dipped his whole head in, then splashed cool water over himself. He no longer felt like sobbing, but his failure was a dull ache he thought he could never overcome. And his desperate attempts to find solace in a woman's embrace now seemed shameful, unmanly. He might not serve the Wanderers anymore, but he also could not meekly offer his "capacities" to a woman's service.

He stood up, shaking wet hair from his eyes, knowing what he had to do. His back toward her, he found his clothes and slowly started putting them on.

"When you were so intent on serving your Wanderers," she said behind him in good-natured tones, "and I thought I could never seduce you from them, I should have returned to the other Hearthkeepers. Instead, I found *myself* with all my feelings changed, and for a mortal!"

Valmar paused in pulling on his tunic, wondering what she could be talking about, then shrugged. It did not matter.

"So I thought if I could not have you for us, I could still have you for *me*. But maybe I was too quick to admit defeat! Your Wanderers will not want you now, after you have killed their creation and run away with me. But the Hearthkeepers still want you! You are needed, Valmar Hadros' son."

He carried his shield and sword to the stallion. Someone had unsaddled him and rubbed him down. Had he done so? He had no memory of it, but then his memories of the last twelve hours were very confused. Perhaps she had done it while he slept. He put on the saddle blanket and saddle, then paused in tightening the straps to wonder if he ought to offer to take her somewhere. But then he shrugged again. She was an immortal being who belonged in this land where it was quite clear he had never belonged. She seemed capable of appearing wherever she wanted; let her appear by herself back with the other Hearthkeepers.

She finally seemed to realize something was wrong. "Where are you going?"

"There is only one way to redeem anything that may be left of my honor," he said, not turning around. "I shall return to the Wanderers and tell them I am ready to go to Hel for them. I do not know if a living mortal *could* return from Hel, but it does not matter. I shall stay."

She took him by the shoulders and whirled him toward her. "What do you mean?" she cried, black eyes flashing. "To give up your life is the path of despair, not of honor!"

"The only path of honor left," he said dully, "is to give my own life so the lords of voima may be reborn."

She kept a tight grip on his arms. He stood quietly, not resisting, not meeting her eyes. "You tried to tell me this the first time we met," she said angrily, "that the Wanderers wanted you to bring them death. At the time I did not believe it. I thought they were only testing your courage. But I should have listened more closely. Hear what I say, Valmar! The Wanderers' time is *over*. Fate has ordained that it is our time now. But they are too cowardly to accept this. Instead they want you to bring them Death, and why? Not so they can be reborn, or whatever story they tried to tell you. But so they can kill us!"

He looked up then. "To kill you? Immortal women? No! That cannot be their intention."

"They did not tell you that you could kill their hollow men—why should they have been any more truthful in this? And think, Valmar! They knew you wanted glory, with trumpets blowing and flags flying high. Would you have followed them if you thought they wanted to murder their competition?"

Everything she said compelled belief. But he could *not* think this of the strong, merciful, shining lords of voima. "Maybe it is too late," he said slowly. "Maybe by coming, a mortal, into this realm I have already brought death here."

She looked at him, considering. "An interesting question. You killed the Wanderers' hollow creatures, but had they ever been truly alive? Immortals have always come from immortals, but since we separated from the men no new immortals have been born. Maybe they thought they could create their own successors, but even they realized that effort failed . . . I know! You can try to kill me."

"What?!"

She had already gone briskly to get her armor. "It's the only way to find out if you have brought death here already, or merely crumbled some beings that could not truly die because they had never truly lived. If death *is* here, then you certainly will not need to take a trip to Hel!" She laughed at his expression, settling her horned helmet on her head. "Don't worry. If you start to inflict real damage on me you can always stop in time."

He slid his own shield on his arm, not sure what else to do, and drew his singing sword. Laughing, she lashed out with a sharp blow which he parried easily. She struck again, harder, and again he knocked the blow away. Her third stroke he deflected on his shield.

"Are you afraid to fight me?" she asked, eyes glinting like mirrors. "You have not landed a stroke yet, Valmar Hadros' son!"

He parried her next thrust and struck her shield so hard she staggered for a second, then he returned to a defensive posture.

"You're afraid," she said tauntingly. "You know you've deserted the Wanderers, and now you're afraid even the Hearthkeepers won't have you if you kill me. Try it! Or are you afraid of being defeated in swordplay by a woman?"

He had defeated her once, disarmed her without the slightest difficulty. Why could he not do so now? He tried to knock the sword from her hand, to strike her sword arm with his shield, but she evaded his blows. Had she let him win that time, or was it his own fear of hurting her that now weakened him?

"If you *do* kill me, of course," she said with a grin, "you will have to get word to the rest of the Hearthkeepers. They will be very interested in knowing an immortal can now be killed. If we ambush the Wanderers—who will not suspect anything—we can kill them all, and then we shall be sure that fate will *never* ordain another end to our rule."

He did not like her repeated suggestions that he had betrayed the Wanderers. Maybe he had, but it was not too late to make restitution, and if he had deserted them it was entirely her fault. He gritted his teeth and started raining rapid blows on her shield.

She had shifted to a defensive position. "Your Wanderers' biggest mistake," she said, panting now, "was trusting another man. They should have known a man could be led by the nose like a bullock by any attractive woman. Maybe they would have done better bringing a mortal woman to this land to do their bidding."

Karin. They had wanted Karin. But she had refused to go with them—and maybe he should have refused as well. What was Karin doing now, he wondered, back in her father's castle? Had Roric ever arrived, and, if so, had he let love for Karin destroy his honor?

The woman before him laughed again, mockingly. "Before, I let you defeat me because I knew it would excite you. But now, you see, I am fighting in earnest. Mortal men have such capacities in some areas, I mistakenly thought they would in battle too!"

How could he have ever thought he loved her? He drove forward, really fighting for the first time, swinging his sword as he had against the hollow men. She fell back, no longer mocking. The black eyes on either side of her nose guard looked alarmed. He struck at her as he had struck at Gizor many times in practice, as he had thrust at the inarticulate weapons-master—had *that* been another hollow creature?—at the Wanderers' manor.

In the distance came the piercing note of a horn.

He stepped back for a second and looked across the meadow. A whole troop of riders were coming toward them. They were still a half mile away, but the sunset light glinted on their armor and horned helmets and shone on the white banner floating above them.

While his attention was distracted she sprang forward, swinging her sword as though berserk. He got his shield up just in time, parried, and thrust, driving her back again.

"We have you now, Valmar Hadros' son," she gasped. "You belong to us!"

He dropped his shield to swing his sword furiously, two handed. Its song was sweet and wild. She saw the blow coming, and for a fraction of a second her eyes widened. Then at the last instant she twisted—was she mocking again?—and lowered her own shield. The edge of his sword struck her in the side of the neck, just below the lip of the helmet, and was immediately bathed in crimson blood.

In the summertime of long, long ago Moikaa the hero sailed his ship alone across the deep and briny sea. There the spray leaped high and the wind tasted of salt, and in the midst of the sea he saw a maiden. Her hair was black, her eyes green, and her waist light and slender, and she walked across the water's surface on shoes of leather.

"Come into my ship, oh maiden!" he called. "Come and rest upon my pillows!"

But she laughed with green eyes flashing. "Let disease rest upon your pillows," she called, "but never I!"

In the autumn Moikaa went alone to the deep woods, timbering. The shadows were deep, the scent of pine strong. And there he saw a maiden, black-haired, green-eyed, walking across the treetops on shoes of leather.

"Come into my cart, oh maiden!" he called. "Come and rest upon my blankets!"

But she laughed with dark hair swirling. "Let destruction rest upon your blankets," she called, "but never I!"

And in the winter the hero drove his sled alone across the ice fields. The sun threw diamonds onto the snow surface, and the wind bit into his lungs. And there he saw a maiden whose waist was light and slender, walking on the deepest drifts on shoes of leather.

"Come into my sled, oh maiden!" he called. "Come and rest upon my bearskins!"

She stopped then and considered him. "And why should I rest upon your bearskins?"

"Because there you shall enjoy a hero's embraces!"

She laughed then as she came to him and stepped within his sled. When Moikaa tried to kiss her she twisted away, as slippery as an eel, as swift as a jay, as cold as a shard of ice. But the hero pinned her though she fought him, embraced her with his mighty arms, and finally she yielded to him upon the bearskins.

They lay then comfortably, and Moikaa asked, "Who are your mother and your father? You must be born of mighty heroes!"

"I have not seen my parents for long, long years," said the maiden. "When I was just a little girl, I went berry picking with my mother. Foolish girl, I wandered far, seeking the reddest berries. When evening came I realized I was alone. I became afraid, but no one heard my calls. For hours, for days, I wandered, until the animals found me. I was raised then by the sturgeons of the sea, the eagles of the air, and the ice bears from the north. But still I carry my father's name, for I am Laaiman's daughter."

When the hero did not answer, she turned green eyes to him and asked, "Who are your mother and your father? You must be born of mighty heroes!"

"Woe!" he cried, "that I was born! That disease did not suck out my life within the crib, that destruction did not fall on me before I learned to crawl! When I was just a little boy, my twin sister became lost, berry picking, when she wandered from our mother. I went to find her, searching far, becoming lost myself, but no one heard my calls. I was raised then by war giants and dragons, but still I carry my father's name, for I am Laaiman's son."

They stared at each other and spoke together. "We have dishonored our parents. We have dishonored the beasts who raised us. We have made the lords of voima turn their backs upon us." And they went, hand in hand, to a cliff that stood nearby, and they hurled themselves over.

CHAPTER TWELVE

1

She was not dead yet. She collapsed at Valmar's feet, holding a hand ineffectually across the gaping wound, but her eyes still flashed at him. "They will kill you when they find what you've done to me!" she croaked.

He stared at her aghast, his sword dangling from his hand and still incongruously singing. Blood ran across the grass, staining her armor and matting her hair.

"The rest of the Hearthkeepers," she said in a slightly stronger voice when he did not answer. "They are coming. Go!"

The horned riders were closer now, and the piercing blast of the horn came again.

"If you still want to serve your Wanderers," she gasped desperately, "you cannot let the Wanderers' enemies kill you! Go! Go now!"

Her words finally penetrated. She was right. The Hearthkeepers were the Wanderers' enemies and—since he had just killed one—his. It would be not honor but utter folly to try to fight a whole band.

He thrust his sword, still all bloody, into its sheath and whirled, half-blind, toward the stallion. He had just destroyed whatever shred of honor he might still have had by killing a woman. The only spot of light left was that he might be able to warn the lords of voima that death was already present in their realm, warn them before their enemies found them.

"Valmar!" she called weakly behind him. "Take me with you!"

He had no time to argue, consider, or even think. The steel-clad riders were only a few hundred yards away and coming fast. He scooped her up and threw her across the horse's neck. She seemed now to weigh almost nothing. The stallion began to run even before he was fully into the saddle.

With a leap, they were across the stream and running all out. Valmar dared a glance over his shoulder to see the riders stop, with cries and exclamations, at the pool of blood. While they hesitated the white stallion gained another quarter mile on them.

For this, he realized, was a true horse of voima. Far faster than it had run yesterday (yesterday?), they soared across the Wanderers' realm, over hills and hedgerows, through woods and valleys. Most of the time they seemed airborne, as if the horse scarcely needed to put down a hoof to remind itself of earth. Not even Goldmane, Valmar thought, could have kept pace now.

He held the woman to him with one arm, his other hand on the reins but not really guiding, for this horse seemed to know where it was running. Her head, still helmeted, drooped, and the blood flowed from her neck onto the stallion's mane. Then slowly the flow of blood ceased.

He expected her to go cold and stiff against him, but she still felt warm, and his hand on her breastplate could feel a beating as of her heart. Unless it was his own.

The stallion's pace gradually slackened. Valmar realized he had not seen the band of Hearthkeepers in what must be hours. Maybe when they realized a mortal could kill one of them they had hesitated in their pursuit.

He pulled up on a hilltop from which he could see miles in all directions and where a spring broke gurgling from the earth. He slid from the stallion's back and gently lifted the woman down.

She smiled, eyes bright as mirrors, and slipped her arms slowly around him. "I hope you are satisfied, Valmar Hadros' son!" she said with a faint smile. "You terrified me as I have never before been terrified."

He lowered her carefully to the grass and removed her armor and clothing. She still seemed very weak, and when he brought water from the spring in his helmet to wash away the congealed blood she lay still, watching his movements, letting him rinse the blood from her skin and hair.

"Don't forget to wash yourself, including your sword," she said, trying to laugh. "And your horse!"

There was now no wound at all on the side of her neck. His shirt, protected by his mail, was the only piece of clothing either of them had that had not been splashed with blood. It was much too big for her, but he slid it over her head and rolled up the sleeves. Karin, he realized with a pang, had sewn that shirt herself; there was the tiny crown embroidered on the hem which she put on everything she made for him.

"How about you terrifying me?" Valmar asked, helping the woman sit up. He found bread and cheese in the horse's pack, food the Wanderers had sent with him, and offered it to her. "I thought I had killed you!"

"Remember?" she said, smiling wider now. Just for a second, there was terror again in her eyes, but she was doing her best to deny it. "I am immortal!"

The wind out of the sunset blew softly and steadily. "So you knew I could not harm you?"

"I did not *know*. And you did harm me, Valmar—when I saw my blood, which I had thought no mortal could draw, I too thought you had killed me. When I challenged you I was fairly sure you could not, but I thought there was only one way to be certain that death had not yet reached this realm."

"You would have let yourself be killed for knowledge?"

"Knowledge to help the Hearthkeepers," she said almost complacently, munching on bread. "Let me have some water to drink—this is dry."

He too had been eating, but the cheese went tasteless in his mouth. "For your people, for your honor, you tried to make me kill you. To serve those to whom you are pledged you were willing to experience a death an immortal should never experience." She nodded, taking another piece of bread. "But why," he added after a moment, "when your own people were there to help you, did you tell me to take you with me?"

She swallowed and looked at him soberly, with no trace of laughter. "This dealing with mortals has consequences I had not expected. Over the years a few Hearthkeepers have left, tired of waiting for triumph, and joined themselves with mortal men, but I had never thought to be among them. I love you, Valmar Hadros' son."

He put his face in her lap, wrapped his arms around her waist, and sobbed. She gently stroked his hair until finally his tears and trembling ceased.

2

Eirik and Wigla blocked the mouth of the sea cave. No diving past them into the ocean, thought Karin.

"Well, Princess," said the renegade king with another supposed smile, "I see you have been reunited with your lover. My offer still stands if the two of you want to join us! So this is the man you prefer to me," looking Roric up and down. "I know he is a good fighter, and I see he is younger than I am, but can he play the lyre?"

"I told you she was not a princess to ransom," said Wigla. "She has nothing to do with that ship down at the river. These are both outlaws—at best we could earn a bounty for killing them."

"Of course, they might be planning to get the same bounty for *us*," said Eirik thoughtfully.

Neither Karin nor Roric had yet spoken. She could feel him at her shoulder, tense and alert, but, she feared, thinking that she herself might have an idea. Had Eirik and Wigla plotted it all from the beginning? Or, more likely, had Wigla set Karin on the path to the dragon's lair to get rid of a potential rival, then gone to tell Eirik about the way into the Wanderers' realm in an attempt to reestablish herself in his favor?

"So tell me," continued Eirik, "are you hoping to find great piles of jewels and rich silks in the lands of voima? Or does one instead bring back charms that guarantee luck in love and conquest over all men?"

"If you are intending to raid the realms of voima for wealth and booty," said Roric suddenly and fiercely, "then let me tell you that you shall find none. I know—I myself have been there."

This brought Eirik up short for a second, then he attempted to reestablish his air of bravado. "Then you think you have powerful help in the Wanderers, is that it, young warrior?"

"*Roric* to you, outlaw," he snapped. "Roric No-man's son."

"Then *King* Eirik to you!" Sun flashed on the waves breaking behind him. "And let me tell you, Roric Slut's-get, in this land we do not fear the Wanderers. The old stories tell us they did not always rule earth and sky, and now there are hints that their rule is coming to an end."

"Then who *do* you fear?"

Eirik grinned broadly, showing gapped teeth. "I thought your princess here would have told you I fear no one. But we *serve* the lords of death."

Roric stepped in front of Karin, his hand on his hilt. "I can help you meet them if you like. I already have three men's blood-guilt on me—I will not hesitate to kill another man, especially an outlaw whose death would bring blood-guilt on no one."

"Be careful, Roric," Karin murmured behind him. "He is trying to make you angry. He must have a dozen warriors outside this cave. He either plans to sacrifice you or else to persuade you at the point of the sword that your best hope is to join his band."

But why, she thought, was Roric trying to make Eirik angry?

"You are very sure of your Wanderers, aren't you," said Eirik to Roric, making no move toward his own sword. "But *we* choose to serve the lords who were there before the Wanderers, who will be there after they are gone. Different lords of voima may rule earth and sky, but only Death was there at the beginning and will be there at the end. The princess tells us you were searching for the door to the Wanderers' realm, but we serve those whose door is never hidden."

Roric had given no indication he had even heard Karin. "What a coward's service," he jeered. "You know that all mortals must die, so you meekly accept the inevitable. You do not fight against your fate but try pathetically to glory in loss. If you want no part of voima, no part of life, why even bother making songs with your lyre? Why even bother noticing the beauty of the princess? Why not sacrifice yourself at once to the dark lords you serve?"

Eirik's mocking all vanished. "I have heard enough," he started to say, the sword halfway from its sheath, but the woman beside him suddenly gripped his arm.

"He is right!" she cried. Her green eyes darted back and forth between the two men. "Listen to him, Eirik! There has to be life that does not serve death!"

Eirik, startled, stared at her a second then gave a shout. There were answering shouts outside, the rattle of weapons at the entrance to the sea cave. The outlaw king turned back triumphantly to them. "The way from here is well guarded, No-man's son. Will your Wanderers guard you if you swim in the sea like seals?"

Roric shot Karin a sudden grin. "The Wanderers keep appearing in mortal realms for their own purposes," he said to her. "We'll see how they like a crowd of mortals appearing in *their* realm!"

He grabbed her hand and sprang at Eirik, his sword out. The king deflected the stroke with his own blade, but then they were past him. Straight out of the cave, where salt spray leaped against the stone, past the startled faces of Eirik's warriors—a *lot* more than the dozen she had expected—they dove like seals into the bitterly cold waves of the northern sea.

And emerged with a thump, not even wet, onto the grass of a hilltop field. Karin stared around wildly, at the sun sitting, bloodred, on the horizon, at the grazing cows who looked at them plaintively, at a cluster of buildings in the lush valley below them. Soft air touched their skin, not ocean wind but an inland breeze of late summer.

Roric jumped up, pulling her with him. "So far the witch has kept the bargain," he said with a laugh. "I see the sun has still not set here—though it's a lot lower than when I was here before. Let's get away from this hill before your renegade king shows up with all his men."

"This— This is the realm of voima?" Karin said. They hurried down the hill toward the manor house.

"Copied after mortal lands by the Wanderers' mother," said Roric. "We should warn the people here that they're about to be invaded. When we do not come back up through the waves again, Eirik will send some of his men diving after us to see if we really have found a door to this realm. He's furious enough now that he won't let us get away. That woman of his—*she* may follow on her own. And if any get through, well, the rest should soon follow."

A woman came to meet them at the manor house door, but only after repeated knocking. "Excuse me," said Karin, "but we wanted to warn you. We think some warriors may soon be—be coming over your hill. I think they are looking for booty."

The woman smiled vacantly and turned back into the house.

"Is she deaf?" muttered Roric.

Two housecarls lounged in the yard. Karin tried them next; they listened as attentively as dogs might listen, then wandered away without answering.

"Roric, what is this?" she cried in frustration. "Do they not see me? Am I not real here?"

The woman reemerged, carrying a tray with milk and bread. She stood stiffly while they thanked her and took some.

"I should have thought of this," said Roric. "*You* are real, Karin. But these people may not be. I met some of them when I was here before but just thought them vague. The lords of voima built a whole world here and had to populate it all, but I don't think there are very many of them, and probably not many of the 'second force' either. And you heard the witch—the Wanderers cannot create new immortal beings without the women. So instead they made manors, complete with animals and people, but people who can no more use reason than can the animals. They're not much more than illusion—no more real than the bear I killed."

Roric had killed a bear two winters back, but Karin was fairly sure this was not what he meant. She would ask him about it later. "How about that 'third force' you were with before?" she asked.

They finished the milk and replaced the mugs on the tray. The woman bore them away with the same vacant smile. "*They* were real and could talk and think," said Roric, "even imagine they could overcome the Wanderers. This time I'd like to find the real lords of voima."

In the distance they could hear loud voices, shouted commands, and heated quarreling. "It sounds as though Eirik has arrived," commented Roric with a grin. "If he is expecting to find piles of jewels, he would have done better in the dragon's lair. We'll let them sort it all out on their own. And while everyone here is distracted by a few dozen murderous mortals, you and I can find Valmar."

As they slipped back out of the manor and through the woods beyond, Karin realized that they had never asked the Witch of the Western Cliffs how, once they reached the Wanderers' realm, they could get back again.

3

The trip through the Wanderers' realm was much slower without Goldmane. And Roric was not sure where they were going. The hills and valleys all looked vaguely familiar, but he saw no landmarks he recognized for certain from his first visit here.

"Well," he said to Karin, "let the immortals find *us*. They seemed so interested in you and me before, and they must certainly know we've entered their realm."

But whether the immortals were no longer interested, or whether they had been so thoroughly distracted by King Eirik and his men that they had no time for anyone else, Roric and Karin spent two days—or a period that seemed to them some two days long—walking through a lush landscape without meeting anyone but more beings without will or thought. The sun, which had been sitting on the horizon when they dove into this land, was now partially gone.

"This would be an easy enough land for a fatherless man to conquer," said Roric as they sat under a tree. He batted at a swarm of flies; there were many more flies here than he remembered. "No one in any of the manors we've passed seems truly alive. They'll do what we tell them, bring us food, and would probably find a bed for us if we asked, though I must say sleeping with them all around would give me duck's flesh! So what do you say, Karin? Shall we make our kingdom here?"

She looked at him thoughtfully. "You would not be satisfied. There is no honor in conquering a people without self-knowledge or will, and there would be nothing but frustration in trying to rule them."

"Oh, I think I could rule them fairly easily once I trained them," he said, keeping his voice cheerful.

"There will soon be nothing here to rule, Roric," she said gravely. "Look at the sun—before long it will be night here, and who knows how many days or years the night will last? In the meantime the cows here all look ill, the fruit is rotting on the trees, and the bread they gave us at the last manor was moldy."

"But a fatherless man can't be picky," he said lightly, "especially one fleeing his own blood-guilt."

She was still looking at him. He found it hard to hide anything from those level gray eyes. "Just because you know now you'll never learn your father's name," she said, "is no reason to settle for what would never satisfy you."

"By the Wanderers, Karin," he said gruffly, looking away, "I am only trying to find a future that holds *any* hope for me, a future that might give me enough that I could ask you without shame to stay beside me."

She entwined his fingers with hers and put her head on his shoulder. "I loved you and pledged myself to you when you were Roric No-man's son, one of the warriors of the king who held me hostage, and I am still pledged to you. What matters a man's father if the man himself is true and strong and honorable?"

"And has blood-guilt on him he can't repay," he muttered.

"I am heiress to my own kingdom," she continued, playing with his fingers. "I can pay Hadros whatever compensation he asks for Gizor and the other men. I would love you the same even if I knew for certain you were the son of a drab and a housecarl."

She slid her arms around his neck and began to kiss him. No man could ask for more than this. He tried his best to embrace her with his old enthusiasm.

But she realized something was wrong. She drew back, eyes glinting in the horizontal sunlight. "There is something else that's happened," she said, "something you have not told me."

"No," he said seriously, "I have told you all that happened."

"You feel even worse about killing Gizor than you have said?"

He tried not to meet her eyes. "No. I told you all about that."

She put her hands on the sides of his face so he had to look at her. "Is it this land, then? You do not feel right lying in my arms in the Wanderers' realm?"

He pulled away and stretched out on the grass. "Nothing like that!" he said, trying to laugh. "If that was a problem, would I be asking you to stay here with me? Maybe I am just a little tired after the last few days."

"And maybe," she said quietly, with an undertone to her voice that he could not tell was teasing or dead seriousness, "there is a woman in this land, a member of the Hearthkeepers, whom you are waiting to see again and love more than me."

"Karin!" he cried in protest, sitting up and clasping her to him. She kept her head turned away so he could not find her lips.

"Tell me truthfully and tell me now," she said in a low voice, angry but with a note that sounded as though she might burst into tears.

He held her against his chest; she leaned limply, waiting. "Karin, I wanted to keep this from you."

"I thought so," she muttered.

"Yesterday or whatever you would call it, I began thinking again about what the witch had said—and what the Weaver told me this spring. Karin, I think I may be your brother."

She went absolutely rigid. After a moment he could feel the front of his tunic growing wet and realized she was crying. He rocked her gently back and forth, his own eyes stinging.

"Why else would the Weaver have told me knowledge of my father would destroy me?" he said after a moment. "I know, I know what the witch said," he went on when she tried incoherently to protest. "The witch tried to explain the Weaver's words by saying that sure knowledge would leave me with no goal to strive for, not even an imagined father to try to emulate. But I think the meaning is far more direct. The Weaver knew what it would do to me if I could never be your lover."

"The Weaver could have meant all sorts of things," she mumbled.

"Such as that I was a warrior's or housecarl's son? That is what I always assumed when growing up. I wanted to know *which* warrior or housecarl, but the knowledge could not have hurt me. For a while I thought I might be King Hadros' son, but Queen Arane told me she was quite certain I was not. That leaves your father."

"It *can't* be true," she said, lifting her head sharply and rubbing her wet cheeks with her fists. "You could have been fathered by a hundred different men. Hadros and my father were always enemies! My father would never have sent him a child of his own, even a child born to a serving-maid."

"Your father sent him you," he said, stroking her hair. He had already thought of these objections and had, he feared, also thought of all the answers. "And they cannot always have been enemies. We do not know what relations were like between them before we were born. They have both long been numbered among the Fifty Kings. They had plans and wars—and alliances—for many years before we appeared and started thinking of them only as they affected *us*. Might I not have been a hostage left over from an earlier conflict? Or might not the war we remember have begun because your father—or, I should say, *our* father—objected to some aspect of how I was being raised?"

"My father would have told me," she said against his shoulder.

"He may have intended to tell you, but remember, you were only home a short time, and he did not know I was your lover. Might this not be why Hadros refused to let us wed?"

"The witch would have told us!" Karin gasped.

"The witch wants to unite everyone, mortals and immortals alike. *That* is why I can never know my father."

She was sobbing in good earnest now. She threw herself on him, giving him tear-soaked kisses. "I don't care! I don't care if you are my brother! I love you and don't want anyone else! It's too late anyway. We'll stay here, Roric, and no one will ever know!"

He held her gently until her wild sobs subsided. "This goes beyond blood-guilt," he said quietly then. "We are both cursed already, and the curse would be made far, far worse if we committed incest in full knowledge."

"Then we might as well die," she said, a little more calmly but in tones of black despair. "In the old stories, the brother and sister who did not recognize each other and became lovers threw themselves over a cliff. We'll find Valmar and send him home, then you and I can go down to Hel together."

"No, remember? The witch did not think that would work."

"I wasn't thinking of seeking death for the Wanderers," she said in a voice lacking all expression. "I would seek it for us."

4

The iron gates of the fortress resounded with the blows of the battering ram, but no one looked out from the narrow windows above or shouted defiance at them.

"Are you all dead in there?" King Kardan yelled up at the empty windows.

"Just cautious," said Hadros, sharpening his knife. "They know we want Roric and the princess back again and are hoping we will pay well for them, so they hope to frighten us with this silence."

The night before, after the terrible day in which they had not found Karin, lost Roric, lost one man to the dragon, and for a while thought they had lost a great many more of their warriors until the final one staggered into camp by moonlight, they had at last buried the dead. They had raised a great mound of earth, sand, and stones above the tideline and sung the funeral songs; the best songs were for Gizor One-hand.

"I should never have told Gizor I wished I was rid of Roric," Hadros had said regretfully as the two kings rolled up in their blankets on the pebbled beach by the salt river. "I am getting too old to do things like that without thinking through the consequences."

Kardan had not been sure whether to be more horrified at hearing Hadros say he had intended to kill his foster-son or at the black-bearded king expressing regret over anything.

Today they had started systematically hunting for the raiders, keeping careful watch for the dragon though it had not reemerged from its lair. "The old tales say dragons only have to eat once a week," commented Hadros. Now, after a long day's searching of the stony lower slopes of the mountains they had found the raiders' fortress, but if anyone was home they were not answering the pounding on their front door.

"Nothing here to build ladders," said Hadros, "but the stone is rough enough that some men should be able to climb up to those windows if no one's defending them. Want to send a few of your lads, Kardan?"

But defenders appeared at last as two of Kardan's men scaled the sides of the gate. They shot at the men from the narrow windows above, missing but sending them scrambling hastily down again, and bringing a flurry of answering arrows from the attackers.

"I could threaten to fire their fields," said Hadros with a sudden grin. "That brought *you* out quick enough, Kardan, as I recall! But I haven't seen any fields except those scorched ones across the river. They must live by raiding ever since their castle burned. A good life for a young man, but no life for someone who used to be one of the Fifty Kings."

Kardan was not interested in how this renegade king

might live. Karin must be inside the castle, and he would set her free if he had to rip it down with his bare hands. "Again!" he shouted at the men with the battering ram, and again the ram smacked into the wood and iron of the gate.

The defenders had disappeared from the windows again. Late afternoon shadows lay across the fortress before them. "They should be shooting at us," said Hadros with a frown.

Kardan glared at him, wondering how the black-bearded king could be so calm about it all, could even joke when his oldest son had been snatched away to unreachable realms, and when the princess he had raised like a daughter was held captive by an outlaw.

But then he noticed that Hadros was still sharpening his knife. He had brought the blade to a fineness that could split a hair yet was continuing to stroke away with the whetstone, now removing half an inch of edge.

"Are they trying to make us uneasy by their silence," said Hadros, "or are they really as confused in there as it seems?" But then he laughed grimly, and the blade snapped in his hands. "Maybe Roric and the princess are leading them a merry chase already! Gizor told us she has a handiness with a knife I'd never appreciated, and *you* told me Roric is good enough to defeat my weapons-master in a fair fight. I'll back those two against any renegade king."

"Again!" yelled Kardan, paying no attention. The frame around the castle gate was beginning to split. The men all shouted as the ram struck again and again. Nails burst out of the hinges. A narrow gap between the two halves of the gate appeared and grew wider with every blow. A final rush with the battering ram, and the gate burst open. The two kings' men rushed through, swords upraised, shouting their war-cries.

Here at last they met resistance as wild-eyed armed warriors sprang in front of them. But the kings' men outnumbered the defending warriors, who seemed strangely disoriented considering they were fighting for their own fortress, and they only had to kill two before capturing the rest with no loss of life themselves.

"I think it's a trap," said Hadros, looking around the dim and echoing hall. "Where are all the raiders who attacked us by the river? This was a defense with no heart in it and no mind behind it."

Kardan was ready to rush wildly down the passages in search of Karin, but Hadros insisted they go slowly. Stepping quietly, looking around every corner before turning it, the kings and their men explored the fortress. The rooms were dug into the rock as much as built on it, and everywhere was comfortless, dank, and bone-chillingly cold. They pushed open the doors cautiously, sent one person ahead alone through every narrow opening with the rest tense and waiting for ambush, and jerked open every chest and every storage bin.

And at the end of the hour they had found a beautifully made lyre, wrapped in rags, at the bottom of a chest; four women; two wounded men; and no one else in the fortress besides the warriors they had already captured.

"Where can they have gone?" said Kardan in despair, a question none of the people here seemed to want to answer. "Where can they have taken Karin?"

"They might be down at the river trying to fire our ship," commented Hadros. "Queen Arane said she could direct the defense quite well by herself—should we go see how successful she's been?"

Kardan shook his head. "Why allow us to take their mountain fortress just for the chance to destroy our ship? Unless they wanted to steal it and go somewhere!"

"It's your daughter who steals ships," said Hadros, but his eyes narrowed. "This renegade king—Eirik, wasn't that his name?—may have decided to get out of here and start over again somewhere further from a dragon. In which case they really *might* have taken my ship." He yelled to his warriors. "Come on, everybody, back down the mountain! Yes, we're taking all the prisoners!"

It was twilight when they emerged from the fortress and full night by the time they found their way, dragging the prisoners and carrying the food and blankets—all the booty the fortress afforded beyond the lyre—down the twisting, narrow tracks to the river. All the way Kardan's heart was pounding hard, as he imagined Karin being taken south in chains by a renegade who would certainly find her more attractive than the slovenly women they had found in the castle. But the watch fires were burning by Hadros' ship when they finally reached the salt river, and Queen Arane's elegantly dressed warriors challenged them with very sharp weapons held ready.

The queen came to greet them once her warriors recognized the kings. "No, I have seen no one all day," she said, looking from one to the other in the torchlight. Night hid both mountains and river, and there was a steady lapping of waves against the pebble beach. "Might they have gone higher up into the mountains, or hidden from you in caves down by the sea?"

"And left just a few men on guard, a guard they hoped would be sufficient and was not?" said Hadros thoughtfully. "That would only make sense if they were terrified of us, or if they were hoping the dragon would corner us in their fortress. But they did not seem terrified when they attacked the first time, and I doubt the dragon does anyone's bidding!"

"Some of these men must know where they took the princess," said Kardan grimly. "Torture should make them talk."

"Too bad Gizor's dead," said Hadros. "He was my best torturer. Let's try the women first."

The first woman they tried needed no more persuasion than being dragged before the two kings and a torch held close to her hair before agreeing to tell them what she knew. "But this is only what Wigla told me," she said darkly, looking up at them from shadowed eyes.

"Wigla?" said Kardan.

"She is *his* woman but she hates him too. She tried to leave last year; that is when Eirik had her lover killed."

This was all very well, thought Kardan, but it had nothing to do with Karin. "But where are Eirik and the princess now?" he demanded.

"I only know what I was told," said the woman sulkily, "and I don't know about that fancy girl Eirik found. But Wigla told us to stay and wait for them. She and the king and a lot of the men were going, she said, to raid the Wanderers. I'm only telling you what she said!" she added as Kardan leaned toward her threateningly.

"One cannot 'raid' the Wanderers," said Hadros sternly. "Was this a code term for some sort of attack?"

"If so, no one ever explained it to me," said the woman, sulky again. "And I must say I was surprised to hear her mention the Wanderers. The king, he doesn't like to hear talk about the lords of voima. He says the only lords he serves are those in Hel."

Kardan had never before known, firsthand, of someone who served the lords of death rather than of voima. A chill went through him right down to the pit of his belly. There were hints of such things in the old stories, but to have his daughter held by such a man!

Hadros sent the woman off, still bound. "What do you make of her story, Kardan?"

"Maybe there *is* a door into the Wanderers' realm here," Kardan suggested slowly, "as Roric said there was. But the lords of voima would never allow someone to rampage through such a door in search of booty!"

"Let's see if we get any more sense out of one of the men," said Hadros.

But the warriors whom King Eirik had left behind seemed to have even less information. Brought bound before the kings with knives at their throats they proved quite willing to talk, but all they could say was that Eirik had taken more than half his men, leaving the rest with instructions to open the gates to no one until he returned.

"We'll find them in the morning," said Hadros, yawning widely. "They can't have gone north because the mountains are too steep, and they can't have gone south or Arane would have seen them, and they can't have gone anywhere out to sea without a ship. They're in a cave down by the shore or hiding in the rocks somewhere. They'll be hungry and come back—unless instead of the Wanderers they were trying to raid the dragon's lair, and discovered that this one likes to eat more often than they hoped! When they return to their fortress and find it standing open and empty, they'll be down soon enough to talk terms."

Kardan felt exhausted and beaten, and yet he kept a core stubborn streak that would not let him believe Karin was already dead. As they rolled up in their blankets, again preparing to sleep by the ship, trying to work indentations into the pebbles for shoulders and hips, he suddenly said, "This all started, Hadros, when you refused to let Karin marry Roric."

"Of course I wouldn't let her," said the other king sleepily. "I had to keep my side of our agreement and send her back to you as the unfettered maid you had sent to me."

"Well, if we find them alive," said Kardan determinedly, "I want them to marry at once. I know, I know, you told me that she had spent the night with Valmar during the All-Gemot when I thought she was with you. And I know a marriage between our heirs would keep peace between our kingdoms. But she prefers Roric, and he must be with her or we would have found him again."

"It was you who was supposed to stay with him yesterday," said Hadros grumpily.

"I do not even care," Kardan pushed on, "that he is a man without a family, No-man's son. If she had married him, fatherless man that he is, she would now be home safe."

King Hadros suddenly rolled over and sat up. "Do you see the queen?" he asked in a low voice.

"No," said Kardan, surprised. "Arane's tent is over on the far side of camp; she must be asleep by now."

"Well, she never wanted to talk about this," said Hadros quietly, "and would never let me ask questions. But I am nearly certain who Roric's mother was. If you're thinking of having your daughter marry him you ought to know. And I also have a very good guess for his father.'"

Kardan thrashed out of his blankets, bit back a shout, then said, "Why did you never tell me this before?" between his teeth.

"It was no concern of yours that I could see," said Hadros mildly.

"But the man my daughter loves! Tell me at least who his mother is!"

"Well, I cannot be completely certain. But Arane and I have been friends for a long time. There was a time some years ago, when I had been married a while but the lords of voima had not yet granted sons to my queen and me, when I had to visit Arane's kingdom. It must have been on business of the Fifty Kings."

"Probably plotting a war against someone," muttered Kardan, realizing that it could not have been too many years later that Hadros had found an excuse to attack *him*.

"As I recall," said Hadros, as though rather surprised at the memory, "I had been going to invade her kingdom. She invited me for a parley, and she talked me out of it. Hard to say how . . . Well, I stayed in her castle for a week that winter," he continued after a brief pause, "and she thought I might be lonely and cold, so she sent her maid each night to make sure my bed was warm. Thoughtful of her—and a very sweet maid."

"And then?" Kardan demanded when Hadros seemed to slip away into pleasant reminiscences.

"Well, it was close to a year later when I was again back that way." Hadros was only a dark shape, lit from behind by the watch fires. "I did not see the maid this visit; I was only there the one night. But Arane took me aside and asked me a favor."

"And the favor?" asked Kardan, already knowing the answer.

"She said there had been a baby born in her court, a little boy. Bright red face when I first saw him and a shock of black hair, and yelling as loudly as any grown man. He deserved a good home, she told me, said he was of a lineage that should not be brought up with the children of the housecarls. A baby was the last thing I needed at that point. But I took him home."

"And that was Roric," supplied Kardan when the other king fell silent.

"He fought me even then," Hadros said quietly. "Small enough to fit in my two hands, but he kicked and yelled all the way across the channel and home again. Poor little chap didn't have anything to eat for two days, though we dripped water in his mouth so he wouldn't be too thirsty—I tried him on ale but he wouldn't swallow it. As soon as we got to the castle I had him put to the breast of one of the serving-maids who had just borne a babe of her own. And my wife liked him. He would quiet for her when he wouldn't for anybody. I didn't want it generally known that I had been weak enough to agree to carry a screaming baby all the way home with me, and it didn't seem right to have everyone know he was mine when my queen was still barren. So I put out that he had been a foundling, a little baby lying in front of the gates when we came up the hill from the harbor."

"Your queen must have known the real story."

"I suppose she did. I suppose a lot of people did. But she accepted what I told her and started taking him into our bed. The old women had told her that sometimes sleeping with a baby will make a woman conceive. Maybe it did work, but it took a while. He slept with us for several years. He never screamed much after I had him home, but he kicked. Once he was asleep he slept hard, nothing would wake him. But let me tell you what I almost told those old women: if you want your wife to conceive, the wrong way to do it is to have her lying every night curled up around a sleeping babe."

"So Roric is your son," said Kardan in wonder. "Did Queen Arane send something with you, some token perhaps you had left with her maid, so that you would be sure?"

"No, and that's the strange thing. There was a little bone charm wrapped up in his blankets, but it was nothing I'd seen before. Arane certainly wanted me to think the baby was mine, and the timing was about right. But if she had her maid entertain all her important visitors, the lass may not have been sure herself."

"But you do *know* that Roric was born to the queen's maid?"

"Well, who else would the mother be? The queen would never have been concerned over an ordinary servant's brat. And she has asked me over the years, not every time the Fifty Kings met but several times, how he was getting on. But she would never answer *my* questions about him, and she did not want to see him herself at the All-Gemot. I'm sure her maid was happy to hear he was brought up as my foster-son."

Kardan lay down and started again trying to make the pebbles a comfortable bed. He had another question, one he was not sure how to ask. At last he said, "If you think Roric is your son, why did you try to have him killed?"

"He wouldn't listen to me," said Hadros sleepily. "He has little room for mistakes, but he keeps making them every time he ignores me. Haven't you ever wanted to kill *your* own sons? But that's right, they're dead already."

Kardan gritted his teeth but did not answer. He still could not always tell when the other king was making a joke.

"Besides," Hadros continued, "I did not in fact want him dead, even if I did suggest something of the sort after drinking all evening. Gizor took me a little too literally! But Roric's always infuriated me. Maybe he picked up a little of my temperament in those years of sleeping with me; I infuriated my father too. But his telling me he wanted to marry

Karin pushed me over the edge. Even if he is mine, he'll never inherit anything from me, so he has to make his fortune on his own. Even aside from wanting to send your daughter back to you a pure maiden, not tied to a man without kin who would acknowledge him, I didn't want Roric to be slowed down by a woman while he's still young. Though I must say, these last few weeks suggest that if anything the princess has speeded him up!"

"So you might allow them to marry after all?"

"Her decision rests with you now, Kardan. But young Valmar—if we find him again—does think he's betrothed to her."

"If he'll have her now," said Kardan slowly. He settled down and soon heard Hadros begin to snore, but his own mind was too active to let him sleep.

CHAPTER THIRTEEN

1

A hand on Roric's shoulder woke him. He was on his feet with his sword in his fist almost before he had his eyes open.

But then he saw who had touched him. A being twelve feet tall, gleaming white in the glow of the sunset, bent over them, and his face—but Roric could not bear to look at his face. He dropped his sword, grabbed Karin and held her to him, his head bowed and his body shaking all over. He would have offered the lord of voima his service and his honor, but no one would ever again ask any of this from him.

"This may sound strange coming from one of those you consider lords of earth and sky," said a voice, faintly ironic, above them. "But I think we made a mistake."

The Wanderers did not want people like him in their realm, Roric thought. One of them—this one?—had originally said they needed him, but they had never wanted a man with unpaid blood-guilt and the curse of incest on him.

Off across the hills moved dark, scuttling clouds, flashing with lightning. Roric looked at the storm so he would not have to look up at the lord of voima, then remembered that when he was here before there had not been any storms.

"We had never allowed mortals in our realm," the voice

330

continued. "When we first opened the rift to make it possible for you to enter, we never expected that *other* beings of voima would use the opportunity to bring you here, much less that so many other mortals would follow."

This was not what Roric expected. So far it sounded as though the lords of voima were more disturbed over having King Eirik and his men in their realm than in the fact that he was Karin's brother. He tried lifting his eyes slowly, but one glimpse of the face, gentle, merciful, and burning with terrible power, made him stagger.

"We are here to help you," said Karin in a high, clear voice. Roric had not yet dared say anything. "We understand you planned to send our foster-brother to Hel on your behalf. Send us instead."

Roric and Karin had finally fallen asleep clinging to each other, exhausted and in despair. How long had they slept? Long enough, Roric noticed, for the sun to slide still lower. Well, they need not worry how long the night might last in the realms of voima—where they were going it was always night.

"We are rethinking that plan, too," said the shining white being. "We should have known after watching you all these years that mortals are unpredictable."

Karin pushed back her tangled hair and looked at the Wanderer's chest. "Then tell us what you want us to do," she said firmly—as though, Roric thought in admiration, she was chiding King Hadros for giving contradictory orders.

"Though it is not what we expected in immortal realms," said the Wanderer, again in that faintly ironic tone, "you may have already brought death here."

"At home," Roric said huskily, "I would try to find a way to pay the blood-guilt. I do not know what I can do here."

"No, you have not brought death personally, Roric No-man's son." The voice sounded, Roric thought, not as calm as when he had spoken to this being, or another like him, outside the manor guest house. Instead the

Wanderer seemed—distracted? "Why don't you sit down, so we can talk more easily?" he continued.

Off in the other direction from the storm, a mountainside suddenly burst into flames. Orange fire went leaping up through the crowns of the trees, with a roaring they could hear even at this distance. The Wanderer extended an arm sharply and the fire went out at once, but the wind brought the smell of smoke to them.

Roric and Karin settled themselves carefully at his feet, and he sat on the grass as well, still towering over them. Roric's heart was pounding as though it would burst from his chest. The little things he and Karin had noticed yesterday, the small changes in this lush realm of voima, the swarms of flies, the sour milk, were intensifying as the sun came closer to disappearing. And might some of this be due to his own presence here?

"We had thought a mortal would need to go to Hel for us," the Wanderer continued, turning away from the scorched mountainside, "a mortal to ask a favor of the lords of death. But it may be that you mortals already have death with you wherever you go. We had not expected you could destroy that which we had created ourselves, or that you could make even an immortal bleed."

The Wanderer was using "you," Roric realized, not to mean him and Karin but mortals in general. Maybe Valmar?—but Valmar would never have destroyed the Wanderers' own creation. Suddenly he grinned to himself through his failure and despair. By bringing King Eirik here he seemed to have stirred up events even more thoroughly than he had intended.

"Now that you have death here," said Karin almost reprovingly, although Roric could feel her trembling, "are you planning to kill the women so they cannot succeed you?"

"There had been some who thought to do just that," said the Wanderer thoughtfully. "I myself do not think it would either work or be desirable. Fate is bringing the time of our rule to an end, but if the Hearthkeepers are gone that does not necessarily mean that we shall succeed ourselves. We tried creating something of our own, sons to rule after us, but they ended up hollow, mockeries of us rather than true sons, and you mortals seem to have disposed of them anyway. It might be if the Hearthkeepers were dead that *no* one would rule the realms of voima, leaving the land here in perpetual night, and dark and chaos in mortal realms."

"Your mother said it would never work," said Karin bravely.

"Oh," said the Wanderer, then fell silent. Karn squeezed Roric's hand until her nails bit into his skin.

"Then if you have spoken to the Witch of the Western Cliffs, as you mortals call her," the voice went on after a moment, "you know that the thought there is to try to reunite us with the Hearthkeepers."

"Why don't you just try it?" suggested Karin. Her voice shook as she spoke, but she still managed a tone of calm reason. Karin could talk almost anyone around, Roric thought in wonder. Was she going to try it on the lords of voima?

"Well, we already did," he answered. As he spoke, all the leaves on the tree by them suddenly fell together from the branches. "We began our rule together. But we had to leave them. And since then they have been our foes, always eager for the end of our rule so that they may dominate once again, bitter that fate ordained the new day here that began *our* reign."

"Were you fated to leave them?" asked Karin, brushing dry leaves from her shoulders.

"Perhaps it *was* the workings of fate, but it was the only decision we could make. As a mortal woman, you may recognize some of the difficulties we had in associating with immortal women. Our eyes were fixed on glory and honor, on wandering far, on ideas and discourse. We sought to discover the secret of creating ideal things through thought alone, not merely reshaping the lumpish stuff of the universe we had inherited. Yet *they* wished to stay in one place, to spend their time trying to guide you mortals, working to mold what is rather than create what is not, more interested in compromise than in deciding what is right, stressing the importance of feelings over reason. . . . Why, several Hearthkeepers have even left immortal realms over the long years to ally themselves with mortal men, and there is one here now who considers herself in love with a mortal."

Eirik worked fast, Roric thought admiringly.

A quarter mile away a chasm appeared in the earth with a great rumbling. Again the Wanderer held out his arm. For several seconds nothing happened, then the chasm reunited with a smack. He kept his arm extended for almost another minute before turning back toward them. "That should keep it under control for a little while longer," he commented.

No use being frightened of this, Roric told himself, staring with horrified eyes at the spot where the earth had split. This realm was disintegrating rapidly around them, but if they were not safe with a lord of earth and sky they would be safe nowhere.

"I must apologize for these distractions," said the Wanderer. "It used to take only twelve of us to keep the realms of voima solid and functioning, with very little effort on our part—indeed, with most of our attention given to mortal realms. Now, even with our best efforts I am afraid these lands may soon collapse around us."

"Nothing you have said," said Karin, getting her voice under control with an effort, "sounds like a reason to kill the women."

"Perhaps not," agreed the Wanderer, "although they have been planning for some time to hold us captive once our powers waned, and they may even now be planning to kill *us*. But I told you that only some of us intended to use death against them and that we were rethinking our plan anyway . . . My own plan all along, which may still come about although there is very little time, was to die ourselves."

Then even the lords of voima could feel despair, thought Roric. He dared a quick look upward, but the expression on the Wanderer's face did not look like one of despair.

"You see," he continued, "when the last upheaval came, the Hearthkeepers became weakened, stripped of their greatest powers; when the sun set, and when the new sun rose, while they were still weak, *we* took control. If fate ordains the same pattern, then we ourselves shall weaken in the same way. But I thought this time to use that weakness. If we were not merely ourselves without our powers, but utterly destroyed, we might be reborn with even greater powers. A seed dies in the earth and gives rise to a stalk of wheat. A tree dies in the forest and gives rise to young and rapidly growing trees."

"A mortal dies," said Roric, "and becomes a voiceless wight in Hel."

"That of course was always the danger," said the Wanderer dryly.

It was all very well, thought Roric, for immortal beings to play with the idea of death. His heart rate had settled down to a steady, rapid pace. He felt Karin's arm against his as he concentrated on the little patch of grass between his feet. No matter what these immortals did to each other, he himself, in a long time or a very short one, would end up in Hel.

And there was only one thing he had to do before then. He had to get Karin safely home. She had said they should both go to Hel, but this he would never allow. Since she had made it clear she was not going without Valmar, then he would get his foster-brother home as well if there was still time before this entire realm collapsed. Maybe if Karin and Valmar made it back to Hadros' court safely the two of them would still marry someday—it would make Hadros happy and would not matter to him, as he would be dead.

"So are you going to try your plan," he asked, "now that you think death may already be here?"

"As the time comes to try it," said the Wanderer, still dryly, "it seems less compelling than it originally did."

"You brought our foster-brother here," Roric said quickly, "Valmar Hadros' son. If you do not need him now to go to Hel for you, then you can return him to mortal realms."

Get Karin and Valmar out of here, he thought. Get them out fast, before the sun goes, before the Wanderers decide to use a mortal to test whether death is really here.

"Perhaps you are right," said the Wanderer slowly. "We chose you, Roric No-man's son, because you were already an outcast, so it would not matter what happened to you here. Valmar Hadros' son chose *us*, but perhaps we should not have let him do it . . ."

"Then let's find him," said Roric, jumping to his feet and pulling Karin up with him. "Where is he now?"

"That," said the Wanderer, "is something of a problem. We had sent him to fight against the hollow men, the ones I mentioned."

The ones I thought for a while actually were the lords of voima, Roric thought.

"But he has broken all contact with us. The Hearthkeepers are looking for him too. He has captured one of them."

Roric shot Karin a puzzled frown. This did not sound like Valmar.

The Wanderer suddenly rose to his feet with a swirl of glowing white garments. "I did try speaking to the one you call my mother, Karin Kardan's daughter. The suggestion there was to try to learn something from the two of you, but it seems that your only wish is to be home again. The best we can do at this point is to gather up all you mortals and return you to your own realm, so that we may face the fall of night and the rise of the Hearthkeepers without being distracted by you. I shall try to find Valmar Hadros' son as well as the others." He gestured with a white arm. "Climb that ridge, and wait for the rest."

Roric wiped the sweat from his face as the being strode away across the landscape, where all the shadows were now heavy and black. Did the lords of voima really intend to send them all back?

"He said nothing," said Karin determinedly, as though trying to convince herself, "about us being brother and sister. *He* would have known, Roric. It therefore cannot be true."

"The Wanderers don't know everything," he said. "And when a change like this is taking place in the immortal realms, a little incest among mortals would not bother them. It does, however," taking her hand, "matter to *me*."

"Then don't take my hand as though you were still my lover," she snapped, pulling it away. "Let's get up on the ridge and wait for Valmar."

She kept coming back to Valmar, Roric thought. He stopped himself just in time from asking sarcastically if the man she called her little brother mattered more to her than he did. Karin was only snapping at him, he thought, because she was so frightened. Besides, it would be best now if Valmar mattered to her more than he did.

There was no way he could pay the blood-fee to Hadros, no way he could again be Karin's lover. He had run from his loss of honor, but there was only so long a man could run. And fate would come to every man whether he tried to evade it or faced it bravely.

The only way to salvage anything of honor was to end his story in glorious battle. Now all he needed was an enemy to fight.

2

Something or someone was approaching Valmar's hill, still half a mile off but moving rapidly. He shaded his eyes, squinting into the distance at what looked like a group of people on foot. "Would those be your Hearthkeepers," he asked, "coming to find you?"

When she did not answer at once, he turned around to see her looking out in the opposite direction. "I don't think so," she said quietly, then came to stand next to him. She leaned on his shoulder, following the direction of his pointing hand. "They would be on horseback."

He looked back then in the direction she had been looking. Against the crimson of the sunset were what appeared to be signal fires on the hills.

"Do you feel strong enough to ride?" he asked.

She laughed, her eyes glinting. "Were you planning to ride into the ambush the Hearthkeepers are preparing for us, or go meet those people on foot? From this distance they look like mortals."

It took a second for this to penetrate. "Mortals? What would mortals be doing here in the realms of voima?"

"Perhaps the same thing that *you* have been doing, Valmar Hadros' son?" she suggested in a tone that made the blood all rush to his face.

"The Wanderers told me I was the only mortal here," he said stiffly.

"The rift that allowed you to pass," she said, "may be widening as their power wanes. I have already seen signs of their weakening. Have you noticed the thunderstorms along the ridges? *We* never allowed such things here."

He expected such things had happened as well when the Hearthkeepers' rule came to an end, but he did not say so. "Let's go meet the mortals."

As he saddled the stallion he asked himself why he chose them. He had lost his honor, betrayed the trust of the lords of voima, entangled himself with an immortal woman, and become so hopelessly lost in an alien land that his life of a very short time ago, growing up as the royal heir in a court where his big sister looked after him, could have been the life of someone out of an old tale. Mortals, whoever they were, however they had come here, were a link with the past he had lost.

He rode down the hill, the woman perched on the saddle behind him, to meet what he could now see were several dozen armed men and one woman, tall and black-haired.

The sight of the white stallion seemed to startle most of them, who staggered back, but one wiry man with a scarred lip watched him approach, hands on his hips.

"If you're a lord of voima, I'm not impressed."

"I am not a Wanderer," said Valmar gravely, "but a mortal like yourself. How did you come to these realms?"

"Is that you inside the helmet, Roric No-man's son?" the man asked suspiciously. He made a strange motion with one hand, a sort of beckoning behind his back.

Valmar removed his helmet. "I am Valmar Hadros' son," he said. "And you know Roric?"

"Never heard of you," said the man dismissively, then hesitated. "Hadros' son? A King Hadros who fought in the north years ago, when he had first come into his kingdom?"

"Yes, that's right!" said Valmar eagerly. "You know him? And you know Roric?"

"Hadros thought he was a better warleader than he really was." The man made the same motion with his hand again. The woman behind Valmar drew in her breath through her teeth, and he looked up to realize that the warriors had them completely surrounded.

Valmar whipped out his sword, which immediately began to sing. The stallion danced under him, turning as he looked to see if there was an easy way out of the circle of enemies—there was none. "Why this attack?" he shouted as the men moved in slowly, their own blades ready. "You have not even challenged me!"

"Outlaws don't bother to challenge anybody," said the man, grinning—or maybe it was just the scar. "Why worry about blood-guilt when anyone can kill *us* unchallenged?"

"I came to you in friendship!" Valmar yelled back. "What can I possibly have that you would want?"

"Your armor and your horse," said the man assessingly, "and that boy riding behind you—I've figured out it's not really a boy."

She laughed and spoke for the first time. "And *I* have noticed that you are a mortal and will die if I kill you!"

The tall woman with the warriors suddenly stepped forward. "Eirik!" she shouted, seizing him by the arm and spinning him around. "I have had enough! You keep capturing other women and expecting me still to be for you alone! Well, I do not need another man in order to leave. I can leave on my own!"

"Wigla!" Eirik said sharply, then, "Wigla?" almost pleadingly, as she stalked away from him, through the circle of warriors, and off across the valley. For nearly a minute he watched as she went, straight-backed, taking long strides. But his men never turned their attention from Valmar.

Then Eirik gave his shoulders a quick shake. "Don't know why I put up with her so long," he said to his warriors, grinning again. "But *you,* my sweet lass in armor . . ."

"This lass in armor," said Valmar, "is an immortal."

"And you, Valmar Hadros' son, are not!" He gave a sudden shout and all the warriors charged.

The white stallion reared, kicking out with iron hooves. Warriors kept an alert eye on the hooves and tried to dart in past them.

But Valmar had been training for this fight for a very long time. He leaned low over the horse's neck, laying about him with the singing sword. These warriors were ragged, with poor armor, but they fought with grim courage. Again and again he deflected a blow, then darted his blade in past the other's guard. The woman behind him gave most of her effort to staying on the horse's back, but twice when someone tried to slip up behind Valmar she stabbed him briskly.

This was a battle out of legend, thought Valmar, as steel rang on steel, men screamed in pain, and he realized dispassionately that any slowing of his reflexes might cost him his life. This was a real battle, such as he had waited for all his life and never experienced, with enemies on every hand and bright blood spurting.

And this time, he realized, he was killing real people.

He froze, tasting bile. He had destroyed the hollow men,

wounded but not killed a Hearthkeeper, and had just now killed half a dozen humans.

In his second of hesitation they were on him, knocking the sword from his hand and wrestling him from the stallion's back. He kicked wildly but they held him down. His sword and armor were taken from him. While Eirik laughed triumphantly they trussed Valmar and the woman with long cords, though the warriors were still having trouble with the stallion.

"There! We defeated you, friend of the immortals!" cried Eirik, his face in Valmar's. He appreciatively hefted Valmar's sword, the one the Wanderers had given him.

"Am I worth six of your men?" Valmar replied hotly over waves of nausea. His father had boasted of how many men he had killed by the time he was Valmar's age; Valmar would never boast of this to anyone.

"This one might be!" said Eirik, licking his scarred lips and leering at the Hearthkeeper.

She, however, seemed very little concerned in spite of being tied hand and foot. "After you taught me fear of death, Valmar," she commented, "I have no further fear of anything. And it may be interesting to see for a while what mortal women have to put up with from mortal men."

"No, don't, it's horrible," he said sickly, his eyes half closed. He had thought he was going to meet other mortals because they represented a link with a happier past, and all that had happened was that he had killed them here in immortal realms, where no one had ever killed anyone until he arrived, and had allowed the woman who obsessed him to lie bound beside him, subject to the crude lusts of outlaws.

Eirik glanced behind him at his warriors, starting to gather up their slain comrades and tending to the wounded. "Maybe you and your friend Roric *have* been more trouble to me than you're worth," he said thoughtfully. "At this rate I won't have any warriors left at all. I don't know what you're doing wandering around here by yourself, but would you like to join us?"

"What?" gasped Valmar.

"It's one way to make sure I don't have to worry about you as an enemy again," Eirik replied. "The alternative of course," with an evil grin, "would be to sacrifice you to the lords of death. The sunset seems to take forever around here, but the sun *is* getting lower. As soon as it's gone we'll sing the songs for our slain comrades and call on death to take them. So start thinking about your choice!"

3

No more chasms opened in the earth as Karin and Roric hurried toward the ridge the Wanderer had indicated. "I know this place," said Roric suddenly. "There was a cave here that led into the back of your faeys' burrows."

Karin looked around wildly at the white limestone thrusting up through the grass, almost expecting to see the faeys here. But— She could not leave without Valmar. She had gone beyond terror to a state where she could scarcely think coherently, but she clung to the knowledge that she had come here to rescue him, and rescue him she would.

"Let's make sure the way is still open while we wait," said Roric. He led her a short distance from where a spring bubbled from the earth to where its water fell over a lip of stone into a sinkhole. It looked disturbingly dark to her, but he started climbing down. "I followed the stream back, and there I was, among the faeys near Hadros' castle."

She leaned over the edge of the little cliff, watching his progress. "The stream flows back here into a pool," he called. His voice echoed hollowly. "And I think if I go back just a little further—"

There was silence. "Roric?" Karin called, then "Roric!" She swung over the cliff edge and was scrambling after him when she heard his voice again below her.

"There's nothing there. There's no way past the pool." His voice was dull, almost expressionless. "I had thought I could get you home this way, but I'll have to try something else."

"There may be no way until the Wanderers open it for us," she suggested.

"There was a way before." He climbed back up beside her. "The Wanderers must want us to stay here, not returning home yet. I wish I knew why."

They sat on the grass on the ridge, looking across the darkening landscape. Only a quarter of the sun's disk, glowing a dark red, still emerged above the horizon.

"What's that?" asked Roric after a minute. "It looks like signal fires."

"Eirik's men?" she suggested. "But who would they be signaling?"

"I don't think those fires are Eirik's," said Roric, suddenly very tense and quiet. "Listen."

From off in the other direction they could hear voices carried on the wind. There was a steady beating, as of a sword against a shield, and the voices were singing to the rhythm. As they came closer, the words gradually became more clear.

> ". . . in fellowship, forged in war,
> Following Eirik and his swift sword!
> Conquering now, and forever more!
> Women all love us, for we brave death,
> Taking in victory with every breath:
> Stronger and truer than all of the rest . . ."

Karin jumped up. "I don't need to hear any more of Eirik's songs!" she said sharply, hands over her ears.

"And after our last meeting I'm not eager to meet him again myself," said Roric. "Let's get down behind those trees."

They watched from hiding as Eirik's men went by, singing enthusiastically. They led a magnificent white stallion that did not seem to want to be led. Karin looked for but did not see Wigla.

"It looks like they have captured someone," said Roric,

"or maybe even two people. Do you think it's some of those beings from one of the manors? You'd think Eirik would realize no one is going to pay ransom for any of them."

Karin gave a gasp and started to leap to her feet. "Roric!" she said in a whisper as he pulled her down again. "They have Valmar!"

He craned his neck, looking. In the heavy shadows of sunset it was growing hard to see clearly. The young man lying passively in his bonds, allowing himself to be carried, did look like Valmar, but bigger, more muscular. A young woman with curling dark hair was also being carried, bound.

Then Karin saw what else Eirik's men were carrying. Piled on litters were six dead bodies.

"Stay still," said Roric in her ear. "It's no use rushing them. When the Wanderer returns we should have a chance in the confusion to rescue Valmar."

"I think I know what Eirik is planning," Karin whispered back, feeling cold from her throat to her feet. "Some of his warriors were killed, and he is going to make an offering to the lords of death. We don't have time to wait. Eirik is going to offer Valmar as a sacrifice."

Roric's eyes bored into hers. "But this is the immortal realm of voima!" he hissed. "They cannot summon the lords of death here!"

She shook her head. "Try telling that to Eirik. Look at how he's having the bodies carefully laid out. He called on death from his fortress—and something answered . . ."

The sun was now only a brilliant red line, pulsing with light. The warriors stopped at the top of the ridge, only a few dozen yards from where Karin and Roric lay hidden by leaves and shadow. "It should be dark soon at last!" Eirik called to his men. "Bring some of the food; we'll need it for the sacrifice."

The men brought a basket of bread and a skin of ale. Taken from one of the manors, thought Karin, who could see even at this distance that the bread was moldy.

"Too bad we don't have any of the women," Eirik

commented, fists on his hips. "The calling should really be done by a woman. Trust Wigla to desert me just when I needed her."

"How about the mountain cat here?" one of his men suggested.

Eirik went to look at the bound woman with the curling hair. "We do seem to be having a run of women who think they can fight like men," he said thoughtfully. "I never did get a chance to teach the princess more womanly ways."

Karin ground her teeth and kept silent.

"So," said Eirik, "how would you like to make the offering and call on the lords of death to take our brothers?"

"They will not hear you here," she replied confidently. "I know the Wanderers had some plan of sending a mortal down to Hel to ask Death to come, but the lords of death are not going to answer a call from our realm."

"What do you mean, *our* realm?" Eirik sneered. "You think you are a lady of voima?"

"That's right."

Eirik paused, then paced up and down for a moment, looking irritably to where the last of the sun still lingered. "If you really are an immortal," he said after a moment, "what are you doing lying tied up here, or riding around with this young man who claims to be a king's son? You should be off ruling earth and sky!"

"Well," she said, a bit uneasily, "our full powers have not yet returned."

Eirik shook his head and grinned. "What good are lords and ladies of voima without full powers? There is only *one* whose powers do not come and go, and that is death itself."

"I will not, Eirik Eirik's son," she said firmly, "help you call on death. I have been thinking this over, and, when our full powers blossom, it would be best if our realm was just as it was before, an immortal realm with no taint of mortality."

"Then how do you explain six of our brothers dying here?"

He stopped in his pacing and whirled toward her. "How did you know my father's name?"

"She already told you. She is one of the immortals."

It was Valmar who spoke, and Karin clenched her fists at hearing his voice—not the good-natured, idealistic boy's voice she knew, but one dull with pain.

"Have you made up your mind, king's son?" asked Eirik. "Do you want to go down to death with the rest or join us?"

"Ever since I came here," Valmar said in the same dull voice, "I have intended to face death for the lords of voima. Perhaps I shall do so now at last—if they will still take anything from my hands."

Eirik shifted his shoulders back and forth a minute uneasily, then shouted, "Let's get some fires going! I think real night is coming on at last!"

"Now!" whispered Karin. "We have to rescue him *now.*"

Roric held her arm tight. "The Wanderers are coming."

But those were not Wanderers. Eirik's band reached for their swords at the sound of galloping hooves. A shadowy group of riders came rapidly toward the ridge, carrying torches. As they approached, torchlight flashed on their horned helmets.

"I fought against these," Roric said in Karin's ear. "The Witch said they are women but I am still not certain— they are small warriors but tough."

The riders swept around Eirik's warriors. One shouted, "Free our sister, mortals!" and it was a woman's voice.

Eirik and his men immediately formed a tight circle, back to back, Valmar and the woman at the center. "More ladies of voima, I see!" the outlaw king yelled mockingly. "And no lords of voima to comfort you? We can help you there!"

Karin's breath came in shallow gasps. Waiting and watching was almost intolerable, but if she rushed out she did not know which side she would try to help.

"Watch their blades!" came a shout from the middle of

Eirik's warriors, the woman they had captured. "Mortals can wound us now!"

"Mortals can do many things!" Eirik yelled in agreement. He leaped forward, sword in his hand. The sword, to Karin's amazement, was singing. A horned rider thrust him back with her spear. But he spun around and leaped forward again, and she was just able to catch the blow on her shield.

And then the battle was joined. Screams and the clang of weapons rose up. And as Eirik's band fought the horned warriors the last burning edge of the sun disappeared. The crimson sky darkened toward the color of old blood, and more thunderclouds moved rapidly toward them.

"They can't hold the circle," said Roric in a low voice, all his muscles tensing. "In another minute we should be able to get to Valmar." He gave a chuckle with no mirth behind it. "Now that I have no honor left, I can plunge straight into the middle of a battle and straight out again."

Karin's eye was caught by something white moving across the twilight landscape. This time it *was* the Wanderers.

But they seemed to be fleeing, not coming to join the battle. The shadows behind them seemed dense somehow— And then she saw they were pursued by the dragon.

They were running, the lords of voima were running in terror. The dragon, seeming even more ferocious on the open plain than in its den, was maybe a quarter mile behind, flying low with its neck extended. Its eyes glowed like a forest fire. In its den it had been slow and inexorable; here it had picked up speed until it moved like an eagle before the wind.

"Take a bite from a dragon's mouth and see how immortal you are then!" Eirik shouted gleefully.

"Mortals are supposed to have extra powers here," Roric commented quietly in a tone pitched below the shouting and the din, edging carefully forward. No one looked in their direction; all the fighters had turned to stare. "I presume that also applies to creatures of voima which are supposed to stay in mortal realms."

There were a dozen Wanderers, all looking strangely shorter, less imposing than had the one who had spoken to them. They called out as they came toward the Hearthkeepers, ignoring Eirik and his men. "Help us! Our powers are failing with the end of day! Destruction is loose in the realms of voima! You must help us!"

This must be the most vulnerable moment for the realms of voima, Karin thought, in all the great cycles that fate ordained. The powers of the lords of voima were waning fast, but those who would replace them had not yet come to power. She expected the Hearthkeepers to laugh derisively at the plea for help, but instead they whirled, their mares rearing, and pounded to meet the Wanderers.

"Look at them go!" Eirik shouted after them. "They've no stomach for a fight with real men!"

He started to turn back toward Valmar and the bodies of his slain warriors, but his men too were off, racing on foot after the mounted Hearthkeepers. "Come back and fight! We've got you now! You're caught between Eirik and a dragon!"

After only a second's hesitation, the outlaw king too ran after them. Roric was in motion at once, hurrying up onto the ridge toward where Valmar and the one Hearthkeeper still lay bound. Karin was only a step behind.

"I should have expected it," she gasped. "Women always have to come to men's rescue when they get themselves into serious trouble."

There was a great bellow from the dragon as the Hearthkeepers reached it, but Roric did not turn his head. Karin closed her eyes for a second as though to fend off a horrifying realization. If somehow, at this moment of weakness, *all* the lords and ladies of voima were destroyed, what would that mean for mortal realms?

Roric went straight toward Valmar, jumping over the dead bodies spread out on the ground, not taking the extra seconds to go around. Karin caught her breath through her teeth. Even in the heat of battle, it was said, warriors avoided stepping across the dead unless they were convinced that they would join them very soon.

Valmar lay on the grass without struggling, his face showing no expression. For a moment he looked so unlike the Valmar she knew that Karin wondered wildly if he might be someone else. But in a second his face changed, lighting up in surprise and delight as he recognized them.

"Karin!" he cried. Then his eyes went wide as Roric leaned over him with a blade in his hand. The white stallion whinnied and tried to rear, but he too was tied.

Roric did not bother saying that he had come to rescue Valmar, not to kill him. The knife slashed through the ropes that held him, and Karin saw Valmar close his eyes, swallow, and resume his stony expression. He had passed in a second from joy to terror to embarrassment and now had again nothing in him of her little brother.

"I can't take time to explain," said Roric fiercely, gripping Valmar by the shoulders. "Just do what I tell you."

But he paused for a second to turn and slash the curly-haired woman's ropes, then whirled back to Valmar. For a moment he smiled. "Attractive woman you found," he said, then was grim again. "I hope the Wanderers remembered to open the way back into mortal realms before their powers went. Take Karin home. Go! Don't worry about me or anything else."

Karin expected the Hearthkeeper to race to join her sisters, but instead she sat quietly, rubbing her wrists where they had been tied, looking at Valmar with a half smile on her face.

Roric glanced over his shoulder. A crowd of warriors was rushing back toward them across the plain. Eirik must have decided that staying away from a battle with a dragon was better for men who had no honor to lose anyway.

Roric jerked Valmar to his feet and pushed him forward. "Along the stream from the spring, then down the waterfall," he said roughly. "Karin knows the way. You'll either tumble through into the faeys' burrow near Hadros' castle,

or we'll be the stuff of story—if anyone ever hears of it."
He tossed Valmar his knife, glittering in the twilight, and
drew his sword. "Get Karin through if you can, get her
through *now*. I'll protect your backs. If they kill me and
there's no way through, take as many of them to Hel with
you as possible."

"They're getting away!" Eirik yelled. "Stop them!" Two
of his younger warriors, already running even faster than
the rest, pulled ahead of the band, coming straight toward
them.

Valmar came to life again. He started in the direction
Roric had pointed, Karin's hand clasped in his, then abruptly
turned back.

"Go!" the woman called. "I shall not follow you to mortal realms." And she was away then herself, running quickly
and lightly, not toward Eirik's band, which was now very
close, but off at an angle, as though she intended to circle
around and join the Hearthkeepers' battle against the dragon.

Valmar stretched out a hand tentatively, imploringly,
either toward the woman or toward his horse. The white
stallion whinnied again, pawing the ground. "What are
you waiting for?" Roric demanded, then gave a humor-
less laugh. "The faeys don't want *another* horse in their
burrows!"

When Valmar still hesitated, Karin tugged at his hand.
"Come on, little brother," she said as she had said to him a
thousand times over the years, forcing her voice to be gentle.
His face was now not expressionless but anguished. After
she had come all this long hard way to rescue him, she
could not let his hesitancy now doom them. She had no
idea what had happened to him in this realm, how he had
served the Wanderers or been taken prisoner by Eirik, or
why he had apparently captured a Hearthkeeper. But if
there was safety for him she had to take him to it.

Roric, much less gentle, gave them both a hard push.
"Get away! Now!" The first of Eirik's warriors had reached
the base of the ridge and were coming fast up the slope.

There was another great bellow from the dragon. Karin, running and dragging Valmar with her, caught a flash of lightning from the corner of her eye. Would the Hearthkeepers and their swords, with the help of the Wanderers and the last of their power to shape this realm, be able to stop the dragon?

And if not, even if they made it safely into the faeys' burrows, would mortal realms even still exist on the other side?

Roric, behind them, shouted defiance at Eirik's men. Karin reached the lip of the little cliff and swung over the edge. Valmar, more clumsily, followed her. She lowered herself downward as fast as she could. At the bottom of the waterfall the water poured into a stream that ran back to a pool, inside a limestone cave.

For the first time in her life, Karin felt no hesitation about a rough, enclosed tunnel. This was not merely safety for her; this was safety for Valmar.

At the top of the cliff above them came the clang of steel on steel. Then Roric came down in one long leap, landing lightly next to the water. He barely glanced toward Karin and Valmar, who were scrambling back into the cave, but tossed back his hair and grinned, looking up at the warriors above them.

Without a final word for him, without a final kiss, Karin plunged into darkness. She had seen his face, alight with a berserk fury mingled with joy, and her heart turned to ice.

Valmar seemed to recover from his blank apathy as they crawled, side by side, into blackness. "There are faeys near my father's castle? And we may be in their tunnels?"

But Karin did not answer. She was listening to the shouts and the sounds of battle behind them. Eirik's men too must have come down the cliff. Unless Roric retreated into the cave, he would be hopelessly outnumbered, captured or killed—and she did not think he planned to retreat.

It seemed as though they had crawled a very long time, on a surface that now felt smooth under hands and knees.

Karin realized the stream no longer ran beside them. She paused and lifted her head, listening, but now there was only silence behind them. Her eyes ached from trying to see in darkness, and when she first saw the green glow ahead of them she thought it was her imagination.

But it disappeared when she closed her eyes, then reappeared when she opened them. The rift between the realms of voima and mortal lands was open.

"I hear something back in the tunnels! But nothing can be back there! Roric came through there. I don't like Roric. He brought a horse in here and took Karin away."

She started to laugh, then realized tears were streaming down her face. "It's all right!" she called in a voice she was not able to make cheerful. "It's me, Karin! And I have my little brother with me."

The oak woods near Hadros' castle appeared unchanged as Karin and Valmar emerged into the cool evening air. The chaos of which the Wanderer had warned had not reached mortal lands—or not yet. They would know that the dragon had destroyed the powers of voima if the sun did not rise again in the morning.

It was a shock to be back, without any period of transition, to a world so familiar, and here Valmar seemed even more fully grown and muscular. Karin felt almost emotionless, as though this final shock, on top of all her recent experiences, had driven all feeling from her.

As they stumbled through the woods toward the castle she told Valmar about their long trip to reach him, about Hadros' pursuit of them, and about King Eirik. She told him of the dragon's den and the cave of the Witch of the Western Cliffs behind it, of the Witch's hope that the Wanderers and Hearthkeepers might somehow be reunited, and of their conversation with the Wanderer. All she kept quiet was the price the Witch had extracted from Roric—and the fear that he was her brother.

Valmar grunted in response as though listening but asked

her nothing. Karin realized as she spoke that she was telling it as though it were a story, someone else's story, and this time might somehow have a different ending.

She listened for any sign of the troll as they walked, not knowing how she would deal with meeting it at this point, unsure she would even bother to try escaping. Valmar had very little to say about his time in the realms of voima, not even how he had become separated from the Wanderers and ended up with a Hearthkeeper.

She had wondered in a daze if she and Valmar, like Roric, had returned from immortal realms invisible, but nothing of the sort seemed to have happened. Dag and Nole were stunned to find them hammering on the castle gates, unaccompanied, filthy, and unable to give any clear answers to their questions. But the serving-maids recovered from their surprise enough to obey Karin's orders, bringing them bread and ale and the last of the evening's stew.

Firelight, ordinary, comforting firelight, flickered through the hall. It must be, Karin thought, because Roric had been with the third force rather than the true lords of voima that he had returned to mortal lands not fully himself.

The household assembled at the far end of the room to watch Karin and Valmar, the maids and the housecarls whispering together. His younger brothers tried to stay quiet and let them eat, but they could not keep themselves from asking questions. Karin told them sharply that they would hear the full story the next day, and Valmar said nothing at all, but that did not keep one or the other from suddenly bursting out with a new question.

"Where have you been all this time?" "Did you see Father?" "Where is your ship? Or your horses?" "Have you had adventures? Did you get into any fights?" "Where is Roric?"

Karin, almost too tired to eat, leaned against Valmar's shoulder. It was strong and solid, reassuring. She wanted to comfort him and protect him, but it came to her as she closed her eyes sleepily that he might also be able to comfort *her.*

Dag dared another question. "Are you two married now?"

Both Karin and Valmar jerked up at that. "No," she said shortly, awake again. What had Hadros told his sons?

Delighted to have at least one answer, Dag tried again. "You left with Roric. Where is he now? Is he still alive? Did Father catch him?"

Karin slumped again, her face against Valmar's arm. Emotion rushed back into her, replacing the numbness which she realized was all that had let her keep moving these last few hours. "King Hadros captured Roric," she said indistinctly, "but he escaped. He escaped to rescue me. And now," she fought unsuccessfully against a sob that threatened to choke her as the full realization hit her of what the silence behind them must have meant, "he has given his life to save Valmar and me."

CHAPTER FOURTEEN

1

Valmar jumped up. "Out!" he ordered. "Everybody out!"

The serving-maids and housecarls took one look at his face, stern and suddenly very like his father's, and made for the door. Dag and Nole hesitated in surprise. "You too," Valmar snapped. Nole began to ask something more, but Dag took him hastily by the arm and dragged him away. Valmar bolted the hall door after them.

He turned back to Karin, who was weeping now in good earnest. She had pushed away her half-finished plate and had her head on the trestle table, her face hidden by her russet hair.

"He's dead, he's dead!" she wailed as Valmar gathered her up in his arms. "I escaped to the faeys and left him to die!" She clung to him, sobbing, as he patted her back.

"Karin, dearest Karin," he found himself murmuring. "Please stop crying. He would not want you to mourn. He loved you. We shall make a great story and a song about him tomorrow so that his name will always live."

Crying harder than ever, she threw her arms tight around his neck. Valmar held her close and kissed her damp forehead very gently, then when she did not pull away he worked his lips down to hers.

She still made no effort to resist, though she was now sobbing Roric's name over and over between kisses. Valmar

crushed her to him. Roric is dead, he thought, trying not
to feel joyous. My father wants Karin and me to marry. He
thinks we already spent one night together. Why then not
this one?

They were alone together with the door barred. He rose,
lifting her from the bench, and carried her to the cupboard bed where she had always slept. He could feel all
her muscles and all her womanly softness against him.

He laid her down and sat on the bed beside her, waiting
for her tears to subside while his heart beat faster and faster.
He kicked off his boots and made a deliberate effort to
keep the hand on her shoulder gentle.

"I'm sorry, Valmar," she gasped, wiping futilely at her
wet cheeks. "But I can't stop crying. I'm so weary and so
miserable! I have tried to be strong for so long— He
embraced death at the end, and I know it was because of
me. And he died without my even saying I loved him!"

She buried her face in the pillow, shaking all over, and
Valmar stretched out beside her so that their bodies were
touching along their entire length. How could he have ever
been distracted by the woman in the realms of voima? he
wondered. She had never been a real woman, he told himself,
only a boy's fantasy come to life in a world very far from
this, the castle he would one day inherit. He had never
even known her name. He pulled Karin slowly closer.

If she realized that the arm around her shoulders was
more than the arm of a comforting younger brother she
still gave no sign. Valmar started trying to loosen her clothing, although it was hard with her back turned toward him.
"Dearest Karin, my sweetest one," he whispered, peeling
off his own jacket, "my own dear love." She only sobbed in
answer.

Abruptly Valmar pulled away and stood up. He could
not take her now, not here in the hall where she had long
been mistress of Hadros' household, ordering around the
maids and housecarls, giving commands even to the warriors, and looking after the boys she thought of as her little

brothers. She had kissed him a moment ago, but she had really been kissing Roric. He clenched and unclenched his fists, looking down at her. He loved her so much that he could not do anything to hurt her.

Dag and Nole—and for that matter everyone else in the castle—doubtless had ideas of their own what he and Karin were doing alone here. None of the men would understand why he did not take a woman when she lay before him on the bed, offering no objection, only tears that were not for him.

He shook his head, then bent to remove her shoes. He was his own man and had to make his own decisions, not do what he thought others expected of him. "Try to sleep, Karin," he said gently, pulling the blanket over her. "Tomorrow you and I can start on a song for Roric."

Her sobs slowly weakened, and after half an hour he heard her breathing grow regular. He sat glumly, not moving, staring into the fire while it burned down to coals.

It was after midnight and the hall was nearly pitch black when Valmar rose again to his feet. He could not retreat back here to safety, where everyone was happy he was the royal heir and would be delighted, as delighted as at a great story of warriors of old, if he told them how many men he had killed. And he could no longer seek solace in the love of women.

Karin slept on. Hadros and his warriors had taken most of the extra weapons when they pursued Roric and Karin, but in the corner chest Valmar was able, after a little quiet rummaging, to find an old sword which he belted on. Eirik had his singing sword, and he did not want to go to fight the outlaw king barehanded.

He felt his way to the door and unbarred it carefully, then stepped out into the courtyard. The rest of the castle was silent. It had been long since Hadros posted guards at night, and the small number of warriors he had left here would not have been enough for constant watches anyway. Valmar crossed silently to the gates and worked the great bolts back.

He had saved Karin and brought her home, but he could not stay here with her as her brother. Roric had traveled hundreds of miles to save him, and he could not now desert him if there was any chance his foster-brother was still alive. The fight with the dragon must be over by now, but if the Wanderers still survived he was still pledged to serve them.

No comfortable inheritance for him of a kingdom he had not won himself, and also no adventure for its own sake, or only in thoughtless imitation of old tales. All that was important was to follow the way of honor in his own heart, even if in the world's eyes his honor was gone.

Now he hoped, hurrying through the dark woods, that he could return through the faeys' burrows the way they had come.

2

Karin awoke before dawn. For a moment she could not remember why she was here, in her own bed. Were all the events of the past few months a particularly vivid dream?

She sat up and remembered. Last night, the arrival at Hadros' castle, the unsuccessful struggle to hold off wild despair, Valmar's attempts to comfort her, were all very vague. But the image of Roric guarding their retreat was vivid. He had wanted to die.

She gulped once, but all the tears had been cried out of her and her sorrow had settled down to a burning ache. With blood-guilt on him and the guilt of incest, no future left for him here in mortal realms, he had saved her and Valmar by letting Eirik's men kill him. All that was left of him was the song Valmar had said they would make for him.

But where was Valmar? In the pre-dawn dimness she could just make out the shapes in the hall, and she did not see him anywhere. Karin pulled on her shoes and went to the door, which was unbolted. She seemed to remember Valmar driving out the others and bolting it when she had begun to weep last night. A thoughtful gesture—the castle's mistress should not be seen to break down so completely.

But *was* she this castle's mistress? She opened the door and looked out into the quiet courtyard. She had ruled here for years, and if she married Valmar she would again.

The thought that now that Roric was dead there was nothing to keep her from becoming Valmar's wife came as a sharp blow, threatening to destroy her aching calm. She took a deep breath and stepped into the courtyard, thinking that she should build up the fires in the bath house— she and Valmar could both use a bath.

Then she saw that the great gates were ever so slightly ajar.

Valmar had gone, then. He had returned to help Roric once he had gotten her home to safety. Men might fight against each other, but they were united in trying to keep the women out of their fights.

She squeezed through the gate and began to run. The sun was not yet up, and there might still be time to reach the faeys' burrows before they retreated underground. The eastern sky was yellow; at least so far mortal realms were still functioning as they always had. Her feet kept stumbling, and she had to throw up her arms against low-hanging branches that appeared abruptly out of the dimness before her, but she never slowed her pace until she tumbled, gasping for breath, into the faeys' dell.

It was not too late. Their green lights still burned as she gave through parched lips the triple whistle to tell them she was there.

"Karin! Karin!" They clustered around her, tugging at her skirts. "We don't understand! Why didn't you tell us last night how you'd gotten into our burrows? Where did the other young man go? Are you going to marry him instead of Roric?"

For a second she relented and sat down, squeezing their hands and patting them on their heads. They had been her friends for years when no one else had been. But then her need to know overtook her again. "Did Valmar come back here? Yes, the man I was with last night. Is he here? Did he go back into the Wanderers' realm?"

In spite of the faeys' insistence that there was no door from their burrows into the realms of voima, they reluctantly admitted that Valmar had appeared in their dell a few hours earlier, had pushed by them to crawl back into the tunnels, and had not reemerged.

"We think he's been swallowed by the earth," said the faeys confidently. "But *you* won't be, Karin, if you stay with us. It's time for us to go inside now. Do you want some raspberries?"

"Don't do anything to close the rift," she said, accepting a handful of berries and stuffing them into her mouth. She immediately began to crawl deeper into the tunnels, the way Valmar must have gone.

When Dag and Nole found them both gone in the morning, she thought, swallowing the berries, they would wonder if they had ever really been there, or if their appearance after dark and disappearance by dawn meant that they were wights from Hel, allowed in mortal realms only to announce their own deaths.

Karin dismissed all thoughts of what the people in the castle might think. She had enough concerns of her own. If Roric was dead, she wanted to bring his body back from the realms of voima, and after having braved so much to save Valmar she was certainly not going to let him go off alone into danger with some thought of protecting her from it.

She crawled rapidly into darkness, keeping her head down, until the sounds of the faeys' high voices faded away behind her and before her came the rhythmic splash of waves.

Waves? What had happened in the realms of voima? The smooth surface under her hands was bone dry. Karin paused for a moment, then shrugged and pushed on.

And felt a cold, salty wave break over her. Struggling, she kicked out, finding nothing but water—no tunnel, no floor or ceiling. She tried to swim, fighting in the direction which seemed to lead upward.

She emerged, streaming and spitting water, in the surf by a rocky shore. The sun was just rising, chasing shadows down the slopes of high mountains. She splashed forward, found a footing, and came ashore dripping wet. Before her a dark cave led into the rocks. She was back in Eirik's kingdom, back to the spot where she and Roric had dived into the sea and into the realms of voima.

No use hesitating now. She spun around and dove back into the surf.

Again salt water closed over her head, and when she got her feet under her and surged back to the surface the dawn light still lay across the steep slopes of the Hot-River Mountains.

She pulled herself up out of the waves. With water pouring off her, she scrambled into the sea cave. Maybe the Witch of the Western Cliffs could help her find Valmar.

But the passage down which she and Roric had come had disappeared. She groped wildly in the darkness, finding what she thought was the entrance, but if so the air had turned to stone. Pounding on it only bruised her fists, The Witch was talking to someone else—or did not want to see her again.

Slowly she turned, emerged from the cave, and made her way along the shingle, walking in the waves half the time, shivering from wet and cold without even noticing. Gulls wheeled overhead, calling sharply. The sun rose slowly higher. The salt water dripping from her hair down her cheeks could have been tears, but she had no tears left.

But there was still her father. At the thought of King Kardan she lifted her head. He had been so happy to see her when she came home from Hadros' kingdom, and she had given him nothing but worry ever since. Then she remembered that he might be Roric's father as well as her

own. If so, he had a right to know that his last son was
dead.

Someone had spotted her. She heard a shout that was
not the gulls and looked up to see a warrior, perched high
above her, signaling to someone. Eirik's men? she thought,
freezing. But it was someone she recognized, one of Hadros'
warriors.

It was nearly evening before they would answer her
questions or even let her speak. Men, she thought disgust-
edly, with the energy that came from sleeping most of the
day and having had hot food again. But Queen Arane was
just as insistent as the kings that she rest.

"We haven't seen this King Eirik or any of his men,"
said Hadros, "or for that matter anyone for the last three
days. I was ready to start for home, little princess, but your
father insisted we wait in case you were still alive. He's
almost as stubborn as you are! Glad of it," he added gruffly.

The sun was sinking over the western sea. When she
looked at the sunset, long ribbons of red-tinged clouds
seemed to carry her hundreds of miles across the waves
toward the dying sun. The moon climbed the sky behind
her. She had not yet tried to say anything about the sun
setting in the realms of voima.

"And where have you been all this time, Karin?" asked
Queen Arane, gently in spite of an irritated undertone in
her voice. "Both your father and foster-father have been
almost mad with wondering and waiting. We waited even
when hope was dulled and gone—your father saying it was
too late to begin again." As the sun set, the long shadow
cast by the burial mound of the slain warriors melted into
the general darkness.

"We were in the Wanderers' lands," Karin said slowly,
deciding to keep the story as simple as possible, "Roric,
Valmar, and I."

"They keep on giving us the same story about the Wanderers," commented Hadros, half under his breath. "At

this rate we'll have to believe the lords of voima really might be interested in people like us." Karin could see her father consciously keeping himself from asking questions.

"I escaped from King Eirik," she went on, "the outlaw king who attacked you here, then Roric and I escaped from the dragon." It did sound in her own ears like one of the more fantastic of the old tales. "Then he and I went through a doorway the Wanderers had opened— But that door is closed now." But the Wanderers had let Valmar back through before closing it, she thought. Men again, acting together against the women.

"Eirik and his men followed us into the Wanderers' realm," she continued, "and Valmar was already there."

"Then that's why the outlaw wasn't in his castle," muttered Hadros.

"We stayed in that realm for a little while. Then, although I do not entirely understand how it happened," which was true, "the lords of voima wanted me back in mortal realms. Valmar, as far as I know, is with the Wanderers."

"And Roric?" That was Queen Arane.

"Roric," she gulped and went on, her voice steady, "Roric is dead."

Karin forced herself to lift her eyes to meet those of the two kings and the queen. All looked startled and, she thought, sorry, but that might only have been sympathy for her. Well, the time for subtlety was long past.

When she trusted her voice again, she said, "Yes, even in the realms of voima mortals can die. I loved him. He was the lord of my heart and my body. And I hope I am carrying his child."

She had expected Queen Arane to give her a reproving glare, both for her frankness and for allowing herself to be with child at all. But the queen's look was distant and strangely expressionless. King Kardan reached out impulsively toward his daughter, as though to draw her in like a little girl, but he stopped.

Once Karin had begun there seemed no reason not to

continue. "Now that he is gone it may not matter—but it does matter to me and to our child. Was Roric my brother?"

"No!" All three spoke at once, Hadros and Kardan and Arane, then became flustered, rewrapping their cloaks against the cool of the evening air, meeting neither her eyes nor each other's.

"Why are you all so sure?" she asked, looking in surprise from one to another. "Is there something you have kept from me?" When they all shook their heads emphatically she added, "Both the Weaver back home and the—well, a creature of voima we met seemed to suggest that, that . . . that I was his sister and for him to love me was incest."

"Like the old stories?" asked Hadros, recovering first. He shot Queen Arane a look, thrust out his chin, and went on. "It wasn't my secret but I don't mind telling it. He was born at Arane's court, though I brought him home as a tiny baby to raise in my own castle. Roric was the son of Arane's serving-maid and, I think, me."

"Oh, dear." The queen put her graceful hands over her face, and the jewels on her rings winked in the firelight.

"*Your* son?" said Karin in bewilderment to the king. This changed everything. "But why would anyone do to his son—" She stopped, not wanting to get into that issue now. She whirled toward Kardan. "Tell me," she commanded, her eyes intense in the shadows, "is there any chance that a baby born to Arane's serving-maid could have been fathered by you?"

He was flustered but certain. "No. No chance at all. I have never lain with any woman at Arane's court." He paused uncertainly. "I can swear on steel and rowan if you like."

Karin looked questioningly toward Arane but the queen had turned her head away. Roric had said he knew for certain he was not Hadros' son—and had he not said Arane herself told him?

Someone else, then, had also enjoyed the favors of the queen's maid, though the queen had managed to make Hadros believe the baby was his to ensure him a good upbringing. Whosoever son he might have been, he was not the son of King Kardan.

Roric's father was another man. She did not know how relieved she was to learn this until she found herself throwing her arms around her own father, just on the edge of sobbing again.

Queen Arane rose briskly, pulling up the hood of her cloak. "The girl is exhausted and drained," she said firmly. "She can tell you the rest of her story in the morning. What she needs now is sleep, which she can best have in my tent."

Before Karin could protest, the queen had her by the elbow and was propelling her across the camp. Now that she had begun telling her tale she would have been willing to continue, but there seemed no chance of that. "Well, goodnight!" came her father's voice, belatedly and behind them.

Karin entered the queen's tent resignedly, ready to be tucked back into the blankets where she had slept that afternoon. Her life seemed rather empty and pointless, now that she knew the lords of voima would not let her rescue Valmar. It would be best perhaps to let others make the decisions for her until the baby within her quickened and gave her again a reason to live.

But the queen put the lantern between them and sat on her cushions, eyes glittering. "Now, Karin. I want you to tell me how Roric died."

"King Eirik had captured Valmar, there in the Wanderers' realm," said Karin slowly, wondering why Arane did not want the kings to hear this. "Roric freed him, but Eirik was such a short distance away that we had very little chance of escape. Roric pushed Valmar and me into, well, a tunnel that led to safety." There would be time enough to mention their brief visit to Hadros' court. "Roric guarded our backs, and there he was killed." She was almost able to say it calmly now.

"Did you see him die?" asked the queen sharply.

"No, but he would have come behind us if he had lived, and he did not."

"I would not yet give up hope of him," said Arane very quietly. "But if he is gone he died to save his beloved and his foster-brother. I shall commission a bard as soon as I am home to put it into song."

When the queen did not speak again Karin asked, "Is there a reason you did not want Hadros to hear about his death? Were you afraid it would reflect dishonorably on Valmar?"

But the queen did not answer her question. "You know I only ever spoke to Roric once as an adult, after he left my court where, it is true, he was born. Tell me: did he carry any charm?"

"He had a little bone charm, cut in the shape of a star. He was told it was in his blankets when he was found—though I gather now he was not a foundling?"

Still ignoring her questions, Arane reached into her belt pouch and pulled out something that she placed on Karin's palm. It was a star-shaped bone charm. "Did it look like that?"

Karin stared at it. "He *gave* you his charm?" She tried to remember if she had seen Roric thumbing it, as he had so often, in the period between when they had been reunited outside Eirik's castle and when Eirik and his men had slain him. She could not remember.

Arane smiled slowly and sadly. "This is not Roric's. But you have answered my question. This in your hand is the twin of the charm that I sent with him, all the meager powers of voima that I dared give him. For you see, Roric was my own son."

Just when Karin thought she had become calm she found herself weeping wildly again. She had not felt entirely sure of Hadros' story, but this—this she believed.

"Oh, Karin," Arane said, stroking Karin's hair as she lay with her face in the queen's lap. "It seems very long ago, but I too can remember how miserable and how wonderful it can be to be young, to feel intense love and great sorrow without the experience to deal well with either . . ."

"If he was your son," Karin brought out, trying to overcome her tears, "why did you send him away? And which man fathered him?"

"He was called No-man's son, I understand," said the queen slowly. "And even if he had lived I would never have wanted him to know his father's name. He was *not* Hadros, *not* your father, only a man who may never even have known he had fathered a son but whom I loved very much . . ."

This, thought Karin miserably, was what Arane had suggested to her back when they had first met, that as long as a queen was very discreet she could enjoy an occasional man in her bed. But she had also spoken of jealousies and rivalries—had Roric's father been killed by some other would-be suitor of the queen, even before the baby was born? Perhaps it was better not to know.

"The Witch told Roric he could never know his father's name," she said through her tears. She had not mentioned the Witch before, but it did not matter. "But it—she—also said that having the name, having the answer, would take away Roric's goal of trying to live up to an image of a glorious father."

"Well, Roric cannot know his father's name now," said the queen reasonably. "And I had never intended to tell him. The man I loved came to me in secret, and I have always honored his secrecy. He gave me these two little charms before we parted for the last time, and I thought his son should have one, but no other information."

Karin felt a sudden horrible suspicion. "Roric's father," she said between tight lips. "Was he perhaps King Eirik?"

Arane managed her tinkling little laugh. "No, Karin, I can reassure you quite certainly on that point. I knew Eirik, of course, from meetings of the All-Gemot over the years, and he was somewhat dashing in his youth in a rather coarse way. But you should give Roric's mother credit for better taste than that!

"King Hadros," she went on, "in spite of an edge of uncertainty, has always assumed that Roric was his. I did not wish to tell him otherwise, though of course that meant he could not know that Roric was born to a queen, not to a serving-maid. My little deception assured that Roric would receive much the same training and advantages any son of one of the Fifty Kings might receive—though Hadros' fatherly methods may be rougher than most! If Roric is indeed dead, I would appreciate it, Karin, if you never told Hadros the truth yourself."

"All right. It doesn't matter now anyway."

"I hope you realize, Karin," the queen continued, "that it is very hard to keep the reputation of a virgin queen if one is seen to suckle a babe! People may have suspicions, but without evidence suspicions are nothing. My household has always been very protective of me and very loyal, but there are limits to what even the most closemouthed servants can keep hid. And of course I did not want Roric to grow up the target for a dagger-thrust from any man who hoped to win me and father his own sons on me."

"Did you think never to see him again when you sent him away?" Karin asked dully.

"If he had lived, I would have told him, sooner or later, that he was my son. A little boy would be in too much danger from his relatives for me openly to declare him my heir, especially when he was a child born to a secret union, when I had never married the man before witnesses or with the consent of my kin. Someone like that the Fifty Kings would be very slow to accept! But a full-grown man, someone with the warrior skills of King Hadros, would have been different. Even as No-man's son, such a man could still be chosen by my kingdom's Gemot as the next king—and accepted by the other kings—if I had no obvious other heir and swore that he was mine.

"But *your* child," continued Arane with the ghost of a

smile, "will be the grandchild of a king and of a sovereign queen, a fine baby boy or girl to rule Kardan's kingdom after him and after you. All you need now is a husband— the Fifty Kings will *still* be reluctant to recognize that the child of a woman who has never been wed may inherit royal rule. Of course, as long as you are married before the babe is actually born, you should be all right . . . I do not, from my own experiences, recommend out-fostering your child on someone else! Now, you said you thought that Valmar may still be alive—"

Karin could not stand it, the plotting, the maneuvering, all ready to begin again and this time around her. "No!" she cried, sitting up abruptly. "Roric is scarcely dead! I cannot start looking at once for a husband, planning whom to fool into thinking Roric's child is his. I would rather—"

She never had a chance to say what she would rather do. There was a great roar outside the tent, not an animal sound but much deeper, a roar of sea and earth.

Karin and Arane scrambled out into the cold night air to see beneath a moonlit sky the Hot-River Mountains quivering as though shaken by an unimaginably enormous hand. The ground beneath their feet began to tremble and sway. As they clutched at each other the moonlight glinted on a giant wave racing up the salt river. It swept across the pebbled beach where the warriors of the two kings were sleeping and spun around the longship that had been hauled up beside them. Splashing and yelling, the men bobbed to the surface as the wave passed by. The few horses they had with them began to scream, and the dogs barked wildly.

"The end has begun," said Karin in a very small voice.

They were not far from the burial mound where Gizor and the others were laid, built well above the waterline. Karin heard Hadros' and Kardan's voices shouting over the din, trying to find out how many men they still had and bellowing orders to secure the ship again.

But she paid no attention, for her eyes were riveted on the burial mound. It moved, but not with the motion of earthquake. One of the horses—Roric's stallion, she thought—had broken loose and was striking at the mound with his hooves. It shook as though something—or someone—was coming up beneath it.

The wave, having bounced off the cliffs at the eastern end of the salt river, came pouring back, lower now but sending the men and supplies anew into swirling confusion. The stallion screamed again. The men, snatching their equipment out of the water, scrambled for higher ground. A number pulled at the ship's mooring lines. Both kings climbed to the top of the burial mound to shout orders. They had not seen the shaking she had seen.

It came again. A great clod of dirt flew from the side of the mound, then another. The dogs went abruptly silent. And someone, black with earth, stepped from within the mound.

That was when the moon went out.

3

Roric glared upward at the renegade king. The sky above was still pale, though everything around them was losing its color as dark came on.

"You're *definitely* more trouble than you're worth," said Eirik with a sneer of his scarred lip. "If it hadn't been for you, I and my men would still be living peacefully in what's left of our kingdom, raiding and capturing those who didn't know better than to come within a hundred miles." He paused for a second, muttered, "Though that life's been getting pretty thin lately," then glared at Roric again. "First you show up with the princess, then it turns out that ship had come looking for you, you free the king's son I was going to offer to the lords of death, and now between you and him I've lost half my men."

"Where's your fair lady Wigla?" said Roric mockingly. "Am I responsible for her disappearance as well?"

Eirik shook his head. "You fight like a berserker, like

someone who doesn't care if he lives or dies—only *I*, Eirik, am supposed to fight like that. And now you act like you want me to kill you in cold blood. Well, I wouldn't let my men kill you, to let the princess make a great song to keep your spirit happy in Hel. And I'm not going to kill you quickly and cleanly now. You're going to be the sacrifice."

They dragged him up the cliff by the waterfall and back to where the bodies of those Valmar had slain were laid out. They added the men Roric had killed before they overpowered him.

Two of the king's warriors had gone back into the cave by the pool but emerged in a moment with puzzled frowns. So Karin and Valmar were safely back home, Roric thought and grinned wolfishly.

The sounds of the fight between the Wanderers and the dragon had died away. Roric peered through the dimness but saw no sign of the lords of voima. "No use waiting for midnight," said Eirik. "The day moves so slowly around here that it might be a week's worth of waiting. We'll make the sacrifices and get back to our own land with the booty."

"How about Wigla?" asked one of his warriors, picking up Roric's question.

Eirik growled and glared over his shoulder at Roric again. "She can do what she likes." He turned back to his men. "Now, we don't have any women so you two will have to do. And this spring will do instead of the boiling pool. Stand there with the bread and ale. I don't have my lyre, but I should still be able to make a song."

He considered a moment, arms crossed and forehead furrowed, then began to sing.

"Outlaws they called us, the men of the south,
Renegade warriors to the Fifty Kings,
But brothers in blood to the band of King Eirik,
They fought, never shirking, till fate struck them
    down.

Come death, take our brothers, to dark realms
      below!
Take them now to the one realm that endures!
In lands of immortals, as in human realms,
Our swords serve the master whom no one evades."

King Eirik snorted and shook his head. "Not one of my
better songs. I really need the lyre. You, there! You have to
do the calling."

Roric noticed that neither Valmar nor he himself got
any credit in the song for having killed Eirik's men.

Two of the warriors stepped forward then while the rest
went absolutely silent. They sprinkled the bodies with bits
of bread and splashed them with ale. "We call on the lords
of death," piped up one in a shaking voice. "We call on
those whose power is greater than all the lords of voima!
Come, nameless ones of the night!"

"We call. We call," went the murmur up and down the
line of the living.

The water from the spring splashed softly. Roric rolled
over to see if there was any change. So far there was none.

"We call on the lords of death to take our brothers!"
continued the warrior in a high, frightened voice when
Eirik elbowed him. "Eat and drink what is offered here.
Strike down those who struck our brothers down!"

"And especially," said Eirik grimly, "drink the blood of
this man." He advanced toward Roric with his knife out.

"You still don't dare to face me in open battle," said Roric
loudly, deliberately breaking the tense stillness. "No wonder they made you an outlaw! Killing a bound man is no
way to show your men your courage, Eirik. You'd lost all
your honor yourself long before the All-Gemot took it from
you!"

But then he went abruptly silent and Eirik whirled away
from him, as the soft splashing of the stream changed its
note. The water rose in a wave that fell back with a boom,
a boom that seemed to say, "We come."

"No man escapes you!" shouted Eirik gleefully, his face transformed. "Even in the lands of voima, we make offering to the lords of darkness!"

"Cut my bonds, Eirik," growled Roric, "and you can be a sacrifice to death yourself."

The earth abruptly shuddered, and a chasm opened directly under the bodies of the slain. The other men leaped backward as the dead disappeared with a roar of falling earth and stone. Roric, trying to roll further from the edge, spat out the sourness in his throat, a sourness of long decay.

And out of the chasm rose a mist, darker than the darkening air and more solid. It grew increasingly dense, seeming to take on an almost human shape, a shape with two coals burning red where the eyes should have been. And the shape had a voice.

"This land is mine," it said, so deep that the split earth vibrated. "Immortal lands are immortal no longer but belong to me. Everything comes eventually to me, and it comes now sooner than expected. All shall end *now*, and there shall never again be renewal or birth."

Eirik's men fled, racing wildly down the ridge, but the renegade king stood his ground. "I've served you all these years," he said, nervously licking his scarred lip. "You should reward me for all the dead I've sent to you."

"No man escapes me, for all die sooner or later," the voice replied, dark, enormously loud, satisfied, unanswerable. "No man comes living to Hel, but death comes to all mortals—and now to immortals as well."

Roric jerked until the ropes bit into his flesh as a touch landed on his shoulder. He rolled around to see a Wanderer bending over him.

This time he could look at the face. It was the same face, burning with wisdom and power, which he and Karin had been forced to look away from before, but it was no longer lit from within by light, and the power was much diminished.

"This plan quite definitely was a mistake from the beginning, Roric No-man's son," said the lord of voima in a low voice, loosening Roric's bonds.

"Kardan's son," he corrected, rubbing circulation back into his wrists, but the Wanderer only shook his head.

"Sending you that stallion originally," he commented quietly, "was the only thing in the entire plan that ever benefited either us òr you."

Roric looked down the hill to see the other Wanderers and the Hearthkeepers, tattered and drooping. A glance at Eirik showed that he had not noticed their approach, having eyes only for the dark forces he had summoned.

They had defeated the dragon, then, thought Roric, rising to his knees. He slipped his hand into his belt pouch and turned over for a moment his little bone charm.

But if even immortals could now die, how much longer could either the Wanderers or the Hearthkeepers rule earth and sky? And if they were not there to bring about birth and renewal, how much longer could mortal realms endure? The sky overhead was now nearly dark, and in it showed neither moon nor stars.

He went forward slowly and silently, three steps, four steps, and still Eirik did not hear him. With a sudden bound he was on him, one elbow tight around the king's neck, the other hand knocking his knife from slack fingers.

Eirik fought back, kicking behind him and trying to heave Roric off balance, but he clung on grimly. "What happens," Roric shouted to the dark red coals before him, "what happens if a man comes living to your realm?"

The mist moved, thickening even more. "This has never happened. Men die in mortal realms and come dead to Hel."

"You came when called to eat what was offered," cried Roric, squeezing Eirik's throat tighter as the king struggled, "but I'll make you a better offer than any mortal ever made to the powers of voima! But with my offer comes a price. If you close this chasm, remove death from the realms of voima where it should never have come, you can have *two* live men in Hell!"

From the chasm came other voices, faint, avid, and cold as ice. "Life! Bring us life!"

"The wights of Hel . . . should have no voice," said the being in the mist, not so loud, not so sure.

"Then if I brought life into Hel," Roric yelled, "would there be voima there even if you had destroyed it in all the realms of earth and sky?"

"Life in Hel . . . would destroy the balance." The voice was even more unsure.

"Yet by coming here, you yourself are destroying the fated balance," grunted Roric, punching Eirik in the stomach. "If you won't take us as an offering, take us as a threat! Close the chasm and leave immortal realms forever! Your balance is changing with every second that Hel is open to the forces of voima!"

Eirik doubled over abruptly, making Roric loosen his grip around his neck. There was no time to wait to see if the forces of death would agree. Roric kicked himself forward with all his strength, launching both him and Eirik over the edge and into the pit.

The chasm crashed shut above their heads. They fell for what could have been five minutes, still clawing at each other. "Don't bother trying to kill me," Roric gasped, getting a grip on the other's head. "You can't send me to Hel since we're both going there already!"

As they fell through blackness, across the insides of his eyelids flitted images of old bones and dried brains. He fought against the images, trying to replace them with a vision of Karin, smiling at him as the wind played with her hair. If he was—even for an instant—to bring life to Hel, let it be the voima of love and triumph.

They reached bottom unexpectedly and hard, but not with the killing smash Roric had expected. They rolled apart, trying to recover their breaths. If no man had ever come living to Hel, he thought, then maybe a living man could not be killed here. It was bitterly cold, colder than a January night with the north wind blowing.

Neither of them spoke at once. Eirik seemed oddly diminished without his ready tongue. He showed no inclination to attack Roric again as both sat up slowly. Roric blinked and blinked again. There was faint light here.

And people. Not quite solid but people nonetheless, reclining listlessly on the dusty floor and looking at them. All were gray, hair and skin and eyes, gray against the gray floor, though Roric and Eirik still kept their own colors. The sound of their heartbeats, fast and hard, echoed through the tunnels, the only hearts here that beat.

"I know these men," Eirik muttered, rising and looking around. "Some of them I killed myself."

Their shapes were slightly misty, but on many Roric could see the marks of a death blow: a slit throat, a stomach sliced open so that the entrails looped out, a deep gash in the chest. "Wigla doesn't miss you at *all*," Eirik said, low and fierce, to one whose throat had been cut so deeply that his head drooped, nearly severed. He was one of the more solid ones. Others had faded so much that they were little more than hints of a shape, through which the next figure was visible. Roric pulled out his bone charm, which had given at least a hint of solidity to the Wanderers' hollow creation, but it had no such effect here.

Eirik and Roric walked slowly between the rows of reclining figures, shivering with arms wrapped around themselves. The dead did not seem to feel the cold. Here were passages that glowed with their own dim light, featureless, stretching on before them endlessly, filled with dead men and women and children who looked at them without moving but with hungry eyes. Roric fought against an increasingly powerful sense of futility and loss. Karin was becoming harder and harder to remember.

He had saved the realms of voima from death, he told himself. He had kept the forces of darkness from immortal lands. It should have been a triumphal shout, but it seemed here no great glory, only a disturbance such as he and Eirik made in the dust with their feet as they walked down unending passages where sprawled the dead.

Eirik stopped abruptly. "Here are the men for whom we just made the offerings," he said in a half-choked whisper. Roric too recognized them. He forced himself to look closely at the men whom he and Valmar had killed, resisting the urge to stumble on unlooking and the feeling that there was no use anymore in doing anything. These men bore their death wounds but they were more solid than any of the others they had passed.

"Eirik!" one croaked.

The renegade king began walking rapidly. "Are they less misty because they've been dead such a short time," Roric asked himself aloud, trying to find the question interesting, "or because of the songs sung for them?"

"The songs, of course," growled Eirik. He seemed either more excited than Roric to be here in Hel—or more frightened. "Don't you know that the dead never truly fade away as long as their songs and stories are remembered? Those others, those that were almost gone—none must have remembered them."

"Why do they keep looking at us like that?" Roric muttered.

"Because we are alive," said Eirik shortly. "Keep walking. Weren't you ever taught not to go near a burial mound at night? The dead, even the dead who live on in story, want life. Anyone alive who lingers too long near them, or near the passage that leads from every burial mound down to Hel, will have the life drained out of him."

Roric reminded himself that he had sought this death deliberately, the one way out of dishonor, even though he realized now there was no honor here. The glory and praise of the songs, which might keep the dead more solid for a little while more, was still only glory in lands under the sun.

Had he indeed saved the lords of voima? Death should be gone again from their realms, but they might still be so weak from their fight with the dragon that neither Wanderers nor Hearthkeepers would be able to rule earth and sky—in which case both their realm and mortal realms would end, either by slow decay or sudden cataclysm. And he knew in the coldness of his heart that even if one or the other of the forces of voima rallied, fate could not ordain their unending power. Eirik was right that there was only one force to whom all came in the end.

As they walked the silence of the halls seemed to alter, just the tiniest amount, but there began to be for the first time sounds as though voices were shouting a very long distance away. It was heard in no passage when they entered, but it built behind them as though they themselves were giving voice to the dead. Roric, experimenting to keep the sense of futility away, discovered that if he held his charm high the effect was intensified.

They kept on walking. He was intensely aware of the blood coursing through him, of the air entering and leaving his body with every breath, and it seemed almost obscene among these shadowy wights. They felt it too, for their eyes kept turning to them, and several spoke Eirik's name clearly, rising on their elbows for a better look, as well as mumbling behind them when they had passed. At one point the renegade king reached for his sword, but he was carrying a singing sword, and at the sound of the first wild and sweet notes the dead began to sit up. Eirik slammed the blade back in the sheath and pushed Roric to greater speed.

They turned a corner and saw a gray figure whose body was a strange mix of solidity and mistiness. His bloody chest, punctured as though by spears or dragon teeth, was vividly clear, but his face beneath a misty crown was almost invisible. His sword too was clear, a long triangular blade and a hilt set with jewels.

"This must be a king out of legend," said Roric in wonder.

"King Thaar, I think," said Eirik in an undertone, "who

killed the dragon many generations ago up in my king-dom—the dragon who first built up the hoard by the sea. Look at his wounds—they're just like in the stories. And this must be the sword Irontooth."

"Then even someone remembered in the stories," said Roric slowly, "will not stay solid here forever, because only a few aspects of his life will be remembered."

"If he's got no face at least he can't try to talk to us," said Eirik grimly.

They could have walked for an hour or for a week. Here Roric felt no weariness, no hunger, even though still alive. The cycles of waking and sleeping, eating and drinking, which ruled mortal lands had no existence here. He almost decided that these passages would never end, that they would wander past rows of the dead until earth and sky themselves passed away.

He kept looking around as they walked until he real-ized that he was looking for Karin and Valmar. If he did not find them it should mean they still lived and were safely home in Hadros' court. Karin they would forgive quickly enough when it was clear that he himself was gone.

But if he stayed here she would arrive some day, gray like all these people, growing more misty as her grandchildren slowly forgot her, at best able to croak his name in recogni-tion. He summoned again the vision of her smile beneath a brilliant sky. He had intended to die for her, his sister, his lover, his life. But being here, surrounded by the dead and not dead himself, he more than anything wanted her with him—or rather to be back under the sun with her.

Roric stopped so abruptly that Eirik, walking behind, slammed into him with a solidity of flesh and bone alien to these halls. Before them lay Gizor One-hand.

He was handless even in death. "Roric," he said through lips that did not move. "Roric," and started slowly to rise. No one else among the dead, not even those for whom Eirik had sung the songs, had tried to stand up.

Eirik was gibbering at his shoulder. "I know that man. I cut off his hand, years ago."

"And I killed him."

"*You* are not dead," said Gizor, half crouching now. "You have the breath and blood of life in you."

"And do you plan to take them from me, wight?" asked Roric. He hooked his thumbs into his belt, and his voice echoed and reechoed down the silent passages.

"Yes, of course he does!" blurted Eirik behind him.

"No," said Gizor. "No." His eyes, gray and hungry, flitted over them. "A wight could not draw the life from a man before he reached his fated end." His voice, the only voice that had spoken clearly more than a word or two, became so faint it was almost intelligible as he straightened up. "But it is good to see, No-man's son, that there is still life beneath the sun."

The two mortals backed away warily. "You tried to frighten me with a children's tale," said Roric to the outlaw king, in an undertone and between his teeth. "There has never before been a living mortal here. Why should the dead be ready to attack the first ones they see? And I have never believed that story about burial mounds. They are places of glory, where we honor the dead. But why," with a sudden thought, "did Gizor call me No-man's son? Why did he not call me by my father's name?"

"Did you think the dead knew anything, Slut's-get?" replied Eirik, but the insult sounded hollow, especially in a whisper. "Why should they in dying gain any knowledge they did not have in life?"

Gizor was standing now, still eyeing them with dead gray eyes. "You are not planning to avenge yourself on me here in Hel?" Roric asked boldly. He reached over and tugged at the sword at Eirik's belt, and again a few notes of the songs of voima rang out before Eirik smacked his hand away.

Seeming to become more solid at that sound, Gizor swayed on his feet. "There is no vengeance in Hel," he said slowly and expressionlessly, "any more than there is honor or voima.

But you defeated me using what I taught you myself. My memory and honor live with you and in the only place they *can* live, in mortal realms."

Roric nodded gravely, then turned to walk on. But there was a faint rustling behind him. He looked back. The wight was following them.

"Faster," hissed Eirik. "He won't keep up." But Gizor did keep up, staying about ten feet back. The murmuring of the awakened voices of the dead grew slowly louder, and when Roric, against his will, glanced back again he saw that Gizor had been joined by other shadowy shapes.

He found himself walking faster and faster and glanced at Eirik to see how he was taking it. But the outlaw king now looked thoughtful and was muttering to himself. "So they do not attack the living. Perhaps a living man could become their leader."

Roric stopped and turned around. "Why are you following us?"

"I thought you might need a guide," croaked Gizor.

"And where will you guide us?" asked Roric. "As you must know," making himself chuckle, "Hel has to be vaster than the earth itself to hold all those who have ever died, and living men would not want to wander its halls forever!"

"I can take you to the lords of death," said Gizor expressionlessly.

"So the dead will guide the living if asked," muttered Eirik as if in calculation.

"Then take us there!" cried Roric. He had already spoken once to Death, but it was either find something different among these endless halls or else lie down himself until he too faded away.

Gizor went before them, shuffling, and more and more of the dead rose as they passed and closed ranks behind them, continuing that faint mutter that had become like a conversation where one could not quite catch the words.

Again they walked through halls that all seemed the same, glowing with the same faint light, for a distance and a time that seemed to stretch out endlessly. But it was not unchanging now, for as living men passed through more of the halls of Hel more of the dead broke from their apathy to follow them. And then they turned a corner and saw a gigantic chamber before them.

Its ceiling was high, its spaces vast. It was wide enough that in the center spread a sunless sea, and on the shore stood a dark tower, its windows not squares of light but of even deeper darkness.

Gizor and the rest of the dead fell back as Roric and Eirik continued warily forward. As they approached the tower they could see within its darkness a mist just a little denser than mist should be. Shining in it were two points of light like coals almost burned out.

Eirik dropped to his knees. "I serve you, lord," he said as though the words were wrenched from him. "I have always sent men to you, and now I come myself."

"With a little help from me," muttered Roric.

Faint and cold behind them, from all the passages they had traversed, came the muttering of the dead who had seen the living walk by. Gizor One-hand and the other shadowy shapes massed together. "You come here alive in blood and breath," said the voice from the mist, colder than any of the voices of the dead. "You have brought life to Hel where life has never been."

When Eirik did not answer, Roric said to the glowing eyes, "I warned you what would happen if you tried to take over the realms of voima. For we are more than living mortals—we are mortals who have walked where only the immortals go."

"You are the only power that all must obey in the end," Eirik was still murmuring.

Roric ignored him. He stood with a hand on his hip, and a line from an old story flashed through his mind, "The hero faced down the lords of death themselves." But he was not a hero, and in spite of his own bold words the one to whom all came in the end could never be faced down.

"The dead should fade, forgotten." Again the voice in the coils of mist sounded uncertain. "If they did not, Hel itself would not hold them all."

"And I have started to waken them?" said Roric. "And does *this*"—he held high his charm—"bring a hint of voima even to the dusty halls of death? Shall I test more fully the effects of the Wanderers' singing sword?"

"The dead . . . cannot wake. They must not wake."

Too bad Eirik didn't have his lyre, Roric thought. This would make a good song. "You hear them. You see them. They *are* waking now. Are two living men too many for you?"

"You do not want it, mortals," said the voice from the mist, expressionless and cold. "You would not want the dead to become animate again, to rise from their burial mounds in mortal realms. If the dead do not stay dead, then the balance will be overturned and the earth shall collapse from too many of the living. *One* living man would not destroy the balance—I should be able to restore it. But two . . ."

"Then listen to me!" Roric cried. "I shall *leave*, so that they may fade again, all those whose stories do not burn in story and song."

"You cannot leave Hel," said Eirik, turning on him, and his eyes too had turned to coals.

"Just watch," said Roric. "First I ran from dishonor, when I knew that love and honor could not be found together. Then I determined to run no more, to fight dishonor by giving my life in battle. When *you* would not take it, Eirik Eirik's son, I came here living. And I have discovered something. There may be honor in how one dies, but the real honor is in living one's life as well as one can, until fate spells the end. There is no honor to be found in fleeing from failure to death."

"Then what *do* you want?" growled Eirik.

"Life itself. All the powers of birth, growth, and love. I thought to find them in the realms of the lords of voima, but I found that even those lords can only guide and reflect that which comes from mortal life. And I shall not find those powers here. Love and birth come only to mortals who still live beneath the sun, but who know that they are not immortal and must seize life while they can."

"All the burial mounds in the world," said the voice so deep and so low he felt the words as much as heard them, "lead to this tower."

"Then one should also be able to climb back the other way," said Roric as confidently as he could. He backed away from the tower, looking around for some way that might lead out of here. "Outlaw! Are you coming with me?"

"No," said Eirik quietly, almost in a mumble, then, "No! I was cast out, made a renegade, with all men's hands against me. The woman I could have loved if she had given me a chance rejected me—and not even for another man, but for *no* one." He lifted his head proudly. "But I have a power here that all the Fifty Kings cannot match. If there is no dying in Hel—as you and your friend Valmar made clear is not the case in the Wanderers' realm!—then I have found the only way for mortals to become immortal. Only here, in the court of the forces of darkness, shall all men and women yield to me in the end!"

"I may be an outlaw too," said Roric, in a voice he deliberately made loud and cheerful to echo through the halls of the dead, "but I know a woman who loves me. If not her lover anymore, I can still be her brother and do all within my strength to ensure her happiness."

"You shall return here!" said Eirik harshly. "I shall be alive, a spot of color and breath and living blood, serving the all-powerful forces, when you come down gray from the mound where they put you."

"Of course I shall return," said Roric. "If life was valueless because short, it would have no meaning at all. If we thought only on the end that fate ordains, of the destruction of even the immortals, none of us would seek love or

renewal. But before I see you here again, I—though not
you—shall have been alive."

Eirik looked at him a moment, an expression that might
really have been a smile on his scarred lips. "I won't need
this sword anymore," he said suddenly, unbuckling it. "Take
it back to the Wanderers. Tell them to send me my lyre
instead! If I could make my songs for the dead here, maybe
I could put a little life in their eyes."

The dark misty shape swirled for a moment, as though
concerned about maintaining the balance with even one
living man here if that man was King Eirik. "I'll see what I
can do about the lyre," said Roric with a grin.

But how was he, in spite of his bold words, going to get
out of here and back to mortal lands? Suddenly Gizor One-
hand stepped forward.

"I shall help you, Roric," he said, his voice almost animate. "Someone who returned living from Hel would have
his song sung for a thousand years—and they will also long
tell the tale of the dead man who helped him. You can
return by way of my burial mound. The way is above you.
Jump."

Jump? Roric looked up without seeing anything but a
distant gray roof, but he had to trust Gizor's word for it.
He buckled on the singing sword and sprang upward, on
legs that suddenly seemed enormously powerful. Gizor
jumped with him, pushing from behind. He grabbed for a
handhold on the ceiling far above the sunless sea and tower
of death. Over him a passageway opened, a passage leading upward, and he kicked his way into it. He looked down
between his feet for a last glimpse of the outlaw king. Then
he turned away, thinking no more of Hel to which fate
would still one day destine him, but would not yet. He
thoughts were of Karin and her love.

The climbing was straightforward, even easy at first. Gizor
was close at his shoulder. Roric went fast, his hands gripping first rocks, then soft earth. Constantly the passsage
opened before him.

But then the climb gradually became harder. Time slowly began to have meaning again, and he thought he had climbed two hours, three hours. As he rose out of Hel hunger and weariness assaulted him, and he thought with a grim smile that this must be a sign he was returning at last to mortal realms. The air here seemed thick and sour, leaden in his gasping lungs.

The passage up which he climbed ended abruptly. He paused, waiting for it to open again before him. But he now seemed surrounded by solid earth.

He turned to Gizor for suggestions, but he had faded again as they climbed and was now only the faintest of outlines, without even a face. Roric knocked at the solid earth before him with his fists, but the dirt was mixed with rocks and sand and packed hard. "Thank you for bringing me here," he said in case the wight could still hear him, for he did not want to be ungrateful although it was hard to sound sincere.

While he hesitated, breathing shallowly the fetid air that surrounded him, the entire earth trembled under him, and the roof of the tiny space in which he stood swayed and swayed again, threatening to collapse. He threw his arms protectively over his head, but the swaying ceased in a moment. He began digging wildly with his bare hands at the earth, and then heard a sound, the first living sound that had reached him: the muffled scream of a stallion. Then the earth again began to sway.

CHAPTER FIFTEEN

1

Valmar saw firelight flickering ahead of him in the tunnel. Eirik's men? he wondered. But he heard no sound, none of the outlaw king's boisterous conversation, not even the snores he would have expected if they were all asleep. He crawled on as quietly as possible, his sword's scabbard dragging behind him.

He came into a dimly lit chamber where something enormous and bulky reclined by the fire. His hand closed around his hilt. Against the far wall was a complicated web woven of string, but it looked as though it had been slashed in several places, for broken ends dangled. Beyond the web was an enormous mirror which seemed to reflect something other than this room. The bulky shape shifted and human eyes glinted at him. "Do not fear me, Valmar Hadros' son."

Valmar emerged from the tunnel and rose to his feet. "Are you the Witch of the Western Cliffs?" he asked cautiously. He made himself let go of his sword hilt. Karin had told him a little of the Witch. "And if you are, am I still in mortal realms?"

He had not been able to get any detail of the witch's shape. She—or it—turned away from him, toward the web, and began slashing. It was impossible in the dim light to see if the witch was using a knife or fingernails. More rents opened, and more bits of string dangled down.

"You are in mortal realms, but not for long," said the voice almost cheerfully. "You humans have given me an idea."

"Humans? An idea?" Valmar found his fingers twitching and clenched his fists. He had come back to rescue or to avenge Roric, not to become caught in the webs of creatures of voima.

"Roric No-man's son and Karin Kardan's daughter," said the witch in a matter-of-fact tone. "They are very unlike, with different goals, different purposes. In a mortal lifespan, there is no way they could ever possibly come to understand each other fully. Yet they love each other. They do not *need* complete agreement. They have learned through facing desperate dangers that even creatures as different as men and women can act together."

The witch was speaking as though Roric was still alive. Valmar fought down shameful disappointment. He should be delighted his foster-brother lived. Karin was not his even if Roric was dead.

But a witch in mortal realms might not know what had happened in the realms of voima. "Are you creating desperate dangers in ripping your weaving?"

"You humans gave me that idea too," the witch continued, glancing quickly at him. "There are too many knots, too many tangles accumulated over the years. Roric No-man's son deals with tangles by trying something desperate and bold. Karin Kardan's daughter does not lose track of the final goal, no matter how difficult the way. The first of the dangers to the realms of voima were those men who went through the rift, being taunted by Roric. At his example, I then sent a dragon through. When a dragon settled at my door many years ago, I had not realized the potential advantages!"

"The Wanderers and Hearthkeepers fought the dragon together."

"They worked together for a short time, it is true. But it will take more than that for our children to join together

permanently. They have known all along that without someone to guide and instruct you mortals, you will lose order
and direction, return to scattered and violent bands roving
through the forest as you once were. But even that danger
has not been enough to make them stop their attempts to
circumvent the other's power. I need something even more
desperate."

"Then what do you intend?" asked Valmar.

"The outlaws and the dragon in the realms of voima were
an excellent distraction while I prepared what I do now. I
am *unmaking*." The voice was harsh and booming, all its
cheerful quality gone. A shiver went up Valmar's back. No
matter how strange and slow this witch might seem, if Karin
was right it had given birth to the chief of the Wanderers.
"We made the realms of voima for them to live in, and
most of us, the makers, built ourselves into the very fabric
of those realms, asleep. But now I who was left to watch
am waking them. If they awake—and if our children do
not ease them quickly back into slumber—then the very
substance of immortal realms shall crumble."

Valmar was swept with a horror that made his whole
body go stiff. "And what will happen if immortal realms
are destroyed?" he brought out between frozen lips.

"Then all the powers of voima will be destroyed, and all
order in mortal realms will go with them."

"You would destroy all you created—" For a moment
he clenched his sword. But then those eyes, human and
more than human, met his and the strength went out of
him.

"We were not the *creators* of mortal lands any more
than the Wanderers were. But yes. We no longer rule earth
and sky, but we can still destroy. This is not a game. The
danger would not be truly desperate if it was not real."

"Then what do you want me to do?"

The witch turned around to face him. The web was now
little more than tatters. "I cannot do this myself, Valmar
Hadros' son. I have tried. Someone needs to bring those

two forces together. If the powers of voima cannot do it, then it will have to be a mortal. If you are no more successful than I have been, then immortal and mortal realms will collapse together."

Valmar crawled back the way he had come. The witch had said he would emerge into realms of voima. He gritted his teeth with the sick feeling that he was being sent back to the faeys to get him out of the way.

But when he saw light before him it was not the green of the faeys' lanterns but the gray of twilight after the sun has set. There was a faint, steady splashing, the sound of a small waterfall. The voices he heard were hoarse, rough, and certainly not those of the faeys.

"That berserker sent the princess this way." "Suppose this is just another path down to Hel?" "Then we'll rejoin our king even sooner than we thought. But even Hel has to be better than what these people keep claiming is the Wanderers' realm."

Valmar rose and stepped forward by the pool, his sword drawn.

His abrupt appearance panicked the outlaws. They stared at him, eyes wide in the dimness. There were not many left of the once proud and desperate group of renegades who had followed Eirik into the sea and out of mortal realms.

And without their leader the courage had gone out of them. Valmar spoke in his deepest voice. "This tunnel may take you to your kingdom if that is your wish. Pass by me quietly, your swords sheathed, and I shall not harm you."

The tunnel was only wide enough for one to pass at a time. The warriors edged by him, eyeing him warily. Valmar wondered without much interest if they would emerge in Hadros' kingdom—in which case Dag and Nole might have an adventure of their own to tell about—or in the Witch's cave. He considered asking them what had happened to Roric but did not want to hear the answer. When several had passed it occurred to him that they might rush him from both directions, but without Eirik they had no one to plot and only wanted to get to safety.

The last of the outlaws disappeared down the tunnel. For a moment, looking after them, he thought he saw daylight and two lichen-spotted standing stones leaning together, but when he blinked the image was gone. He shrugged and turned away.

Valmar went by the pool and out into evening. He had to find the Wanderers and warn them.

He sheathed his sword and scrambled up beside the waterfall. At the top of the cliff he paused, blinking and trying to see, then started walking along the ridge in the direction the Wanderers and Hearthkeepers had taken to fight the dragon. After a short distance he made out something huge and streaked with black, sprawling across the rocks for dozens of yards.

For a second he thought it was the witch again, grown to enormous size. Then he realized it was the dragon. It was dead, lying in its own black blood, its mouth sagging open and the tongue loose over the needle teeth. So the lords and ladies of voima too could kill, he thought grimly, even in their own realm. He was just wondering how to locate them, before the last of the witch's web was unmade, when he heard voices.

The loudest voice was that of the woman with the dark curling hair. "When the new sun rises, which it shall do very soon, our time will come. Since fate has ended your rule, we must be fated to take again the direction of earth and sky. Now that the last of the mortal men are gone from here, there is little more for you to do but retreat to your manors, because if you do not yield willingly you will be forced to yield at the point of the sword."

"And you always complained that *we* encouraged mortal men in violence." It was the deep, slightly ironic voice of the Wanderer who had first brought Valmar here.

"In which case," she answered briskly, "there is nothing

you can say against us if we use your own weapons to reimpose *our* vision of the world."

Valmar could now see all of them in the last of the light, the lords and ladies of voima sitting on the ridge top looking off toward the east. They all seemed battered from their fight with the dragon. There was a great scar in the earth nearby, as though it had opened and closed again.

He hesitated, wishing irrationally that Karin was here. How was he supposed to reconcile the rulers of earth and sky before earth and sky themselves were destroyed? The last daylight was fading behind them, but there was no hint of dawn in the east in spite of the Hearthkeeper's confident prediction that the new sun would rise very soon.

"I do not like your inviting a mortal woman to join you," said another of the Wanderers. "We have always been equally matched with you in numbers."

Valmar counted quickly. So far no one had noticed him. There were twelve Wanderers but thirteen women, including, he realized with a start, the tall, green-eyed woman who had been with King Eirik. "I have no intention of returning to a world that includes mortal men," said Wigla firmly.

"Were you Wanderers suggesting that *I* instead should return to my husband and children in mortal realms, to bring the number back down to twelve?" asked one of the Hearthkeepers. "*He* will be protected by the powers of voima, and my children will lead long and happy lives even if they are still fated to die. But why should I not stay with my sisters and rule over mortals and over you? After all, there have been even lords of voima who have visited mortal women in disguise! If I care to I can still visit my husband, who already knows well who I am."

The ground suddenly heaved and swayed under them. Valmar lost and regained his balance. "And I cannot say I like these earthquakes," commented the leader of the Wanderers.

"You men just didn't do enough to make our world firm

while you were ruling it. As soon as our powers return, we will end these problems. I must say, I thought we would feel them returning by now . . ."

Valmar stepped forward. The immortals, with their full powers either eroded away or not yet come to fullness, were entirely capable of being surprised.

All spun around to face him. "You said you had sent all the mortal men back!" one of the Hearthkeepers started to say accusingly, but Valmar did not want to hear any more of their bickering.

"I come," he began and found his voice cracking, which it had not done for several years. "I come," he tried again, "from the one called the Witch of the Western Cliffs."

Everyone stared at him, but he could not afford to be overcome with awe or shyness now. He had pledged himself to serve the lords of voima, and if saving them meant forcing them into something they had not wanted, he would still do it. Besides, he would not merely be saving the Wanderers: he had to save his younger brothers, back in mortal lands, and had to save Karin.

"I come to warn you," he said, high and clear. "The reason for the earthquakes, the reason none of you have your powers now, is because the Old Ones who made this realm in the first place are now destroying it."

A storm came rumbling across the plain while he spoke, spitting rain, and came up the ridge to drench all of them. He wiped wet hair away from his eyes with one arm and stared at the immortals. They *had* to listen to him.

"Valmar!" It was one of the Hearthkeepers, *his* Hearthkeeper, and she sounded both delighted and calculating as she shook the rain from her hair. "We never thanked you properly for showing us that even immortals can be wounded and made weak. We shall be able to use this knowledge as soon as the new sun rises."

"You aren't listening," he said desperately. "The sun is *not* going to rise!"

"The Witch sent you to threaten us?" said the leader of

the Wanderers sharply. Then for a moment his face, no longer overpowering but still thoughtful and wise, smiled a little. "You have always tried to serve us truly, Valmar Hadros' son—in spite of these women!—but you are too easily influenced."

"It's not just a threat. She—it—told me that unless the two of you come together—completely, reunited—it will be impossible for you to put immortal realms back together. And if the realms of voima are gone, there will not be much hope for mortal men and women."

He finally had their attention. All of them jumped up. "We fought the dragon together," said the curly-haired Hearthkeeper. "They held the dragon imprisoned with the powers of voima while we used our swords on it. We can all work together again for just a little longer and stop this."

"That won't be enough," said Valmar despairingly. "Before the Witch sent me here, she—it—made it clear that only if you join together *completely*, neither ever trying again to overcome the other, will you be able to stop the unmaking."

"This sounds—" one of the Wanderers said but never had a chance to finish. A mile away, a volcano exploded in the middle of the plain.

Wind rushed up the ridge, stinking with sulphur. The earth trembled as molten rock, glowing orange with heat that could be felt from a mile away, bubbled out of a rapidly growing cone. Rain turned to steam in an instant and boiled up in great clouds, lit orange from below. Hot ash settled glowing just a little lower on the ridge, igniting the wet grass. Trees swayed and toppled around them as the earth shook again, and the limestone heaved its way out of the earth.

The lords and ladies of voima, scrambling to keep their balance, conferred rapidly, and several held out commanding arms. Nothing had any effect. In the light of the molten rock, in the trembling of the earth, Valmar seemed to see giants coming awake, sitting up, tossing back the blankets

of grass and earth under which they had slept. A cracking
and roaring was loud in the distance, as though the solid
earth itself was being broken off and cast out into nothing-
ness.

He was *not* just a boy to whom the warriors did not have
to listen. "You have no choice," he shouted over the roaring of the earth. He seized the closest Hearthkeeper by
the arm and dragged her to him. He recognized her when
she smiled, eyes bright as mirrors even in the near-dark-
ness.

But she was not for him. "You won't be any longer a
woman who might love a mortal," he gasped. "But I cannot try to hold on to what we shared." For a second he
went still, meeting her eyes. "I did love you." With his other
hand he snatched at the arm of a Wanderer.

He had never before dared even brush against them,
but he had no time for awe. All of them, even Wigla, he
pulled and pushed together into a tight, dripping group.
Mortal muscles were effective against immortals who had
lost their powers. "You were once one!" he cried. The lava
was pouring toward them and the volcanic cone had already
risen higher than this ridge. "You must know how to unite
your powers again!" He kept trying to push them close
together, make them hold hands, make them embrace each
other, but they remained a group of separate, frightened
people who had always thought they were immortal.

What else could he do? What else had the Witch meant
him to do? "You were created as *one*! Remember that creation! Humans somehow find a way for very different people
to work together, even if not in full agreement: men and
women, old and young, men who are enemies, the honorable and those who love. What mortals can do the immortals *must* be able to do! We shall still reverence you—if we
still exist!"

And then, as the shaking of the earth beneath them
became so intense it was hard to keep his feet on the wet
grass, there came a change. Where he forcibly held their

hands together he felt jolts, shocks as though touched by lightning. They were all forming a circle, a circle of twenty-four lords and ladies of voima and of two mortals, himself and Wigla. He forced reluctant hands together until they were all united, alternating men and women, the curly-haired Hearthkeeper beside him. Joined in hand, joined in thought, they turned their powers on the disintegrating realm around them.

Racing through his mind came images that he knew were not his, yet seemed joined in him. He saw himself striding high on a mountain, watching the mortals far below. The mortals he could see clearly in spite of his distance from them, and he seemed to remember himself hearing their requests and tasting their offerings, holding out an arm to bring them new hope through the forces of voima. Then he was riding, unseen, in the prow of a ship cutting through a storm on a dark night, where the men fought desperately and coura-geously to save the ship and each other. And most strangely of all, he seemed to remember lying with his own weight on top of him, his legs wrapped around his own waist, and realized he was partaking in the Hearthkeeper's memories.

The lava glow lit up the sky. More memories that were not his, more images of immortal power flashed through his mind, of helping a woman in childbirth, of encourag-ing a man in glorious battle, of guiding the sun and rain of mortal lands, of lying with a chestnut-haired woman who wore a jeweled pendant on her forehead. He could see the immortals moving, writhing, growing closer and split-ting apart. Jolts still passed through him as he tried to force them back together whenever the circle threatened to split. If any of them spoke he could not hear it over the roaring of wind and cracking earth.

Then, abruptly, they pushed him away. The powers of voima surged between them, restored at last, stronger than any mortal could bear. All of them seemed to grow and to glow with their own white light, and he had to squeeze his eyes shut against their faces.

Valmar staggered backward. Then, with their memories still fighting for prominence inside him, he raced through driving rain for the waterfall. These beings, these enormously powerful lords and ladies of voima, turned toward the volcano, but his only thought was somehow to get back to mortal realms if they even still existed.

Stones had cracked off the cliff leading downward toward the pool and the cave that had—twice—led to the earth he knew. He slid more than climbed down, bumping bruisingly as he went. More stones had fallen from the roof of the cave, but the passage still seemed clear. He pushed into it, trying to keep from thinking the thoughts of the rulers of earth and sky, trying to think only of crawling down this passage before it fell in.

The earth quivered again and more of the roof collapsed. He was past the pool now, feeling in heavy darkness for the way to safety. His hands found only solid rock with no way past.

He heaved himself up into a tiny opening between ceiling and wall, bracing himself and holding up his arms as, with another shudder, more stones broke loose. A flying shard caught him on the temple, and he knew no more.

2

Karin screamed as absolute darkness covered the earth. She clung to Queen Arane, feeling her knees turn to water in sheer animal terror. And from the yells around them she was not the only one.

The only voice that was not one of fear and horror was the stallion's, whinnying as though in recognition.

The darkness might only have lasted a half minute, but afterward, when she thought back to it with chills walking down her spine, it seemed that it might have been much longer, that there had been a period outside of time when there was no thought, no event, and no light.

Abruptly the moon was back. It shone down from a cloudless sky as though it had never been gone, lighting up the salt river and all the dripping wet men along the bank—and the person stepping out of the burial mound.

Just for a second, there seemed to be a faint fluttering, of a wight emerging shadowless into moonlight then disappearing into the mound again. But the person who came forward, shaking the taint of earth from him, was Roric.

Karin tore herself from the queen's clutching hands and began to run. Even dead he was Roric, and she loved him.

He felt reassuringly solid as she threw herself, gasping, into his muddy arms. She could understand now the stories of the women who offered anything to have their men back.

He was laughing, loud, joyous laughter to sparkle in the moonlight. She had not known the dead could laugh. "I am no wight but alive, Karin," he said, holding her to him, his embrace not cold but warm around her.

"I thought you were gone," she said, sobbing now for no reason at all. "I thought you had died to save Valmar and me. But, oh, Roric," pausing to kiss him hard, "I have learned you are not my brother."

3

He opened his eyes with only the vaguest idea who he was.

He was a Wanderer, watching as men rode into battle in search of the glory that he encouraged in them. He was a Hearthkeeper, tending the tender shoots in the barley fields, sitting unseen by women as they rocked their babies. And he was a king's son, born to rule at some vague future time that seemed it would never come.

He turned over his memories while delicately rubbing his temple and looking around. He was in a cave, not far from the entrance, and outside it was morning. He heard bird calls and water splashing. He was jammed into a tiny crevice among fallen rocks, all his clothing damp, but he felt well-rested and comfortable, with none of his joints stiff, and the bruise on his head the only wound on him. His clearest memories were of a childhood in a yellow sandstone castle set in oak woods above the sea. But were these his own memories, or was he a ruler of earth and sky who had acquired some of the memories of the mortal who had brought Wanderers and Hearthkeepers together?

He worked his way out of the crevice and stepped toward the pool. Perhaps his reflection would tell him.

There was enough light that he should be able to see. A drop of water fell from the cave ceiling, sending ripples across the surface. He knelt and leaned over, seeing the wavering outlines of a human shape. But whose face would he see? He waited for the ripples to subside. Just another moment and it would be smooth enough—

Another drop fell from the cave ceiling, and again the pool's reflections dissolved into ripples. He waited again while the ripples subsided. But just before the pool was smooth enough to use as a mirror the ceiling dripped again.

He rose and walked toward the cave entrance. If he met someone he might be able to tell from their reaction who he was before they realized he did not know himself.

He should have emerged from the cave at the bottom of a little waterfall, but instead as he went forward he smelled salt spray. The splashing water he had heard no longer sounded like a waterfall but like waves breaking against the shore. As he stepped into sunshine the singing birds he had heard all became gulls, wheeling with sharp cries overhead.

Frowning, he climbed out of the cave mouth and started walking slowly along the shingle. He was quite sure he had never seen this stretch of coast before. Sunlight flashed on green waves and white foam. He had to walk carefully amidst great boulders, packed between with pebbles and wet sand.

He came around a boulder and saw a young woman sitting on a rock before him. Her hair, tousled by the sea wind, was black and curling, and the sunlight glinted in her eyes. She smiled, showing a row of sharp little white teeth. "Greetings, Valmar Hadros' son."

Then he *was* Valmar. His identity swirled for a second, then settled itself. He was the heir to the yellow sandstone castle, but he also knew that within him now, and for the rest of his life, was a fragment of the wisdom of the immortals. But she—

"You can't be here," he said. "You *can't*."

"Why not?" She rose with an amused smile and came to take his hands in hers. She appeared younger than he remembered.

"Because you and all the other Hearthkeepers have been joined with the Wanderers, to rule earth and sky united. You must have restored both mortal and immortal realms before they were unmade, or neither we nor this shore would even be here."

"But I am not a Hearthkeeper!"

"Then what are you?" asked Valmar, trembling between fear and delight, hoping he knew the answer.

"I *think* I am a mortal." She grinned up at him. "We were thirteen sisters, including the one who had just joined us. Only twelve of us could join in the new union to rule earth and sky. Since we had just told her she could be one of us, it would be hard to eject her from our numbers! The sister who had most recently been living in mortal lands had come back to rejoin us as the sun set in realms of voima, and she had no intention of leaving. That left me. I was, after all, the only one carrying a mortal child. Twins, actually!"

She laughed at his expression. "Are you not flattered, Valmar, that I left the realms of voima to become a mortal's wife—even if I did take care to choose a man who had saved those realms from destruction?"

He crushed her to him, one hand around her small, straight back, the other plunged into her hair. He felt too full of joy even for desire. "If you are now mortal," he was able to gasp at last, "be careful about daring people to cut off your head."

She caught her breath as he held her a little away from him to look at her. "By the Wanderers!" she said with a laugh. "That *is* what mortals say, isn't it?" she asked as an aside. "Since I have become mortal, your embrace is so strong it could keep me from breathing! And you haven't even said yet you'll have me."

They sat down together on a stone, his arm around her shoulders. "It will be, how shall I put this, interesting to have you as a wife," he said with a smile. "You won't be like the queens of any other of the other Fifty Kingdoms."

"Is that a problem?" she asked with a quick, sideways look. "You wouldn't perhaps prefer to have—Karin?"

His eyebrows shot up. He had not known she even knew about Karin. But then—she had until very recently been an immortal. "No," he managed to say in an even voice. "Karin is my foster-sister. I have given up any thought of making her mine. She would never think of me or treat me as other than her brother—not like you!" He pulled her to him, tickling her until she shouted with laughter. And he realized with his new wisdom as she tickled him back that he spoke truly: when he left Karin sleeping in his father's castle he had put off any love for her other than a brother's love.

When they had caught their breaths again, Valmar said, "There *is* one problem. If you are going to be my wife, you have to have a name."

"You can call me Wigla," she said promptly.

"Wigla?! But—"

"Well, I never had a name the way you mortals have names when I was a Hearthkeeper. Now that the woman you used to know as Wigla has become an immortal, she won't need her name anymore. Since we have, you might say, changed places, I have taken her name."

He took her face between his hands and kissed her. "Well, Wigla, if you are a mortal now you'll have to learn that you can't just decide to be one place or another. And we humans need to eat. Unless you care to swim in the surf and eat raw fish, we had better start trying to find a house or manor around here."

4

Early in the morning the two kings, Queen Arane, Karin, and Roric all sat together by the shore of the salt river. The men had bailed out the ship and had nearly finished salvaging what could be salvaged from the tidal wave. Counting and checking had yielded the good news that no one had drowned.

King Kardan looked assessingly at his daughter. She nearly glowed with joy. She had Roric's hand clenched in hers and kept looking at him as though not able to believe the good fortune fate had brought her. The man who had been chosen by the Wanderers to save their realm and had walked living through Hel had returned to her, and she did not even care what glorious deeds he had done as long as he was with her.

"We don't need a formal Gemot," she said. "Since Roric did not kidnap either me or Valmar, there is no reason to outlaw him."

"I can certainly outlaw him for stealing my ship," said Hadros fiercely, thrusting out his bearded chin.

"Roric did not do that," she said coolly. "*I* did. To outlaw a future sovereign queen would take the All-Gemot of the Fifty Kings, which means you'll have to wait until next year. Unless you planned to declare war on me? I've heard you say, Hadros," with the faintest smile, "that you do not war on girls."

"He still has the blood-guilt of three men on him," the king said roughly, "and we have not seen Valmar."

For a second Karin's face became clouded—thinking doubtless of her little brother. Kardan answered for her. "I shall pay the blood-fee, Hadros, for my future son-in-law. Karin has told me she is ready to swear on steel and rowan that when Roric killed your warriors Rolf and Warulf they had attacked Roric as three against one, and I witnessed his single combat against Gizor."

Karin unexpectedly smiled. "Roric and I can pay the blood-money ourselves. We know where there's a dragon hoard—and the dragon is not coming back."

The other king grunted and stretched out his stiff leg. "Even if the money's paid," he said, "I don't like a man who's forsworn his loyalty." He kept glancing at Roric as though extremely proud of him, and then he would make himself scowl again.

"I think," put in Roric, sober but with a hint of laughter at the corners of his mouth, "that Gizor has forgiven me."

"The wight that appeared on the grave mound," commented Kardan, "was said by many of the men to be one-handed . . ."

They all looked at Roric for a moment. The story he had told them, how he had gone from what Karin had been sure was a fatal fight against Eirik's men to stepping alive out of Hel, was hard to believe yet impossible to doubt. They had already dug into the mound where Roric had emerged to bury King Eirik's lyre next to Gizor's body.

Karin seemed determined to make Hadros agreeable, or as agreeable as he could be given that his heir was still missing. "Are you two the first man and lord ever to quarrel?" she asked with a smile. "The Gemot would be busy indeed if it had to hear about everything said in a fit of anger."

This would be much easier, Kardan thought, if Hadros would acknowledge that Roric was his son rather than treating him like a rebellious warrior. But perhaps he did not want to tell him the truth until the blood-guilt was cleared away. Or perhaps he did not want to appear too quick to claim parentage of a man about whom they were already telling stories and would soon be making songs.

"All three of you," said Karin, looking at the kings and

queen, "came north seeking a lost daughter or son, and two of you have found them."

"Valmar had better just be lost in the woods at home," growled Hadros, then stopped, raising his eyebrows. "All *three* of us?"

"I think," said Karin, looking levelly at the queen, "that it is time to tell Roric his real parentage."

Roric clapped his hands over his ears. "I told the Witch that I renounced all knowledge of my father."

Queen Arane took a deep breath. "You shall not learn of your father from me. But I think it time that you learned of your mother."

The telling took a while. Hadros was at first furious, then abruptly began to laugh. "Fooled by a woman!" he said, slapping his knee. "You knew I was ready to believe, *wanted* to believe my own wife's barrenness was not due to me. And you also knew that a king's son, even if not acknowledged, would be brought up fit to rule. Are you going to tell us more about that winter when *somebody* fathered this lad?"

Roric mostly looked stunned. "This is not the kin I thought I had. I always assumed I was the son of a serving-maid, not a queen!"

"How about it, No-man's son?" Hadros said, clapping him on the shoulder. "Ready to conquer yourself a kingdom as I've been trying to persuade you to do?"

"How about mine?" asked Queen Arane.

Roric stared at her. "You are suggesting that I bring warships and pillage—"

"Not at all," she said with a smile. "I am suggesting you appear before my kingdom's Gemot and have them elect you as my heir. It will be difficult enough persuading some of my powerful lords, especially the ones who have long hoped to become heirs themselves, for you to find all the glory you want."

Hadros reached into his belt pouch and pulled out something. He flipped it to Roric who caught it one-handed. "If you're planning to become a king," Hadros said gruffly, "I guess you won't want to be my sworn man anymore. But you might as well have your ring back."

Roric suddenly grinned at Arane. "I presume some of the potential heirs to your kingdom would not mind trying to assassinate me? I'll do all the sword can do to persuade them I'll make a good king. And my queen," with a squeeze of Karin's hand, "will do all the persuasion at which women excel."

By late afternoon they were ready to leave. Roric and some of Arane's warriors had climbed up to the dragon's den and come away with as much treasure as they could carry, but before they left they levered huge stones into the entrance. All the old stories agreed that a dragon's hoard was always cursed, and that if any man tried to carry away more than a reasonable amount he would become consumed himself—by greed, or by the next dragon to scent the gold.

The ship had been afloat for three hours without leaking any more than might be expected, and Hadros declared it ready for the sea. "We're too far from home for a raven-message," he said, "but in a few days we should be able to send one to Dag and Nole and reassure them they were not visited by wights from Hel." He added, half under his breath, "But if Valmar is there they already know that."

"If any of the Fifty Kings were planning to conquer Eirik's kingdom," commented King Kardan cheerfully, "we should tell them this is no fit place for a man to rule. I'm glad you set the prisoners free, Hadros; trying to live on here is the worst punishment anyone could wish on a band of outlaws."

With Karin with him again, he thought, he should be able to end his sorrowful worry, to enjoy watching her and the grandchild he should have sometime next year. He could rule as king for a few more years, give her time to gain a little more knowledge of the kingdom and its governance before becoming sovereign queen. Home was a good place to be.

But he had, he thought, strangely enjoyed this trip, now that it was ending happily—at least for him. Next time, perhaps he should invite Hadros to go somewhere a little more civilized in *his* longship.

They were about to push the ship out into the channel when Kardan saw someone coming along the salt river from the direction of the sea: two people, he realized, a man and a woman, walking with hands clasped. The woman was young and dark haired; the man had a full red beard and was powerfully muscled. King Hadros beside him let out a gasp.

"I know I am not yet of age, Father," called Valmar. It *had* to be Valmar, Kardan thought, but he seemed both bigger and older than the boy he remembered. Hadros had sprung from the ship to the beach and was pounding toward him, stiff leg or no stiff leg. "So I shall have to ask your permission. I would like to be married."

5

Roric and Valmar stood at dawn in a circle formed by all the warriors. Each of the two held a gold ring and waited for his bride.

Men always waited and women always came, to make it clear that the women were not being married against their wills. But Roric thought that Karin and Wigla seemed to be taking their own time about it, having chosen as the starting point for their procession a rock a quarter mile away and coming at a leisurely stroll, talking and laughing with each other.

Hadros, grumbling, had agreed that another day's delay would make no difference. Now that Valmar was back and the blood-fee paid with the dragon's wealth, Roric was freed from his blood-guilt, and since Valmar most definitely did not think himself betrothed to Karin there was no reason for the two couples not to be wed at once. Hadros had mumbled that he was not sure he wanted his heir to marry a woman without kin who looked to him like a siren, but there was no force in his objection.

"So you think there will be fewer wars in mortal realms now?" Roric asked Valmar as they watched the women slowly approach.

"There should be. But mortal realms were not remade, only the lands of voima. It may be generations before the change is complete, before humans are able *both* to follow the wandering paths of glory and to keep hearth and home— theirs and others'—safe and secure."

"Eirik's men may have trouble adapting to the change," Roric commented.

"I'm looking forward," said Valmar with a grin, "to hearing how my brothers did defending the castle against them." He paused for a moment, then added, "They will be surprised when we all arrive, married to those they will think are the wrong people."

"Oh, I think I can keep there from being talk about my wife," said Roric lightly, tapping his fingers on his sword.

"And I can assure that no one says anything against the purity and constancy of my sister," said Valmar.

The two women were slowly drawing closer. "Men and women have never been as clearly separated in their abilities as the Wanderers seemed to think," said Roric thoughtfully. "Why do we men wander far, after all, if not to return at last, at the end of adventuring, to make a secure hearth and home?"

Valmar glanced at him sideways. "I think I figured that out myself."

"It would be good," Roric continued, "if more men could have women like Karin along with them, doing the plotting and planning, rather than thinking honor required them to be left at home."

"And I think you shall find, if you face her in the practice ring, that Wigla's as good a warrior as most men." Valmar hesitated for a moment, then asked as though casually, "In your experiences in Hel and in the realms of voima, did you ever learn your father's name?"

Roric shook his head. "I have renounced knowledge of my father. I had thought it would be hard knowledge to give up, but in fact it frees me. I have kin now and a mother, but I have no father, glorious or inglorious, either after whom I have to mold myself or else whose shame I have to overcome. My identity as No-man's son will satisfy me well."

"Maybe you *are* freed," agreed Valmar quietly. "I feel as though I have only now truly become myself, yet I still have to go back and live in my father's castle—with a wife he'll be wishing was Karin."

Roric laughed. "You can come help me plot against my newfound relatives if Hadros' castle wearies you too much. But I do not fear you will return to your boyhood. The last time I talked to the Wanderer, he did not sound as though he would *ever* agree to joining with the Hearthkeepers. I'm impressed with you, foster-brother. They are making songs about me for coming back from Hel, but the real songs should be for you. Death is easy—it's life that's hard."

Karin and Wigla had finally reached the circle. The warriors stepped aside to let them through, then closed in again. Both women had small smiles, as though still trying to make up their minds whether to accept these men.

Roric and Valmar stepped forward to meet them, rings held out. "If immortal men and women can join together," said Valmar, "we should be able to find a way to live happily with our wives."

TALES OF THE WIZARD OF YURT
C. Dale Brittain

A young magician earns his stars the hard way in these engaging, light fantasy adventures.

A BAD SPELL IN YURT   72075-9 ♦ $4.99 _____
The tiny backwater kingdom of Yurt seems to be the perfect place for a young wizard who only barely managed to graduate wizard's school (especially after that embarrassment with the frogs) as a result of inspired (if not disciplined) magic-wielding. But Daimbert senses a lurking hint of evil that suggests someone in the castle is practicing black magic.... Soon Daimbert realizes that it will take all the magic he never learned to find out who that person is, and save both the kingdom and his life. Good thing Daimbert knows how to improvise!

THE WOOD NYMPH AND THE CRANKY SAINT
                                72156-9 ♦ $4.99 _____
Wizards should be careful what they wish for. Daimbert, for example, wished for more independence and authority. After dealing with the mysteriously connected crises of the cranky saint of the shrine of the Holy Toe, a plague of magical horned rabbits, a scandalous duchess with a fondness for young wizards, and zombielike creatures made with spells they never taught at wizard school, Daimbert learns that there is a great deal to be said for the quiet life!

MAGE QUEST   72169-0 ♦ $4.99 _____
Daimbert and five guys from Yurt are on a quest to the Holy Land. They will encounter intrigue, treachery, black magic, and a big blue djinn—and only Daimbert's ingenuity might be able to save their lives, as the line grows thin between a fatal curse and finding one's heart's desire....
